Finding Jessica Lambert

Finding Jessica Lambert

Copyright © 2020 Clare Ashton

All Rights Reserved

This is a work of fiction. Names, characters and incidents are the products of the author's imagination or are used fictitiously. Any resemblance to actual events, locales or persons, living or dead, is entirely coincidental.

Editor: Jayne Fereday

Cover: Fereday Design

Published by:

BREEZY TREE

For Jayne

1

The woman's frantic movement through the window caught Anna's eye first. As her Tube pulled in at the underground station she looked up and caught her own reflection – pale and features slack with inattention, her blonde hair draped around her face – then the Tube doors slid open. The young woman's figure, moving fast in tight black jeans and smart jacket, was distinct for a moment against the tiled walls of the underground, before she barrelled into the carriage, eyes panicked and gleaming white against her brown skin.

"Come on," the woman rasped. She backed away from the closing doors, squeezing next to Anna, her shoulders hunched and diminishing her otherwise tall stature.

"Are you all right?" Anna said. Her response was instinctive and her stomach tightened. She thought she recognised that fear. She knew that kind of panic.

The woman didn't respond and stared through the doors, anxious about someone outside, and as the Tube juddered into motion she clung to the partition. The train pulled out of the station, clacked quicker into the dark tunnels and passengers spilled back to the section by the doors. The chatter, the attention, the bodies squashed tight in the tin can of people, sent the woman cowering further towards Anna.

"I need to get out of here," she breathed, seemingly to herself. "I need to get out."

Anna modulated her voice in a way she'd perfected, so that it would soothe and imbue confidence. "Would you like me to help?" she said. Then when the woman didn't respond, "Are you having a panic attack? Was someone following you?"

The woman peeked up. "Yes," she panted.

The train lurched on the track around a corner and the lights flickered at the same time a flash burst from behind the woman. When the carriage lights relit, a group of teens were giggling and playing with their phones.

It seemed to send the young woman's anxiety rocketing and she clutched her head, her long fingers buried deep into her short black hair.

The woman had caught the attention of a young man across the carriage. He leered and checked her up and down. The woman was undeniably attractive, Anna had taken in that much as she'd careered into the carriage, but she was obviously stricken. What was wrong with people? This wasn't a time to ogle. A nearby businessman, peering down with disdain from his newspaper, was no help either.

Frustrated at the response of her fellow passengers, Anna said, "It's about half a minute to the next station," and she offered a reassuring hand without thinking how the woman would react. She immediately buried herself into Anna's trench coat and began counting in short breaths, "One, two, three," swaying as the Tube curved around a bend.

The carriage jolted and lights flickered again. Another flash bleached Anna's vision.

"Four, five, six," the young woman counted louder.

"Excuse me," Anna tutted in the direction of the flash. It must have been the teens again. She shuffled around the young woman's body to shield her. "Nearly there," Anna said.

The throng heaved against them from behind, pushing Anna against the woman.

"Ten, eleven, twelve," the woman gasped, and she buried her face into Anna's chest as the Tube slowed, and almost on the count of thirty the train stopped.

"Follow me," Anna said, determined and taking the woman's arm. Her companion followed, checking over her shoulder every second.

"I don't usually go this way," Anna said, hesitating, "but it's quieter and we can get you out quicker." The woman gave the slightest nod of approval and Anna tugged her towards the inconspicuous archway and stairwell.

"Count the steps if you find it comforting," Anna continued. "I tried it once upon a time. There are seventy."

It was one of Anna's little reassurances. One of her checks.

The woman nodded and mumbled numbers as they climbed with a quick, fluid pace. A few moments later, the humidity and stuffiness of the Tube, the oil and sweat that lingered in the tunnels, was diluted with the freshness of autumn night air. An archway of orange streetlight opened up ahead and the exit emptied into a quiet side street and freedom from other passengers.

"There," Anna said. "You're out." And she dropped the woman's arm.

"I don't know where I am," the woman blurted, her anxiety climbing again. "I haven't got a bloody clue."

"It's OK," Anna said. "Do you think you're still being followed?"

"I don't know." The woman peered behind her, but who could tell what was down in the darkness of the tunnels. "I touched in with an Oyster card and ran to the nearest train. I don't even know what line that was."

"You were on the Northern Line," Anna said, using all her training to project calm. "Where did you need to go?"

"Anywhere." It was like the woman's body burned with stress.

"It's all right," Anna murmured and she moved closer, catching a vague smell of liquor. "Have you been drinking?"

"I'm not drunk," the woman shot back. "I don't usually drink. It's just… Yes, I have." She deflated. "I wanted to calm my nerves. A quick vodka. Then another. Maybe another after that. But people were looking. And this guy approached. Panicked. I was sure he followed me into the subway."

"I didn't mean for it to be judgemental," Anna said, purposefully slowing her voice. "Nothing like that at all," she carried on, seeing its calming effect on the woman. The woman's tension subsided whenever Anna talked. "I thought that perhaps we could find you a coffee, to sober up."

"Oh. That's probably a good idea. But…"

"Somewhere quiet?"

"Yes, please show me. Somewhere I can rest for a while. Somewhere to hide."

The young woman trembled when Anna took her arm and led her from the side street, perhaps coming down from nervous energy. Now that Anna had time to think, she would have guessed the woman was in her twenties. Her voice, although broken with anxiety, had a deep timbre that suggested some maturity, but in moments of calm it had the clarity of youth and her face, though strained with distress, had a flawlessness that only the young enjoy.

Anna led on with a confidence that she didn't feel but, with her practice, projected. The young woman stood as tall as Anna now. She had a firm grip around Anna's arm, a presence in fact, no matter how much she'd tried to hide it on the train. It seemed ludicrous somehow when she'd attempted to make herself small in Anna's chest, her thick black hair buried against Anna's shirt.

But Anna knew what it was like to feel vulnerable, to have that fear, and she'd despaired that not one person was willing to help.

"Let's try Costa," she said.

"Is it quiet?"

It was Friday evening around eight o'clock Anna guessed. "Perhaps," she replied, not hopeful. "Let's take a look."

She winced as they broke into the main street with the glare of streetlights and assault of taxis, buses and bikes buffeting past.

"It's this way," she said, drawing breath.

She made a mental note, as she always did, of the shops along her familiar route. First was the nail bar, where best-friend Penny used to work years ago, with a dark alleyway down the side that Anna always checked. The convenience store where she bought her food. Flicks the hairdressers where the trusted and much appreciated Lucca kept her practical bob in perfect trim. A few doorways to offices, shadowy this time of night, but empty Anna registered with relief, then on the corner a Costa, which she sometimes frequented.

She pushed the café door open and the wave of harsh chatter and incessant chink of crockery told them straight away that it was full.

"Jesus, it's packed," the young woman said.

"Shall we check at the back?"

"No, I can't stay here," she said, and she was already tugging Anna towards the street, more agitated than ever.

"It's Friday," Anna said. "Everywhere is probably busy. Let's check for a table."

"I can't. There are hundreds of people in there. They were already staring at me. I need a break."

The woman's expression was taut. Was it fuelled by paranoia? Anna wouldn't blame her, but it was useless trying to ask above the noise of the café and with the woman's anxiety on the rise. It would likely cause further agitation, so Anna remained calm. Every time she'd offered help, the woman had responded well.

Anna racked her brains. Pubs were a poor place to leave someone who needed sobering, restaurants would be full with Friday night diners, coffee shops on the main street packed, those less frequented on side streets already shut. Apart from Zehra's. But she'd been avoiding there.

Anna sighed. "There's a Turkish coffee shop not far away. It closes in an hour so it'll be quiet. We could go there."

"Please," the woman breathed.

They turned and Anna reached out again for the woman's arm, but was met with the warmth of her naked hand. The sensation was vivid and intimate, the woman's soft fingers clinging around the edge of Anna's palm and when Anna met her gaze, the young woman's eyes were wide and intense. Anna realised the woman had placed her faith in her. She was trusting Anna to take her to safety.

2

Jess's brain fizzed, her stomach clenched and her body wound tight. The sensation of the woman's fingers wrapped around her own was her only anchor and she clung on.

"Is it far?"

"Not at all, although I take a long way around I'm afraid." The woman had the kind of voice Jess found herself trusting, like a doctor's. It had a reassuring quality, mature and confident with quiet authority and it held Jess's attention in her sea of anxiety.

Jess had lost all sense of direction. They'd crossed several busy roads, playing Russian roulette with the zebra crossings, headlights of cars and buses flashing in every direction, horns shrieking, and all the while the woman continued her steady pace.

They turned down a side road, the streetlights becoming sparse and traffic quieter, and into a narrower lane towards a small café with ochre awnings. There were a scattering of tables and chairs outside, each accompanied by an elaborate Middle Eastern pipe.

"Come inside," the woman said, and with that velvet voice Jess didn't question her. "Go to the booth at the back. I'll be with you in a moment."

Jess kept her head low, sheltered her face with a hand, pretending some annoyance with her fringe, and dived into a quiet booth by a window which overlooked a dark alley. She sank onto the padded bench seat.

At last. Somewhere quiet. Somewhere she wouldn't be watched.

She'd been stupid earlier that evening, diving into a pub to steady her nerves with a quick vodka, then another, and a larger one to follow. Voices of recognition had whispered around the pub, the young clientele picking up on her presence, and her back had prickled as she became aware of all eyes upon her. Faces from dark booths had peeked out to get a glimpse and a man had approached. Of course she'd started to slur and that flamed her panic.

She'd fled, and the sensation of being watched had followed her down the street into the subway, Jess too fraught to discern whether the threat was real or imaginary. Then on the Tube, the group of teenagers had giggled and pointed. A young man tried to hide his urge to stare with a sideways glance. Jess had feared everyone knew who she was, but the businessman, from a different sphere, peered down at her with disdain. He probably equated her with the anonymous giggling teens who were ten years her junior. Then a handful of others frowned in confusion, perhaps noticing that she was noticed but couldn't put a finger on why.

Of all the crowd, the blonde woman paid her the most attention, but at the same time showed the least recognition of who Jess might be. It was sobering and engendered trust and Jess, lost and breaking down, had taken the offered hand.

Now, at last, the tension dissipated, leaving Jess's body leaden with fatigue. She propped her elbows on the café table and let her head drop into her hands. Her breathing slowed and the gridlock of thoughts and cacophony in her head began to clear until there was only a muffled sense of chatter and clink of cups, which she realised was simply the background noise of the café.

Jess was finally calm enough to take in her surroundings with some kind of objectivity. Half of the café was dimmed, ready to close, the other loud and bright with colour. The counter was filled with trays of tiny sweets and cakes behind glass, and shelves of illustrated tins lined one side of the café. The walls blazed with pinks and yellows and greens, a mosaic trim around the whole room, and tinted photographs of, Jess assumed, movie stars and singers smiled with impossible glamour from the walls.

The woman from the Tube chatted at the counter to a young man and middle-aged woman with long black hair streaked with grey. There was an exchange of handshakes and a kiss on the cheek from the older woman who held Jess's companion's arm and chatted with a warm intensity. The familiarity was comforting, as was their disinterest in Jess, and she let go of another wave of tension and shuffled into her seat.

The woman concluded her chat and slid into the booth seat opposite and Jess only had a moment to take her in while she made herself comfortable. A white woman, late thirties or early forties, she guessed. Naturally pale skin or skin that hadn't seen the sun in a while, high cheek bones and a patrician demeanour.

"You can relax here," the woman said, her voice doing as much as the setting to soothe Jess. She was well-spoken, as Jess's mother would have described. "Posh" her nan would have cackled. It was nothing like Jess's accent, or as it had been. Its corners had been rounded over the last few years, only coming out in full force on the phone to her parents, slipping into Brummie and saying "Mom" instead of "Mum" and lapsing into Northern idioms with her dad, with a few choice Jamaican Patois phrases from her Nan's early life. Jess's accent was a blend with the flavour of many places and unmistakably British.

This woman sitting a metre away, perhaps existed in a completely different world. She came from a different generation and class, probably shopped in places Jess still wouldn't dream of frequenting. Jess may be one degree of separation from a millionaire on the other side of the world but many from this fellow countrywoman. Was it possible, but for that chance meeting on the Tube, neither would have known of each other's existence?

That seemed incredible and exciting all at once, and the possibility filled Jess with a strange hope. Perhaps this was the only person in London who didn't have an ulterior motive and had simply offered help to a young woman called Jess.

"I've ordered a dessert mezze with your coffee," the woman said. "Eat as little or as much as you like but I thought sugar and caffeine might help steady you. I'll wait until it arrives and you feel comfortable."

"Thanks," Jess said. At least she was capable of speech now. "Thank you."

"You're welcome," the woman said, a picture of ease and decorum. "Do you know where you are?"

Jess shook her head. She hadn't a clue.

"You could use your phone to see on a map?"

"Oh. Yes, of course. Sorry." Her brain was still sluggish. "I switched it off."

She dived into her jacket pocket, squeezed the side of her mobile and a light glowed in her hands. It took a while to start, but as soon as it displayed the home screen notifications beeped incessantly and didn't stop for several seconds.

"Jesus." Jess dropped the phone on the table as if it burned and the woman shuffled in her seat, perhaps disconcerted at Jess's reaction.

"Are you in trouble? Who was following you?"

Jess's brain began to cease again, the pressure building as soon as she began to consider her position. "I've really messed up," she muttered. She gripped her head. "I was already running away. I've let so many people down."

Her phone beeped again and buzzed on the table. Then again and again. Jess snatched up the phone, reduced the volume and threw it down. It was silent but glowed on, off and on and didn't stop.

The woman remained in her seat, her voice even. "Is there someone you can call? Someone you trust?" Perhaps she was looking for a route out.

"No," Jess snapped. No-one. She couldn't think of a single person she wanted to see right now. Everyone she held dear, everyone who was important, would be livid with her.

"Anyone who could take you home?"

"I don't live in London. I hardly know the place," Jess blurted. "There's a hotel room with my stuff, but…" Her hands hurt. She hadn't realised she had been wringing them, but they clenched together until they ached.

Jess ceased wringing her hands, and regarded the stranger across the table, one who clearly had no idea who she was. She was just a woman who'd been kind, who was probably alarmed at Jess's behaviour.

"You don't know who I am," Jess said, unable to take her eyes off her companion's.

"No." She was studying her too, the epitome of calm.

Jess wondered out loud, incredulous, "You don't know anything about me?"

"That's right."

The air was tense.

"But you helped me."

The woman nodded.

Another pause.

"You were in trouble," the woman offered. "I didn't like that no-one offered to help. I don't make the best Good Samaritan I'm afraid, but I couldn't stand by and do nothing."

Jess stared at her companion, a well-dressed woman in a Burberry trench coat. An actually beautiful woman, now Jess could see clearly, with poise and consideration and apparently no motivation for helping Jess other than her obvious need. An hour ago, the existence of such a person seemed impossible.

"Thank you," Jess said, her voice at last controlled enough to convey her sincerity. "Really, thank you."

Now that Jess was calmer and perhaps appreciated the oddity of the situation, the woman relaxed, sinking more comfortably in her seat.

The woman opened her mouth, then paused. "I'm Anna, by the way," she said and she offered her hand.

"Jess." She smiled, relieved at the woman's contentment. "I'm…" The waiter approached their table. "Just Jess," she finished.

They released each other's hands with the arrival of the drink and mezze. Anna, Jess had only just got to know her name, was shuffling as if to leave.

"Will you stay? A bit longer?" Jess heard the rawness in her own voice and a wave of guilty embarrassment engulfed her. "Sorry. You've done loads already. Thank you."

Anna hesitated. The more mature woman stood perfectly poised but for so long it made Jess smile.

"Please. You don't have to be polite," she added. "I've spoiled your Friday evening and I'm grateful for you bringing me here."

"I do want to make sure you're safe," Anna said, her voice sober with responsibility. "What will you do? Where will you go?"

"I…" Jess's head filled with nothing. Of all the things she could have done, not one appealed or was possible without repercussions.

"I'll join you for a coffee at least then help you on your way. Sorry, Yusuf?" Anna took her seat and called towards the retreating waiter. "Could I have another coffee please?"

She turned back to Jess, a warm smile lingering on her lips, and Jess couldn't help her gaze flicking there. Full, deep, pink lips, free of makeup so that you could see all the tiny delicate lines, making her mouth all the more tenderly appealing for it. Jess felt the inappropriateness of her gaze and switched her attention to her drink.

"What is this?" she said, pointing to the small gold-trimmed china mug.

"Turkish coffee," Anna replied. "I can order an Americano or something else if you prefer. You didn't seem in the best frame of mind for deliberating when we arrived. I thought a hit of this might revive you."

Jess nodded and pinched the delicate china mug handle between her finger and thumb and lifted it to her lips.

"If you haven't tried it before, don't glug down to the bottom. It's unfiltered. You leave the sediment."

Jess took a tiny sip. Fragrant, roasted, rich coffee flowed across her tongue and aromatic vapours filled her nose. It had a fruity tang and a bitter strength that shrunk her tongue. She couldn't help the gasp of pleasure after she swallowed.

"That hits the spot," she said. "And these?"

"A small selection of their baklava and sekerpare."

Jess recognised the flaking layers of diamond-shaped baklava and supposed the round syrupy biscuits with an almond on top to be the sekerpare. She pinched one of the latter and nibbled. The moist sugary dessert was a perfect follow up to the bitter coffee and the flavours blended in her mouth, the fragrance of lemon surfacing deliciously.

"Nice?" Anna murmured, a smile playing on her lips.

Jess found herself gazing again. Anna had the beginning of faint lines, little semi-circles at the sides of her mouth where her smile filled her face. She had the perfect soothing voice for Jess – mellow and shaped by education but with hint of regional flavour.

"Edinburgh," Jess said.

"Sorry?"

"You come from Edinburgh?"

"Yes, I do. I didn't realise I still had an accent."

"It's very faint. I have an ear for them," Jess said proudly. "One of my skills."

Jess admired Anna's profile as she turned away with a laugh, her elegant jawline displayed to full advantage and her slim neck tantalising in the shadow of dark blonde hair.

"How about some more food?" Anna suggested, amusement pinching in the corner of her mouth, perhaps aware of Jess's scrutiny.

3

Anna was sitting in her favourite café, almost a daily haunt, a few steps away from the sanctuary of her flat, two pillars of her ordered and private life, with a woman she didn't know, who was troubled by god knows what, and god knows who.

The intrusion was unnerving. But at the same time Anna had to acknowledge the thrill. It was something the old Anna might have done, having the self-confidence to offer help to a stranger. It had taken a powerful dose of empathy when the woman fled into the carriage to tempt Anna, as she was now, from her shell.

She'd have to tell Penny. Her best friend would be proud of her digression from her routine. In fact Penny would be overjoyed and heartened at the progress. Too heartened and Anna decided perhaps she wouldn't confess.

The young woman sipped at her coffee and checked out of the window. She was stunning, Anna had to acknowledge. Brown eyes, Anna thought, so deep they appeared black in the dim light of the booth, long eyelashes with a touch of makeup, a face so shapely and beautiful it was hard to think the woman hadn't been created by an artist. And, yes, she was young, her brown skin smooth and made real only by a small scar on her cheek. When the woman relaxed and refrained from biting her bottom lip, her mouth curved in a generous bow. Anna wondered at who pursued her.

Jess's eyes settled on Anna for a moment, flicking away again as if caught trying to study her. Then she smiled and lifted her cup.

"This is delicious," she said.

Did Jess's gaze have a tendency to linger? It was rare for anyone to really take Anna in these days. Attention may not have been uncommon, but it was unwelcome, and she'd become adept at deflecting that which came her way. But tonight it was refreshing to have someone, this person, perhaps look at her that way. That it made Anna feel warm inside was a surprise. The confidence the woman placed in her was novel too, pleasing and reassuring somehow.

"Do you want to talk about what's troubling you?" Anna offered, with some of the assurance and authority she used to have. It was clear that the young woman's stress was caused by more than someone following her. "Would you find it helpful?"

Jess's shoulders slumped. "I'm so tired," she said, and the fatigue was evident in her voice as well as her demeanour. She seemed to find it difficult to speak when her anxiety was heightened, her phrases becoming monosyllabic. "I'm running on empty, I'm exhausted, my brain..." Anna could hear the struggle. "My brain's not working right."

Anna didn't interrupt. Jess was clearly distressed and Anna gave her time to recover.

"I've been working non-stop for seven years," Jess continued, "ever since I left school. God, it seems like decades ago. You're going to laugh aren't you if I tell you I feel old." The young woman waited for her to answer.

"No, I won't laugh," Anna replied. Honestly, she knew the feeling.

"I don't think I've been home to Mom and Dad for more than a handful of hours the last few years. And..." She groaned. "I know I should be having the time of my life, but I'm not. I couldn't be further from it."

Jess's head drooped, and her eyelids seemed so heavy as if she might simply stop.

"What is it you do? Can you take a break?" Anna asked.

"No." Jess's voice broke with desperation, her smooth youthful features knotting. "My schedule is packed. Do you know, this," she held her arms out, "this is the closest I've come to a break in, I don't know, months." She shook her head. "I'm going bloody crazy. I mean," Jess hastily added, "I'm tired of the constant demands and people wanting stuff all the time."

Her phone glowed again on the table.

"And this," she said, holding her mobile up. "I don't get a moment's peace. Even while you sleep people are demanding."

Anna was torn between asking for more detail and not wanting to add to the pressure.

"Tonight," Jess carried on before Anna could enquire, "I was meant to be at an interview. I arrived from France today and tomorrow I'm due in Manchester and I can't think of anything worse than some stranger interrogating me."

Anna bit her tongue and reconsidered. "Will there be anyone worried about you? Is there someone you should call?"

Jess shook her head. "I don't want to."

"Family who might be worried?"

"You're right. I should text my mom."

Anna nodded encouragement and Jess turned her attention to the phone, holding it in both hands and tapping with her thumbs. She was about to put the phone down when it lit up again.

"Fuck," Jess whispered.

"What's wrong?"

Jess had gone rigid. "Look." She thrust the phone towards her and Anna flinched as the shape filled her field of vision.

"Someone's in here. It's us. Jesus."

An indistinct picture of Jess and Anna in the booth filled the screen. It had been cropped and enlarged but it was clearly them.

"This is what I mean," Jess's voice pitched higher.

Anna's heart rate rocketed and she didn't dare turn around. "Who was it? Who sent it? Can you see them?"

"It's anonymous."

"Is it the person from the train?"

"I don't know." Jess's voice tightened. "I wasn't sure if I was being paranoid. I ran from the pub, from a man at the bar. I was scared he... But others too... The drink...I didn't know whether to trust myself."

Anna was beginning to freeze. Threat filled the air. She felt exposed from every direction and fear ran its chilling fingers over her body. How quickly it rushed in again, her whole being sensitive to this kind of terror. It was horrifying how one moment you were part of civilised society, safe in a city, surrounded by diners enjoying a Friday evening treat, the next you were vulnerable from every angle.

"Can you see him in the restaurant?" Anna said, her face locked forward. "Is he here? The man from the pub?"

Jess moved back and forth, craning around the booth. "I didn't see him properly. It could be anyone. I want to get out." Jess's voice became strangled.

"OK," Anna said. "OK." She was whispering it to herself.

This is what she feared most, that and panicking so that she couldn't judge a situation for herself.

She reached across the table and her hand was immediately engulfed by Jess's. The young woman held on for dear life. Anna could feel her fright. Jess's desperate grip communicated every frayed nerve. Every urge was to flee.

Anna breathed out slowly, its jittery staccato betraying her. "I can help."

"Please."

Anna steeled herself. She was a long way out of her comfort zone, but the momentum of the situation had her in its grip.

"There's an emergency exit out the back, past the loos," she said quietly. "My flat is a few metres away. You go first, I'll pay the bill and follow you. You can wait out a while there if you want to."

"What if he follows?"

"We can be out of the building and home before he realises."

"Shall I go now?"

Anna nodded and when Jess left the table she waved towards the counter for the bill. The curvy figure of Zehra wandered over and squeezed Anna's shoulder with affection.

"Did your friend not like my baklava?" she said with mock indignation, waving her arm grandly across the table.

"Sorry, we need to go," Anna said, grasping Zehra's hand on her shoulder.

"What's wrong?" Zehra said, immediately picking up on Anna's anxiety.

"I need to leave through the back. I think my friend has a stalker. I don't know for sure." Many things didn't make sense. "Because," and a hollow chill settled in her stomach as she voiced her admission, "I hardly know her."

This was too far beyond her comfort zone, so much that the world began to lurch and her head reeled. She closed her eyes and gripped Zehra's hand until the spinning stopped.

Not for the first time she cursed her fear and limitations. But the compulsion to help the woman built inside her again. No-one had helped her on the train, and just as Anna couldn't stand by then and ignore the woman's clear need, she couldn't hold back now when she sensed the woman's fear so keenly. Jess, she said to herself. The woman was called Jess, and she wanted her help. Anna released her grip and opened her eyes.

"I need to take her to mine until she feels safe."

"Are you sure you should do that?"

"No," Anna said with an ironic laugh.

"Hmm," Zehra pondered, her mature face crinkling with thought. "If you want my opinion, although it is difficult to tell, she looked fine to me. Worried, yes, but not worrying. To tell the truth, I wonder if I've seen her before. Can't for the life of me place her though. Would you like me to call on you and check you are OK after we shut?"

Anna squeezed Zehra's hand. "Thank you," she said and she began to rise from her seat.

"No problem. Can't be too careful. Do you have any idea who was troubling her?"

"Not completely, no," Anna shook her head helplessly.

"I will watch for anyone leaving."

"Thank you."

"Go. We'll settle up tomorrow." And Zehra cradled her head in both hands, drawing her forward and kissing the top of her head.

Anna slipped out under the cover of Zehra clearing the table and found the corridor empty except for Jess pacing back and forth.

"Straight on," Anna said.

Anna hit the emergency lever down and they broke out into the dark side street and Anna slammed the door behind them.

"Straight ahead," she said, and Jess scuttled alongside her, down the side-street, and Anna prayed that nothing hid in the darkness of her usual path home. "Left here, and first house we come to."

Anna felt for the shape of the front door Yale lock in the dim light and dived into her trouser pocket with the other hand. Her fingers trembled as she fumbled the keys and the pair almost fell into the hallway of the end terrace house. "Close the door," Anna said. "I'm on the top floor."

She led the way, hauling herself up the rail, sprinting up three flights of stairs and she found herself shaking as she opened her studio flat door. They burst in, both breathing hard, and stood in the dark room, the only light coming from the wide balcony window and the orange glow of the city outside.

"Please, sit down," Anna panted, and she put her arm out towards the foot of the bed as she slumped into the armchair beside it. "I need a minute," she gasped.

Jess collapsed onto the bed and curled up small, her arms and legs tucked into her belly. Anna watched her dark shape, taut on the bed, and waited for her own heart rate to calm.

"You're safe here," she murmured.

Jess curled up tighter with a moan, her anxiety so acute she seemed to have lost speech entirely. Anna waited, for Jess to recover and open up, expecting her to explain in her own time. She waited too long in fact, Jess's words all now apparently gone and the young woman shut down, and sometime later in the night the tense shape eased and Anna could hear deep regular breathing.

Her heart sank as she watched the sleeping stranger, stunned by the intrusion into her ordered world and her sense of control slipping away. It was thrilling and terrifying.

4

When Jess opened her eyes, she felt a surprising calm. She was cosy under a duvet and her body was relaxed with a pleasant heaviness from deep sleep. There was an emptiness from exhaustion too. After her acute anxiety last night, she'd reached a threshold and was unable to panic anymore.

The worst had happened and she was fine. She'd hit rock bottom and the fallout was settling outside somewhere, but she was still here. She'd freaked out in front of the whole of London, fucked up the interview, so many things she'd feared, and now there was nothing else to go wrong. It was like she'd taken a drug and was light and carefree at last.

She sat up, blinking, and stretched her arms, which ached in that satisfying way on awakening.

Daylight shone through thin blinds across the dormer window that spanned the width of the small flat. Jess could search the entire place without moving from the bed. A small kitchen area and island in the left corner by the window. A sofa, bookshelves and TV forming the three sides of a snug living area on the right. The bed was backed against a wall and faced the flat's front door, and the roof of the attic sloped into shadows at the back.

There was no movement or sign of Anna, then the pitter-patter of water running in a shower became apparent. Another door set back from the front must have led to small bathroom.

Jess could scarper if she wanted. Last night she'd been careless on vodka and desperate. Could she trust her judgement of Anna from a few hours ago? Her gut said she could. But photographs of Jess sleeping on this bed might be all over social media and gossip sites she realised with a reluctant fatigue.

She turned over her phone beside her, the battery icon low and red. There were hundreds of notifications, missed calls, re-postings of her cowering on the train or nursing a coffee. Little else though, and nothing taken in this room, and her heartrate remained quiet as she gazed at the shower door.

Perhaps her bold vodka-self had judged well after all. The woman either had no interest in Jess's celebrity or was unaware. Jess smacked her lips together. Her post bold vodka-self could do with a glass of water and a toothbrush.

She checked for messages on her family filter. There was one message from Mom, "Call as soon as you can", and another from Nan which consisted solely of emojis and Jess suspected the cat had been pawing at her grandmother's phone again.

An email pinged on the screen from her manager with the subject line "WTH – underground picture?"

A nugget of panic tightened in her gut, the chill threatening to crystalize up her spine and seize her brain.

"No." She squeezed her phone, its hard edges pressing into her fingers, until the screen went dead and she held the mobile to her chest as if to suffocate it.

The sound of the shower stopped and Jess sat up straight, expectant.

She waited and fiddled with the duvet over her legs. Anna must have covered her last night after she'd nodded off. The bed linen was a yellow ochre, quite garish for someone like Anna, but the flat too was vibrant – a rich terracotta for the walls with wood cut prints of seascapes in chunky wooden frames then a palette of blues for the kitchen cupboards. Jess would have expected something more muted, perhaps a Victorian room of chalk white paints and modern classic furniture.

And it was orderly. "Bloody hell," she whispered.

It struck Jess how symmetrical and particularly arranged the flat was. Not just the precision rows of containers on the kitchen surface and the range of Pantone mugs hanging below the wall units. The matrix of small drawers embedded in the island. The dust pan and brush clipped to the end unit. The bust, and literally it was a headless pair of boobs, Jess noted, on the book shelf that ran along the sitting area, aligned with a vase of irises and a curvy Polynesian sculpture.

Jess had a fleeting suspicion about Anna's sexuality before dismissing it. Did every queer female household have a nude? But, everything had its precise place, nothing was simply cast aside, all apart from the explosion of vegetation that hung in the kitchen corner of the long window. Spider plants. "Impossible to kill," Jess heard her Nan say in her head. "Couldn't if you tried." Funny how she'd been thinking of her family so vividly the last few hours.

"Good morning."

Jess's heart beat faster at Anna's voice, not only at her surprise presence but its mellifluous quality that Jess found appealing in more than one way. It calmed and reassured last night and flooded Jess with a sense of ease now, but it also delighted.

Anna stood before Jess, her blonde hair in dark tendrils from the shower. She seemed paler this morning, even though her white skin showed a slight tan against her classic linen shirt. Slender arms were revealed by the rolled up sleeves and the sunglasses tucked tantalisingly into her cleavage drew Jess's attention.

Perhaps it was Anna's lack of makeup – none at all as far as Jess could make out. She had enviable dark lashes, which accentuated her blue eyes, but no, no makeup at all. There was nothing to mask the deep pink of her full lips, no concealment of the sprinkle of tiny freckles across her nose. She was just a beautiful woman in a white shirt and jeans. A confident woman, thoughts impenetrable beyond her calm expression. An assured woman. A woman patiently waiting for Jess's response, she realised.

"Hi," Jess said, shy and giggly at the situation.

Anna waited, a twitch curling the corner of her mouth.

"I'm so sorry," Jess burbled. "I don't remember getting here very clearly. I mean if I had, if I'd been anything like I usually am, I wouldn't have stayed for a start, but you know…"

Anna tilted her head to the side.

"I might have…at least…you know… perhaps…." Jess drew breath. "I completely crashed in your bed, didn't I?"

Anna's face brightened with amusement and their eyes met. "You needed it."

A burst of elation sang through Jess as Anna's eyes shone bright azure with their shared recognition of the situation. It was enough to make Jess lose herself for a moment in those twinkling blues.

"Oh," she said, coming to. "Did I even pretend to leave you any room?" Her sprawl when she'd woken made this unlikely.

Anna laughed. "No. And I took the sofa." She gestured towards the living area near the window and a pillow and blanket folded on the end of the couch.

"I really did impose, didn't I?" Jess said, shoulders sinking.

"Yes you did." Anna might have agreed, but her voice was full of delight. "I was perfectly comfortable."

"I'm so grateful. And believe me, my Mom would have a fit if she knew I'd been this rude."

"Well, if your mother enquires, you can tell her you were a well-behaved guest, after presumptuously taking the only bed."

Jess groaned inside. It may have made it outside too.

Anna smiled once more, her head tilted to the side, and the warmth of her expression seemed to shine on Jess and make her glow inside. She probably wore a goofy expression of appreciation. It's not like she didn't wear everything on the outside, and Anna dipped her gaze perhaps out of politeness.

Anna unhooked her sunglasses from her shirt and for a moment looked as if she intended to put them on, before setting them on a bookcase. She sat next to Jess on the bed, in that measured way she had, not close enough to touch, but intimate and comforting.

Anna's manner was the perfect tonic for Jess. Her memories from last night were a jumble but her impressions of this woman were the same. Safe, responsible, kind without overbearing. It's funny how you picked up on cues from a person. There was something about Anna's assured but careful movements that engendered trust. That and the lack of recognition. The whole world had an ulterior motive when befriending Jess.

She had nothing like the panic when she'd woken in a strange hotel room with a vague memory of paying for it, a woman under her arm and too much alcohol in her veins. The lack of clothes in the morning she remembered though. Knickers, bra, T-shirt all gone, taken as souvenirs and sold on eBay, complete with tag line of "genuine scent included". She shuddered at the memory and shrank inside. Everything was so public. It felt stripped bare and stretched out for all to see. Not even her worn knickers were beyond scrutiny and were treated as fair game. She'd learned caution from that, hadn't she?

"How are you feeling?" Anna's presence beside her, respectful but close, was everything. It soothed away her troubled memories.

"Safe," Jess said. An odd response, considering. But it was exactly what she felt – relaxed, quiet with tingling through her entire body.

"Have you thought about last night and what you should do?"

"No."

Which part did Anna mean? There would be significant fallout from the night before. She wasn't sure how much she'd blurted to Anna.

"About reporting the man who followed you to the police?"

"Oh." That's the piece she meant. "I don't think I have enough detail to give them."

"You have the online account," Anna said, "and I've been thinking. Zehra has CCTV at the café. You may be able to identify him from that?"

Jess's throat tightened. She didn't want to think about it. How many people could it have been – there were so many crank accounts trolling her these days. Who knew what was behind any of them? She wanted to hide here, the only place of late where the weight of the world disappeared from her shoulders. She was anonymous in a secret sanctuary with a mature thoughtful woman. An attractive mature woman. Jess rolled her eyes at herself. Is this why she'd placed her trust in Anna, inclined towards older, usually straight, women and thinking with her heart and hormones?

"Think about it?" Anna squeezed her knee. "We should at least ask Zehra to keep last night's recording."

Jess nodded. No, there were good reasons to have faith in Anna.

"Thank you," Jess said. "For the suggestion."

"I will come with you. I know Zehra well and will explain, but she won't be in for a little while if she was working last night."

"Oh."

"You could wait here and we'll go down in an hour or two?"

Jess opened her mouth. "Sorry. Am I getting in your way? You must have plans. Do you have time to do that? I can be out in a second." Although her heart lurched at the thought of tumbling outside exposed into the world. And again at tumbling out without Anna's company.

Anna hesitated and Jess couldn't see her expression behind a curtain of hair that had fallen over Anna's face. She stared, waiting for her answer. Anna stroked the locks of hair behind her ear with slender fingers. "It happens," she said, her voice a soothing murmur, "that I have time this morning."

And it was the best answer Jess could have imagined. A couple more hours with this woman with the honeyed voice and aura that made Jess warm inside. The woman with the enigmatic smile and eyes as blue as the sea. The woman with smooth skin and freckles sprinkled across her cheeks and that trailed down her cleavage.

A little demon of conscience tutted inside. "Jess Lambert. You and older women," accompanied by a shake of the head. That little demon had her Nan's voice. She blinked and the demon disappeared in a puff of smoke.

"Thank you," Jess said.

She hoped she didn't grin too much.

5

"Have you found your bearings?" Anna asked.

Her guest seemed remarkably at ease this morning, right down to the big goofy smile. She lounged in bed in her tight black jeans and jacket.

"Have you told someone where you are?" Anna continued.

"No, do you think I need to?"

Anna puzzled. Perhaps it was the invincibility of youth talking. "You've woken up in strange flat with a woman you didn't know the day before."

"I'm twenty-four not sixteen," Jess laughed, and the deep timbre of her voice reinforced her statement. Then she added, "Although I woke up in plenty of strange places when I was."

The response was laden with innuendo and with Jess's looks Anna was in no doubt about the statement's veracity. The abrupt silence that followed perhaps spoke of Jess's embarrassment at overstepping the mark. Her guest peered away for a moment. Anna still wasn't certain, but did Jess's attention sometimes more than linger? Not that it mattered. Any partiality wouldn't flourish past the awkwardness and her limitations. Anna wouldn't allow it for a start. But for now? Could Anna let herself enjoy it for once? It frightened her, but Jess would be gone soon enough.

It was surprising how relaxed Anna was too. After Zehra had quietly popped round to check on her after the café had closed, Jess sleeping through it all, Anna had slept deeply and woken refreshed in the morning. She thought she'd have a wretched night with a stranger in the flat, but it had been reassuring to have company, the regular breaths of sleep lulling Anna into slumber too. For once she hadn't triple locked the door. And here was her troubled visitor too, calm if a little flustered.

"Um," Jess cleared her throat, "I like your flat." The grin that accompanied it spoke of genuine appreciation even if the change in subject had been clumsy. Jess got out of the bed. "Really beautiful. I love the colour scheme." Her large eyes shone with enthusiasm.

"It was my aunt's apartment," Anna said. "I bought it from her when she moved into a home. A friend of mine, actually a set designer, decorated it for me a couple of years ago. I was lucky."

"Very lucky. It's gorgeous."

Anna hesitated, not wanting to explain. "I wanted a complete change. I wanted a bold and saturated colour scheme." To feel safe, contained, nurtured, her world away from the real one. Dominique with her artistic eye had presented Anna a palette of rich yellow and red ochres for the bedroom and snug spaces, and Prussian blue for the kitchen cupboards. The rows upon rows of pots on the kitchen surface were arranged in colours from the whole palette. It was all complementary and pleasingly harmonious and sumptuous.

"I love it," Jess said. "The colours make me smile and want to roll around in your bed enjoying the luxury of it all."

Jess stopped, her smile frozen on her face while the words hung in the air, cut off at the realisation of what she'd said. So, was there something more to Jess's compulsion to roll around in Anna's bed, not only enjoying the décor? Anna dismissed the notion, for Jess's and her own sake, and persisted with, "I had to share it with two others to afford the mortgage."

"Three people in here? Blimey. Where did you all fit?" Jess spun around, her expressive and beautiful features in entertaining shock.

"I shared with two others from college and we were all broke," Anna replied. "We hardly had any belongings and managed to squeeze in."

"Did you all squeeze into one bed too?" Jess joked and pointed towards the bed that Anna sat upon.

Anna tilted her head to the side. "Yes. Three of us. All snug in the bed."

"Oh," Jess said. Was there a gulp?

Anna could swear she could hear the wheels turning in Jess's mind. Was she piquing Jess's curiosity about her sexuality? Anna had to admit she had a few questions about Jess, questions she had a decent feeling she knew the answers to.

"They were good friends," Anna said. "Some of the best."

Still silence from Jess. Still the wheels.

"Right," Jess said. There was slow nodding and a "hmm"-ing to make light.

Anna had definitely sparked her interest.

"Penny and Elizabeth," Anna offered.

"Women," Jess mumbled, it seemed without thinking. Then silence. Still those wheels.

"Three years. Three in a bed," Anna said.

"That's um," Jess picked at a nail, "a long time to share a bed."

"Yes."

"A lot of nights."

"Hmmhmm."

"Though I suppose nice to snuggle up in winter…"

Anna let the suggestion hang there a moment. Was she mistaken, or was Jess a little hesitant and coy. Was she tripping over mental images? Anna was picturing three women all cosy, so she'd bet good money Jess was doing the same.

She decided to move the conversation along for Jess, who was possibly catatonic with awkwardness.

"Lot warmer in summer though," Anna said, attempting to shift the mental images out of the bed.

"Really?" Jess said, with a politely interested question.

"Definitely. Come spring, the sun shines through these windows until evening. It's gorgeous."

"Yeah?"

"An attic like this, at the top of the building, with the heat rising in the day? It's like a greenhouse. I think we were down to our undies in June."

Oh dear. Jess definitely gulped. Anna hadn't intended the image, but it tickled her now her companion was so obviously affected.

"I bet it was hot," Jess gasped.

Anna had to cover her mouth to stop laughing. "Absolutely." She decided to clarify, "Sometimes I stayed with my boyfriend at the time."

"Oh."

It was a light "Oh," but tinged. Anna's could hear it and see a little of Jess's spirit sink. Was she fooling herself or was Jess disappointed that her ex had been male?

"Must have been good friends by the end of three years though," Jess giggled. "Very intimate sharing this space."

Jess's subconscious was making itself very vocal indeed.

"They were great," Anna said soberly, but with amusement bubbling inside. "Penny, my best friend, and Elizabeth did start seeing each other."

"Oh?" It was said lightly, as if uninterested, but so very high pitched.

"Right." That too was an octave awry.

So they'd established Anna knew lesbians.

"But," Anna added. "I was never involved with either."

It said something about her though, didn't it. Jess's mind was ticking over again, perhaps rejecting the suggestion that Anna had ever been either's lover but not protesting the possibility.

"Hmm," Jess said, again, with clumsy nonchalance, swinging her arms round her back. "Awkward."

Anna laughed. She didn't know if Jess meant her reaction or Anna sharing with two friends who were lovers. She imagined both.

Jess's now blatant interest in her sexuality entertained her. Whether she was interested in Anna or not, Jess's gaydar was beeping, and surely that said so much about her.

"So," Jess stuttered. "Is she still alive?"

"Which one?" Anna asked.

"Sorry?"

"Which lover?"

"Whose lover?"

"Not mine, but the two I shared a bed with." Anna's cheeks twitched trying to supress her amusement.

"Oh! Ha!" Jess padded from foot to foot. "No. Not them. Not your not-lovers. I wasn't thinking of them. Honestly."

"Honestly?"

"Honestly."

Anna bet she was. In all kinds of ways.

"No, really," Jess said. "I meant your aunt." Jess sounded relieved to have finally steered away from that minefield. "Is she dead?" she said with great delight.

Anna raised her eyebrow.

"Oh, I mean." Jess's chin dropped and her voice lowered with solemnity. "Is your aunt, who I'm sure you adored and probably doesn't deserve my disrespectful tone, is she alive?"

Anna paused, her lips parted, pondering. She shouldn't be drawing it out, but Jess's open-book mind and ability to entangle herself was adorable.

"Yes." Anna relented.

"Oh good. What a relief."

"Actually it's something she's rather livid about."

"What?!" Poor Jess. The exasperation hit two octaves higher and her eyebrows touched her hairline.

"It's just that she was expecting to be in a home for a year at most. She smoked and drank her way through life but she's one of those rebellious souls who defy even carcinogens. So she's still kicking about, something I'm very happy about. But I think she envisioned dying young and gloriously and didn't intend going gently into that good night. Her words. Her borrowed words at least," Anna added.

"And is she in a home?" Jess asked, peeping from beneath her bouncy fringe.

"She's happily sharing a house with five old friends in Epping, with a garden and a view over the forest. They can afford a full-time carer between them and run up a riot because they make the home rules."

At last Jess relaxed, her shoulders dropping with a satisfying sigh. Safely out of territory where she'd mentally rolled around in Anna's bed, possibly visualised Anna with two female lovers and wished death on her dearest of relatives.

"She sounds like a big personality," Jess said, delight in her voice. "She sounds like my Nan."

And those big beautiful eyes stole Anna's.

6

"You have CDs." Jess was wandering around the flat, perhaps shaking off a little of the embarrassment she'd brought upon herself. Anna felt a twinge of guilt at her enjoyment.

"You have, like, honest-to-god CDs."

It sounded as if Jess had unearthed a relic or ancient treasure.

"They do still sell CDs you know," Anna said.

It smarted a little. After Jess's interest in Anna's sexuality, it was a disappointment to be reminded that it didn't mean Jess was interested in Anna, a middle-aged woman, living secluded and alone and clinging to her CD collection. Even though Anna would never encourage Jess's interest, the frisson of attraction was good for her esteem.

"Yeah, why is that?" Jess said, running her finger along the collection and wrinkling her nose.

"Why is what?" Anna said.

"Why do they sell CDs?"

"For old buggers like me probably."

"I still don't get it."

"You're meant to say 'you're not old'," Anna jested.

"How old are you?"

"Thirty-nine."

"Like nearly forty?" Jess faced her and gasped theatrically.

"Yes."

"Jesus."

"Oi." She'd deserved that. So Jess could play too. That was good. It made Anna smile and fill with satisfaction. When was the last time someone had teased and made her feel like that, so full of delight from her belly to her ears?

"I'm kidding," Jess said, and shrugged off her quip. "It's weird though. I don't often see people's music taste on display. Or their books. I have everything on my phone. My parents got rid of their CDs after they'd copied them. Not their books though. Never the books." She frowned. "There are a lot of female artists here. I mean, a lot of female artists. Queer too…"

Again the suggestion. This time Jess said it without blatant innuendo, more a realisation of her own thoughts.

"Do you always think out loud?" Anna asked.

"Oh," Jess stood up. "Sometimes." She grinned, that great big smile with beautiful lips like a bow. "Gets me into trouble."

"I bet it does."

There was a silence. Again Anna could almost hear the cogs ticking over in Jess's head, wondering what Anna's impression of her might be, perhaps anxious that she'd overstepped the mark.

"I don't think I could throw the CDs away," Anna said to break the silence. "I love the artwork. Sometimes, when I'm tired, it's nice to recognise the picture of a favourite album and put it on." She wondered if the woman from a different generation would understand.

"There's like a thousand dance albums here," Jess said.

"Were you expecting the complete works of Bach?"

"Yeah."

"They're on that shelf."

Jess laughed out loud, throwing her head back, that generous mouth open wide. Anna was beginning to love that sound – joyful, fearless and full of song like her voice when it was confident. Anna found herself smiling, too much.

"So what are you listening to at the moment?" Jess asked.

"It's probably Kylie in the player."

"Kylie?"

"You don't know Kylie?"

"Of course I do. My mom listens to her. But I keep thinking you'd be listening to something like opera."

Anna would have liked to have dispelled that assumption by saying there were many sides to her character but she was reeling from being lumped in with Jess's mother. Composed on the outside though, Anna raised an eyebrow.

"What?" Jess said. She'd turned to Anna, eyes and mouth wide.

"If I said, have you heard of Madonna, I suppose you'd say your gran listens to her?"

"No.... Oh." Jess beamed. "I didn't mean to suggest, you know."

"Tell me." Anna let her voice crack into an aged croak. "What do young people listen to today?"

Jess grinned. "I haven't got a bloody clue. I just listen to whatever catches my ear." She ran her finger further along the shelves. "Wow, you really are organised."

Anna winced. She'd rebelled against it for years, but had to admit it was her saviour. Her mother was delighted at it, Anna embracing her regimentation, the new job too, and the loss of disapproved friends. "In some ways this is all a blessing you know," her mother's voice intruded. Anna mentally waved her away.

"I had a clear out when the flat was decorated a few years ago," she admitted.

So many memories thrown or packed away. Items from her past that she couldn't bear to part with, but of which she didn't want the daily reminder. Things that would trigger a cascade of memories and impressions, floods of emotions, lovers, arguments, friends, pinnacle achievements of her career, hopes, dreams all safely contained in the darkness of the void under the roof.

And the rest. "It's all labelled and organised." In neat boxes with big tidy letters.

"I'd expect nothing less."

So Jess had already picked up on the order.

"Actually," Anna said, "my meticulous mother helped with the flat, and I'll admit that order runs on her side of the family."

"But you're nothing like that?" Jess teased.

Anna opened her mouth. Had she ever been messy, even when she'd shared this studio flat with two other girls? She had always been the responsible and organised one, before she used it to regain her sense of control and it became so critical.

"Being prepared and organised does come naturally," Anna admitted.

"Wow," Jess's voice was muffled from bending over.

What had she found? Anna tried peering around Jess's curving bottom to see what she'd spotted.

"OK, if you find anything odd or embarrassing, don't tell me," Anna said.

"Like the vibrator?"

This time Jess's voice held no embarrassment, not a hint that she might be crossing a line.

"What?" Anna coughed.

"So you do have a vibrator hidden away in here." Jess peeped back towards her, smile shining and the accompanying giggle too catching not to lighten Anna's mood.

"Don't delve," Anna said, delivering her best schoolmarm voice.

"Oh." Jess replied. "I like firm and commanding Anna." She drew out "like" so lasciviously that Anna's heart did a little flutter. Jess's flirting wasn't only good for her ego. It was reaching other places too.

"Stop it," Anna said, schoolmarm again, a little fearful of all the places Jess was reaching. And Jess laughed and desisted.

Anna stood up from the foot of the bed, her heart tumbling over and fearful of where all this was leading.

"It's still a while until Zehra will be at the café," she said, briskly. "How about some breakfast while we wait? If you want a shower, feel free while I make pancakes."

"Pancakes?" Jess said, with a hint of incredulity, and just like that her flirtatiousness switched to awe. "Proper, home-cooked pancakes?"

"Yes?"

"Real pancakes, like from eggs and flour and stuff?" Jess said, her bright smile getting bigger.

"Yes."

"Do you know how long it is since someone's cooked me proper, honest-to-god, pancakes?"

"No?"

"Me neither, it's that long ago. Must have been when I was a kid."

"So would you like some?" Anna said.

The brightness got even bigger as Jess turned fully towards Anna and that smooth voice was full of joy. "That would be the best thing in the world."

"How would you like them? Honey and fruit? Syrup? Chocolate sauce?"

"Chocolate sauce," Jess said, like there was no other legitimate accompaniment. "You don't have squirty cream as well do you?"

"Yes, I do."

"Oh really? What do you get up to with that?" Jess's tone was so blatantly suggestive that Anna laughed out loud.

"Excuse me?" Anna said it just as suggestively.

"I mean." Jess's features dropped. Was there blushing this time, her skin tone deepening ever so slightly? There was definite stuttering. "Sorry. I am not being appropriate this morning. But squirty cream? I thought you'd be more an organic honey and rare Himalayan berries kind of woman."

"Actually, I am. I have the rest in for Bibs."

Jess paused.

"Sorry," Anna added. "I usually have a breakfast date Saturday mornings with my best friend Penny, who I used to share with, and her daughter Bibs.

"Are they going to be here soon?" Jess twitched.

"No, Pen's gone to a wedding that her partner had forgotten to tell her about. She'll be sending me livid messages all day."

"Oh. Good," Jess said. "I mean. That I'm not getting in your way."

"Not at all." Anna stared at Jess.

The young woman's head was dipped down, then she peered up to attempt to catch Anna's eye perhaps, before looking away again.

She seemed an unusual mix of confidence and maturity, cheeky attention then crushing bashfulness and anxiety. She could stand tall and full of presence, then the next moment shrink away. Anna couldn't quite make her out yet. But she had no wish to have her gone and plenty of compulsion to get to know her better.

"Get that shower," Anna said, "and I'll make breakfast. There's a clean towel on the radiator and a packet of new knickers on the side – bog standard M&S but you're welcome to take a pair."

"I don't know, I jump into your bed and your knickers..." Jess stopped. "Shit. Sorry. My mom would be dying if she could see me. And Nan would have slapped me round the calves."

Anna could only smile.

"I should tell you," Jess said, brushing her fingers through her thick black hair. "Maybe I should have mentioned it before. I don't know if it makes people uncomfortable sometimes. Especially when I make crappy jokes and flirt. Which I do a lot. With people I feel comfortable with anyway. Only by telling the truth. But....look, I should tell you..." She took a deep breath. "I'm gay. Lesbian. Actually I had a boyfriend when I was a teen if you really must pin me down, and I'm most comfortable with queer. Just so you–"

"Me too. Bi if you must pin me down."

"Oh."

It was as if Jess was sent gently reeling from the confirmation. Anna waited for her to adjust and when Jess did there was a comfort in her expression and knowing in her eyes.

"I'd wondered," Jess said quietly.

"I'd wondered about you too," Anna murmured.

And with the certainty, the air between them was suddenly charged with real possibility.

7

So, Anna was bi.
Jess caught her own reflection in the bathroom mirror. She hadn't seen that expression in a long time. Her large brown eyes were bright and her face eager with delight for all the implications. It wasn't with the expectation that something would happen, simply that it was a possibility at all. She filled her lungs and breathed out with a great deal of satisfaction.

She felt free of people's preconceptions of late and the pervading sense that she was being courted for favours more than her company.

She stared at her image, seeing it as her own for the first time in a while. Her warm brown skin and heart-shaped face, high cheekbones, slender neck which she was often ordered to display by tilting her chin. She didn't have to today. Her generous lips curled in a smile and she blinked lazily. Her inky eyelashes were free of mascara this morning and she wore her small gold hoop earrings, more than enough decoration for the role of just Jess.

She was a woman, who'd met another queer woman, with a definite spark of attraction. To feel that again, without the dread of ulterior motive or betrayal, was elating.

She rubbed her fingers up the short hair at the back of her head then tousled the longer locks on top. They were starting to curl into their natural wave.

She checked around the small room, bright with sunlight beaming through a window in the sloping roof. A shower in the corner. Orange towel folded crisp and clean on a rail. A shelf with a bright green bottle of shampoo and coconut conditioner beside it, ideal for Anna's strawberry blonde, not the usual treatment for Jess. She bet Anna didn't have a pair of straighteners and there was no sign of a shower cap either.

No matter. Jess smiled once more at her natural reflection. She would leave her hair and her loose curls, which would spring back with a drop of water, would have their day instead. She wondered if Anna would like the look.

Wait. Did Anna have a partner? The flat was her own but that didn't mean she was single. Jess hadn't noticed any photos. There were no pictures of her arm draped around a handsome lover or cheek to cheek with anyone special. Anna hadn't mentioned anyone either.

Still. Jess should be cautious and respectful. That didn't quell her smile though. Her reflection grinned at her.

"Stop it," she chastised herself.

It's not like it could go anywhere with everything on Jess's plate, and although there was that palpable excitement when Anna said she was bi, it didn't mean that Anna was interested. Jess's smile was still there though, the twinkle in her eye brighter than ever.

"Have a bloody shower, you maniac," she said to her reflection.

She was enjoying that flirting though. That wasn't out of bounds.

—

Anna was standing in the kitchen, board, knife and bananas laid out in front of her, when she heard the shower door thud shut from inside the bathroom. That was no surprise as she had suggested a shower to Jess. What did surprise, with the sound of water spraying on the glass surround, was the visual her brain concocted for her. A steamy image of a tall, nude woman popped into her head.

Anna cleared her throat, as if someone was present and could see her thoughts, and warm embarrassment bloomed on her cheeks. And it wasn't only the embarrassment that was warming.

Anna wondered if, for anyone, it was possible to listen to Jess in the shower without picturing her naked. Apparently it wasn't for her, and the steamy picture of a tall shapely woman in her bathroom intruded again. Anna didn't let herself dwell on the detail, and decided that as she couldn't accurately form Jess because she'd never seen her naked, that it didn't count as indecent. And after one last mental peek, she reined in her imagination.

Not that the likeness of Jess's upturned face, with eyes closed and glistening water trailing down smooth dark skin, didn't flash in her brain whenever the water broke for a second. Or Jess's long fingers massaging her skin in a way so satisfying as to make the imagined Jess open her mouth in rapture.

"Oh." Anna said it out loud. She dropped the knife with a clatter onto the worktop.

She covered her mouth and the smile that spread there. Excitement tingled inside. A slight flutter of interest thrilled her body. She had been closed off for so long, she'd forgotten those feelings were possible.

Was it because Jess had said she was gay? Or was it the fact, obvious now to Anna, that the younger woman flirted and her gaze always lingered more than it should?

"Stop it," she muttered, and she picked up the knife from the surface.

Would it linger if she knew? Would Jess's expression, her whole body language and tone, change as soon as she realised how small Anna's world was?

A heaviness threatened to descend and Anna shrugged it off. She could enjoy the flirtation this beautiful morning with the sun shining diffuse through the light blinds. It was not often she enjoyed the attention of someone she was partial to. Of someone who was just, well, nice. It was a treat.

The running water stopped and was followed by the creak of the shower door opening. Try as she might, there was no way Anna could stop herself from imagining Jess's long toned leg stepping onto a white towel. The image was indistinct, but went too high, way too high, round a curving buttock high.

"OK, that's enough," Anna said, and she chopped a banana, very slowly, very deliberately using every part of her conscious brain, hoping to keep those subconscious parts in check.

"Hey," she heard over her shoulder a few minutes later, and she realised she'd cut enough banana for ten people.

Anna turned and blinked to behold Jess. The T-shirt she'd put out, loose on her, was snug around Jess's well-toned physique and now more obvious bosom as she stood in profile. Anna was glad her imagination hadn't had that to play with earlier, and her cheeks felt the heat once more.

Jess's hair had sprung into a mass of waves, bouncing on her head. It accentuated her heart-shaped face. Attractive. To Anna, very much attractive. As if conscious of the change, Jess tugged a curl away from her face.

"Did you find everything you needed?" Anna asked, taking a deep breath as if that might cool her cheeks.

"Yes, thanks." Jess beamed and she stepped closer.

She smelled of familiar and borrowed soaps, but of someone different too. It was odd having someone unexpected in her flat, someone not from before, but her presence was comforting and exciting all at once.

"Looks like a beautiful day," Jess said. "What's the view outside?"

"Sorry," Anna said. "I keep the blinds down first thing in the morning." She stepped forward and pressed a button and the thin white blinds whirred upwards. She blinked at the bright light.

"That's posh," Jess laughed, then, "Oh wow. What's that over there?"

Beyond the tall terraces and streets, they could see the trees and grassy expanse of the park, the beech trees that Anna knew so well a blend of deep summer green to burned tips of yellow and the plane trees a blaze of rubies and gold.

"I don't know why I ask," Jess added. "It's not going to mean much when you tell me."

"It's Regents' Park," Anna obliged. "Does that ring a bell?"

"Not really." Jess peeped at her. "Don't tell anyone, but I'm a bit of country bumpkin. I know Oxford Street, Hyde Park, Piccadilly Circus and the train stations, but I have no idea where they are on a map."

Without thinking, Anna wrapped her fingers around Jess's arm above the elbow and encouraged her to step closer to the window.

The sensation of Jess's naked skin gave Anna a jolt. She'd forgotten Jess wore her T shirt and a soft bicep was vividly tender within Anna's palm and delicate on her fingertips. For a moment, all Anna was aware of was the intense point where they connected and the warmth of another human in her hand. Jess seemed more present, like she was more real – a sketch suddenly flushed with paint and colour. It was so powerful that Anna couldn't speak for a moment. She wanted to apologise. "I'm used to being a physical person," she would always say. It had been part of her easy character, but she rarely felt comfortable enough to be that person anymore.

She didn't let go and Jess didn't complain so Anna stayed her hand, letting herself become accustomed to the proximity.

"Over there," she pointed across the rooftops. "Do you see a group of trees? That's London Zoo."

"Zoo?"

"As in the world-famous London Zoo?"

"Oh," Jess replied, but stared ahead.

"And then beyond that, Primrose Hill."

"Uhuh."

"Don't worry." Anna laughed quietly. "I didn't realise it was in Regent's Park until I moved here from Edinburgh."

"Good."

"I know the whole park like the back of my hand now," Anna said. "I take a stroll round most days."

"Nice," Jess replied and she nodded, still staring towards the group of trees in the distance.

"It is," Anna said, relaxing and turning towards the view, a movement that only brought them closer and Anna's breast pressed against Jess's arm.

"Very nice," Jess murmured.

And if Anna could have spoken she would have agreed.

8

Jess hadn't understood a word from the moment Anna took her arm. Anna's fingers had slipped around her bicep and inadvertently stroked the side of her breast. The tingles that shot through her body rendered Jess immobile and her brain inert, in the best possible way.

Unexpected physical contact sometimes made Jess flinch, but this she welcomed. Dozy and relaxed in the warm sunshine and balm of Anna's company, a glow thrummed through her body and if an inane smile spread across her face, then that couldn't be helped. Such a small, innocent gesture, and Jess was captivated in this moment of accidental intimacy.

She stood snug next to Anna, hoping she would stay and keep the gap between them cosy. She tried, very hard indeed, to concentrate on the enviable London view that Anna presented – grand terraces, the park beyond, trees rich with autumn hues and the bright green jewel of a hill beyond that. But all she wanted was to take in Anna. She turned her head with the slow awkwardness of someone attempting the surreptitious to peek at her companion. The sunlight reflected off Anna's hair in a multitude of colours. Golds glistened, subtle reds glowed and darker blonds contrasted with her natural highlights.

Anna had nice eyebrows. The thought tickled Jess. How often did she notice eyebrows? They were smooth and the colour of golden straw, the fine tips fading to nothing in the bright sunshine and a satisfying arc making them expressive. She couldn't see Anna's eyes clearly from this angle, but she could admire that sprinkle of freckles again across her nose and the plump lips that were open as if on the verge of speaking.

"So," came Anna's voice. And what a blissful lazy soothing sound it was. Jess may have literally sighed, before realising she was required to be present in a conversation.

"So?" What had she missed?

Those captivating lips curled in a smile. "Would you like breakfast?"

"Oh. Yes. Great. Please," Jess replied. Maybe she hadn't missed anything. Not any words at least.

Anna continued her gaze through the window, her amusement seeming to intensify.

"Perhaps you'd like to make yourself comfortable while I cook the pancakes. I'm not a fast cook I'm afraid, so make yourself at home."

"Yeah. OK." Jess still had the feeling she'd missed something. "But do you need some help? I mean if you're slow?"

"Thank you," Anna said. "The batter's all made and everything's on the table."

Jess turned to see the island laid out with crockery, cutlery, sauces and fruits. She hadn't noticed a thing when she stepped in the room. Anna had commanded every ounce of her attention.

"Oh, I see," she said, grateful that her skin tone hid much of the blush that was warming her neck.

"But," Anna looked over her shoulder, "you could pour the coffee. The cafetière's ready on the top. I like mine with milk please."

"Great," Jess said, bouncing on her feet. "I'm on it."

She didn't have to ask for anything. The graded pantone mugs were hanging above the kettle. "Sugar, sugar," she muttered, but that was in a scarlet storage pot with "sugar" written in enormous letters. Teaspoons were in a cutlery drawer beneath, as convenient as you'd expect in this well-ordered flat.

She dug out two heaped spoons of demerara sugar and dumped them in a mug, then glanced towards Anna beside her, warming a frying pan on the hob.

"I'll eat you out of house and home when it comes to sugar," Jess said. "I blame my dad."

Anna raised an eyebrow.

"He's a tall skinny bloke and been an electrician all his life. I swear he's powered by sugary brews alone. He switched to decaf though so his heart rate doesn't go through the roof."

"Do you take after him?" Anna said, swirling a melting knob of butter carefully around the pan with a wooden spatula, not a careless movement indulged. She was always so elegant.

"Yeah, yeah," Jess said, "That's where I get my height from at least. The padding," she slapped her thigh, "that's all my mom's side of the family. Here." She pulled her dead phone from her pocket and pinched out a photo that was tucked inside the case.

"My nan gave me a print of the last family photo," Jess explained, "so I don't have to get my 'bloody phone out', as she says, to see her 'beautiful face', as she also says." And Jess was glad of it now. She didn't want to see the onslaught of notifications that she knew was imminent if she switched on her mobile.

Jess held the print in front of Anna then hesitated. "I don't show anyone anymore."

She hadn't brought this picture out in a long time. She'd stopped talking about her family – too many anecdotes turned up in the media one way or another and she didn't want them used as fodder for articles. But that was another part of herself she'd sacrificed. She clammed up whenever her family arose naturally in conversation and their powerful presence in her life dimmed. The realisation made her feel thinner and unsubstantial. She wanted to share this with Anna, this precious nugget of the real Jess.

She peeked up at Anna and found her bright blue eyes attentive. "I'd love to see," Anna murmured, "if you want to show me," and she stepped closer so that her thigh gently nudged into Jess's and she felt surrounded and bathed in Anna's presence.

There they were again, in another accidental moment of intimacy, not just physical but where Jess felt like she was letting in another soul.

"Tell me about them?" Anna said, her voice quieter.

"So." Jess engaged her brain. "So there's Mom here." She pointed to the quiet black lady with a large impact on Jess's life, although physically nearly a foot shorter. Eyes that didn't miss a thing. Hair gloriously braided and beaded. She was at the end of the row of family in the garden in their village home. The leaves were gone for winter and the family wrapped up in scarves and new woollen jumpers.

"It was taken at Christmas, although not last Christmas." Or in fact the one before. "Too busy last year," Jess added soberly. "Then this lady," she said brightening, "this is my Nan. The spitting image of my mom, but with the gift of the gab."

White streaks smoked through a mass of black curls, and Nan was always a reminder of what lay in store for Jess's mother.

"Then me of course." Jess pointed to the middle. "Then the skinny white dude is Dad," the only one who matched Jess's height, "and this scrawny git is my little brother who's pissed off that he's not as tall as me, even though he's fourteen."

Oh god he might be now, she suddenly thought. And a coolness swept through her as she realised how much he'd likely changed since she'd last been home.

"Where are they? Where's home?" Anna asked.

"Middle of nowhere in the middle of England." Jess laughed. "Seriously. South of Birmingham. Nowhere tourists would go. Just fields, woods and villages of old brick cottages and not much else."

"Sounds nice."

"It is," Jess said. And a longing for both family and the ordinary sat heavy in her heart. "It is."

Then she looked at Anna, who'd started to carefully ladle mixture into the pan, swirling the batter round into pools of pancakes so equal that Jess couldn't have done it better with the aid of a ruler.

This had the magic of the ordinary too, a treat breakfast in a real home in the company of someone who didn't know her from Eve. Jess sighed watching bubbles form on the surface of the pancakes and again when Anna flipped them over perfectly golden.

"Those look wonderful," Jess said.

"Shouldn't be long," Anna replied. "Sorry, I did warn you I was slow. But speaking of slow, how about that coffee?"

"Ha! Yes." Jess shone an apologetic grin at Anna. "Milk next. So fridge…?"

A turn to the left. Jess didn't need to take a step, she simply swivelled round. She opened the larder fridge door to the most systematised sight. Rows upon rows of Tupperware of every colour. Little boxes on the top shelf of butter and cheese. Larger boxes containing small yogurts. Three containers the next shelf down for strawberries, apples and grapes in different states. The same meticulous order applied to a shelf of pickles and jars. Even the bottles and cartons in the fridge door had stickers on, for a reason Jess couldn't fathom, but knew would be logical in a way beyond her.

"Jesus. Do you alphabetise the contents of your fridge too?"

It wasn't considered, and it wasn't subtle, but this was a whole new level of regulation and Jess couldn't have held back if she'd tried.

It was fortunate that Anna burst out laughing, and when Jess turned Anna was pinching her lips together.

"Which relative do you get your tact from?" she said.

Jess grinned. "My nan."

"The current milk is closest," Anna said, her smile irrepressible. "Pancakes are ready."

Until the pile of pancakes was laid in front of her, steam rising in a fragrant swirl, Jess hadn't realised how hungry she was. She'd plonked herself on a stool opposite Anna and didn't wait to be invited to start. She squirted cream in a fluffy nest then liberally spiralled chocolate sauce on top.

"This is amazing."

"Tuck in," Anna said, the pinch in the side of her mouth poorly hiding her amusement again.

Warm buttery pancakes with silky cream and velvety chocolate melted in her mouth. Jess audibly hummed this time. Several bites in she managed to mumble through a divine mouthful, "This is delicious."

Anna rested her elbows on the table, her chin elegantly propped on her entwined fingers.

"And which relative is responsible for your eating habits?" she said, a plummy accent coming to the fore.

Jess was unapologetic. "That's all my own. I'm going to blame that on having to work out for two hours a day, several months of the year."

Anna's brow pinched in a frown. It was a revealing detail and they both seemed to know it. Jess stared at Anna afraid of what she might have given away. Neither moved, but unlike Jess, Anna was the epitome of tact. Not a word escaped her.

Jess slowly put down her cutlery, the clatter on the plate deafening in the silence. Where could she start with this?

"Your earring," Anna said.

"Sorry?" Jess replied. Anna was staring to the side of her face.

"Don't move. Your earring's coming out." Anna slid off her seat. "If it falls, you'll lose it down the floorboards."

Before Jess could react, Anna had leant forward with her thighs pressed into Jess's and reached up to cup her hand beneath her ear. The warmth of her body this close was difficult to ignore. Jess could feel the intimacy once again. Anna's breath on her face, the heat of her body over hers, her fingertip delicate on her earlobe. Jess swallowed, acutely aware of Anna's touch. Such a tender fragile moment, the sensation of Anna's skin at that tiny point of contact. Her whole body thrummed alert at that sensitive nakedness and the thrill radiated down her neck.

Anna removed her earring, the slight tug on Jess's earlobe exquisite.

"There," Anna said, offering the gold ring in her palm. She stood, still snug against Jess's thigh, very much in her personal space. Jess was aware of her own breathing, deeper and slow, her chest rising in the small space between them, almost touching.

"Thank you," Jess said quietly. She took a moment or two to meet Anna's gaze.

"Sorry," Anna whispered, blinking over those startling blue eyes. "I'm naturally a physical person, although I understand that not everyone is comfortable with that. When I'm feeling confident I tend to relax into my old ways. Tell me if I overstep the mark."

Would kissing her be overstepping the mark? Would Jess slipping her hand behind Anna's back and pulling their bodies close be inappropriate? She couldn't speak.

9

Anna had leapt without thinking, so relaxed in the young woman's company she'd forgotten herself. And now she stood too close to the beautiful young woman with eyes so large Anna couldn't look away.

That gaze captivated Anna. She didn't know whether it was the openness in Jess's expression or the sudden intimacy of being near. The aching temptation was to reach out again, this time to stroke Jess's cheek and entice her chin towards her. Anna's whole being wanted to pull her in. She blinked, unsure whether she'd actually drawn Jess to and kissed her, the desire was so strong. She blinked again and was relieved to find they remained a small distance apart, the earring in her palm.

Anna had stared too long, her whole body alight from the tentative contact with Jess's earlobe and her smooth neck, which Anna had inadvertently stroked with her fingers. Without her training, Anna would not have covered her reaction at all, but she gazed deep into eyes that contained laughter and the joyful, sometimes fragile, character who had surprised her.

Anna may have restrained her reaction, but there was no way to ignore the moment. "You have nice eyes," she admitted, her heart beating too strong.

"Brown," Jess said, "like conkers."

Anna delighted inside. It had been an odd simile but a vivid one, the natural variation on a dark conker as natural as the shades in an eye. Beguiling, beautiful, something to behold and Anna felt their pull again. She'd already stared too long, but she couldn't turn away.

"It's true," Jess said. "My mate Maisie told me when I was ten, so it must be."

Anna smiled at the innocence of the description, then a smile on top of that so that her cheeks ached because Jess's expression creased in laughter and those brown eyes twinkled. They were caught up in a little bubble, two people tentatively enjoying each other's company. Anna could feel it. Oh it was dangerous.

A buzzing interrupted from the island top and they both flinched. Anna's phone vibrated and lit up with a new message from Penny, the short sentence visible in the notification.

"Already pissed as a fart. Miss you. Bibs too."

"What?" Anna gasped incredulous.

Jess giggled. "Sorry, I shouldn't have looked."

"Oh Pen." Anna covered her mouth. "It's not even lunchtime."

The phone announced another message and they both peered over. "Bibs misses you that is. I don't miss Bibs. She's here with me. Well with Lana anyway. I think. Will go and check."

And again. "Yes, she's asleep, dribbling on Lana's shoulder."

And again. "Can't believe we're at this pissing wedding. Save me a pancake. Love and snogs."

There, at last, the messages ceased.

"Sorry, I only saw the first one," Jess said, grinning. "Is that your best friend?"

"Yes." Anna sighed, put her hands on her hips and stepped away from Jess's side. "My ebullient, loving, slightly inebriated, even in the morning, best friend."

Anna swept her phone off the surface. She swiped up a photos app and searched for Penny at a birthday party. "This is my BFF." She turned the screen towards Jess. The photo showed a short curvy woman, with a mass of red curls, arms thrust into the sky with two bottles of Champagne and an ecstatic look upon her face. You could feel the energy of the woman through the screen it was so potent.

"She looks awesome."

Anna nodded. "She is. An absolute handful, but the best friend in the whole world."

They relaxed apart and Anna put her phone away. The moment had gone. She was safe. Both luckily and regrettably safe.

Anna checked the large clock on the kitchen wall, and sighed, too obviously. "We should see Zehra," Anna said. "She should have started her shift. Let's make sure the CCTV footage is kept."

—

Last night's anxiety had seemed decades away and the reminder rudely brought Jess to.

"Yes," she said, unable to keep the regret from her voice. She had no compulsion to leave Anna's company. Quite the opposite. She wondered if Anna could sense her disappointment. It would have been written all over her face but her body too sagged with despondency.

Jess tried to say, with as much lightness as possible, "Yes, we should."

Anna fetched her coat from a stand by the flat door and slipped on a pair of boots. She unhooked a set of keys, dropped them in her jeans pocket and glanced back. "Ready?"

"Yes," Jess said, her throat constricting. She felt nowhere near.

This was it. She had to leave. This was the end of her time with Anna. No more sanctuary inside this airy flat in the sky. No more gentle company of this intriguing and beautiful woman.

Jess couldn't move.

She had to go outside, into the cold, into the harsh noisy reality where everyone would stare. She would be on her own again. The demands would start from her manager, her agent, on social media, everyone clamouring for her attention and time and devotion and favours. She clutched her phone in her pocket, squeezing it tight, as if to keep the world from intruding.

Anna was disappearing down the stairwell. Jess made it as far as the door, but no matter her intention her body wouldn't follow.

A cold numbness crawled over Jess's back, seizing her body in panic. It spread up her neck and enveloped her scalp as if anxiety were encasing her in ice. She stood, unblinking and not breathing, staring after Anna's figure. She willed her body forward, to move at all, but it refused and she froze, acutely aware of her beating heart that pounded in her chest.

"Jess?" Anna called from the stairwell.

Mouth hung open, jaw aching, everywhere aching, as her muscles cramped like a statue, she couldn't release her breath let alone issue words.

"Are you all right?" Anna said, more urgent. She emerged from the stairs, her movements uncharacteristically rapid. "Jess?"

Cold sweat broke on Jess's back in a rash of pin pricks. She gulped in air but it caught in her chest. Desperation threatened to burst, but she couldn't even look at Anna's face, and Jess stood trapped inside her own body.

"I'm here if you need me," she heard. That soothing voice again, murmured beside her ear. Then warmth on her cheek. It was the soft human touch of Anna's face beside hers. Arms encircled her waist, their tenderness melting Jess in their wake, and her body suddenly released its tension, becoming fluid in Anna's embrace. Jess gasped as her whole body shuddered desperate for air.

"That's it," Anna whispered.

"Oh christ," Jess said, before her throat throttled her words and she fought to inhale.

"You can sit down," Anna encouraged, and Jess succumbed to her words as Anna walked her back towards the bed. She collapsed more than sat.

"Concentrate on breathing," Anna said, calm but eager. Her hand cupped Jess's cheek, and the delicate and gentle care almost made Jess cry.

"Sorry," she croaked, and her throat moaned as she tried not to sob.

"You're fine," Anna soothed. "You're safe."

She cupped Jess's face with both hands, a soft finger stroking across her cheek. Jess closed her eyes, and let her head drop, heavy with fatigue, but steadied by Anna's caress. It made everything disappear, like her head was the whole world, and her body shrunk away to insignificance. Her head floated in a warm concoction of hormones, coming down from the attack, and the dreamy sensation of Anna holding her face in her hands.

When she opened her eyes, her first controlled action, concern was written all over Anna's face and her eyes flitted over Jess's features, perhaps trying to take in her condition.

"Sorry. Am I worrying you?"

Anna's features relaxed into a beautiful smile. It was utterly bewitching. Jess hadn't appreciated how expressive Anna's face was before. Sometimes, she realised, Anna was guarded and reticent. But in the intensity of the moment everything came flooding through and the concern had burned in her eyes and bored into Jess in a way that anchored her then brought her back gently to reality.

And when that face, so full of apprehension, had relaxed into relieved joy, well, didn't Jess's heart do a little flutter that was completely unrelated to anxiety. That was a face that engendered love and devotion, especially when Anna's blue eyes glistened with tears.

"Sorry," Jess said again. This time staring too long and admiring more than a little.

"You did have me worried," Anna said, quietly. "Is it always this bad? The panic attacks?"

"Oh." That's what they were. Her anxiety had spilled over into a full blown episode. "No," Jess said, unnerved by the diagnosis. "Never like this." She couldn't think of a time when she'd been so paralysed, unable to move, think or react.

"I mean, often I get so tired I almost stop. I get worried about things, but never..." She felt fried. Her hands trembled and her whole body was jittery and drained in the aftermath.

Anna placed her hands over Jess's in her lap, and the trembling lessened but didn't stop.

"Do you want to see a doctor?"

"No." Jess said it too sharply. It would be another person to scrutinise and judge her. People were always watching and examining. This was the problem, there was never a break from prying eyes.

"These attacks," Anna said, squeezing Jess's hand. "They're quite severe. The doctor might be able to give you something." Jess twitched and Anna must have felt it. "Just to get you past a bad spell if you need it."

Jess's throat constricted again, this time with despair. This is how bad it had got. The exhaustion, the schedule, the constant attention, the judgement, the life that wasn't her own anymore. As soon as she'd tried to follow Anna out of the door, it had all descended. If she set foot outside, away from this sanctuary, the world would be spinning out of control with her manager after her blood, sponsors and TV shows clamouring for reimbursement, contracts torn up, the public demanding attention.

"Are you worried the man who followed you may still be around?"

And then there was that.

"Oh god," Jess moaned. "That and everything else."

She gasped again and tension seized her hands, crept up her arms and radiated into her chest. Her teeth clenched as the spasm overpowered her and the world swirled.

She closed her eyes and let it take hold, knowing she was safe, sat on the bed with Anna, sure she would come out the other side.

When Jess came to, Anna was holding her hand and a stillness descended. It was like Anna was the calm centre inside the storm, cupping her cheek in one hand, Jess's fingers in the other. A frown pinched Anna's forehead but as Jess's breathing settled the frown relaxed and attentive regard remained.

"We should definitely request the CCTV footage from the café," Anna said. "I can ask Zehra to make sure it's kept. You can stay here if you like, if you need more time, and request a copy later. I'd hate for it to be lost, that's all."

"Please don't go out of your way for me," Jess said. Guilt gnawed at her. "I'm not even sure someone was following me last night. I was a mess from so many things."

"But you thought you were followed on the Tube?"

"Possibly... Maybe... I think so." Her head spun again.

"And someone took that photo."

"Yes."

What had the caption said? She didn't want to check. Not such a hero? Degenerate Jess? Worse? They got much worse. Everything that people thought of her, everything they planned to do to her. It had been an account with a blank profile picture like so many others. They could all be the same person for all Jess knew. Or there could be tens, hundreds of them denigrating Jess from the mildest troll to those who were explicit about what sticky end she deserved. She shuddered as she thought of her phone, an innocent little box opening a door onto the worst of the world bursting with toxicity.

"I think I need a few minutes," Jess said.

"Take as much time as you need," Anna replied, the kindness in her voice washing over Jess. She wished she could bottle that soothing tone. It would be a balm for anyone.

"Sorry."

"Don't worry about me," Anna said. "I've spent enough time trapped here, too anxious to go out."

"Really?" Jess frowned confused.

Anna looked down for a moment as if gathering herself.

"I had a stalker once," she said, at last. "A very persistent one."

"What?" Anna had said it so calmly. "When?"

"A few years ago."

"What happened? Who was it?"

Anna hesitated and pondered in that way she had, always considered. "A man who was delusional about his relationship with me."

"Someone you knew? Sorry," Jess caught herself. "This is none of my business."

"I brought it up."

"And is he still following you?"

Again Anna hesitated. "No. He died in prison."

10

It came out a surprise. Anna hadn't thought she'd tell the young woman. She hadn't expected her to be there still, or to be comfortable enough to tell her. Anna kept people at arm's length and further these days, but this woman had entered Anna's life unexpectedly and with the kind of fear she recognised as her own. It's what had drawn her to Jess's plight, recognising that terror.

Anna could hear Jess's confusion and doubt about the man who followed her and Anna could guess at the thoughts and feelings that swirled inside her. Revulsion when someone assumed an intimacy that wasn't there. The persistent and incessant need for attention and a reaction. The simple danger of the situation and threat that clouded over everything, then doubt and denial that it was happening at all. She knew them all. But there was guilt too, unjustifiable guilt at driving someone to irrational behaviour. Had she encouraged it somehow? Then fury at being made to feel you were to blame.

"What happened?" Jess said, her eyes upset and forehead crinkled in concern.

"He was a friend of a friend, more an acquaintance I learned later." Anna stopped, her mind reluctant to resurrect the experience and remember her life how it was before – that was neatly packed away in the eaves.

"I chatted to him at a party, that was all," Anna shrugged. "He placed more importance on our conversation than I ever meant and, believe me, I have replayed it often in my mind, wondering how he got it so wrong and what I did to give him that impression."

"I can understand that," Jess said, her eyebrows furrowing in sympathy.

"Then his attention escalated."

It seemed innocuous enough initially, phone calls and messages that were a nuisance and to which she politely replied then ignored.

"Then, he was at every party I attended. I didn't want to say anything to the hosts – I assumed they were friends."

So she'd stayed away. Her first retreat inwards.

"When he missed me at parties, he started turning up near my work. That's when I realised it wasn't just my paranoia and mentioned it to others."

She'd gained some sanity for a while when people could see what she feared. Friends had rallied round and the man was barred from places and parties. How sympathetic they'd been, at first, then they were scared at how she reacted. "This isn't healthy, Anna," her mother's voice came through. "You need to get over it."

"The fear had me by then," Anna said. "I couldn't go out without him being there, either in actuality or in my imagination. It does something to you, having that threat lurk over your shoulder day and night. Your life is dictated by the cruel whims of another." She breathed out. "It was the unpredictability of his behaviour that shook me most I think. I felt like a prisoner in someone else's world."

Anna paused. She was finding this more difficult than she'd envisaged.

"Your flat?" Jess said, reaching out and holding Anna's hand. "The tidiness, the order?"

Anna nodded. "I retreated from people and places, until I only felt comfortable here, the one place I had some control over, to the point of obsession."

It was her well-guarded sanctuary, an attempt to regain control over her life and fears. It had become a different kind of prison, albeit one that kept her safe.

"Did you get help, from friends, family, anyone?" Jess asked.

"No, not straight away." Anna tutted at herself. "I bottled it up, developed unhealthy coping mechanisms and a stomach ulcer. I was very British about it," she smiled and Jess's face lightened like a mirror. "What about you?" she asked.

"I was thinking of doing the same."

Anna chuckled. "Please try to see someone." She hesitated, wondering at what else bothered Jess. "For everything. I wish I had earlier."

"Maybe I will," Jess replied. "God, everyone needs help sometimes."

"The reason I mention all this and why I'm keen to go to Zehra's is that I had a restraining order put on him. Later, when he broke it, my solicitor relied on CCTV footage to prosecute him."

"Oh."

Anna smiled. "So, please let me ask Zehra to hold on to it?"

"Yes, of course," Jess said, as if coming to.

"The CCTV company can send you a copy of any footage, although they will blur out the faces of customers apart from you. You might find it useful. But most importantly it needs to be kept in case the police investigate – they'll be able to see everything."

"Thank you," Jess said, her expression attentive and searching Anna's face. "You seem so calm and capable about it though, after all that."

"What you see now," Anna said, "me, the organised flat, my regular haunt at Zehra's, the Tube trip to work, my daily walk in the park where it's open and safe, that's my comfort zone. It took a lot of effort to establish my independence within even that boundary and feel like myself again. Beyond it…" she trailed off.

She hadn't trespassed further for a long time. She would go for days without thinking about him. That had been the case for months, extending into years, but she hadn't ventured far from her well-guarded world had she?

Jess smiled. "So, we're trapped here?"

Anna laughed.

"What a pair we make," Jess added.

The phrase fluttered pleasantly through Anna's mind. Did she like the idea of Jess pairing them together? She rather enjoyed the young woman's company, but Jess had probably not meant it like that, not now that she knew the extent of Anna's world.

"So," Anna sighed, not wanting to examine her feelings and wishes about the young woman. "There you are. That's me. And while I rarely think of him anymore, my life has changed. It's why I'm hesitant. Why I keep to familiar places. Why where once I was outgoing and confident, now I'm more circumspect. Why I have difficulty letting people in…"

And for the first time in so long, Anna realised, she wanted to.

She stopped, feeling ashamed of what she'd become.

"And yet…" Jess's voice was more thoughtful. "And yet," she continued, "you helped me. Out of everyone on that carriage, you were the one who asked me if I needed help."

"Of course I did," Anna whispered. "I know what it's like to be followed and to feel vulnerable."

Jess hesitated. "It was one of the nicest things anyone's done for me in a while. I'm very grateful."

Anna didn't doubt her. Jess had said it choked with gratitude. Anna was compelled to add, "If it hadn't been in my neighbourhood, where I'm confident, I might not have been so generous."

"Then I have more faith in you."

And Anna believed her.

"I'm sorry," Jess said. "I'm sorry you had to go through that."

Anna squeezed her hands to acknowledge it. "Now," she said, not wanting to dwell on her experience, or the hopes she harboured about Jess. "I may have something to help you."

Jess stared at her blankly. "Help me?"

"Something that will give you confidence when you go outside."

This was something Anna could do. In fact she was a bit of a pro.

11

It had been all Jess could do to stop herself from flinging her arms around Anna. After all the shitty things people had done to Jess over the last couple of years. After all the times she'd been taken advantage of, here was Anna with nothing to gain, but fear to overcome, who'd been kind to a complete stranger.

She noticed in Anna's demeanour that overblown attention wouldn't be welcome. Such simple emotions Jess could read easily, better than others in fact.

The incident was hard to believe looking at Anna, this understanding woman who was so capable. There was a calmness about her, a serenity. While the world hurtled round outside, there she was going about her life at her own pace, hiding away, and Jess slowed in her presence. The rest of the world disappeared to a blur of white noise in the stillness of Anna's sphere, so much that Jess had forgotten about the chaos waiting for her outside.

Perhaps this was why Anna hadn't recognised her, tucked away in this sheltered world, that and perhaps the age difference so that they inhabited different cultures.

Anna retrieved numerous boxes from the void beneath the roof, all labelled with large clear letters: wigs, hats, accessories.

"A different lifetime," Anna countered Jess's exclamations.

The hats were everything from Anna's aunt's top hat to a bowler, equally theatrical and incongruous. The wigs had been bought as complementary to Anna's white skin and were stunning and too eye-catching on Jess for a disguise. So they settled on a few items from Anna's ordinary wardrobe.

"What about these?" Anna said, lifting the fashion glasses to Jess's face.

Jess took them, their fingers touching and faces close. Anna looked at her intently, trying to see if they were a good fit, a little ripple across her forehead as she concentrated.

"I think they change the shape of your face," Anna offered, in adorable concentration so that Jess wanted to kiss her. She wanted to hold her and kiss her and never let go, and a mix of deep empathy flooded through her, together with fear about her own life. But she held back her touch, because Anna clearly wanted to move the conversation on.

"And this." Anna stretched out a beanie and slid it over her head. Jess relished every inadvertent stroke of Anna's fingers. "There."

"Different," Jess said.

Anna laughed, probably at the simplicity of her statement.

Outside, Jess stood in front of the corner shop, her reflection grinning at her in the window, while Anna locked the terrace front door. Jess looked like a student. Glasses with dark purple frames, striped beanie hat over her hair, hands tucked into the pockets of a faded denim jacket. She even slouched a little, which made her smile. It was funny how a change of outfit could switch a person into a different role. It didn't feel like a disguise, but Jess certainly didn't resemble her publicity photos. This was more like a Jess that could have been.

She'd skipped university, not something that she regretted often, but she rather liked the idea of playing a student and she twisted from side to side to take herself in.

Anna slipped on a pair of sunglasses and they walked together down the hill, while another couple walked towards them. Jess flinched as the pair passed by, but neither person gave her a second glance. She tried to relax and turned to face oncoming pedestrians. A man shuffled by, engrossed in his phone. Two young women approached arm in arm, speaking in words she couldn't quite catch. Croatian Jess decided. She recognised the odd word from her own basic tourist use. They brushed by, perhaps not noticing her at all, and she let them pass with a relieved elation. Jess was anonymous, for the first time since she'd arrived in London.

"How are you doing?" Anna said beside her.

"Good." She felt like she could breathe again.

They ambled down the hill, Anna's steps nonchalant and Jess jittery and tentative, not sure that her freedom and anonymity would last.

This was more like when Jess was abroad. Arriving in London had been a shock. Perhaps it was timing, perhaps it was exposure, but everyone seemed to know her face. Maybe people expected to recognise celebrities in the street here.

It became busier as they descended the hill, out of the residential streets and nearer the shops and Tube station. Jess leaned towards Anna, so close that Anna took her arm and smiled reassurance at her.

Still no-one paid attention. If anything, it was Anna who received the odd second glance and gradually the tension dropped from Jess's shoulders. She was outside, sun shining on her face, arm in arm with a beautiful woman, just an ordinary girl in London on an autumn day.

"Do you want to come in?" Anna said as they reached Zehra's.

Jess hesitated.

"I wondered if you'd feel uncomfortable after last night," Anna continued. "I can talk to Zehra if you like."

Jess nodded. "Please."

Anna squeezed her hand and disappeared into the coffee house, hidden for a moment by the reflections of the street in bright sunshine in the café window, then reappearing by the counter in the clarity of Jess's shadow. Jess's stomach gnawed at her, anxious at the distance between them. And it wasn't only because she was nervous at her vulnerability, not quite sure yet of her disguise. Jess was undeniably and irresistibly drawn to Anna.

Jess felt the pull in her chest and shuffled impatient on the pavement. She was raw after Anna's confession and didn't want to leave her. She wanted to protect her but also craved her company. Perhaps Anna would understand her. Perhaps Anna would appreciate why, with all the attention, Jess was coming to pieces.

As Anna chatted to Zehra, Jess saw the very specific care that the older café owner took now, holding each other's arms and Zehra's face a picture of concern. She gesticulated with a flourish, every emotion perhaps made more sympathetic for Anna's benefit, perhaps her natural style. The detail had passed Jess by last night.

Then Anna smiled and hugged Zehra around the shoulders and made her way back towards Jess with a piece of paper in hand.

"Here's who you need to contact," Anna said, when she came out. "Zehra will get in touch with the company to make sure the footage is kept."

"Thank you," Jess said, pocketing the paper in the jacket. Then in awe, "Thank you for everything."

"You're welcome," Anna said, her Mona Lisa smile returning. It was both intriguing and frustrating, that serenity, which Jess suspected was the calm surface of very deep waters.

"You've been amazing," Jess blurted. "Way beyond being a good Samaritan."

Anna laughed.

"And, of course, I'll return your things," Jess said, clutching at the jacket.

"Don't worry if you can't. You sound," and Anna's eyebrows flickered with consideration, "busy."

"I am, yes." Jess deflated. "Insanely busy."

Anna took a step forward, as if to say good bye.

"You know I...." Jess started.

It was all such a mess, an impossible mess, the world she had to go back to now, and she had no compulsion to return at all.

"I've really taken the mick with your help," Jess said, staring at her feet and shuffling on the pavement, "but I was wondering." She hesitated.

"You were wondering?"

Jess peeked up to see Anna considering her, head tilted to the side, smile playing at the corner of her mouth.

"Well, I know I stole your bed."

"Yes?"

"And I was very grateful for that."

"You're welcome."

"It's just, I don't know, do you fancy, I mean, tell me if I'm overstepping the mark here."

"I will tell you." Anna's delivery was pitched to gently rib and her smile was so catching that Jess's cheeks lifted.

"So, like I said, I'm already grateful for the bed." Jess grinned. "And shower. And breakfast. And T-shirt. And jacket." She tugged at the latest garment. "The knickers which I assumed you meant me to keep, and the form from Zehra, but..."

"But?"

"I wondered if you'd show me your walk?"

"Walk?"

"You said you took a daily stroll around the park?"

"Oh."

"Like I said, I know I've really overstayed my welcome by a night, shower, breakfast—"

"Yes, I'd like that."

"Yeah?" Jess's voice was so full of blatant hope it would have been embarrassing if that hope hadn't obliterated her self-consciousness too.

"Yes." Anna murmured, with that voice that made Jess giddy.

12

"You seem to be recovering from your panic attack," Anna said, amusement bubbling inside. Jess was almost skipping by her side.

"It's a beautiful day, I'm in a beautiful place," Jess said as she spread her arms wide towards the park that opened at the end of the street, "and I'm with a beautiful woman."

Anna laughed out loud.

So they were still doing this, the flirting, despite Jess knowing the extent of Anna's reclusiveness. Despite the years having passed and Anna finding herself a middle-aged woman, they were still doing this.

"Oh, the crossing's out," Jess said. "Work on the pavement or something."

Anna began navigating the way round in her head, her usual pedestrian crossing blocked. It was a long way to another park entrance.

"Let's dash across here," Jess said with glee and she reached back and took her hand. "There's a space."

It was a tiny gap in the traffic on the busy London road. A blur of turquoise whizzed by, a cyclist, then a red double decker bus, then they hurtled across the two lanes as a taxi buffeted behind them.

They grinned at each other, breathing hard when they reached the pavement on the other side, then cut into the park, Jess not letting go.

Anna looked down at their entwined fingers. So, still flirting and apparently holding hands.

Jess hadn't skipped a beat. She'd been surprised and affected, god knows she was in a position to empathise, then allowed Anna to move on as if it were the most natural thing in the world – all part of the course of getting to know someone. For the first time in a while, Anna didn't feel embarrassed about what she'd become.

The trees inside the park were at the peak of autumn colour. They ambled beneath a canopy of glowing golds and reds, the roof above blending into kaleidoscopic colours. Leaves shushed beneath their feet on the pathway and leapt into the air from enthusiastic kicks from Jess.

"There are conkers here!" Jess said, stopping a moment and releasing Anna's hand. She picked something up from the ground and struggled with it for a moment then opened her hand to present a shining treasure.

"I bet that would make at least a tenner."

"You played conkers?" asked Anna.

"Yeah." Jess made it sound obvious.

"Who plays conkers these days?"

"Oh, were we too good for conkers in Edinburgh?" Jess raised an eyebrow in jest.

Anna opened her mouth, had a vision of her mother sitting on the edge of her antique spoonback chair, hands resting in her lap, in a relaxed pose attainable by only the most uptight, and closed her mouth again.

"I'm a country girl," Jess continued. "My Nan kicked us outside at least once a day. 'I can't be doing with you round my feet and tapping away at that computer all day. Go play in some mud'." Jess deepened her rich voice and let it crack at the edges and Anna had the vivid impression of an older woman.

"I used to collect these beauties from the fields behind our garden," Jess said in her usual tone. "Just for treasure. Here's one for you." And she passed another shining nugget to Anna. It was fresh and cool in her hand and flawlessly smooth where she stroked her finger, then her skin tingled where she toyed with the rough eye of the nut. She slipped it into her coat pocket. A little memento of the day.

They ambled on and Jess reached for her hand again while engrossed in her find in the other.

Anna smiled. No-one held her hand except for Bibs, her best friend's toddler, a precious wee girl who sought her hand for comfort. When was the last time an adult had taken her hand for any other reason?

Anna let herself acknowledge it was intimate and Jess swung her arm. This was like a date. Anna's smile broadened, then a pang of anxiety made her question whether the feeling was one-sided. What would a vivacious woman like Jess be doing with Anna?

"We're safely across the road now." She offered Jess an exit.

"I know." Jess leant so close, Anna could feel the humidity of her breath on her cheek. "Don't tell anyone, but I dashed across the road as an excuse to hold your hand." And Jess looked at her with a brazen grin so large you could have seen it from space. Anna laughed in disbelief at Jess's cheek.

So, actually, like a date. Anna's heart quickened. They were still doing the flirting thing and Anna had to admit she was very susceptible to this clumsy, obvious charm that Jess had.

"Oh," Jess suddenly stopped.

"What is it?"

"I kept meaning to ask." She sounded unnerved.

"Yes?"

"Well, I mean, a little while back I thought to ask, not straight away, but…"

"What?"

"Do you have a boyfriend?"

Anna stared at her.

"Girlfriend?"

Anna didn't know whether she was silenced by the forwardness of the question or the idea that Jess would think she'd have one. Anna worried a moment that Jess hadn't comprehended how sheltered her existence had become.

"Anyone who'd mind me holding your hand?" Jess finished, her tone rising in alarm.

It was rather sweet. Her bold flirtatiousness had become tentative and the answer had importance to her.

"No, it's just me. And I don't mind you holding my hand either."

Jess chuckled and the gentle squeeze she gave Anna's hand was delightful.

"Well, what about you?" Anna asked. It was far more likely the younger woman was involved with someone.

"No. Not for an age."

"How long's an age?"

"It's, like, six months," Jess said, sounding oppressed with the enormity of that period.

"Half a year," Anna murmured.

"I know," Jess said incredulous. "What about you?"

Anna breathed in, but it caught in her throat. How long had it been? She knew very well. The perfect storm of entering middle age, her retreat from her customary social circles and imploding self-confidence, all had contributed.

"I can't believe you've been single for a minute," Jess carried on.

"Why?" Anna snorted. Did Jess not see what others did?

"You're gorgeous," Jess said, throwing up a hand. "Kind. You have a witty sense of humour. Honestly, your voice is a honeyed aphrodisiac. If you could bottle it, you'd make a fortune. And that's before we even get to the killer pancakes. I imagine you're usually with some rich, suave, city type."

Well that honeyed voice was silenced for a moment. Jess did see something quite different to others. Anna stopped, her heart heaving.

"Thank you," she said.

"For what?"

"The way you described me."

"All true. So why? Why single?"

The knot in Anna's stomach tightened. There had been interest, it was true. A client last week had asked her to dinner, a respectable businessman, distinguished in his forties, his chest taut beneath her hand and toned in his suit. "He's a bit of a dish," her partner had said with a nudge to the ribs.

The idea had terrified her. There was the pressure of a date outside her sphere, the impending threat of familiarity, the thought of his strong thick fingers, nails short with rounded pads at the top, running around her waist and exploring up towards her breasts, feeling for her sensitivity. She flinched and shuddered at the thought.

And yet it hadn't been him. He'd been polite and understanding when she'd turned him down. It was the idea of allowing anyone that close. She froze at the thought and found herself gripping Jess's hand. Jess squeezed back in reassurance and delicately held on when they both relaxed.

Anna looked up at her companion, walking slowly and surely beside her. Here was this young woman, holding her hand with more intimacy than Anna had allowed anyone else. She'd snuck under the radar. This intriguing young woman had slept at Anna's flat, worn her clothes, made blatant innuendos and could flirt like she was in training for an Olympic sport, and Anna kept walking beside her, unable and unwilling to remove her hand.

Was it because Jess had been vulnerable when they'd met? Had she quietly built up trust? Was it because, although she was evasive at times, Jess was transparent and honest at others?

"You turn heads you know," Jess said.

"I wouldn't be so sure."

"You turn mine."

And there it was again, a compliment delivered in a tone deep with honesty and Anna's chest lifted with an intoxicating mix of pride, hope and longing. The young woman seemed to have a gift for it when it came to Anna. She imagined Jess did it to everyone. Didn't she admit as much? It was probably a universal charm she had.

"Warned you I can be a terrible flirt," Jess said gently. "I'll cut it out, if you like."

No, don't. Anna's reaction was immediate and loud in her head. Her chest heaved with the prospect that Jess would stop. It was wonderful, this gentle flirting by this woman, like the first sunshine in spring when the world comes alive with warmth and colour. Anna hadn't enjoyed someone's company like this in so long. The thought of Jess stopping her flirtation and being gone left a chill inside, even though Anna had become numb to her habitual loneliness in recent years.

She was unable to speak. Anna squeezed Jess's hand in return, hoping that said the right words.

13

This was almost ordinary, so wonderfully ordinary, to Jess, a day rich and glowing with autumn sunshine, whispering trees above, strolling along with a companion who made her feel like it was OK to be herself again. It was a morning of simple everyday things. Jess had missed those. Things like finding a new song. Listening to an old one. Making someone laugh until they snorted.

She'd left school at seventeen and worked ever since, intoxicated by ever higher-profile offers and scared that it would all dry up the moment she took a break.

When she was little, she thought being famous would be amazing. "I bet she gets her weight in cake for doing that" her Nan had said of someone on an advert, and that had seemed the pinnacle of human achievement to young Jess. She'd never appreciated that you lost your life and privacy, or how important that would be to Jess in particular.

But here was a delicious piece of reality and freedom, a walk in the park with this beautiful woman. Anna's hair was swept back as they strolled and her sculpted face was revealed in all its elegance. Anna tucked one hand deep into her woollen coat, the other in Jess's, and her chin lifted as if enjoying and embracing the day as much as Jess.

Anna hesitated. "Chestnuts?"

"What was that?"

Anna stopped and tilted her head to the side. "I can smell hot coals and roasting. Is there a chestnut cart nearby?"

The aroma drifted into Jess's consciousness and she checked around. The path curved into trees and out of view.

"Let's have a look," she said as she looped her arm through Anna's.

And sure enough, this ordinary day had a touch of magic too. A bicycle and cart beside the path was undeniable temptation. Sweet chestnuts roasted and smouldered on a griddle and Jess couldn't resist.

"I've got to get some." She jogged up to the seller and gleefully handed over a few coins to the woman with a flat cap behind the cart. The bulging paper bag was scalding in her hands and they walked over to a bench.

"Ouch, they're hot." Jess shuffled the bag between her palms. "Do you want some?"

"Please." Anna grinned.

Jess didn't know if Anna was caught up in her enthusiasm or amused by her.

Jess hopped onto the bench, crossed her legs and tucked her feet beneath her knees to face Anna, the bag of chestnuts between them. She dug in, passing a nut to Anna and keeping one for herself, and peeled back the chocolatey shell to reveal the golden food beneath.

"I love how relaxed you are," Anna said, laughter bubbling beneath that silky voice.

Jess looked up. So she was amused by her. "I don't know how I give the impression of being relaxed after stressing on you several times."

"I mean," Anna considered, "how casual you are. You're at ease with yourself."

"Really?"

"See how you sit?"

Jess was hunched over, elbows resting on knees that were wide apart. It's how she'd sat as a kid, reading a book or playing on the tablet. It was still the most natural position for her, the chestnuts replacing the book. Anna was right, in some ways Jess couldn't help being herself and that did make part of life more straightforward.

"It's so casual and relaxed," Anna said. And it was funny then, the difference between them – Anna reclining on the bench, her long slim legs crossed and the heel of her boot making the whole line pleasing.

"Would you pull a muscle if you sat like this?" Jess challenged.

Anna raised an eyebrow. "I do a little yoga to keep supple."

Jess tried not to visualise or think of the benefits.

"It's more," Anna said and turned towards Jess, her arm graceful over the back of the bench, fingers posed as if in a painting, "sitting properly, as my mother would say, is so engrained I think something might break in the universe if I hopped up to join you."

"Don't you want to slouch sometimes?" Jess chuckled.

"I even cross my legs and place my hands in my lap in front of the TV."

"Isn't it exhausting, sitting properly and having good manners all the time?"

"It's so habitual, I suppose I don't think about it. But then," Anna paused, sadness rippling across her face, "I used to have an outlet and a break from it all." She drifted to a place that Jess didn't think she should follow or question.

Jess snapped off the last bit of shell from a nut and offered it to Anna.

"Sorry." Anna shivered as if reviving herself, and offered her open palm to receive the offering. "Thank you. Tell me more about your family please. They sound lovely."

"Oh," Jess said. That would be no hardship. They seemed to be on her mind this last day, a flood now that she'd let them in again. It was always the same with her – either nothing to say or everything.

"I come from the Midlands." Jess couldn't say it without lapsing into the accent. It was the same when she asked after anyone. "Yor'roit?"

"I grew up in a village near Solihull, which counts as posh round us, though Mom always described us as Brummies. She won't have a bad word said against Birmingham." And the way she said Birmingham rang true, as well as the idiosyncrasy of 'Mom' instead of 'Mum'.

Jess cracked open another chestnut and handed it to Anna. "I feel like such a country bumpkin in London, I'm telling you."

Whether Anna was delighted with the roasted chestnut or Jess's conversation, she didn't know, but the glow of her smile definitely thrilled Jess. She tripped over her words a moment, taking her in – the rose on Anna's cheeks, her lips that curved with pleasure, the creases around her striking eyes, which settled intently on Jess.

"My family are all the kind to call London the 'big smoke' or the 'big city'. You won't catch any of them here. In fact, before my first job, I'd only been once on a school trip. Dad is a lovely bloke, just a straightforward guy. He loves my mom, loves reading sci-fi and fantasy and loves his fish and chips. That's where I get it from." And at that, she clammed up.

"Which?" Anna asked, gently.

"What was that?"

"Love of sci-fi or chips?"

Jess hesitated again. "Sci-fi and fantasy," she stuttered. "Because Mom," she tried to carry on as naturally as she could, "Mom and Dad were both bonkers about sci-fi shows. That's how they met. They were fans of *Doctor Who*, *Star Trek* and *Blake's 7*."

Jess remembered her mother wittering on about the gorgeous Dayna from the last. The actress Josette Simon was on the telly when she was last home and the sigh that had accompanied "She hasn't changed a bit," made Jess doubt her mum's heterosexuality and issue an appalled "Mom!"

"We used to watch the new *Doctor Who* together." Jess's cheeks ached, beaming as she reminisced. "Mom, Dad, Nan on the sofa and me and my kid brother tucked in wherever we'd fit. I wanted to be Martha Jones."

"I had a crush on Rose."

"Really?!" Jess shrieked. "I did not have you down as a *Doctor Who* fan."

"Honesty, I'm not that into it. Just Rose."

Jess laughed. "God, I miss my folks," she sighed, and they fell into silence.

"Did you call them?" Anna asked, gently.

Jess came to. "What? No. I messaged Mom to say I was all right."

Anna waited, then led her again. "Why don't you go and see them? Call them at least. You seem to miss them badly."

Jess's heart filled with sudden longing and tears threatened. "I don't get the chance…" She stopped because her voice was cracking. "And," she swallowed and her vision blurred with a tear, "my phone's dead anyway."

When she'd blinked away the imminent tears, she found Anna offering her a phone. "Use mine?"

"It's all right… I mean I could… They still have a landline and the same number from when I was a kid. Bet they're the last in England to have one."

"Go on," Anna said, her face entreating her.

The ringtone purred in Jess's ear as she paced across the path a little way from the bench. It had taken a few tries to work up to it, pressing cancel as soon as it had rung the first time. But this time, the fourth attempt, she stole herself for whoever picked up the phone.

It clicked and the ringing stopped. Jess opened her mouth to burst in with "It's me." But the loud and lasting beep stopped her in her tracks. A recorded message played. "All right, bab." It was her mother. Jess grinned so much tears were squeezed from her eyes. "Leave us a message and we'll get back to you."

Jess laughed out loud, elated at the familiarity of her mother's voice, her wonderful accent full of song and home, and someone calling her "bab".

"It's me!" she found herself shouting. "Jess!"

She paced faster, not knowing what on earth she wanted to say.

"I'm just saying hello and that I'm fine." And she said "foin" as if she were right back there in the Midlands. "I'm sorry if you've been worried. But I'm OK. And I love you. I love you Dad. I love you all. I'll try again. OK. OK. And everything's fine. Bye."

She pulled the phone away from her face, taking a moment to work out how to end the call and shouting "bye" at the mobile one last time.

She clutched the phone to her chest. She had a vivid feeling of being connected to her family and it filled her whole body with poignant elation. A few recorded words from her mum and she was pulled home, and her sense of self grew and swelled with pride as she stood there. She could have been dancing in the kitchen with Nan and Mom, bumping hips along to something on the radio.

"Thank you," she said, handing the phone to Anna. She sniffed. "I didn't get through, but," she couldn't help smiling while sniffing and wiping her tears away. "Thank you."

"I'm glad," Anna said, reaching for the phone.

The expression on her face spoke of tenderness and generosity. Their fingers met, and for a moment the warmth of Anna's naked skin on Jess's fingertips was the most explosive sensation.

She could have kissed her.

14

The park was a well-practiced walk for Anna. It was already a familiar space from her life before, and one of the few open spaces in which she could truly relax. She knew every fork in the path, where the fountain was, the playground, the boating lake, the zoo, the winter gardens. She knew the paths with a full view from every direction, and those she would only walk with company.

When she'd first tried to adjust to life after her stalker, full of anger and determination, she'd struck out with GPS on her phone, exploring London, but one anxiety attack after another had forced her retreat and now she stayed within her comfort zone.

Jess stayed beside her as they ambled on, their arms looped through each other's. The young woman had relaxed and Anna could feel her full presence when she was at ease. It was as if Jess grew when she was happy. Her arm was strong through Anna's and whenever they brushed together, their hips bumping gently, Jess felt solid and powerful.

"What's over there?" Jess said, her voice carrying. Even that was stronger the more at ease she became.

They'd reached the edge of the park. "The canals," Anna replied.

"Oh wow, is there a tow path?"

"You can walk all the way to Camden Market that way." Anna pointed along the silvery trail to the right. "And Little Venice if you follow it the other."

"You're kidding?" Jess's eyes expanded bright. "We're near Camden?"

"Fairly, yes."

"I've always wanted to go to the market," Jess blurted out.

"Really?"

"Does that make me sound provincial?"

Anna laughed. "More like a tourist."

"I don't care." Jess grinned. "See, my coolest mate at school always went on about London markets when I was a teenager. She used to stay with her cousins in Harringay during the holidays and buy all the best clothes from the markets. She'd tell us how she'd bartered for this, that and the other. I would have killed to have gone with her."

Anna was hesitant and Jess picked up on it straight away, her smile subsiding.

"Do you ever walk down there?" she said more gently.

"I used to." Anna dug her hands into her pockets for comfort. "Will you think it stupid if I tell you I've been too afraid?"

"Not at all. Is it the canals that worry you?"

Anna nodded. There were long stretches of water with no escape route. Then the bridges hid who knows what beneath them in the shadows. But it wasn't just that. It was beyond her world, where every deviation was known, where she knew what was around every corner. She'd quickly retreated from places where a mistake would leave her exposed, and walking with her phone would announce that she was lost.

"Do you want to have a look?" Anna said.

"Are you OK with that?" Jess replied, hope mixing with concern on her face.

Anna intended to simply say yes, but she stared at the glint of the canals running into the distance, her mouth open, but the word left unspoken.

Her heart rate rocketed. When was the last time she'd taken any road that wasn't to the Tube station, to work, the journey home or the amble round the park. She suddenly saw how small her world had become. It hadn't varied for months. She felt like she was a specimen trapped in a jar, a pet fish that had explored every tiny crevice in its bowl, every piece of gravel and the one plastic toy treasure chest, and the weight of her small existence felt like it might crush her. She had a horrible image of her face, expressionless and gawping for water like a goldfish and Penny coming to visit each day to sprinkle on a little food.

"I want to," Anna whispered.

But her feet refused to move.

She'd been getting by. She had Penny. She had a new job that didn't trigger her anxiety and enough money to look after herself. She hadn't had to high tail it back to Edinburgh to live with her family. God, her mother would have loved that. But was Anna doing much beyond existing? Was there anything beyond the splash of colour in her week that was Penny and Bibs?

Jess held Anna's arm to her chest. "We don't have to. It was just a whim."

"But I want to," Anna whispered, "very much." But still her feet wouldn't move.

"I'll hold your hand," Jess said, a brazen grin blooming on her face. Anna's cheeks twitched. Jess's laughter was so catching.

"Yeah?" Jess said, peering up from beneath her fringe. Anna's mouth pinched in amusement.

"I'm giving you my best smile," Jess said. One where her eyes sparkled, her joyful cheeks glowed and her mouth was open on the verge of giggling. "Is it working?"

"You have an astonishing smile," Anna sighed. It seemed Jess's honesty was catching too and Anna almost reached up to caress Jess's face, but she refrained from the telling gesture.

Jess laughed that larger-than-life laugh. "It's my bestest winning smile."

"And it's pretty potent."

"Another of my talents."

"I bet you have women eating out of your hand," Anna said, before she could stop herself.

Anna flinched, realising she was giving away her growing inclination. Was she as open a book as Jess when it came to emotions?

"Yes," Jess said, hesitating. "Sometimes." The answer was loaded. Perhaps having people flocking to you wasn't all it was cracked up to be. In fact, Anna knew it wasn't.

Jess slipped her arm around Anna's back, and Anna let the warmth ease her anxiety.

"Let's go," Anna whispered, and they headed towards the road.

She felt light as they descended the slope to the canals, a nervous energy wriggling in her belly. Jess was almost bouncing next to her.

"It's gorgeous here," Jess enthused.

Anna had forgotten how appealing it was. The canals were covered in autumn leaves – golden speckles on a bright blue bowl of sky. The big red pagoda of the floating Feng Shang Princess restaurant was moored at the side. She could have pictured the scene with some accuracy, but it would have been missing the full flavour of the place – the saturation of the sky, the frailty of the crisp leaves balancing on the water surface, the breeze through her hair, the sound of a bird unfamiliar in a tree. And Jess. The balm of good company.

"Can we walk a little further?" Jess asked.

Anna hesitated at the thought, but Jess's arm comforted around her. She wasn't sure if she was still breathing, but she was – short, shallow breaths in the pit of her belly that fluttered with butterflies.

"A little way perhaps," she said, taking a tentative step forward.

"Now that is a den to die for," Jess said.

There was a house and garden across the canal that backed on to the water, a weeping willow casting its leaves over the surface and a little wooden den hidden by the trunk. She was sure it hadn't been there but a handful of years ago. Life had moved on without her knowing, just a stone's throw beyond her usual world.

"I bet that kid's popular at school," Jess said. "What a place to play."

Without Anna realising, they were walking at a casual pace with Jess encouraging her with the lightest touch at her back.

"What is that sound?" Anna asked. "That bird?" It cried in the trees above.

"Which?"

"The squawk."

"Oh," Jess said excited. "It's from up there." She pointed to the trees ahead. "There are a couple of bright green birds, a bit like parrots."

"Parakeets?"

"Hey, maybe."

Tiny little details others would pass by were fresh and exciting to Anna, like piquant drops of flavour in what had become a stale world.

"I hadn't noticed that," Jess said, and she snuggled in, not to comfort, just to, what? Anna wondered.

This wasn't a stroll with a friend. Jess's arm enclosed and pulled Anna gently to her side. There was an undeniable warmth between them. Anna took a chance and slipped her arm around Jess so they walked like a couple and she heard Jess's breath hitch. Jess glanced at her and Anna couldn't catch her expression, but the familiarity didn't fade; if anything Jess came closer.

There was a building and thrilling sense of intimacy. They were past flirting and into new territory, getting further with every step.

"This is nice," Jess said, barely above a whisper, and Anna's heart beat faster.

Anna nodded. "I like this too."

She wasn't sure if either of them were aware of their surroundings anymore. They kept on walking, Anna tingling where they met. She was in the comfortable bubble of Jess's arms, as if the world outside had faded and her conscience was filled with the exciting presence of Jess and nothing more.

Then her arm slipped down Jess's back and her fingers encountered naked skin beneath her jacket. It was as if everything was obliterated and all she could think of was the tenderness above Jess's belt. The human touch was debilitating in a most delicious way. She couldn't have pulled away if she'd tried.

They walked on as if frightened to acknowledge the change, but it had happened. Suggestion and urgency were building in the air. That naked touch, at the small of Jess's back, the toned muscle relenting to supple skin around her sides that teased and promised greater delicacies beyond.

Anna had lost so much confidence, given up so many things, and all those years flooded out in yearning now. Anna's whole body seemed to come alive, a liquid warmth filling her inside and rising through her torso. She was overcome with longing. She stumbled and her breath came shuddering out.

"Are you OK?" Jess said, reaching around to steady her. Her arms slipped around Anna's waist and it was all Anna could do not to throw her arms around Jess's neck. She hadn't come anywhere near this with anyone else. It wasn't even a kiss and Anna was overwhelmed.

"Four years," she blurted.

"Sorry?" Jess replied, gently.

"You asked me how long it had been? Earlier."

Jess still didn't respond.

"Since I had a partner. It's been four years."

"Oh," Jess said. It was filled with sympathy.

"I…" Anna clutched Jess. "It's been so long, I don't even know how to start trusting anyone. It scares me. Letting go. Letting my vigilance down. I don't know how to do it anymore."

Jess held on.

"But I don't want to be alone," Anna said, and she failed to keep her voice under anything like control. "I'm sick of being by myself and detached from everyone."

Jess's arms encircled her.

"I want to be touched again," Anna murmured.

Her hand tingled where she touched Jess's back. She stroked her fingers around to her belly and the tenderness of Jess's stomach made her close her eyes with the intensity of the sensation.

"I want to be with someone." She dipped her head onto Jess's shoulder, dizzy with the intimacy. The fragility of another human and their flesh against hers – she'd forbidden it and had forgotten how intoxicating it was. This moment had been building all night and day and she was consumed by it.

Then Jess tensed. All the warmth seem to evaporate, their bodies separated and the spell of longing disappeared.

Jess didn't move and she stared into the distance.

"What is it?" Anna said, looking up at Jess's frozen face. "You have to go, don't you," Anna realised. "You have to leave."

15

Jess stared at the canal bridge where the double decker bus had passed over so quickly that Anna hadn't caught it.

Jess's hair and suit were very different, but there she'd been, plastered large across the side of the bus, hands on hips, chest jutting out, her organic black suit moulded to her toned physique that took two hours daily at the gym to perfect. Her prominent breasts were the subject of several hashtags and the intensity of her gaze a meme already. The character's hairstyle had made it onto the streets and been photographed everywhere from a gay bar in Hamburg to Hong Kong.

Characters and threats leapt out from the twisting dark background of the poster. Jess played a hero that no-one knew they wanted until the first *Atlassia* film five years ago. Now they couldn't get enough of her and the phenomenon had spilled into the mainstream. The larger-than-life image had towered above them for a moment. The posters were new, but how long until Anna caught one? No doubt they would be unveiled in every Tube station and on the side of every bus stop. Jess could feel the moment, this glimpse of the wonderful ordinary, slipping through her fingers.

What the hell was Jess doing? Anna hadn't caught the image on the bus, and remained ignorant of who her companion was, and guilt and grief at the loss of the moment caved in Jess's belly. Why was she flirting with this kind and vulnerable woman? And it had gone beyond flirting now.

"I'm sorry," Anna said, her face becoming stony. "I shouldn't have said. I had no right to–"

"You don't understand," Jess said, clutching Anna on either side of her waist. "I have had the nicest day…" She gazed into Anna's eyes, struggling to communicate everything she felt. "It's been one of the best in a long while. Eating pancakes. Taking a walk in the park. Holding hands."

It must have sounded so mundane to Anna, but for Jess each had been blissful. She could see hope drain from her companion.

"I'm not just saying that," Jess said, hating to see Anna pale. "I haven't had a better day for…years."

Anna looked down. Jess could see all kinds of emotion flit across her usually controlled face: embarrassment, disappointment.

"My work," Jess struggled on. "I move all the time. I'm told where to go and I have no control over any of it."

It was on the tip of her tongue: I'm an actress. I'm famous. I can't walk out the door without someone staring. I'm photographed at restaurants. I'm sent worn knickers in the post. I haven't made a real friend in years.

But Anna would change, wouldn't she? Jess couldn't bear to imagine it. This tentative getting to know you would be blown away and replaced with the juggernaut of Jess's public persona and every preconception and expectation that came with it. She could picture the look that would take over Anna's face – the false friendship, the deference, the awe that would evaporate with one failed film and Jess's descent into obscurity.

People always wanted something and not for the sake of her company. She was desired as an escort to a party for the cachet, to recommend a product in front of the media, for introductions to a director. Gone were the days when the price of friendship was simple camaraderie. Loyalty, support, enjoyment were a thing of the past. Favours, nepotism and guilt were the currency in Jess's circles and the duplicity of it all had her reeling with incomprehension.

She rarely understood when someone was flirting or buttering her up, the why of it all being further from her understanding. It was like a game to which everyone else knew the rules. It's show business, they said.

But here was Anna, a woman who'd helped Jess for no other reason than help being needed. They hadn't left each other's side because they enjoyed their company, and sprinkled on top had been that magical thrill of attraction. The longing for these simple things, the stuff of everyday lives of millions of people, had eluded Jess for much of her adult life and she yearned for it with an ache that made her want to crumple into Anna's arms.

It all sat there, building inside her chest, wanting to burst out, but she dreaded the consequence. The trouble was, Jess often didn't know where to start and if she did she didn't know when to stop.

If she opened up she wanted to tell the truth, the whole truth, about herself. That's what open and honest Jess wanted. But that had gone badly wrong in the past. Why couldn't she say something flippant – a half-truth like everyone else did, no matter how misleading? So she attempted a real truth.

"I can't stay."

Anna visibly sank before her, and Jess's heart ached.

"If my life was different," she said, drawing Anna closer. She hesitated, trying to make sure it came out right. "If my life was different, I would be working up the courage to ask you on a date. I'd be standing here hoping you'd say 'yes'. I would be wanting to kiss you and touch you and would take it as fast or slow as you wanted." Her hands at Anna's waist tingled with warmth and the temptation to pull Anna in. "But I'm never around. I shouldn't be in London anymore. I'm leaving the UK on Monday, then Paris and Barcelona next week, and maybe back to Croatia. I don't know after that."

"What takes you away?" Anna said, quietly.

"Promotion," Jess said. It left out a lot. The rest squirmed in her belly – words that would destroy this gentle to-and-fro of getting to know each other and end this piece of heaven. How much more time did she have? With Jess's ever growing popularity, how long until her face was known by every demographic, not only the youngest fans and those who'd grown up like Jess with the graphic novels on which the films were based.

She couldn't speak and Anna didn't ask any more.

"I should talk to my manager," Jess said, resigned. "He's probably going wild."

Anna breathed in and composed herself, a slight smile lifting her face. She placed her hand on Jess's chest and Jess could feel the warmth of it over her heart.

"I would have said yes, you know," Anna said.

"To what?"

"To a date." She looked up at Jess with those beautiful blue eyes. "And to the possibility of more."

Jess could have kissed her.

"But, you have to go," Anna whispered.

"I do." Jess hung her head.

And for a while neither could say any more. It seemed their meeting had affected Anna as much as it had Jess.

"I know nothing can come of this," Anna said at last, "but would you like to come home? You could charge your phone. Make your call. I can give you some privacy on the balcony."

Jess hesitated.

"I would like more of your company, while I can," Anna said, all her refined composure restored but her words so filled with honesty it broke

Jess's heart. Jess ached for a little more. Just a little bit longer before this small piece of heaven was extinguished too.

"I'd like that," she murmured.

They turned towards the park and Anna's home. Jess didn't think she could bear the cold distance of walking apart and the relief was intense when Anna slipped her arm around her waist. They kept walking, the warmth buzzing between them, and every inch of Jess's body yearned with unfulfillable desire.

—

"Where the fuck have you been, Jess?" The deep voice boomed even on the phone. It was an understandable greeting given the circumstances.

"Hi, Femi," Jess replied, amused but mainly resigned. She pictured him, sharp suit taut around his muscled arms, pacing with the phone against his ear.

"Have you any idea of the shit I've had over the last twenty-four hours?"

Honestly, she did have an idea and she didn't envy him.

"A no show with the top host isn't something I can clean up after."

"Did they manage to get another guest?" she said, weakly.

"Yeah, course they did. Anyone, and I mean anyone, would kill to get on that show. The likes of Mirren would jump at the chance."

"Oh."

Jess peeked towards the balcony window, wondering if Femi's voice carried that far. Anna sat outside, legs crossed and gazing across London, a cup of tea at her lips, apparently unperturbed.

"What the hell's going on Jess? Where are you?"

"I'm, erm, at a friend's."

"What?"

"I'm in London, don't worry."

"Don't worry? Don't worry?! Have you any idea how many contract clauses you're breaking."

"No." She shrugged.

"Well, neither do I, and I don't even want to think about it."

Jess had to laugh. Things were such a mess, she had to.

"It's not fucking funny. Now, how quickly can you get ready? You're meant to be in Manchester. Gina's up there with all your stuff from the hotel. If we get you back on schedule the studio lawyers might not be quite so rabid."

"Femi—"

"Then Matt's going to meet you in Paris. He's worried and frankly so am I. You can't sink this film. They've already spent millions on the next."

"Femi—"

"Get your arse in gear and get up to—"

"Femi!"

That had shocked him. There was silence on the other end, or at least only the background chatter from a café or street.

"I can't," Jess said. Anxiety didn't rise or strangle. The situation was too obvious now and the calm of realisation and acceptance pervaded her tone. "I'm breaking."

"What?"

"If I carry on like this, I'm going to collapse. I can't soldier on."

"But…what the fuck?"

Jess swallowed and took stock. "You can't push me on this one."

Far too many times she'd been persuaded by her agent, producer, Femi, everyone. Squeeze in this film. Take another sponsorship. A fashion show for a favour. She needed quiet, much more quiet, and she needed time. She was exhausted by years spent doing the things that drained her – publicity, socialising, disrupted routine – and small interludes no longer revived her.

"I'm burning out, Femi. I need a rest."

"Not right now!"

"Then when?"

There was the background chatter again, but no Femi. "OK," he said, more gently. "What's going on?"

"You know publicity drains me," Jess started. "I need to be on top form for interviews and being in public."

"Yeah, I know, but this is part of the game, Jess."

"It's a part I'm not good at." She hadn't gone into acting for fame and adulation. If anything it was a deterrent. "It's exhausting at the best of times and I'm already empty."

"What do you need?"

"Time," she gasped. "To see Mom and Dad. To do normal stuff again. Not live out of a suitcase, travel across the continent and come home to see my face plastered over everything." Her hand trembled. "I'm sorry, Femi. I can't help it. But if I carry on I will break and it will be a lot messier."

She was impressed with her resolve. Her shy side was too often overruled by others with more confidence. Too often she believed them when they told her how she should be rather than how she knew she was, but her sojourn with Anna had given her perspective and clarity.

"OK," Femi sighed. "Well… fuck."

Jess laughed.

"It's not bloody funny," he said, but she could hear the smile in his voice. He wasn't an insensitive manager. Far from it. It was why she'd chosen him. He was efficient, effective, but human.

"OK," he said. "I've already cancelled several events, so you've got at least a couple of days. I'll see what I can do about shuffling the rest."

"Thank you," she said. "I need it. But I'm going to have to take it slower in future too. I need more time to recharge."

"Let me have a think," he said. "Take a couple days while I sort this out. See your family and whatever. But I want to see you on Monday to chat face to face."

"OK," Jess said, relieved.

So, she had a couple of days respite at least. She sat on the end of the bed staring at her phone and the ludicrous number of notifications. She swiped to her apps and began removing them. All social media. Any messaging that wasn't used by her family and colleagues. All news apps but one and the world was suddenly a quieter, safer place, for now.

"Are you all right?"

Jess looked up at the sound of Anna's voice. She couldn't help smiling at the elegant woman who stood before her with kind concern on her face.

"My manager's bought me some time."

"Good," Anna replied.

"He's cancelled my UK events. He said I should go and see my folks and meet him on Monday."

"I'm glad. Sounds like you need to." The entreaty to take care of herself made Jess long for Anna more. "You seem to miss them terribly."

"I'll take the train and drop in at home tomorrow."

Anna nodded.

"Then Monday. I leave…"

They were silent, until Anna suggested, "So stay? For now?"

Jess opened her mouth to ask if she meant the night, but it was obvious. "I shouldn't."

"I don't mean anything by it. It's late. I know nothing can happen and I don't think I could anyway."

That almost broke Jess's resolve and she wanted to rush to Anna, hold her, kiss her and hope that Anna burned as much as she did.

"But if this is the only time you have in London," Anna continued, "I'd like any you can spare."

Whether Jess thought it a good idea or not, she couldn't refuse. "I'd love to stay."

They were quieter that evening. They watched the sun go down, the red orb sinking below the buildings and baking London golden. And when the light extinguished and the city glowed with street lights they remained on the balcony under a blanket listening to the sounds of the metropolis.

They ate takeout and when Jess was too tired for words, they listened to music from Jess's playlist and Anna's antiquated CD collection, then laughed about everything and nothing until Jess fell asleep for a second time on Anna's bed, this time cuddled up with Anna spooned in front of her.

When Jess got up, she brushed her teeth with a spare toothbrush, had a quick shower and took another pair of knickers and T shirt. Then, it was time to leave.

"So?" Anna said. That voice. Jess was going to miss it.

"So," Jess replied.

Anna looked as if she brimmed full. Their meeting seemed to have left both of them raw and yearning for what they couldn't have.

"Do you think you'll have any time," Anna asked, "before you leave England for good?"

"I don't think so," Jess said, full of regret. "If I did, this would be the first place I'd want to be."

Anna attempted a smile.

"In that case..." Jess said.

"Yes?"

"Could I... you know... Is it all right... if I have your phone number?"

Anna laughed quietly. "Phone number?"

"So I can call you if there's time?"

"That's a bit forward isn't it?" Anna's smile lifted her face but it was tinged with sadness, her heart not quite into her usual teasing. "So you get into my knickers, stay two nights and now you want my phone number?"

Jess smiled, and it hurt at the same time.

"Of course," Anna relented, and Jess tapped the number into her phone while Anna recited it and they did the same for Anna.

"OK," Jess said. And still her body didn't turn to leave.

Anna stepped forward, put up her arms around Jess's shoulders and drew her body against her to say goodbye. Jess's whole being sighed with the intimacy and she was filled with powerful attraction and desperate sadness.

Anna tilted back her face from Jess's shoulder and lifted a hand to her cheek in a tender gesture. She hesitated, her finger poised, apparent and warm above Jess's skin.

"May I?" Anna asked.

Jess nodded and closed her eyes.

"I want to remember you," Anna murmured.

Her fingers caressed Jess's face gently and her skin delighted where she traced. Anna explored delicately across her eyebrows, over her eyelids, making out the shape of her cheeks. Jess giggled when Anna stroked her top lip. It tickled.

"Sorry," Jess said.

"You are beautiful," Anna said, her voice like velvet. It made Jess's heart beat deeper.

Anna ran her finger over her lips once more, so that Jess's head swam with the sensation and her lips pulsed expectant. She felt Anna lean closer. The warm humidity of her breath on Jess's face made her heart beat quicker still and when Anna's fingers slipped behind Jess's neck she opened her mouth to receive Anna's kiss.

Did Jess moan when those tender lips slipped over hers? Did she pull Anna in and hold their bodies together with eagerness? She certainly couldn't help the groan as her hips undulated between Anna's.

Oh, Anna could kiss. It was the kind of kiss that reaches in and consumes the body. Jess opened her mouth to let their kiss deepen, her legs weakening as Anna took command and slipped her tongue inside.

Jess couldn't help her desire and her hands exploring, and she drew Anna in tight, wanting to crush her arousal but at the same not wanting to let go. They gasped in each other's arms, Anna's breath urgent beside Jess's ear so that Jess was left in no doubt about the passion that flowed in Anna's veins.

As their breathing stilled, Jess held her more tenderly, and at last had to let go. Jess opened her mouth but no words came out, and she stared at the woman she'd kissed and whose beauty was heightened by glowing cheeks and dark eyes.

Anna cupped her face. "Don't worry," she whispered. "It's only a kiss. If you never see me again, it's just a kiss."

16

That kiss was going to keep Anna on a high for a long time. Jess had left an hour ago and Anna couldn't help smiling and dabbing her fingertips on her lips. The touch of Jess tingled there.

What a difference two nights had made. Anna stood in the middle of her flat, bathed and euphoric in morning sunshine. She could still imagine Jess's hand on her belly. She'd woken in the night, Jess spooned and wrapped around her, fingers on Anna's bare stomach where her T-shirt had ridden high. Anna had jolted awake at the realisation, so unused to contact on her naked skin, and she'd lain there frozen. Jess hadn't stirred. The cosy sensation of her, rising and falling with slow sleepy breaths, had calmed Anna with its soothing motion.

Anna had let her spine, taut like a metal wire, relax and allowed her body to sink back into Jess's embrace. Her tense shoulders eased down and she lay there feeling nothing but Jess's soft fingers resting on her belly. They gently stroked as Anna inhaled, then slipped lower when Anna's breath hitched, and lower again at that movement, and all kinds of sensations celebrated lower still at the seductive touch.

Anna gulped at her body's reaction. It had been a long time. It was frightening how rapidly she reacted to the barest contact with this woman. In the park, her inadvertent caress of Jess's back had sparked a torrent of feelings and Anna's outburst. She'd blushed again in bed, then clutched Jess's hand at the embarrassment, subconsciously wanting her reassurance again that she hadn't stepped too far.

Jess had stirred at the motion, snuffling a little as she wriggled in her sleep. She woke enough to perhaps realise where her hand lay and Anna stiffened at the realisation. Jess lifted her hand away and Anna's heart sank. But Jess had reached up for Anna's T-shirt, pulled it down to cover her stomach, before drifting back to sleep. Anna squeezed Jess's hand, warmed through this time at the young woman's consideration. A person, at last, she could trust with closeness, and Anna lay awake, her body humming with the contentment.

If only she could trust herself though. She hadn't meant to kiss Jess when she'd left. Not like that. Not at all.

She'd asked only to hold her face for a second, to commit the full sense of the beautiful woman to memory. Then, seduced, Anna meant only to place her lips on hers. But Anna had flooded with desire and when Jess had pulled her close, their legs entwined and bodies joined, that had been all kinds of wonderful. A wave of heat rose again through Anna at the memory, all the way to her cheeks and she took a deep breath and exhaled noisily, then fanned her face when that wasn't nearly enough.

She smiled again. The world was a better place this morning, a bigger place. Her body was alive. Jess had found her hiding in this sheltered existence and burst it wide open.

Jess was only a message away. Anna patted for her phone but she mustn't message though. That's not how they left it. If there was time before Jess departed for good then she would call and Anna should leave it at that. She clutched her phone between her hands and it was comforting to know Jess was in there.

A harsh buzzer interrupted her reverie and Anna pressed the button on the intercom. "Hello?"

"Thank christ you're in."

Anna grinned. That would be Penny.

"Please. I'm begging you. Could you take Bibs? Just for an hour. Say yes."

"Of course. Door's–"

"Great." And the small woman topped with a frizz of long copper curls had already disappeared from the intercom screen.

Anna heard stomping up the stairs and opened the flat door to the whirlwind that was Penny MacFarlane, her very best friend. The woman barely cleared Anna's shoulder in height, but there was much personality packed into that petite, round figure.

"I have got," Penny dumped a small child into Anna's arms, "the shittiest hangover ever."

"Pen!"

Anna cuddled Bibs to her chest and gave the blonde bundle a smile. Smiles were impossible to deny with a squashy two-year-old in her arms, especially one who reached up and put her tiny hands on her cheeks and tried to say her name as something between "Anna" and "banana".

"She'll pick up swear words now," Anna said in a harsh whisper to Pen.

"Really couldn't give a flying monkey's arse at the moment. Oh, Jesus Christ. This headache." Pen put her hand to her head and the tight expression on her face gave the vivid impression of a splitting headache. "Lana's gone to the shitting office already, so she's no help."

Anna was going to question it, being a Sunday, but this was Lana they were talking about.

"She has no idea," Penny rattled on, "how appallingly wretched it is to look after children with a hangover."

"You let Bibs drink? To excess?"

"What? No, of course… Oh…Please. This is not the time. Really, you haven't experienced the truly hellish depths of a hangover if you haven't done it while entertaining a two-year-old."

"She's so insensitive." Anna had trouble not laughing. "Works round the clock to keep you in the manner to which you neither deserve nor appreciate, and refuses to do childcare at the same time."

"I know she does all that bringing-in-the-money business. But does she get up in the middle of the night to clean up vomit and escapee turds? Hmm? Feed Bibs when she's on a growth spurt? Read her Fluffkins the fucking Rabbit for the ten thousandth time at two o'clock in the morning?"

Actually Pen looked as if she was about to cry.

"I. Just. Need. Some. Sleep," Pen said, throwing her hands towards the heavens.

"I know," Anna relented. "Come here," she said and she leaned forwards, Bibs in one arm and the other wrapped around Penny to give her a kiss on the cheek.

"Can I crash?"

"Go for it," Anna said.

"Thank Christ for everything that is good and holy." And Penny stomped towards the bed, fell face first and rolled over with the duvet wrapped around her.

"She's eaten by the way," came a muffled voice from the cocoon. "Breakfast. Second breakfast. And a snack. And she's pooed…"

And it was like Penny was asleep and snoring in the same breath. Anna sighed and turned to Bibs. "Mummy's tired," she said gently.

"Kwee have story?" Bibs said.

"You betcha."

Anna settled into the corner of the sofa with Bibs on her knee, snuggled into the crook of Anna's arm.

"Which shall we have first?"

"Animals," Bibs said, clapping her chubby hands together.

"Can you get it from the shelf for me?"

Bibs shuffled off her knee, waddled over to the shelves that divided the kitchen space from the lounge and returned with a large picture book. She hopped onto Anna's knee and opened it at the first page of bright colourful snakes. The book was well worn and Anna read to a captivated Bibs, who sometimes pointed to the page and pretended to read too.

They followed up with a stack of *Winnie the Witch* books.

"What can you see in the picture? Tell me about your favourite bits." Anna smiled.

"Wormy." Bib giggled. "Wormy's eating Winnie's food."

And Bibs pointed to the detailed and distinctive illustrations and Anna loved the emerging person that was Bibs talking to her. Anna knew the books by heart, given her aptitude for memorising presentations and lines, but being snuggled up with this squidgy toddler was a highlight of many days.

Bibs shuffled on Anna's lap and rested her head on her shoulder. After the tenth book, Anna felt her slump and become still, all cosy in her arms. Anna remained quiet, taking in the gentle rise and fall of the toddler's ribs, listened to the slight whistle from her tiny nose and watched her eyes roll back and lids finally remain shut. Anna picked her up and walked carefully, agonisingly carefully so the toddler didn't wake, towards the bed.

Penny suddenly sat up and stared at them.

"Ssssh", Anna said.

"I need a wee!" Penny said with a frantic hiss. "I'm going to wet myself!"

She fled off the bed while Anna lay Bibs down, replacing one slumbering MacFarlane with another, and covered Bibs up to her shoulders with the duvet.

Anna rolled her eyes at the sound of Penny on the loo.

"Sorry! Didn't have time to close the door," came a loud whisper.

Anna didn't know why she bothered apologising. She'd experienced far more personal moments with Pen, none of them romantic.

"Ooooooooohhhh," Penny sighed as she shuffled back into the room, adjusting her snug top and pulling her tight skirt around her bum.

They both leant over the sleeping child and Penny sighed.

"Oh my wee girl." The adoration was obvious in Penny's voice. "I love you, sweet thing," Penny said to the oblivious Bibs. "But I had no idea I was going to kiss goodbye to bladder control when you erupted from my womb." And she tugged the duvet up to her daughter's pudgy chin.

17

"Thank you," Penny sighed as Anna placed a steaming cup in front of her on the kitchen island. "I'm starting to feel human again after a nap." Penny paused. "Jesus. How ancient do I sound, having a nap?"

"Bibs is having a nap, so that makes you on a par with a two-year-old," Anna replied.

Penny shrugged and seemed satisfied with the analogy. "Oh god," she moaned. "I wish you'd been at that bloody wedding yesterday. Instead of me would have been good."

"That bad?"

"Wall-to-wall toffs and suits. You would have been fine. You always knew how to charm in any circle. Benefits of an uptight upbringing," Penny raised her mug, "ability to politely charm in that strata of society. Can't stand doing it. The number of scathing looks Lana sent my way for swearing."

Anna smiled indulgently at her friend. "It's what I've always loved about you. You wear everything on the outside."

"Well apparently Lana doesn't appreciate that."

Anna was diplomatic and held her tongue. She couldn't reassure Penny. Since Bibs had been born, cracks had appeared in the MacFarlane family, circumstances, personalities and pressures no doubt all contributing, and Anna did all she could to support Penny and Bibs and help take the strain.

"And the couple we were sitting next to," Penny carried on, "honestly, when Bibs filled her nappy, you know with that little grunt and straining red face, because when she's in a high chair it needs that extra push because she's basically sitting on it, but if you take her out she'll stop and be constipated for days, well you would have thought she'd got up and shat in their soup."

"Fuck 'em." Anna grinned.

"I love it when you swear." Penny's face was full beaming satisfaction. "It's so much dirtier with your sophisticated accent. Do it more often please."

"I'll indulge you once in a while."

"Hey," Penny leant forward and grabbed Anna's hand. "You've got to come to the cinema with me."

Anna tried not to groan, but apparently failed.

"I know you avoid it, but Lana's always tapping at her phone answering emails if she goes and is wretched company. Pleeeeeease." Penny drew out the entreaty for several seconds.

"I've never liked superhero films."

"This one's not a superhero film."

"OK, fantasy action film."

"I have broader taste than that. But, yes, it is fantasy and there's so much more to it than another fictional world. It's an epic saga with drama, family tension, politics. It's gripping and this one's really captured everyone's imagination. And, most importantly," Penny inhaled dramatically and put her hand over her heart, "it has a super-hot sexy heroine."

Anna groaned.

"No, honestly. That woman." Pen gurgled and drooled over the word "woman" and her open-mouthed poleaxed expression was indecent. "She is sensational. She has the most fit body ever and you can see every inch of it when she wears that suit. Frankly, her tits are magnificent."

Anna must have tutted because Pen followed up quickly with, "Yeah, yeah, I know, you never understood people falling for someone's body. But her eyes, imagine deepest dark pools of hazel deliciousness. And lips, they look like they could kiss you into oblivion in the filthiest way possible. She'd have your knickers wet in seconds."

"Pen!" Anna swallowed away a hint of nausea and wrinkled her nose.

"You have to watch the new one with me so I can lust after Jessica Lambert without Lana sending me disapproving looks."

Anna laughed. "How about I babysit Bibs and you go by yourself?"

"Naww. If I was sitting by myself, I'd feel like a perv."

"Well…?" Anna raised her eyebrows, accusingly.

"Oh, you're no fun."

"I can't," Anna said sadly.

"But the voice!" Pen said, suddenly animated again. "Her voice. That'll seduce you all on its own."

"What's the film then?"

"*Atlassia, Part 3*"

"Never heard of it or parts 1 and 2."

"Well that's disgraceful, mainly because I've told you about it tons of times before and you clearly weren't listening."

Anna sighed with guilt. Her loss of enjoyment of cinema trips which were beyond her regimented world grieved her from several perspectives and she suspected she'd switched off as a defence mechanism.

"I'll owe you," Penny sang, with all the guile and subtlety of a four-year-old needling for sweets. "I'll do anything."

Anna took Penny's face in her hands and leant forward. "You," she tutted. "Look at your mischievous twinkling eyes."

"Don't look too close, otherwise you'll see all these bloody wrinkles too. 'Pregnancy makes you bloom,' everyone tells you. Yeah well, they don't mention how shit tired you'll be afterwards and how your face will age like an elephant's arse."

Anna laughed out loud and kissed Penny on the forehead. "I love you."

Penny squeezed her hands. "I love you too."

Bibs snored sweetly from the bed and they both gazed in her direction, Anna noticing Penny had the same besotted smile she wore herself.

"Hey," Pen said, turning back and squeezing her hand. "How was your day yesterday? Did you chill out?"

"Actually." Anna found herself treading carefully. Pen was a terrier when it came to sniffing out gossip. "I spent it with a friend."

"Did Marcus get his arse in gear and call round?"

"No, not Marcus."

"One of your cousins? Oh, Dominique said she was going to call you."

"That's good."

"So not your cousins either?"

Oh god. She'd already piqued her friend's interest. Pen sat up alert on the bar stool.

"A new friend," Anna said, trying to keep it light.

"Someone new?" Pen said, tight faced, with a high-pitched nonchalance that was anything but.

"Yes, I..." Shit. "She was lost, on Friday."

"Oh yes?"

"On the Tube."

"Uhuh?" Pen was leaning forward, elbows on the top and head perched on hands. Anna was beginning to sweat.

"And we got talking and..."

"And?"

"Hung out."

"Oh," Penny deflated. "I'm just playing. You know I always hope that…well, you know….And I know you worry and don't want to….well, you know. I know."

Good. There. She'd confessed to Penny who was too good a friend not to tell.

"So, a woman?"

Dammit. Penny was fake-nonchalantly sipping her coffee again, eyes hawk-like on Anna.

"Yes, a woman."

"Good."

"What?" Anna laughed. "Why?"

"I will never understand your attraction to men. All that…hair." Penny wrinkled her nose.

"Not all of them are hairy."

"And they smell funny."

"Everyone smells different."

"No breasts."

"Not always true."

"And great hairy bollocks and dicks. I really don't like those."

Anna snorted. "You don't have to sleep with them. And you adored Marcus."

"Well, he was like a lesbian."

At least they'd moved on from the topic of Anna's latest friend.

"So are we talking hot new friend? Young, hot, new friend? Rich older friend?"

Bugger.

"Does any of that matter?" Anna said, with amused despair.

"To me it does." Penny leaned forward, insatiable and enjoying her tease.

"OK," Anna relented. "She was twenty-four. Does that count as young?"

"Like, yeah," Penny tutted. "Pretty? Attractive?"

"I suppose, yes."

"I know you don't like reducing people to their looks, but come on, was she…?" and Penny carved out the shape of a curvy woman in the air with her hands.

"She was attractive." Anna had a sudden flash of caressing Jess's face and then appreciating those luscious lips with her own. Oh my god she was attractive.

"You're not having a fling with some young thing are you?" Pen nudged her.

Anna really was sweating. "Going to open a window," she said, and got up.

"Anna?" Pen was calling after her, more earnest now. "Anna? Seriously? Did you meet someone?"

Anna fiddled with the window and tried to keep talking as if none of it was as earth moving as it felt. "She was someone who needed a place to stay and we chatted and–"

"She stayed the night?!"

Damn.

"Yes. On Friday." Anna held her breath. "And Saturday."

Silence. Anna didn't dare turn around.

"So you met her on Friday?"

"Yes."

"And she's stayed here ever since?"

"It's not like that."

"Because moving in on the first date would be some kind of record even in lesbian circles."

Anna laughed at last and turned round. "It wasn't like that at all. I offered help and she was wonderful company." And now that Jess was no longer there, Anna began to doubt herself. "She was funny, and charming, and young and attractive. And also not available. She works abroad, so nothing can happen even if she was interested in middle-aged women who barely leave their homes."

Penny got up and came towards her.

"I'm certain she would have been interested." Penny held her hands, gentle sympathy suffused on her face.

"You couldn't know that. You haven't met her."

"Anna Mayhew, you are one of the most beautiful women in England. She would fancy the pants off you."

Anna squeezed Penny's hands, grateful for her friend's biased compliment.

"Anyway," Anna sighed. "She works all over Europe apparently, so nothing can happen even if we both wanted it."

"OK." Pen, at last, seemed satisfied.

Anna's phone buzzed beside them on the kitchen top. Message from Jess. Oh god, no.

The message notification was lit up on her phone.

"Jess? Who's Jess?" Pen asked. "Is she the new friend?"

Please leave it there. Please don't read the message. Don't say anything else. Anna prayed that the phone would fade to a black screen again. Anna peeped to the side to read the message that was very clear, very obvious, and that said, "That wasn't just a kiss."

Crap.

Anna and Penny stood clutching each other's hands, as still as statues, apart from the ever widening hole that was Penny's mouth. Any moment now, a great noise and consternation was going to come out of that gaping cavern.

"Anna Mayhew!"

Anna smiled sweetly and gripped Pen's hands.

"You!" Penny gasped. "You lied!"

"No. No. No. It's not like that."

"Kissing!"

"Really I didn't."

"There was kissing. And it sounds like serious kissing." Penny growled to make sure that it sounded salacious.

"It was when we said good bye. Only then."

"Really?" Pen eyes narrowed to slits.

"Honestly. Nothing happened."

"A kiss happened."

"Nothing apart from the kiss. I swear to you."

"But." Penny's body went slack and her face softened. She drew Anna's hands into her chest. "That's amazing."

Anna swallowed. Yes. It had been amazing.

"I mean it." Penny was almost tearful. "That's brilliant. Was it ok?"

"The kiss?" It was fucking phenomenal.

"I mean. Were you OK with being close to someone?"

"Yes." Anna nodded. "Actually, yes."

Pen reached up and bear hugged her, rocking from side to side. "It's been too bloody long," Pen said, muffled into Anna's shoulder. "I'm so happy for you."

"Nothing will come of it," Anna said, trying not to sniff over Penny's shoulder.

"But that doesn't matter. This is a huge step for you." And Penny squeezed her again.

At last she let Anna go and stood before her, holding her hands with a big grin on her face. Then the grin disappeared.

"Did she know who you are?" Penny asked, cautiously.

A sadness settled in Anna's belly. "Sorry, what was that?" She knew what Penny had said and what she alluded to.

"Did she recognise you?"

Anna shook her head. "Of course she didn't, Pen. No-one does anymore."

18

"That wasn't just a kiss." The thought had filled Jess's head ever since leaving Anna's flat. She'd walked away like she glided a foot in the air.

She bounced her knees up and down, hidden away on a fold-down seat in the end carriage of a train with bikes, buggies and one other person for company. It definitely wasn't travelling movie star style, but she didn't want to relent and have Femi order her a private car all the way from London to Birmingham, and he knew better than to offer. "I know, your green principles," he'd said.

So the none-too-salubrious carriage for bulky items and the loo was her choice and that of very few others, which was the point. Nervous energy charged through her veins, wary of recognition and now doubly anxious after caving into her urges and sending that message to Anna.

Jess wore the glasses and hat which so far had proved effective as a disguise. She hunched over listening to her favourite playlist on headphones, periodically shoulder bumping the guy next to her as the train swayed along the tracks. She let a string of beads flow from one hand into the palm of the other and back again, something that was pleasing and usually calmed her, while she tried not to think about exactly how long it had been since she'd sent the text to Anna.

She peeked at her phone in her jacket pocket. Still no reply.

She'd tried to resist sending it. But that kiss. It had filled her mind, body and soul and it was all she could think of as she'd floated along the streets to the train station, hardly taking in her surroundings in a daze and with a giant grin on her face.

She'd been kissed, by someone who knew her only as Jess, and who enjoyed her company and found her a little bit sexy. It made Jess as giddy as a teen and she let her mind savour the memory of Anna's soft fingertips trailing across her cheeks and circling her eyelids with a feather-light touch in a way that had surprised Jess with its intimacy. It was a delicate area of the face often neglected and it had sent a signal to everywhere else, leaving a glow inside. Then Anna's lips had delicately slipped over Jess's and her body flooded even at the memory. She'd breathed out with heady exhilaration and dashed off the text while high on the reminiscence, saying exactly what was on her mind.

And now she waited.

She wouldn't call Anna though.

Talking on the phone to her manager or agent or anyone from the set was as natural as the sun coming up in the morning and she would answer their calls without thinking. With anyone else it was an unnatural event of catastrophic order, which would cause her to regard her phone with horror. Whatever they needed, they could say it to her answer phone or text, unless they were Mom or Nan who would ring incessantly until Jess answered. You didn't say no to them, or pretend to be out, or busy, because they just knew.

Still no message.

"Hey, bro." The young bloke next to her, with shoulders three feet wide, gave her a nudge. "What you listening to?"

"Sorry?" Jess pulled out a headphone and sat up straighter. "Do you want me to turn it down?"

"Whoa," the guy said checking her up and down. "Sorry, thought you was a dude." And he raised his hands in apology.

Jess shrugged, not particularly bothered by the mistake. "No worries."

"It's that tune," he carried on, "I've heard it before. Wanted to know what it was like."

"It's just a Dua Lipa track." Jess scrolled down her screen to show him the song title.

"That's it. Knew it was something like that. My girlfriend loves it."

Jess looked up at him and smiled.

"Hey, what?" His face fell and he leaned away. "You look just like Jessica Lambert! Like mirror image."

"Sssh," Jess said, frantic, and held her finger to her lips. "Keep it down, please."

"What? No way!" he said in the loudest whisper Jess had ever heard. "You serious? Are you really like, the Jessica Lambert?"

Jess put her hands up. "Please."

"Oh, right," he said, lowering his voice. He leant in conspiratorially. "You don't want no-one to know, right? Travel quiet?"

Jess nodded and her heart rate settled as the man checked around for people listening with a comical lack of subtlety. "I think we're all right". He might not be the most discrete but he seemed a decent guy.

He turned back and whispered. "I'll leave you in peace, but I have got to thank you first."

Jess crinkled her nose in confusion.

"See, my girlfriend watches soppy films, which I don't mind, like, but it was all the time. Until," he paused for effect "the *Atlassia* movies. She's nuts about them. In fact she's going to be so pissed off when she hears I've met you."

"Thanks," Jess said.

"In fact...." He was suddenly coy as he realised he was getting ahead of himself. "Sorry, I'll leave you be."

He sat straight, attempted to act casually, slapped out a beat on his knees with his hands, looked determinedly in every direction but at Jess and opened his mouth periodically as if to speak before snapping it shut again.

Jess smiled. "Do you want a selfie?"

"Yeah," he said, breaking out into a huge grin.

Jess took off her hat and glasses and swept her hair into a style that more resembled her character's. The guy took out his phone and leaned in shoulder to shoulder with Jess.

"Kit's going to go mad when she sees this," he said.

A grin took up permanent residence on his face for the rest of the journey and he left Jess to her music. From time to time, another passenger might pass by and stare at Jess, until her companion made a show of being her friend or said "What you looking at?" dropping his voice an octave and the words booming from his considerable chest. At Jess's stop they exchanged a fist bump and she left a very happy man in the carriage. If only all her encounters in public were like that. At least it had taken her mind off Anna, and what that wonderful woman was thinking.

Jess plunged her hands into her denim jacket pockets and wandered through the village. The air was cool and her breath billowed in clouds. The village green was peppered with yellow and brown leaves, although the group of oak trees in the centre still retained theirs. The church beyond peaked above its perimeter of yew trees, a pale limestone anomaly in the village of old red brick cottages that surrounded the green.

The family had moved here when Jess was seven after her grandad had died. It was perhaps a few months after his funeral that Nan had thrown a wobbly and it was only now that Jess realised that Nan had channelled her grief into frustration and changing her life and that of her family's.

"I can't be doing with the city no more," Jess remembered Nan announcing in their tiny terrace front room. "I've had enough of tarmac and tower blocks. I want to see green again. I want to see trees not pylons and telegraph poles. I'm sick of the smog and fumes."

Jess's mother had rolled her eyes. "Mom. This is Acocks Green, not flipping Victorian London." Jess had tucked away the mild swear word for future reference. It was rare her mother let one slip.

"I don't belong in this urban sprawl. I grew up with mountains, palm trees and blue sea."

Mum had glanced at Jess and muttered. "She grew up in Kingston, Jamaica, the capital, which has about as many people as Manchester."

"I heard that. And I could see mountains. It wasn't like this endless grey." And Jess distinctly remembered her Nan with her hands on her hips staring out into a day that was indeed very grey.

"I'm moving," Nan said, which meant they all did.

It was with Nan's sheer force of personality that she settled the entire family in a small village to the south of Birmingham, which may not have been the most welcoming of places at first, but Nan's conviction had enough momentum to steamroller any uptight second looks from the residents, for which Jess was eternally grateful. She wished she had her Nan's determination and confidence. Any bigotry aimed at Jess personally made her want to crumble.

Jess started at the tiny local primary school with the best ever teacher of Miss Powell, who had time and a kind word for every child. Jess sat between Maisie Green and Sandeep Mehta – a girl with white skin and freckles who eschewed pink and preferred her brother's hand-me-downs and a boy with straight black hair and brown skin who was obsessed with superhero comics. They became school-long friends and Jess was established in this village locale.

Jess smiled at the memory and approached the white wooden door of a cottage overlooking the green. She raised the lion's head iron knocker and let the sound reverberate inside the house.

"I'll get it," she heard muffled inside. Her Nan. Jess couldn't help grinning. "If it's one of those window sales people I'm going to give them what for," came louder towards Jess.

The door opened and a grey-haired lady of modest height scowled over little half-moon glasses with a ferocity that would have sent any door-to-door salesperson running.

The expression soon changed.

"Oh. My. God!" Nan screamed, and her mouth and eyes expanded wide and her arms shot into the air.

19

"I thought you weren't going to have time to see us!" Nan shouted and she tugged Jess's shoulders down so that she could envelope her in comforting arms.

That squeeze from her Nan, its strength had not diminished over the years, if anything it had got stronger as Jess became bigger and more able to withstand it. Nan pulled her into her padded and reassuring hug, which felt as if it could protect Jess from all the ills in the world.

"I can't believe it!" Nan yelled. "Everybody! Jess is home!" she shouted into the house.

"Hi, Nan," Jess said, muffled by the considerable upper arm of her grandmother. Jess wondered if she imagined the aroma of sweet spices, the comfort of it all was so consuming.

"I'm baking," her grandmother said.

Oh. It actually was the smell of spices.

"I'm making parkin for bonfire night, my own recipe. Come in quick. I need to take it out the oven. Trisha! Jess is here!"

Jess ducked her head under the doorway and followed Nan into the low-ceilinged kitchen.

"Give me a moment," Nan said, "then I'll get to you properly." She lumbered towards the range oven. Jess frowned. Nan hadn't hobbled so much when she'd been home last. She'd left it too long and a pang of guilt and regret pinched in her chest.

"People never put enough ginger in," Nan said, shaking out a T-towel then folding it thick. "It needs to burn your throat if it's going to warm you up on a cold November night. Your father always mutters about the traditional recipe, but I'm not having that. I know a good cake when I taste one."

Nan bent down as if her back creaked with every small movement and slid out a loaf tin, brown lining paper curling over the top and the rich dark ginger cake peeking out from within. A warm, humid, spicy cloud enveloped Jess's face.

"That smells delicious," she said, unable to resist the temptation to inhale it all.

Nan let the tin clatter onto the iron trivet on the farmhouse style kitchen table and flopped her tea towel beside it.

"Oh my girl." Nan came back to squeeze Jess's cheeks in her big hands. "We should eat this now. You need fattening up." And she slapped Jess on the bum. "Too much bone on them hips. You wait until your mother sees you."

"I can see her," came a voice. Jess squinted further into the cottage, struggling with the dimness in the middle of the house then the bright contrast of the window beyond in the sitting room that overlooked the garden. Her mother stepped out of the stairwell and into the kitchen. "She's perfect the way she is," Trisha said with the kind of smile that fills you right up to the top with love.

"Mom," Jess murmured and she wrapped her arms around her. Her mother's hug was less ferocious than Nan's but no less comforting.

Jess couldn't hold back any longer. She thought she'd steadied herself over the last day in Anna's company, but tears sprung into her eyes and they wouldn't stop. "I missed you all so much." And that's all she could say, now that she was full-on blubbing. Her mother squeezed her gently and rocked her from side to side.

"Come here, bab," she said, and she cradled Jess's head with one hand, and that made Jess blub some more.

Jess sniffled and was only half aware when she drew herself up that she wiped her nose on her hand like a five-year-old.

"You had a haircut!" Jess said, beaming and still crying a little.

"Do you like it?" Mom said, grinning so much she was obviously thrilled with it. Gone was her weave and braided extensions and she sported a short pixie cut of tight curls.

"You look amazing, Mom."

Jess didn't have to even try to think of the compliment. The short hair suited her mom's face and accentuated her cheekbones. Jess knew she owed her looks to her mother, with her dark skin, deep brown eyes that didn't miss a thing and a curve to her body. Her Dad had given her height but everything else she owed to these two ladies.

Jess sighed. There were too many changes. Her life was so fast-moving and all-consuming that she sometimes forgot change went on for others too.

"You do not need fattening up, or slimming down, or any other change my lovely girl," Mom said with eyes full of adoring sympathy, "but I bet a cup of tea and some cake would go down a treat."

Jess nodded, a lump still blocking her throat. "Yes, it would."

"Tell that husband of yours to get home," Nan said with the flick of a sharp knife towards Trisha before she resumed cutting through the rich sticky treat. "His daughter is home and there's cake. That son of yours too."

"I'm trying," Trisha said with such a strong Brummie twang it made Jess grin.

They sat round the kitchen table, mugs of tea in front of them and tendrils of steam drifting towards the low-beamed ceiling. Trisha was tapping at her phone then waving it around the room, attempting to send a message against the will of the temperamental service.

"You can say all you want about the benefits of country living, but for once I'd like to be able to send a message without having to be a contortionist."

"All this modern technology," Nan said with a dismissive wave of her hand.

"You're the one who wanted me to send a message."

Nan tutted and Jess couldn't stop beaming, back in the company of their habitual bickering.

"Jack's on his way to a friend's," Mom said. "I'll tell your dad to turn round and bring him home."

"It's OK," Jess said quietly. "I didn't give you any warning. Don't bother him if he's going out."

"Rubbish," Nan snapped. "You're a busy woman. He should come home to see his famous sister."

Jess swallowed and took an interest in her tea.

"We were worried you know," Nan said, peering straight at her.

"Mom!" Trisha hissed.

"Well we were. We were all round the telly expecting you on that talk show, then some comedian comes on instead. We didn't know what to think."

Jess squeezed her mug until it started to burn her palms. "Sorry," she said.

"Nothing to be sorry for," Mom said and she patted Jess's hand. "Thank you for leaving a message yesterday."

Jess looked up to see concern creasing her mother's forehead which she immediately disguised with a smile that wasn't quite convincing but was nonetheless full of regard and no blame.

"I…" The words stuck in Jess's throat again. "I'm tired," was all she managed.

Nan thrust a small plate with a large piece of cake towards her and Jess took a nibble as an excuse not to say anymore.

"You sounded happy in that message. Who were you with, huh?" Nan said, peering down her nose through her glasses so that she had Jess in sharp focus. How did she do that? How did she sniff out gossip like that?

"What?" Jess said, putting none of her acting skills to use.

"You heard me. Who were you with? Some nice lady?"

"Mom!" Trisha shot Nan another look.

"Well, I wouldn't blame her for skipping a TV show for some nice woman."

"Or man," Mom added.

Nan tutted and batted that possibility out the room with a wave of the hand. "If she must," Nan said. "If I'd ever known about lesbians when I was young, you might never have been born. That's all I'm saying."

It was one of those snippets of conversation that Jess was never sure whether she should be heartened or disturbed by. But her grandmother had been one of the most supportive people in her life when she showed signs of being queer as a teen. Her Nan had told her straight away that she'd seen enough bigotry in life not to entertain other kinds when it came to Jess, and when she'd tugged her into that crushing hug of hers it had gone a long way to extinguishing the fear that had built up inside young Jess.

"I…" Jess nursed that tea some more. "I freaked out," she said, watching the steam twist and curl out of her mug. "That's why I missed the show."

Mom and Nan were quiet, Trisha's hand resting against Jess's.

"I've been working hard lately."

Her mother nodded encouragement.

"Travelling, interviews, reshoots and last-minute dubbing." Jess took a deep breath. "I think I'm exhausted, that's all."

"You need your quiet don't you, bab." Mom smiled. "You always did. Too much time with people and you'd need to hide away with a comic or go into your own world outside in the woods."

"Yeah," Jess sighed. She didn't feel too far away from that young girl that Mom referred to.

"And where did you find quiet time in London?" Nan said, spitting out the name of the capital.

"A friend helped calm me down," Jess admitted. "She was very kind. I only met her on Friday, but she was so helpful." She glanced up to see two faces that were trying very hard to be diplomatic.

"She's a friend." Jess tutted. Only a friend, she tried to tell herself.

Her phone beeped on the table and Jess peeked at the screen. "Anna: Yes. More than just a kiss."

Jess couldn't help grinning. "That was her," she said, swiping the notification out of sight of prying eyes. "She was just checking in. Like I said, she was really helpful."

When she looked up, Nan and Mom were staring at her, their eyebrows almost hitting the ceiling.

20

Jess was saved further scrutiny by the front door opening and the tall figure of her father ducking into the house. He pulled off his woolly hat and ruffled his greying fair hair and beamed at her.

"Hello love," he said, his Yorkshire accent intact after all these years in the Midlands.

"Dad!"

Jess leapt up and crossed the small kitchen in a couple of strides and threw her arms around his shoulders.

"Steady on there," he said, chuckling. "When did you get so strong?"

Jess laughed and squeezed him a little more.

He leant out of their embrace. "Jack's going to be livid. He's still not as tall as you and I doubt he'd beat you in an arm wrestle too."

"Is he here?" she asked, excitement bubbling inside at seeing her little, probably not that small, brother. He would definitely have changed.

Her Dad's face dropped and he peered down at his hat that he rolled in his hands. "No, he, um. Well, we were almost at his friend's so… He's been looking forward to it and all, staying over like, so um…"

"Oh," Jess said, unable to hide the disappointment that had sunk like lead in her stomach. "OK."

"That boy's not coming home to see his sister?" Nan shrieked. "The one day we get to see our Jess in two years and he can't be bothered with coming home?!"

"It's all right, Nan." Jess tried to placate. "I didn't give you fair warning. I don't want to spoil his plans."

"Rubbish!" she shouted. "You're a busy woman and we're glad to have you home. That boy needs to learn some respect and priorities. Family first." She slapped the table with her hand.

"He's…." Dad sheepishly tried to catch Jess's eye.

"He's got another thing coming!" Nan shrieked some more.

"It's all right, really," Jess said, feeling doubly bad that her brother didn't want to see her and that, in his absence, she was landing him in a whole load of trouble.

"Trisha." Nan pointed at Mom. This was always a bad sign. "You need to have a talk with that boy, before he turns out all disrespectful. I see the people he hangs around with."

"What?" Mom engaged. "Fred? The doctor's kid?"

"Him and those other ones."

Dad tugged on Jess's arm. "Shall we go out back?" and he nodded towards the sitting room.

Jess nodded, the disappointment lingered in a knot inside.

"You all right?" Dad asked.

She was gutted. He could probably tell.

He gave her a squeeze and they ambled through the kitchen, leaving Mom and Nan to bicker.

He shrugged off his coat and sat on the sofa by the window. It had turned darker outside, the heavy clouds threatening rain and the wind toying with leaves on the lawn, the wind chimes on Nan's annexe at the end of the garden tinkling.

"Come sit down, love," he said shuffling to get comfortable. "Oh," he said, once she'd joined him. "Thanks for the *Broken Earth* trilogy." He lifted the three books that she'd ordered for him a few weeks ago from a bookshelf. "Not got far yet, but really enjoying them." He stroked the cover of *The Fifth Season* reverentially.

He wasn't the most talkative of men, but Jess and he could always rely on their shared love of reading for conversation. He'd introduced her to Tolkien as a child then Ursula Le Guin and Anne McCaffrey as a young teen. Now she returned the favour with NK Jemisin.

"And thanks for the offer of more," he said, still looking at the books.

"I wish you'd accept some money," she said, knowing exactly what he was being coy about.

"We don't need it love."

"Wouldn't you like to retire early?" she said. "I can help with that."

While Mom appeared as vital as ever, especially with her new haircut, her dad's older age was showing. He'd always stooped a little, aware of his height, but it seemed accentuated with age.

"Oh aye, I'd love that, but…" He pawed at the book as an outlet for his awkwardness. "It doesn't feel right and, besides, we've paid off the mortgage and your Nan keeps us on a tight budget." He grinned, and they both peeked up at the bickering parent and child in the kitchen.

"Think about it though," Jess said. "And you can always ask if anything comes up."

"You'll need it, pet." He squeezed her knee. "You never know when work will dry up in that line of business, I'm sure. You might need what you've got for decades yet."

"I'm twenty-four, Dad. I'll find a way to earn money if I'm never offered another role."

"You might be right there," he said, giving her a fond smile.

Jess stared out of the window, hesitating at her next offer, because of the return to the subject of her brother.

"What about a college fund for Jack?"

"Well..." Her dad gave her sheepish look. "Honestly, we're struggling to put money aside for that. I mean, we had a small pot saved up towards university for you. So there's that. But," he drew in breath between his teeth, "by heck it's expensive. And I don't want the lad burdened with all that debt for the rest of his life just to get a decent education."

"Is he interested?" Jess said, still looking out of the window.

"Aye, he's a bright lad." Dad tried to catch her eye. "Get him in a quiet moment, and he'll admit that he wants to be doctor."

"Really?" Jess said.

"Despite what your gran says, the lad works hard. And, yes, he loves his XBox and he and Fred probably won't sleep tonight, playing all hours, but he's a good boy. She just worries he'll need to work twice as hard as some of his mates. You know."

Jess nodded and averted her gaze, the disappointment sinking her belly again at her brother's absence.

"Would he accept money from me?" she said, quietly.

"We'd not tell him," her father chuckled. "Not until he stops being a stubborn arse."

Jess opened her mouth in surprise. Her father didn't usually come anywhere in the district of a swear word.

"Oh, he is though." Dad laughed. "I remember being that age. He's so full of hormones and wanting to prove he doesn't need us anymore, least of all a big superstar sister."

Jess tried to smile.

"Be patient with him. He has it hard sometimes. Every time one of your films comes out it's all he ever hears about at school, people wanting to know if he's been to the premiere or met some of the stars. And of course," Dad looked at her sadly, "you're never home to see him, so he has nothing to tell them."

Oh.

Jess felt several tonnes of guilt. "It's difficult. I'm rarely in the UK."

"I know you're busy, love. You won't get complaints from me. But please see it from his point of view too. He feels a fool when he knows less about you than what some of them read in the papers."

Jess nodded. "I will try." She sighed. "Can't see where he gets that stubbornness from though," she said pointedly. "Can you?" and she bent round in front of her father and stared accusingly at him with wide eyes.

"Bugger off," he said, chuckling.

She found herself thinking of Anna then, wishing for her company to soothe away the guilt. That wouldn't be an option soon, how soon depending on what her manager had lined up for her on Monday. Was it all worth it?

She sat back, arm round her Dad's shoulders, gazing fondly at her Nan and mother who'd found several other topics to bicker about while actually agreeing with the essence of what each other said.

"Did I make a mistake, Dad?"

"What, love?"

"Leaving school for that film? Missing out on uni. Not seeing Jack. Doing something normal."

"Now don't talk rubbish. All you ever wanted to do when you were little was be in a story. Do you remember how many days you spent playing in the woods with Maisie and Sandeep? You three came up some with incredible games. Whole worlds. A cast of amazing characters. Then you'd come home for your tea and write comics. We've got them stored somewhere."

"That was playing, Dad. Kid's stuff."

"It's what's made you a great actor."

Jess blushed and hoped it didn't show.

"Honestly, it is you know. It's like you're completely immersed in the story and you embody those characters. I don't see you on the screen, and I'm your Dad. You're that convincing when you're playing Kalemdra. Even when you were the Bond girl, I couldn't believe it was you."

"I still love that part of it – making a story come to life," Jess admitted. "That'll never change. In fact it's magic." She gave her Dad a smile. "But...what's the point of it all?"

"The point?" he said with exaggerated consternation. "You of all people are asking me about the point of stories?" He looked horrified. "Escapism if nothing else; you know that, love. But stories help us make sense of our worst fears and the terrors that life can throw at us. In fact, cataclysmic films like *Atlassia* establish new folk tales and narratives that frame the dangers of the climate change era and greedy corrupt governments."

Jess opened her mouth. "You...What...?" She narrowed her eyes. "Did you read that somewhere?"

"Yes," Dad grinned. "Dead proud I remembered it too."

Jess laughed. "I do know, but..." She sighed.

"Being famous?"

"Yeah. That."

"An introvert's nightmare?" he suggested, his eyebrows raised.

Jess opened her mouth, to disagree with her Dad's categorisation. She'd always needed her quiet time to recharge like her mother said, but also hated being alone. She loved nothing better than raving about films with Matt, best mate and producer of *Atlassia*, or cheeky flirtation with Anna. But a large group? In fact a large crowd, screaming at her for attention at a premiere? Yes, it was exhilarating but it would leave her depleted for days. And there were no quiet moments when everyone recognised you in the street.

But it was more than that.

"Yes," she said at last. "That covers some of it."

—

Jess would have kicked herself, but she would have fallen flat on her face on the muddy track. She'd dug out her old trainers and clothes from the box room that had been Jack's old bedroom and left the cottage to run off the frustration before the autumn light faded. Besides, with her training regime she became twitchy if she didn't exercise most days, her limbs filled with a nagging energy that needed to be burned away.

She'd run across the green, through the copse of old oaks, around the churchyard and into the woods beyond. The path curled through silver birches and bushes of holly that gave way the further Jess ran to more ancient woodland. Beech trees and gnarled oaks, with trunks wider than Jess's arm span, towered above, cutting out the light to the forest floor. Dusk was falling and the golden leaves glowed eerily in the twilight, the floor a bronze carpet of old beech leaves.

"Stupid," she panted as she ran, her feet stamping on the trail and rustling the brittle leaves "Stupid, stupid, stupid."

What did she expect? She'd left home at seventeen, leaving her seven-year-old brother behind. And how many times had she made it home in the last handful of years? Her mind closed, not wanting to admit the answer to herself, and the odd video call had hardly made up for it.

She remembered waving goodbye to Jack when she'd left to film the first *Atlassia* movie, his face grinning and waving his arm in that goofy and enthusiastic way he had as a younger boy, excited that his sister was going to play the character in the graphic novels everyone talked about.

Then every time she returned he was a little bit bigger and a little more sullen. Then he didn't wave goodbye anymore.

She had to stop. She'd run faster and faster into the woods, as if avoiding the memories, and a stitch stabbed her side as the several slices of ginger cake made themselves known.

Jess bent over breathing hard. "Shit."

She took great lungfuls of air, trying to stretch the pain beneath her ribs away, standing up to let her lungs expand. She'd run further than she'd thought and found herself in a spot that was particularly familiar. She stepped over brambles away from the path and through the trees. If she was right, a fallen oak hollow with rot should lie a few trees further in. Twigs snapped beneath her feet, sharp and loud in the still air, and a disturbed blackbird flitted through the trees chattering with alarm.

She was right. The great tree slumbered here, not much changed in the last decade. She knelt down and peered through its hollow stem. Could she still fit through? She put her hands forward, tentatively, and crawled in. The wood was soft and spongy beneath her fingers and little woodlice scuttled away on all sides. The musty, earthy smell filled her head and she closed her eyes. She could imagine the shuffling footsteps of Maisie and Sandeep running around the fallen oak. Their shouts and cries rang in her ears.

How many days, weeks, months even, had they played here? Her chest filled with sudden longing to go back. This was the place that had changed everything.

Jess crawled through the tunnel and sank onto the forest floor on the other side, her back and head slumped against the trunk.

This is where they'd filmed their version of *Atlassia*, all three of the teens obsessed with the new series of graphic novels that had become a youth hit and threatened to spill out into mainstream consciousness.

Jess had dressed in head-to-toe black Lycra to resemble the prodigal Kalemdra coming home to save her arboreal lands from the threat of destruction, a character she related to so strongly and resembled so completely that kids at school ribbed her for it.

She'd stuck up her hair into the iconic style with cheap gel Maisie had nicked from her mother and Sandeep had filmed them on an old mobile phone. They uploaded their clip, in all its variable focus glory to YouTube, and played it over and over on their parents' computers, buzzing with excitement.

Then Maisie had shared it. And it snowballed.

Soon Jess's athletic leaps and dashes though the local woods had been viewed thousands of times and it didn't stop there.

The first she heard of an independent studio making a modest-budget version of *Atlassia* was the phone call to her parents from Matt the producer. Jess's dad had taken her to London to see him and she was thrilled when she met the young wife and husband team who dreamed up the story and illustrated her favourite epic.

Jess and Dad had walked into the hotel meeting room: Matt, all little and lithe in his skinny jeans and Converse, Kuniko who was tiny next to her colossal husband Jacob who looked as if he could carry the other two in his arms. They'd all stood when she'd entered, their eyes wide. It was Matt who stepped forward, his hand reaching out.

"Good god," he said. "You are Kalemdra."

And here she sat, three films later, each a bigger budget version than the last. She was now such an integral part of the story that Kuniko and Jacob wrote further volumes of their originally conceived arc to encompass Jess's age and growth. The enormous pressure of just that was overwhelming. And to think, if Sandeep had never shot that little film, if Maisie hadn't stolen her mother's gel and made Jess resemble Kalemdra so perfectly, if she'd never shared the link and let the clip silently lay there, everything would have been different.

Jess stood up and started walking back, kicking through the leaves that shushed with every step. Her thoughts swirled through her head and she wished she could escape to Anna's flat and pretend none of it existed.

21

"Your new friend wants sex."

"Pen!" Anna checked towards where Bibs was sitting on the rug, apparently unperturbed by her mother's background conversation and playing with a wooden alphabet board. They'd been out to the playground in Regent's Park then on to a greasy spoon to feed Penny's hangover with every fatty food imaginable in the form of an English all-day breakfast, and had now returned to the flat. They sipped at the umpteenth coffee of the day at the island, while Bibs had a quiet play in the sitting area, looking sleepier with every moment as the light faded outside.

"Believe me, she wants your bod," Pen continued, smiling lasciviously over her coffee.

"Not necessarily," Anna replied. She squirmed on her seat.

"What? A pretty young thing who you, Anna Mayhew, kissed and believe me I've heard your kisses are legendary and it quite clearly worked on Miss, what did you say her name was, anyway, that got her churning inside so much she started grinding your nether regions."

Anna made a face. That was not how she'd related it at all. "I so regret telling you."

"Believe me, people don't do that without wanting the whole dirty." Penny said it with a grotesque shimmy that made it gleefully obscene.

"Pen! I might not see her again."

"She'll be back." Pen said, knowingly. "That young thing will be back."

"She's busy."

"She wants sexy time with you."

Anna screwed up her face like she'd bitten a piece of apple with a whole convention of maggots inside. "You are putting me off sleeping with anyone."

"Charming," Pen said, high pitched and affronted.

"Just because she's a young thing…" Anna tutted at her use of Penny's lingo. "Just because she's younger than us doesn't mean she's…" She searched for a delicate phrase.

"Gagging for it."

Anna sighed with frustration. "Yes, for the want of a better word."

"Come on," Pen said. "What were we like in our twenties?"

Anna recalled. "We were working so many badly paid jobs that we were too exhausted to even think about sex."

"Well, there was that." Pen shrugged. "What did you say she did again?"

"Publicity of some sort. Marketing I think. She clams up whenever she talks about it. She travels a lot and it doesn't seem to suit her and it's stressful, so," Anna sighed, "we tend to avoid the topic."

"Hmm. So, an exhausted, stressed, hot, young thing?"

"Exactly. So she might not be 'gagging for it' and might not be back in any case," Anna said, satisfied with her riposte.

Penny groaned and took a sip of coffee, then her face wrinkled into naughtiness. "But she will be." And her face broke out into a blatant grin.

Anna growled her frustration.

"Why would a hot young thing not want sex with Anna Mayhew?" Penny shrieked.

Any number of reasons. Anna's worst fears could list a lot. But Penny would counter them, one by one, to logically dismiss them from the argument if not from Anna's deepest fears.

Pen leaned forward and squeezed her hand. "I understand your anxieties, I really do," she said gently. "But who you are and what you look like shouldn't be the cause of any of them. For a start, physically, you walk for miles and do yoga. You haven't had a young child stretch your body to oblivion then let it sag like an old party balloon. You look great."

"You haven't seen… you know… me naked for years."

"You wear summer dresses so I've had a good letch at your pins."

Anna made a mental note never to wear summer dresses again.

"And your arms are in spectacular shape. Honestly." Pen ran her hand up Anna's arm. "I've always been envious of these elegant long things. And your tits…"

Anna wondered if this assessment was actually worse than having sex.

"I would put good money on her wanting to ravish you," Penny said. "So. Be. Prepared."

And Penny made a self-satisfied noise and leant back. At last, Anna could relax.

"Oh god," Penny said, sitting up alert again.

"What?"

"Your bush."

For the love of all things sacrosanct.

"You need to get that in order. When did you last attend to that for anyone?"

"I'm not talking about my...that."

"When did you last bother? I imagine it's way out of control," Penny said with too much gusto. "I bet your bush is so overgrown it's under the jurisdiction of The Forestry Commission."

"Pen!"

"You could probably get a grant for it as a rewilding ecology project."

Anna wanted to die.

"I..." Anna closed her eyes and steeled herself. "I am not discussing the state of my...."

"Vulva? Poonani? Vajayjay?"

"Exactly."

Penny leaned forward and kissed her on the forehead. "I think my work here is done, although I've always loved grossing you out for fun."

Anna said a noncommittal "hmm" and finally realised what Penny was doing, an odd sort of desensitisation therapy, and the knowledge made her want to hug her friend and maybe pinch her a little bit so that it hurt.

"You like her don't you?" Penny said, more gently. There was a sincerity in her voice and Anna's heart beat faster at having to answer.

Whenever Anna thought of Jess she had a sense of longing and comfort all at the same time. There was that simple compulsion to be with her and loss whenever she wasn't near so that Anna would seek her out again, even if they were in the same room. Like when they walked home from the canals, neither of them could bear any distance between them.

"She's funny and flirty," Anna said, a smile creeping across her face, "not brash or loud, or in an overconfident way. If anything I would describe her as quiet. Then she'll surprise me," Anna's smile bloomed into a grin, "with a cheeky compliment or forward suggestion, a grand movement and burst of showmanship, then..." Jess would say something that resonated so poignantly with truth and meaning that Anna's heart would skip a beat and she would be lost for words. She didn't say this to Pen. She didn't trust herself not to become choked.

"She's different to me. Very different. Down to earth, only withdrawn or quiet when she lacks confidence. She's more open like you otherwise," Anna said, looking up at Penny who had remained motionless and attentive.

"She's full of charm, not like you'd describe my well-mannered version, not the kind that drops a compliment for decorum's sake, but the charm that comes from saying the best feelings from the heart.

"I say she's different to me, but only in ways that make me want to know everything about her. I could spend all day and night doing just that, talking to her about everything and nothing. Time seems to fly when I'm with her and I'm shocked when the sun comes up and I've spent two nights and days and never wished for a moment that it went faster or had been spent in any other way."

Anna stopped and cleared her throat. "Yes," she said at last. "I like her."

Penny didn't say a word. She slid off the stool and came to Anna's side and clutched her head to her bosom.

—

It was late. Penny had gone. The flat was quiet and it was dark outside. Anna sat on the floor, hugging her knees.

With the light and Penny gone, the thought of someone out there wanting to have sex with her was terrifying and overwhelming.

Anna held her breath and closed her eyes, holding back the rush of fear.

"Stop it. Think," she told herself.

Her heart skipped several beats then lurched into action again. Oh god. This was going to take renewed effort, the kind of energy she poured into rehabilitating herself a handful of years ago.

What was the worst that could happen? She summoned her therapy. Really, when she thought through the scenarios, visualising them and preparing herself to keep the panic at bay, what was the worst? That Jess would be over-solicitous? But then Jess didn't seem to have time to think straight let alone turn overly attentive. If anything she was skittish and Anna wondered if she scared easily herself.

But what if they saw each other again, if Jess was indeed a young thing intent on jumping into bed with her? Would Anna freeze, shake, vomit in the sheer terror of it all. Yes, that might happen. She could see it clearly. That might indeed happen. Could Anna cope with Jess seeing all that? Actually, she thought she could. If anyone had to see that, Jess is who she'd choose.

Another option – what if Jess never came back? And this made Anna's mind trip over and her heart stop. What if Jess wasn't interested in the reclusive and older Anna? Was that what she feared most? After the piquancy of Jess's company and a vivid glimpse of life – the possibility of being intimate and close with someone – that it might not happen after all left Anna cold and desolate.

Her phone vibrated on the floor. Message from Jess. Anna twitched, as if she'd been caught thinking of her, then smiled, picking up the phone.

"Hi," was all the message said, but it conjured warmth and Jess's presence and the desire and taste for life flooded through Anna again. Anna pictured Jess somewhere, she had no idea where, but somewhere thinking of her and Anna was comforted and her world full of light again.

"Hi," Anna replied. "Hey, are you busy? Can I call you?"

Anna smiled at the prospect. Then smiled in puzzlement when Jess didn't immediately reply. Then her smile turned wry. "You don't talk on the phone often do you?"

The phone rang and Anna answered straight way.

"Busted," Jess said. "You're right, I'm definitely a say-it-with-a-message kind of girl."

Anna laughed. Jess's voice came through loud and clear and filled her imagination so that it was like she was in the room again.

"How was your day? How are your folks?" Anna said, not able to keep the laugh from her voice.

"They were great. I can't believe I haven't been home for so long. I've missed them."

"I'm really glad."

"They're all in bed now and I'm trying to get to sleep on the sofa bed in my Nan's annexe, except she's bonkers about wind chimes and there are so many hanging up it's like trying to get to sleep with a kids' triangle band playing outside."

Anna's cheeks were aching. Yes, Anna liked her. Yes, she wanted to see her again.

"I need to be in bed too," Anna admitted, "but I wanted to say hi before getting some sleep. I've got a client early tomorrow."

"Hey, I never asked," Jess said. "What do you do?" And she went quiet on the other end of the line, as if reminded of her stressful job.

"I'm a voice coach," Anna said.

"Oh, like for actors?" Jessa replied.

"No. Everyone always assumes that. But no, not actors if I can avoid it."

"…oh?" Jess said.

"My partner and I run a consultancy that helps people improve their presentation and oratory skills. I know acting seems the obvious application, but our main revenue is from business people, politicians, anyone who has a professional role where they need good presentation skills to get their point across."

"Right," Jess said, full of understanding.

"So that's me early tomorrow," Anna said. "How about you?"

"Ah." The reply was laden with dread. "I have to meet my manager and take it from there." Jess was quiet and the air was heavy. "I'm not looking forward to it. You can probably tell."

"Yes I can," Anna replied. "And," her heart beat quicker wondering if she should mention it, "is this in London?"

"Yes."

"Do you think… you'll have time to see me? Afterwards?"

Jess hesitated again, and Anna suddenly felt foolish for raising it.

"I hope so," Jess said, so full of honest longing that Anna drew breath.

"Call me if you can," Anna said, "or message if you must."

Jess laughed. "I would love to see you again."

Anna's spirits lifted, soaring way too high so that she inhaled sharply to try to keep them under control.

"Good," she said.

"Really," Jess said, "I can't think of anything better than hanging out with you. I…" and she suddenly cut herself off as if she was about to say too much. "I'm looking forward to it."

Anna sensed Jess being coy and couldn't help herself, some of her old playfulness often coming out with Jess. "Anything you're looking forward to in particular?"

"Sorry?" Jess sounded intrigued and a little alarmed.

"Is it the pancakes?" Anna suggested with a hint of irony.

"Um, yeah?" Jess offered.

"I do make particularly good pancakes, even if I say so myself."

"You definitely do."

"Or perhaps you'd prefer relaxing on the balcony with a cup of hot chocolate?"

"Yeah. I'd love that. Snuggling up under a blanket would be…erm." Again Jess sounded like her mouth had run away with her and given away her thoughts and desires.

"That can be arranged," Anna said, her face aching with delight. "And perhaps after all that," she paused. It was like she could almost feel Jess leaning in with anticipation. "Perhaps I should kiss you again?"

Silence.

Absolute silence from Jess.

Anna leaned into her own phone, dreading that she presumed too much. Those nagging doubts wriggled deep down and clawed their way up. All she could hear from the other end was wind chimes.

"You promise?"

Anna's grin shot wide. The relief was intense and the prospect more so.

"I promise," she said, her delivery the epitome of poise and nonchalance, while her tummy fluttered and her heart went wild.

22

That there were two studio execs sitting with Femi in the restaurant was the first bad sign. That her agent, Celia, was also in attendance was the final nail in the coffin.

The foursome sat in a semi-circular booth at the back of the restaurant which was empty post-lunchtime. Two execs in pristine suits sat straight and rigid, scrolling through their tablets. Jess had met them before. They reminded her of Mr Neat and Mr Tidy, two white middle-aged men in suits from a children's book. Opposite, Femi leant forward with his elbows on the table in his 'I'm listening and trying to be accommodating but also showing my biceps and steely resolve' pose. Celia sat coiled beside him, as if about to strike at any moment. The woman terrified Jess. Her eyes bulged a little even at rest and seemed to grow when agitated. Celia had decades of experience and, though she never raised her voice, she had an enviable range of tones from unnerving velvet to acid sharp. She was brilliant and exactly who Jess would choose to have in her corner every time.

Jess removed her hat and glasses and approached the table with her stomach leaping into her mouth.

"Good morning," she said. "I mean, afternoon."

"Ms Lambert." The nearest exec nodded.

Femi put out his arm and gestured for her to sit beside him on the curved seat of the booth.

"As I was saying," the nearest exec said, "the studio signed a publicity schedule and any changes must be agreed by all parties..."

Jess's brain was seizing with anxiety already. She shuffled next to Femi, beanie hat in hand, fidgeting and rolling the material in her fingers.

"At this crucial stage," the exec continued, "Ms Lambert's lack of cooperation has a detrimental financial effect on the film and calls into doubt her capacity to fulfil future obligations. And I should remind you, which is why I requested the presence of Celia Hartingham, we are negotiating the finer details of the contract for Part 4 of the *Atlassia* Series."

Jess shot her agent an alarmed look. Celia raised her hand, her long fingernails threatening.

"Now," Celia said, using her mother-cat purr. "For the sake of clarity, are you suggesting Ms Lambert could be dropped from the rest of the series?"

So Celia had heard the same as Jess.

The exec paused. "I have the authority to rescind the agreement that we've been drafting, yes."

"What?" Femi shouted. "Does Matt know about this?"

"We do not need his agreement. The contract allows the studio, not the director or producer, final say in casting."

Jess's head swirled. How had it escalated into this? She'd been expecting a meeting with Femi and some uncomfortable words and maybe agreeing a less packed but still hideous publicity schedule. But this? She hadn't been expecting this at all. Was there something else going on?

Femi and Celia desperately talked over one another to the impassive execs and Jess couldn't process it all quick enough to follow. This is what she hated, groups and meetings like this where she couldn't keep up and by the time she thought of anything cogent to say business had moved on and she'd missed several important details.

But being dropped from the *Atlassia* series? It was like someone had taken away the earth beneath her feet and she was falling. Her stomach reeled as if she were actually plunging. But at the same time, a little part of her said, "Let go. Just fall." Her thoughts and fears slowed at the realisation and a little clarity came into focus.

She looked up and cleared her throat. All four were startled at the contribution.

"The *Atlassia* series will likely die if I'm dropped," she said, quietly. "Maybe not straight away with the next film, but after that."

The nearest exec pulled himself up, affronted.

"I'm not saying this as the actor," Jess added quickly, "or with any ego, but as a fan. I have lived that series since the first volume was published. Kalemdra is on a journey and you cannot change the human at the centre of that story."

"There are plenty of actresses who fit your type, Ms Lambert," the exec said, coolly.

Jess wasn't immediately sure of all the nagging insinuations of that and decided not to process it until she'd made her point.

"Have you ever seen that work?" Jess asked. "There's always some adjustment. Maybe there's time to recover the viewer's suspension of disbelief if the character's part of a series. But the protagonist of a film mid-arc? You don't have the same chance for the audience to invest in the character again. Yes, if the story needs it, say time has passed, a new actor would work. But this? You will lose the heart of the story and the hearts of the audience."

The exec was silent. Celia peered around Femi's shoulder with kind of smile that a proud parent might have.

"She's right." Celia cackled. "And whether you know it or not, you should listen. Another actress cannot be slotted into Jess's place. She is not a prop or studio building. You will lose goodwill, and even the best actor in the world would have a hill to climb to regain the audience's loyalty."

The exec faced Celia. "That is as may be. But if Ms Lambert sinks this film, it's all academic."

The look on Celia's face turned venomous and she engaged and the scene erupted into a squabble. Jess wanted to cover her ears but stared at the table instead. Femi's hand reached for hers beneath the table.

"Have you told them?" she murmured, while Celia and the execs argued.

Femi nodded.

"I can't help this," Jess said. "I'm exhausted. I'm going to break."

"I know," Femi said in a low rumble.

"If I'd broken a leg, wouldn't they have a plan to work around it and accommodate me?"

Femi looked her in the eye. "Yes, they would."

Jess didn't want to listen anymore, and her flight response was building inside. She couldn't even take in the conversation. Every time she had a chance to relax – her break going home, the sanctuary of Anna's – she thought she could recover, but any stress and she hit maximum immediately.

"I want to go," she muttered, as the tension crept over her skull.

"Sorry, I wasn't expecting this," Femi muttered. "I think you should. Let me and Celia lay into them. You don't need to hear it."

Jess nodded. "I don't want to let Matt down," she said, "or Kuniko and Jacob. But the rest of it, do whatever you think best. Tell Celia."

Femi nodded, and when Jess stood up, she was already too burned out to vocalise goodbye and Celia and the execs too occupied to notice her exit.

Jess was shaking when she stepped outside the restaurant. She walked in a daze before noticing people staring, and a couple of passers-by took photos on their phones before Jess realised she was carrying her hat and glasses in her hand. She dipped into a shop and bought a long woollen winter coat, the denim jacket from Anna not keeping the bite of the frosty afternoon at bay, then reapplied her alter ego.

She caught her reflection in a window. It was remarkable how such everyday accessories had changed her. The hat disguised her characteristic hair style and glasses detracted from the large dark eyes that beguiled and invited adulation in the media, both the most distinctive elements of her look, so a first glance no longer invited a second of recognition. Anna had chosen well. She clearly had a knack for it and Jess wondered if that was a trait she used in her job.

There was a little time before Anna was due back home so Jess turned up the collar on her navy coat and called up a map on her phone and started to walk across Central London to Anna's flat. She switched off the vocal instructions, never taking information well aurally and certainly not in this state. She was approaching burn out and preoccupied and distracted by the concerns that tumbled through her head.

It turned out to be quicker to walk than negotiate the other-world geography of the Underground and her stomach was still in free fall from the threat of losing her role in *Atlassia* when she pressed the buzzer for Anna's flat.

"Jess?"

She was in.

"Hi," Jess stuttered. "I didn't know if you would be back."

"I'm here." That voice, like honey. "Come on up."

Jess pocketed the glasses and hat in her coat as she climbed the two flights of stairs and Anna's door was open when she reached the top.

"Oh my god," Jess gasped out loud. That was a sight for sore eyes. Anna smiled at her, arms outstretched in welcome. She looked divine. Her hair was tied up so that Jess could appreciate the elegant sculpture that was her face. Her tailored pale dress suited her slim tall physique and lay bare her arms that Jess hadn't had opportunity to admire until now. She moved towards Jess with a grace that was so refined its elegance must have been innate and Jess couldn't help but move to meet her.

Anna's soft hands cradled her cheeks and for a moment Jess assumed she wanted simply to reacquaint herself. But Anna swept Jess closer and in a single smooth movement placed her lips over Jess's with the most delicate touch.

It was the softest of kisses that made every other seem clumsy and hard. Jess couldn't have imagined a way to make it more perfect. Anna's mouth slipped over hers with a tenderness that removed every ache from Jess's body. Every tortured thought melted away. Every knotted muscle relaxed as if soothed by a liquid panacea that flooded through her entire body. Those exquisite lips that touched hers drew her in so completely it was as if her feet had left the ground and she was powerless to Anna's every whim and desire.

It was the kind of kiss that made you fall in love.

Anna leant away and gazed at her, lightening blue eyes full of desire and admiration for Jess.

"Hi" Anna murmured.

And that velvety voice made Jess's liquid body almost collapse at the knees.

23

Anna didn't need to open her eyes to know the effect of her kiss. When Anna had slipped her lips away, Jess had sighed "oh" as if she could have floated like a cloud with the release.

Anna linked her hands lightly behind Jess's neck and smiled. "I keep my promises."

"Muh?" Jess opened dozy heavy eyelids.

"I promised you a kiss."

"Mmmm." Jess nodded with a goofy smile.

Anna was unable to suppress her laughter at the delirious Jess. "So, how was your day?"

"Not the best," Jess said, shoulders sagging.

"Do you have to leave straight away?"

"I don't know," Jess replied. "In fact, I'm less sure than before the meeting."

Jess's neck tightened beneath Anna's fingers. "But we have now," Anna said, trying to lighten the mood. "I have you tonight?"

Jess nodded.

Just one night. Anna yearned for very much more of this young woman. But, "I will take that," Anna said. "If that's all we have, I would like it." When Jess's spirits didn't lift she added, "Do you want to talk about anything?"

"Not really," Jess murmured, looking deep into her eyes. "I'd rather do this," and she dipped her head and took Anna's mouth with such seductive finesse Anna would have been proud of it herself.

So Jess could disarm with a kiss too. Anna would have been amused if she'd been able to think with anything like that clarity, but her body responded so completely her mind was a pleasant void.

Her fingers massaged Jess's scalp, stroking through her hair and tugging her closer. Anna's mouth watered as Jess's full lips slipped between hers and she was deepening the kiss before she'd realised they'd begun. Anna loved the touch of her, the taste of her. Kissing Jess felt so natural it was if she was reunited with a favourite seasoned lover and it was shocking how much Anna had missed this simple human interaction. Yes, that first kiss between them, when Jess had left, it had breathed on embers Anna hadn't realised were still alive. But this? Flames were consuming Anna already.

She hadn't thought about it over the years. She'd been so preoccupied with her anxiety about sex. But kissing. How could she have forgotten how delicious it was? There was the kiss that tingled all the way to your toes and made you feel as light as the air itself. It was always a favourite of Anna's and that she could still elicit that feeling in someone was a mischievous pleasure. And there were kisses that soothed and made the world a better place, all warmth and comfort. Then there were kisses like this that obliterated the world and made you forget everything but the sensual being you devoured.

Well, Anna's mind may have forgotten the pleasures of a kiss, but her body had not. It arched into Jess, betraying any semblance of reticence and when Jess's hands slipped to either side of her waist she gasped and her heart cantered.

Jess stroked her thumbs in small circles as if eager to explore and Anna's body awakened with anticipation. Anna could almost feel what it would be like if Jess caressed higher and willed her to take her breasts and tease her with those desperate fingers. She imagined Jess flicking her thumbs across her nipples and the thought alone sent thrills down her whole body and warmth pooled down low.

She broke the kiss.

"Too much?" Jess whispered, her eyes wide and dark.

Jess wasn't being too much. It was Anna.

"No," Anna gasped. "I just…" Her body was way ahead of her.

She blushed at her chest heaving, such a blatant clue to her enjoyment. She didn't want to say anything. If she admitted it was too fast, Jess would step away and a cool gap would open between them. At the same time, she wasn't ready for this. It scared Anna how quickly her body reacted and how she would be in too deep before her head had time to catch up. She could be naked and exposed in the bright beams of the setting sun streaming through the windows before she could say "stop" and the thought made her tremble.

Jess relaxed but didn't pull away. She let her head drop to the side of Anna's so her cheek rested against hers. Jess's hands, so eager a moment ago, drew Anna in tenderly and held her with reassuring strength.

"Are you OK?" Jess whispered.

Anna nodded, unable to voice exactly what she wanted or needed. Jess seemed to have anticipated, and Anna clung on to her, grateful for her understanding.

"Tell me if you're ready," Jess murmured. "But I want to point out that…"

Anna tensed, unable to anticipate what Jess was about to say.

Jess blurted her answer as a single word. "Oh my god you're good to kiss."

And Anna laughed.

She squeezed Jess, appreciating with a poignant pinch in her chest the young woman who adapted to her, prepared to slow and wait when necessary.

But she would be gone soon. How long did they have? The urgency thundered in Anna's chest but she was too intimidated to move quicker. Instead she stepped back, needing the space and time for her confidence to grow.

"I wonder," she said, "Can I trust you with a small adventure?"

"Yes?"

They held hands, neither wishing to break the connection, and Anna felt the afterglow and remnants of the seductive pull of their embrace.

"I wondered if you fancied a walk this evening up Primrose Hill."

"Of course," Jess said.

"I haven't walked that far in a long time," Anna said, "especially late in the day."

The park's lamps would be lit. Plenty of people of all ages would be strolling through today, but the thought of going alone in the failing light was too daunting. Yet Anna wanted to break out of her comfort zone and she'd set herself this challenge.

"I have a soft spot for this place," she carried on, "because it was one of things I always wanted to do before I moved to London. It's funny when you live somewhere, you forget about the major sights. And recently…"

She'd abandoned any exploration.

"I might choke," Anna warned. "I might need to turn back."

"OK." Jess squeezed her hand in reassurance. "Where else was on your list?"

"Tower of London, of course. That's been a top-ten since childhood. All that blood-thirsty intrigue about beheadings." She smiled.

"I've always wanted to go to Buckingham Palace," Jess said.

"Really?"

"Yeah, my Nan's mad about the queen. Perhaps it's a matriarch thing."

Anna loved every detail Jess sprinkled in her conversation about her family and how those big eyes sparkled with life and love when she mentioned them. Anna had the impression of a loving base supporting Jess.

"I wanted to go to St Paul's Cathedral most of all," Anna continued. "I know it doesn't sound the most adventurous destination, but there's something about a childhood dream isn't there. See Venice before it's swallowed by the sea. Gaze across the Grand Canyon. I always wanted to test out the Whispering Gallery. Can you really hear someone whisper from the other side of that enormous dome around the curving walls? It'll nag me until the day I die unless I try."

"I know what you mean," Jess replied, excitement filling her face. "My life will not be complete until I buy a five-pound Amy Winehouse top from Portobello Road market to match Daisy Smith's T-shirt at school. That has always been the ultimate London experience for me."

"I would love to take you one day," Anna said, before she could think. Would there be another day? Would she get the chance with Jess again? Anna blinked, trying to keep the urgency of the evening from overwhelming her.

"But tonight," Anna made herself say, "most of all, I want to walk to the top of Primrose Hill at dusk."

Outside, Anna was dressed in the same classic woollen coat as Jess. She joked about Jess keeping her beanie and retrieved another when Jess stuttered guiltily in response. It was a night for scarves and hats, but Anna found herself wishing to hold Jess's hand without any barrier and left behind her gloves. Their breath billowed in huge orange clouds, illuminated by the street lights when they stepped outside.

"Come here," Jess said, reaching out. "I'll keep you warm."

Her hands entwined with Anna's, tickling the delicate skin between her fingers. Just this naked touch seemed intimate now, the human warmth of Jess's skin triggering need in Anna. She wanted to pull Jess's fingers to her lips and kiss their delicate pads. She wanted to explore the warm palm of her hand, the soft fragility of the wrist, the whole length of Jess's arm, tasting, touching, enjoying her whole body. Anna's resolve evaporated and she almost turned right there to drag Jess back up to her bed.

"I can't believe how dark it is already," Jess said.

And Anna laughed, distracted from her quandary. "I think you have to be the grand old age of forty at least before you're allowed to say that kind of thing."

"Nah," Jess grinned. How Anna loved that big smile. It elicited joy every time. "I remember walking home from primary school with my mate Maisie." Jess looped her arm through Anna's and they set off down the street, the need in Anna complaining a little and hankering after her bedroom. "We must have been about nine," Jess continued, "and we were complaining about how rubbish it was that when you got home there was only ten minutes to play before being called in. I remember moaning that it was 'bloody ridiculous' then my Nan heard me."

"Were you in trouble?" Anna replied.

"Actually, no. My mom was though." Jess giggled. "My Nan knew I'd picked it up from her." Jess inhaled deeply. "Trishaaaaa." Jess had dropped her voice an octave and given it an earthy growl then pitched it high at the end. Anna had a vivid sense of her Nan's power from the impression. "Your daughter is picking up on your swearing," Jess bellowed and waggled her finger. It was as if she'd brought her whole family along and Anna loved the world Jess conjured for her.

"So," Jess said in her own voice. "I've been complaining about the weather and the nights drawing in from an early age."

Anna reached up and stroked Jess's cheek. She really had the most pleasing shape to her face, the wonderful jaw line and those cheeks with fine structure and a lovely fullness. She smiled indulgently.

"Earnest young Jess sounds very sweet," Anna said, meaning every word and they walked on.

They edged around Regent's Park, lights from the zoo twinkling through the trees.

"Thank you for coming with me," Anna said, squeezing Jess's arm. "I find it a bit too daunting at night on my own and I don't usually want to bother anyone for company in case I panic and need to go home."

"Why?" Jess said, with an incredulous tone. "This is no hardship. We can take the evening as it comes."

Anna took a deep breath. "Perhaps I have less accommodating friends and family than you."

"But." Jess hesitated. She seemed genuinely confused. "Everyone needs accommodating in some way. My Nan can't do steep steps so we might miss out on some sights when we're on holiday. My Dad's always been rubbish at heights. Mum can't for the life of her navigate, not even from her bedroom to the front room, without a satnav. So what?" Jess shrugged. "It doesn't matter in the end. We can muddle through the days having fun if we help each other."

Anna smiled at the thought of Jess's family that supported and understood each other. It sounded like they all got a say, although Anna had an inkling her Nan more than others.

"Doesn't mean it always goes smoothly or without a squabble," Jess added. "But there's no end to the fun we can have without leaving anyone behind."

It was a lovely picture Jess painted and Anna thought back to all the times she'd wanted to spend this evening of the year on Primrose Hill. Anna's mother's voice snapped in her head from two years past. "Don't be ridiculous. You can manage on your own. It's about time you got past this paranoia." Anna twitched at the recollection.

A firework popped overhead.

"Bonfire night," Jess murmured, and the burst lit up her upturned face.

"Yes," Anna said.

"I was gutted I couldn't stay home for it," Jess said as they walked on.

"Do you usually go to a display?"

"Yeah, it's one of the biggest nights in the village."

Anna could hear the enthusiasm from Jess as she recollected and she held her closer, wanting to bask in that comfort.

"There's an old quarry at the edge of the woods," Jess said, a distant look in her eye. "There was a little outcrop of rock used to build the church hundreds of years ago and it's been disused since. They'll be setting off fireworks later and old Gracie Brown will be selling cups of hot soup to warm your hands. There'll be sausages on a fire. And of course a bigger fire with a Guy on top."

"I always think it strange how people encourage their kids to burn an effigy with such enthusiasm."

"Weird, isn't it," Jess laughed. "And my Nan made parkin." Anna could hear the disappointment in her voice. "Actually we'd eaten most of it by the time I left."

"So you have a soft spot for Bonfire Night?"

"Definitely."

"Come with me," Anna said, encouraging Jess forward. She could make out the outline of the top of the hill. "Let's go right to the top without turning round."

They marched up the hill, Anna's legs burning with the swift walk up the incline. It was a novel feeling, enjoying the exertion in Jess's safe company. They were breathing hard when they reached the top, Anna's cheeks glowing simultaneously from the cold air and her hot body.

"Now," she said, between panting. "Turn around."

"Oh my god. This is amazing!" Jess yelled.

The sky had darkened to indigo in the dusk and the city glowed orange in the band beneath it, the distinctive London skyline a silhouette.

The dark curtain of grass swept down the hill and little pools of light from lamps along the pathways glowed in a pattern across the swathe of park.

"You can see the London Eye," Jess said. "And what's that tall building over there? "

"That would be the BT Tower."

"This is incredible," Jess enthused.

A firework bloomed in the sky above them and Anna thrilled at the sudden sparkling burst.

"Wow!" Jess shouted. "It's as if someone's thrown gold into the sky."

Jess hugged her tighter and pointed over the skyline.

"And over there to the left."

There were fireworks exploding in the sky all over London, exploding with a muffled crack in the distance and rockets squealing louder overhead. Anna felt invigorated, alive, Jess's enthusiasm and the bursts of multi-coloured lights that she hadn't enjoyed for years lifting her high. Jess held her tight around her shoulders, drawing Anna into her soft chest, surrounding her with exhilarating energy.

Anna beamed at Jess waving her arms and going wild beside her, beneath the sky that bloomed in colour. The chill of the night air kissed Anna's face. The distinctive smell of smoke from fireworks filled her head. The squeal of rockets and yelps of delighted children and grownups filled the air around her. She closed her eyes, revelling in all the sensations of bonfire night, and it was beautiful.

24

Anna's face shone in the light of the fireworks, her eyes wide in awe. Jess gazed at her, captured by her magnetic elegance and flooded with desire. How quickly it came back after their earlier kisses, which had tantalised.

Under the concert of fireworks and kind cover of darkness, Jess felt free. People had gathered on the hill to marvel at the displays that bloomed over London, not one interested in Jess or the woman she accompanied.

"You are so beautiful," she whispered, more a thought out loud.

Anna turned to her, her face heightened by the smile that was full of regard and, Jess recognised, desire too. Anna reached out and caressed Jess's cheek, her eyes dark pools that flashed with the illuminations scorching the sky above.

With just the slightest encouragement, the soft pressure of Anna's fingers stroking around her neck, Jess melted into another kiss.

Her whole being sighed with longing. She kissed Anna deeper, letting herself go, perhaps safe in the knowledge they were outside, both cocooned in winter coats, where Anna couldn't be exposed. They could only kiss, but it was a kiss that commanded her completely. Jess ran her fingers through Anna's silky hair, her intense urges seeking release as she pulled her closer and their delicious kiss deepened further.

This is what she wanted – this woman, evenings in the park, to see fireworks, this ordinary life that so many couples and families were enjoying on this hilltop. It was wonderful.

If someone had asked her right now to give up fame and money for this existence, she would have thrown it all away. To stop playing the character's role. To put aside the mask of the movie star. To put aside every mask. To be herself with this woman who'd seen her at her most broken, this was all Jess wanted and her heart and body were overwhelmed.

Jess was breathing hard when she leaned away but when she saw the same need in Anna's eyes and her chest heaving with the same power, the longing built again.

"Let's go home," Anna whispered.

They walked with nervous haste, senses heightened, the movement jarring against bodies which were readied for passion. Fear coursed through Jess, not wanting to lose the moment but at the same time anxious at the prospect of what was to come.

They didn't say a word as they hastened around the park, bodies pulled tight together, faces glowing with excitement, clouds of moisture from breath or Jess's steaming body, she didn't know which.

Anna's hands trembled with lock and key clattering together, metal scraping against metal. They climbed the stairs, Jess's legs jittery with nervous energy.

Anna shut the door behind them and the noise and cold night air were locked outside. The cosy room enveloped them, the only light from the glow of streetlights through the window. Anna faced Jess, her features softened in the kind light, although her expressions were clear enough to Jess. Craving consumed Anna's whole body, but apprehension flittered across her brow.

"We don't have to–" Jess started.

"But I want to." Anna stepped forward and reached for Jess's cheeks, her fingertips light on her skin so that they elicited the most tender and thrilling of sensations. "Oh, I want to," Anna whispered.

Her fingers trembled as they danced over Jess's cheek, played over her lips and for a moment Jess thought Anna would kiss her, but she paused. "I want to touch you." She looked into Jess's eyes. "I want to touch you everywhere."

The thought alone was exhilarating.

Jess took Anna's hand and kissed her fingertips, then gently let it drop. She unbuttoned her coat and jacket, lay them over the arm of the chair, and stood before Anna in her T-shirt and jeans, lifting Anna's hand again to invite her. She needed to let Anna set the pace.

Jess had never been so transfixed by someone's attention. The care and devotion Anna took as she traced the shape of Jess's neck and the curves of her collarbone. It was as if Anna had found a jewel and was entranced, her eyes wide with appreciation.

She traced down the open V of Jess's T-shirt, her finger's progress slowing as she dipped into the shallow of Jess's cleavage. Her fingers spread as if to take in her breasts but instead she lowered her hands to Jess's sides.

"Can we take this off?" Anna murmured, her voice thick with excitement. Jess crossed her arms and lifted away her T-shirt, Anna's gaze and attention not wavering for a second as she sloughed off her own coat to the floor.

Anna reached up, her arms bare with only her dress remaining, and placed her hands upon Jess's shoulders as if admiring them. The temptation to embrace Anna and seduce her was powerful, but Jess must wait, let Anna become comfortable with her presence and let her take her in. Jess hoped her body could withstand it.

Anna ran a fingertip over the bumps of her shoulder, into the sensitive dip by Jess's collar bone, and tantalisingly massaged the rise of her neck. It was soothing and inflaming all at once.

"You have wonderful shoulders," Anna said, a smile playing at her lips, "shapely, toned, appealing."

Her fingers travelled down Jess's chest and played at the top of her bra, as if desperate to explore further but embarrassed to admit it. She teased her fingers beneath the strap.

"May I?"

Jess nodded, desperate for Anna to explore quicker.

Anna ran her fingers beneath the straps and stretched them gently over Jess's shoulder. Jess closed her eyes as Anna slipped her arms around her back to unhook her bra and shuddered with delight as Anna brushed over her breasts as she threw it aside.

Jess kept her eyes shut, aware of Anna's proximity, the tempting warmth of her body near and her gaze seeming to burn through Jess. She twitched as Anna placed her fingertips either side of her cleavage then slowly, agonisingly slowly, stroked around her breasts.

Jess held her breath, fearing she might give away how aroused she was and how much she ached to touch Anna. The sense of Anna taking her in, savouring every inch of her body while tenderly cupping her breasts was overpowering.

She nearly groaned when Anna lifted a hand away but when succulent lips enveloped her nipple she couldn't contain her reaction any longer and she caved in anguished pleasure and let out an audible gasp.

Anna's response was immediate. She closed her lips eagerly around Jess and massaged her breast further into her mouth. Jess groaned again. All the tension built by every kiss, every caress, every embrace celebrated this intimate touch. Hours of heightened sexual tension released in her body with wonderful relief.

She put her arms around Anna's shoulders to steady herself and encourage her nearer, Jess's knees almost giving way when Anna's hands dropped lower and slipped inside the waist of her jeans.

"Can I...?" Anna was breathing hard, her obvious excitement driving Jess further.

Jess couldn't trust herself with words and tugged her jeans down for her answer. She let Anna guide her to the bed, delirious with want.

"And these–" Anna's words were strangled as she dipped her fingers beneath the band of Jess's underwear.

"Please."

Jess lay down and lifted her hips from the bed, letting Anna tug down her underwear. That Jess was already wet was obvious as the garment slid down her legs.

Anna knelt between her knees and Jess hardly dared look down. She could see the full naked length of her own body, gently writhing in the glow of the city, the stunning Anna staring down at her mesmerised, her hands on Jess's thighs, slowly caressing higher and higher.

Jess quickened. She closed her eyes again, almost unable to take the building sensation. She peeped once, wanting to take in Anna's almost incapacitated expression of exaltation, and it made her pulse between her legs with more intense desire.

Higher Anna caressed, stroking firmer into Jess's thighs as if losing herself to arousal, the tormenting pressure reaching where Jess wanted her most of all before her fingers even arrived. It was heavenly torture, the anticipation of Anna's soft fingertips. They almost made contact. Just a light resting of Anna's thumbs either side of her centre. A tantalising circling motion parted her lips and Jess panted with every movement, willing Anna, pleading silently, as if she might burst if Anna didn't touch her. Then Anna stroked into her slick moisture and the sensation struck every part of Jess's body.

She moaned, her back arching with the thrill that shot through her body. Anna circled her clitoris with firm, slow, enthralled appreciation.

"You beautiful woman," Anna gasped. Then, as if every layer of artifice was gone, "I want to feel inside you." How intoxicating that honeyed voice became under the spell of arousal.

"Please," Jess said. It may have sounded as if she was in agony but she was beyond caring. She tensed until Anna obliged, slipping her fingers inside, then Jess's mind went blank and she thrust up to meet her. Her arms searched in hope for Anna and found her leaning over her.

Jess was close and ached for the intimacy. She gently and clumsily pulled Anna in, losing coordination and a sense of where she lay.

Then the words Jess had been waiting for, "Touch me?" Anna whispered.

Jess's eyes shot open. "Yes."

Anna pulled her dress up to her hips and unzipped beneath the arm. She lifted Jess's hand and placed it inside the slit and with delight Jess's hand encountered Anna's bare breast on her palm. She had to shake her head to remain conscious of where she was and looked for Anna to anchor her, but Anna's face betrayed her. Her arousal was catching up with Jess's.

Jess lifted away Anna's underwear and Anna agitatedly kicked it away. She straddled Jess's leg and Jess groaned as she became aware of how soaking Anna had become.

"Touch me," Anna pleaded louder and Jess rapturously obliged.

She felt light as her fingers slipped inside Anna. It was exquisite. Soft and tender warmth of the woman who'd consumed her now surrounding her and she was dizzy at the sensations that whirled inside. She stroked her fingertip over where Anna was slick and swollen, and Jess's arousal began to grip every part of her body.

They tried to kiss. It was probably clumsy but Jess was too lost to know or care. They were noisy. They were uncontrolled. They held each other as they climaxed. They still kissed desperately even when the moment was past, as a myriad of emotions burned through them and not wanting the intensity of passion to end.

25

Darkness still clung to the sky when Jess stirred. She had the faint memory of a ping on her phone waking her and she opened her eyes but didn't move. Her body felt balmy and fluid, it was so relaxed. She must have slept well for all anxieties to have been so pleasantly purged. She smiled at the thought. Last night's activities had pushed everything from her mind except for the wonderful woman who lay spooned in her arms, holding Jess's hand tight to her chest.

Anna looked divine, her features frozen with sleep and perfect in the soft light through the windows. They'd neglected to pull down the blinds in their haste to come together and the room was bathed in the glow of streetlights, the pale blue halo over the city outside a hint that the sun was about to peek over the horizon. What would Jess give to wake up like this every day.

Anna had risen in the night to remove her dress and hide her body again under a generous T-shirt and returned to bed apologising for her reticence. Jess had told her she shouldn't fret and reassured her in more ways than one and Jess smiled again enjoying her own nakedness wrapped around the partially dressed Anna.

She reluctantly rolled away from her slumbering lover and checked her phone. Six-thirty and she had a message from her agent, Celia. It must have been the notification that had woken her. Did the woman never sleep? Actually she knew Celia didn't. "Bloody thyroid," she heard Celia croak in her mind.

Jess sat up and opened the message. "Call me as soon as you wake up. And I mean, as soon as you wake."

Jess dressed quickly, throwing her coat around her shoulders, and padded out to the balcony, sliding the door shut behind her. She shivered in the near freezing air and swiped to Celia's number.

"Good god, darling. I didn't expect you to be up at the crack of dawn," Celia answered.

"Good morning, Celia." Jess sniggered at her agent's insistence of punctuality then berating her for complying.

"What's stopping you sleeping dear?" Celia asked.

"Your message."

"Oh. I was rather hoping for something more interesting than that. We live in hope." Celia chuckled. "Right, to business."

"OK," Jess readied herself. Celia sounded serious.

"So this is a bit of curve ball, but I have my reasons. Theatre."

"What about theatre?"

"How do you feel about it?"

"As in, watching it?"

"Oh, don't be dense. You really are slow for someone who is very clever in so many other respects."

This was the story of Jess's life. Thinking on her feet wasn't her forte, but submerging herself in the depths of a subject and emerging with something novel definitely was.

"I meant," Celia tutted, "performing."

"Oh," Jess frowned. "I haven't done any stage work for, well, since school, just amateur dramatics."

"That's what I thought."

Jess could hear Celia's sharp nails drumming on her desk.

"How do you feel about an four-week run in the West End?"

"London?"

"Yes, dear. That would be the West End I would be referring to."

"When?"

"Starting in a month's time after intensive rehearsals."

"But–"

"Femi's sorting your publicity schedule, but he's wrangled some remote interviews along with personal appearances and social media events with the studio and that's keeping them, if not sweet, from suing at the moment."

"Oh."

The phone was silent.

"I know it's unexpected," Celia said, "but let's just say, if you did this, Matt and many others would be relieved."

Jess didn't know if it was early morning brain fog or her inability to process Celia fast enough, but she didn't have a bloody clue what she was getting at.

"I can't really say much yet," Celia continued, "but a theatre board member would be very grateful if you, with your high profile, could save the day and in return they might save yours."

"Right."

Clear as mud.

"You see, one of the cast has toppled off a bus and broken a leg and the understudy really isn't cutting it, and frankly the play is dying on its arse anyway. So some injection of star quality around Christmas, to bring in curious punters who'd like to see you in the flesh, should revive its fortune and get it back on its feet to continue its run. Actually I'm tasked with signing up several guest appearances. And Femi and I were listening when you said you needed to stay in one place for more than a day. So–"

"Yes."

"Yes? Yes what?"

"I'll do it."

"I haven't even told you about the play and the rest of the cast."

Oh. "I don't care."

"Don't you want to think about it?"

"I have."

"But are you up to it?"

Jess blinked and shook her head. Was Celia trying to sell this to her or not?

"I mean," Celia continued. "You'll have to audition with the director, but she'd be a fool not to take you."

"Celia," Jess smiled. "I haven't had coffee. It's six-thirty in the morning and I don't do talking on the phone."

"Bloody millennials," Celia chortled.

Jess ignored that. "Please tell me what I need to know. Clearly. Succinctly."

Jess heard another chuckle at the other end of the line. "OK. The play's *The Return*. An ensemble piece. Are you familiar with it?"

"No."

"Fine." Celia didn't seem surprised. "I didn't have you down as a theatre buff. It's a fairly new play and has already been on tour and is in London for what should have been a long run but it's hit a few problems. There's a high calibre stage cast, so you will have to expect some superior attitude, but none of them have your audience pulling power so dismiss their snooty little noses if they get priggish about it."

Jess could imagine what Celia meant. That Jess had been catapulted to stardom from an unknown school girl didn't always go down well with seasoned actors who'd been to drama school and put in years of auditions and work. Actually it hardly ever went down well.

"It'll be hard work," Celia continued. "If you get the heebie jeebies on stage or don't put in the rehearsal hours it could all backfire spectacularly of course."

"Are you still trying to encourage me to do it?" Jess asked, wrinkling her nose in confusion. Her humour belied her nerves. Her heart beat with hope in her chest. The sense of relief was huge at the possibility of staying in the same place for weeks at a time. And Anna. She could see Anna again. Jess peeked through the windows. Anna remained in bed, a sleeping beauty.

"I'm surprised that you're so eager to take it," Celia came to an end.

"Honestly?" said Jess. "I'm desperate. I'm at the point where I want to quit acting and bury myself at home, wherever that is."

Celia was silent.

"I know I'd regret it in many ways, but right now I'm ready to throw in the towel."

"OK." Celia said. "I do understand. I hadn't appreciated how far you'd been pushed. I'll send you the audition details and the script. Let me know what you think."

"I—"

"Don't worry, I'll send a provisional yes, but mull it over while you're away. And call me any time. Seriously anytime. I'm always awake."

"Thank you," Jess said.

"Oh my dear, you're welcome," Celia said, amused. "You really are by far the most straightforward and polite of all my clients."

Jess laughed.

"While at the same time bringing in the most money. So thank *you*."

"OK," Jess said, trying not to apologise or thank her again.

And they rung off.

So.

Theatre.

That's not what Jess had been expecting. She gazed across London with her heart in her mouth. The prospect of theatre, with a real live audience, no retakes, nothing, was terrifying. But, and her heart cantered at the thought, it opened up the possibility of seeing Anna again.

She peered inside the window. Should she tell Anna now? Jess was desperate to tell her everything, but this wasn't a quick conversation after a night like that. Femi had indeed emailed with the week's hellish schedule, then who knew where she would be after that. But if she could stay in London, well, there would be months to talk and spend together.

The sky was getting lighter by the time Jess returned inside. She warmed her hands on a mug of coffee before waking Anna. She gently squeezed her shoulder. Anna's eyes opened slowly, taking a little while to settle on Jess's, then she smiled the most beatific of smiles.

"Good morning," she murmured.

Jess beamed. "It's a bloody amazing morning. Here, I made you a coffee," she said and she carefully handed it to Anna, who dutifully sat up to take a sip and set the mug down on the low bookcase beside the bed.

Was it the hot coffee that brought colour to Anna's face, the slight flush, those large eyes, or was it something else? Jess grinned, sure of the answer.

Anna reached up to her face "Last night." She smiled. "That was…" Anna was unusually lost for words, her lips parted, and that gorgeous full mouth captivated Jess.

"Wonderful", Jess whispered and she leaned down to kiss her.

Despite staying awake well into the early hours, appreciating those lips and much more, she couldn't tire of them.

"It's been a long time," Anna started. "I'd forgotten how close you feel to someone."

"Someone you're mad about," Jess finished in her head. When you've fallen for a person. When it's not just sex but opening up your whole being to share and be able to enjoy another's.

Jess kissed her again.

"Are you leaving?" Anna said, looking down at Jess's coat.

"I have to. My manager has scheduled several meetings but," she braced herself, metaphorically crossing everything, "if I get a chance to stay in London for a while, would you, you know, like to spend some more time together?"

"Is that possible?" Anna blinked and sat up higher.

The air seemed to flutter with excitement.

"I don't know yet but there's a possibility and I would really like to spend more time with you. Proper time, without having to rush off or fear never seeing you again. There's so much I want to tell you and I love every minute we've had, so if you–"

"Of course." Anna reached up, an unbridled look of happiness on her face, and drew Jess closer. "I would love that."

Jess blinked and let herself be drawn in and fell victim to another of Anna's delicious, infatuating kisses.

26

Anna smiled, a lot, and she knew exactly why and that made her grin more.

She caught herself before stepping inside Zehra's coffee house to meet Pen for breakfast. She pursed her lips, attempting to appear serious, but her mouth twitched and she couldn't stop her whole face lifting with rapture. Was she imagining it or were her cheeks glowing? She checked her face with the back of her fingers. Yes, she radiated heat.

She fanned her face with her hands, let them rest, felt the cool air on less obviously euphoric cheeks, which then slowly filled with a rosy glee. Damn it. Afterglow was written all over her face and Penny would know exactly what the glow was after.

But Penny was flapping when Anna entered the café. She heard her first and found her best friend and daughter at their favourite booth by the window. Bibs was sitting in a wooden highchair pulled up to the end of the table, a ring of Turkish simit bread brandished in one hand and something squelchy in the other.

"Stop squeezing that egg, Bibs," Penny snapped.

Oh, that was it. Vaguely yellow mush was emerging from in between Bibs's fingers. The girl seemed unperturbed by her mother's fussing and looked up to say "Banna".

"Hello, lovely girl," Anna said and she stroked the toddler's wispy hair and kissed her on the forehead. She risked egg all over her clothes, but she wasn't missing out on a cuddle from her favourite kiddo. Besides, Anna was leading a more informal class today, open to everyone who needed voice coaching, and she was dressed in jeans and a long jumper in which a bit of egg could conceivably blend.

"Sorry," Penny blustered. "We started without you. Bibs was wailing and we couldn't wait."

Penny was behaving as if she had the most cantankerous, demanding child on the planet while Bibs sat quietly getting on with the business of being a toddler.

"Banna want some?" Bibs said and she spread out her yellow fingers accompanied by another little squelch.

Anna smiled. "No, thank you, Bibs. I will order mine in a minute."

Penny was tugging a bib that resembled a mini raincoat onto the child, seemingly a little after the fact, but Anna didn't want to point that out.

"Oh god," Penny groaned. "We've been up since four. And it's not like we spent much of before that sleeping."

That would explain Pen's grouchiness.

"What's up?" Anna said, sliding into the booth seat.

"Bibs is snotty again." That would account for the nasal "Banna" greeting. "And she's been having night terrors." Penny fussed and tugged at the bib. "I'm trying to pass off these dark rings under my eyes as smudged makeup after a good night out, rather than a terrible night in sharing a bed with a toddler."

"Any idea what's causing the nightmares?"

"No," Pen replied, relaxing as a popper button finally snapped into place. "Poor pumpkin," she said with genuine sympathy. "I wish I could see what was going on in that little head." And she kissed Bibs on the forehead while the toddler obliviously licked food off her hands.

"Right," Penny sighed and she plopped down onto the booth seat opposite and at last focussed her attention on Anna. Penny's mouth dropped and continued to widen until it peaked at maximum stretch. It was accompanied with an excited and indignant inhalation.

"You got laid!"

Shit.

"It's written all over your face."

It *was* written all over her face and now that it was heightened with a blush it was written in bold.

"Who got laid?"

It was Zehra who sidled up with an order pad. She abandoned the pad on the table and shuffled her bottom next to Anna.

"You got laid?"

Oh god. Was nothing secret in this world for long?

"Stop!" Anna cried. "Just….stop." She put her hands up.

"So?" Pen said, eyes as wide as her mouth.

"Yes, I saw her again last night."

"And?"

"Well, let's just say she was still here this morning." Anna sat back, relieved that she'd managed a tasteful answer.

"And?"

Oh come on.

Pen tutted. "She managed to stay two other nights and show a disgusting amount of platonic behaviour. So?"

Did she really have to do this?

"I…"

"You are definitely glowing," Penny said.

Apparently she did.

"That grin of yours stretches from ear to ear."

"True," Zehra added.

"And," Penny said with finality, "you walked in here with your titties thrust out like weapons of mass seduction." Penny shook her own bosom for good measure.

"I did not." Why did Penny do this to her – maul her experience over with such crudity she wanted to die?

"Did too." Penny strung it out to make it the last and final word. "Oh come on. I get to spend the night with a tiny snot monster. I want to live vicariously at least."

"OK." Anna smiled. She couldn't bring herself to use Penny's diction and answered succinctly with, "Yes."

"I knew it!" Penny punched the air. "Anna Mayhew had sex!"

"Jesus, Pen!"

Zehra chuckled beside her. "Oh, I've missed your morning-after conversations." And she put her arm around Anna's shoulders. "You two have entertained me over the years."

It had usually been the other way round though, Anna and Zehra the listening ears and shoulder to cry on after Penny's exploits. It had been a quiet spell over the last five years, with Pen settled with Lana and Anna quiet at home.

"My money," Zehra tugged Anna towards her affectionately, "is on that beautiful girl from the other night."

"You've seen her?" Pen gasped, aggrieved.

"Am I right?" Zehra asked.

"How…?" How did Zehra know?

"The one sprawled on your bed when I came to check on you?"

There was that.

Anna pinched her lips together. "Yes."

"Aaaaaah." Zehra enjoyed the satisfaction of being right. "I thought so."

"How though?" Anna said.

"The way she looked at you."

Again, "How?"

"Yes, she was worried and in a state, but those little looks in unguarded moments, taking you in, those are always such a giveaway."

"But she was only getting to know me. People regard others when they meet."

"Do they?" Zehra cried with high-pitched disbelief. "A few seconds is all they take to categorise a new person, put them in little boxes then move on. But this girl, always peeking up, those big brown eyes, admiring, searching."

"I can't believe you've already met her," Pen huffed.

"I didn't speak to her, but I saw enough."

"What was she like?" Pen leant forward, with the eagerness of a hound.

"Gorgeous," Zehra said, like she was sampling a new dish. "Tall, brown skin, beautiful eyes with long lashes. Natural too I think. Lovely lips. Not covered in makeup. She was kind of, how would you say, soft butch maybe?"

Pen nodded with the speed of a drill.

"You know," Zehra had her hands cupped in front of her as if weighing large fruit. "Fit, with short hair, and great big–"

"I am still here," Anna said. "You are talking about someone whom I respect and have a high regard for."

"Yeah, yeah," Pen dismissed. "You were always far too considerate with your lovers and hardly ever dished the dirt, so I need to sniff around elsewhere for details."

Anna crossed her arms and rolled her eyes and let Zehra and Pen carry on their discussion and conjecture.

She gazed through the window and wondered where Jess was now. She'd left soon after waking but not before they'd kissed once more. And Jess's kisses had trailed down Anna's neck, and eager hands had teased her nipples beneath her T shirt. Jess had eased on top of her, Anna wrapping her legs around her back while Jess slipped her fingers inside and sensationally circled her thumb around Anna's centre.

She breathed in sharply to stifle a moan that was desperate to escape.

It was quiet. Too quiet.

She turned to find two faces directed at her.

"Anna Mayhew," Pen was tutting and slowly shaking her head from side to side, and Anna's face engulfed in flames.

Penny balled up her fists with excitement. "This is so good," she squealed.

Zehra stroked Anna's hair. "You are definitely glowing. It's lovely to see."

Damn it. But honestly she felt revitalised from her head to her toes, like she'd had a shot of delicious energy.

"Did you tell her though?" Penny said, more quietly. "Who you were?"

Anna paused. "No. I didn't." She heard Penny sigh. "Why would it matter? I'm not that person anymore, and I wasn't a big deal anyway."

"But it was important to you," Penny said. "And it's not like it doesn't have an effect on you. It was a huge part of your life."

"Maybe, some day," Anna said.

Penny was silent.

"We've spent one night together," Anna continued, trying to keep calm and stop everything from bubbling to the surface. Her stomach was in knots. "You can't tell someone everything in one night."

"You've spent three nights together."

"OK, in three nights."

Anna noticed she was squeezing her thighs. She clenched her fingers then stretched them to relax.

"It was a long time ago," Anna said, finally. "I'd rather she got to know me first, who I am now."

"It's only five years since you went all Greta Garbo," Penny muttered.

"Pen!" Anna shot a pleading look to her friend.

"Well you did." Penny was equally pained.

"It's not like I wanted to."

"I know it's hard for you," Penny said. "Honestly, if you'll let me acknowledge the fact, I'm in awe of how you managed. If someone had treated me like that I would have lost it completely and run home to Ireland. But you have withdrawn in so many ways."

Anna was about to get annoyed, but realised where Penny was coming from, one of the benefits of being so familiar and knowing her friendship and loyalty were unwavering. Penny missed Anna. She missed their old lives.

"The point is," Penny said. "It was only five years ago."

"Plenty of time to fall into obscurity these days," Anna answered.

"You are still known. It's why your classes are popular."

"Penny's right," Zehra said. "You cannot escape your past entirely, not when people recognise you."

"But they don't anymore."

"Oh, they do. I see people look at you when you come in here sometimes. They're always respectful, I keep an eye out for that. Besides I have your signed photo on the wall."

"Really?" Anna had forgotten.

"Yes."

Zehra got up and Anna followed her away from their favourite booth to the back wall which was covered with glamourous photos of all kinds of star. A smaller picture than most, snug between better-known faces, was Anna's portrait. It was of her younger self, ten years ago at least, when her generous hair fell to her waist, before she preferred to keep it shorter and less eye catching to avoid attention. Back when she applied makeup and let those blue eyes shine across a room, and in this photo, deep scarlet lipstick that enhanced her classic smile. "Dazzling," people had said.

27

The two weeks, as it turned out when Femi let the schedule grow, was exhausting, but all the while Jess kept thinking of Anna and how soon she would see her again. They talked briefly a couple of times on the phone, Jess enjoying Anna's remedying voice and the delicious promise of what waited at home.

France was the highlight with the film premiere at Le Grand Rex in Paris. The crowd outside was raucous and large. Jess had breathed in deep and thrown back her shoulders like Kalemdra and for once it worked and was enough to power her through two hours of signing autographs and shaking hands with the crowd. She was careful to avoid the intimidation of journalists with their onslaught of prying questions, which could break the spell, and saved her limited tank of words for fans who wanted to talk about their mutual obsession with *Atlassia*.

Her heart now belonged to two sisters, around eight to ten years old, who had matching thick glasses. They were dressed in clothes like Kalemdra's, their black hair shaped like the character's, with their Mum beaming with pride behind them. Jess had signed their graphic novels and apologised in her school-girl French for not being able to converse fluently. The mother and the eldest told her not to worry in embarrassingly perfect English and the girl spent five minutes, without a pause, telling her how much she loved the character and showing her favourite parts of the story. Her younger sister twirled on the spot and buried her face in her mother's armpit.

"Sorry," the mother said. "We've been waiting a long time and this one's tired and about to have a meltdown, otherwise she'd be chatting to you as well. She'll be talking about you all day tomorrow when she's had time to take it in."

"She's autistic," the eldest chipped in, "and she forgot her beads that she shakes to relax."

The younger girl made a noise and shot a look of exceptional displeasure that only a sibling can provoke. She whined something in French that Jess made out as being upset that her sister was talking about her as if she wasn't there.

Jess hesitated, taking the girl in, the child's bottom lip pulled and her scowl both furious and upset. Jess squatted down beside her, but didn't try to catch the eye of her kindred spirit.

"Me too," Jess said, and she reached into the pocket of her tuxedo jacket and drew out her string of smooth green beads. She let them unfurl and swing in the air between them.

"These are mine," Jess said, considering the beads and careful not to insist on eye contact or to bombard the girl with questions.

"I have several of these," Jess continued. "When I was young I had a special set. I always played with them when I got anxious or tired. But I'd lose them or forget them and that would make me more stressed." The girl unwound from her mother's chest.

"So," Jess said, "I make sure I have several sets so it doesn't matter if lose one. I like the feel of them," she said, letting the beads stream into her palm, then running them into the other hand. "I like their spherical shape on my palm and the way they flow. It's mesmerising and pleasing all at the same time. It makes everything quiet, my mind and outside, and I can think again."

The girl's face was in the open, her expression blooming, and eventually she stepped forward with a confidence that things of importance imbue.

"You have beads," she said in French. She stared at Jess, then incredulous wonder brightened her eyes and a goofy smile spread across her cheeks.

"Yes," Jess said, the pleasure at their similarity infectious and her own face lifting. "I used to shake them like this when I was little." And she held one end and flicked the string so that it snaked in a blurred figure of eight. Other kids had mocked her and she'd adapted to the more socially acceptable flowing beads between her palms and it had never felt the same again. But she didn't relay that.

"I do that!" the young girl said, her face radiating sensational delight. Not an ounce of emotion was hidden. Jess could swear she could sense the warmth of that joy.

"They might not feel right," Jess started, "but do you want to have mine?" and she offered the beads.

The girl nodded. She took the end and flicked her wrist so the string of beads snaked in the air. "They're a bit light," she said earnestly. "I have large wooden beads at home."

"Say thank you, Michelle," said the mother, mortified.

"That's OK," said Jess. "If they don't feel right, then they don't feel right."

The girl experimented, putting them from one hand to the other. "But they sound nice," she said and she looked at the beads in her hands reverentially. "Can I have them anyway?" she said, peering up with wide excitement in her eyes.

"Yes, you can," Jess replied, and the girl jumped on the spot with unfettered glee. She showed her sister, refining the movement so that it became hypnotic and the girl was lost in its soothing rhythm.

"Thank you," the mother said, tears brimming and twitching on the verge of giving Jess a hug. Then with a look of fondness at her daughter and one of apology to Jess, "We might not get her attention again."

"There's no need," Jess shrugged.

"*Merci,*" the mother said, hand on her heart.

"You're welcome." And Jess had to move on.

Matt, the producer, was conspicuously absent and that was a loss. Jess had missed being able to download without reservation to someone who knew the stresses of the business and the series in particular. Seeing the rest of the cast lifted her though. They were a professional and amiable group, even A-lister Chris Smith, especially when intoxicated by the energy of the premiere and then literally drunk at the after party.

Jess couldn't remember when she'd handled a glitzy event this well. A little Champagne and a good dose of camaraderie with the familiar cast, and the thought of her family at home and Anna in London, had given Jess a confidence boost, a base of happiness, a promise of respite. She played to the cameras that flashed everywhere at the party but avoided the nosy hacks.

Then, after a whirlwind fortnight, she stood nervous and hopeful outside a theatre on Shaftesbury Avenue in London. This was the kind of place she'd only entered on school trips and it had been daunting enough stepping foot into this world to see a matinee performance of *Macbeth* with her classmates, let alone knocking on the doors to audition for a role. It was a world to which she didn't feel she belonged in many ways.

That didn't mean she was going in unprepared.

The auditorium smelled of history: dust, the sweat of generations of audiences and actors, and spilt coffee. She tapped the seat at the rear of the stalls and it squeaked as it rocked back. They must have been the originals, small and tightly packed together, even the velvet covers decades old and wearing thin from thousands of bottoms. It was the kind of dishevelled chic that attracted actors from overseas, top directors and a loyal audience, despite the cheaper seats being obscured by pillars and suffering the odd spring in the rear.

It was a sizeable theatre too with a few hundred seats in the stalls, Jess guessed. She turned round and gazed up at the ornate and gilded balcony above, the royal gallery, and up again to the gods. It was awe-inspiring despite its shabbiness and Jess imagined that when the lights went low the anticipation and atmosphere must be on another plane.

"Ms Lambert I presume," came a female voice, the kind that could cut glass. It came from the front of the stalls and Jess finally noticed a tuft of iron grey hair peeking over the top of mid row.

She strode towards the stage and found the diminutive figure of the director, cross-legged and pale fingers entwined, on the front row. She considered Jess over the top of scarlet, cat-eye glasses.

"Yes," Jess said pleasantly. "Jessica Lambert." Then she realised, always a step behind, the director was toying with her. She undoubtedly would have recognised Jess immediately. Jess put out her hand in any case, but it was ignored.

"Hello, Ms Warwick," Jess said and she casually withdrew her hand, as if she took no offence, because in general Jess took less than most.

Deborah Warwick continued her silent appraisal. She was a stalwart of the Royal Shakespeare Company although her productions were innovative and controversial, at least in her heyday. Her rehearsal process was rigorous and experimental and expensive, which sometimes led to productions, as Celia would say, "dying on their arses". Jess wondered if she was the kind of director who would not appreciate a rookie film star imposed upon her. It seemed her suspicions were correct. Deborah Warwick gave Jess the kind of look a cat might give when offered a bubble bath with a spaniel.

The director glanced at her watch. But Jess had been punctual to the second and Ms Warwick was slightly aggrieved.

"So," Deborah said, flicking open a script. "I assume you've read it."

"I have."

"Memorised your part at least?"

"Yes."

Deborah hesitated a fraction of a second. Was Jess's preparation unexpected?

"A little presumptuous, don't you think? You don't have it in the bag just yet," Deborah snapped.

Oh. It was a bad thing. But Jess suspected that every possible answer would have reflected badly.

"Well, let's get on with it. Hop up on the stage then." Deborah tossed her a script.

Jess caught it and took the stage in a single bound.

For a fraction of second, it had been fleeting, Ms Warwick looked impressed, then she downgraded with, "You'll need that fitness if you're going to catch up with the rehearsal schedule and perform twice a day."

Jess turned away to hide her smile and walked centre stage.

The set design was reassuringly minimalist: a menacing dark background to expose the characters, Jess had read in a newspaper review. It was rather like being in a green-screen studio, which Jess was more than used to, conjuring a performance in an imagined world, where the rushes contained only your raw performance with nowhere to hide.

Doors clattered at the entrance to the stalls.

"Sorry I'm late," came a powerful voice with precise enunciation.

A young white actor entered, Jonathon Bates, who Jess recognised as playing the part of her character's husband. His tardiness was apparently tolerable and Deborah waved him onto the stage.

He at least gave Jess a welcoming smile after he'd clambered up. "Bloody good to meet you," he said with a grin and firm handshake and Jess was comforted by the gesture.

"From page twenty, would you please," Deborah said, her voice ringing though the auditorium. "From where Jonathon enters. So as you should know, if you have indeed read the script, your character has had an affair and Jonathon has found you out."

Jess flicked to the page. "Got it." And she let the hand with the script drop to her side. She had memorised a good portion of the script and it had stuck easily, but she was glad of the reassurance of it in her hand.

Jonathon paced the stage, his presence large and footsteps thudding on the boards.

"When did it begin?"

She twitched at how loud he'd pitched his voice. It came so naturally as if his barrel chest was a powerful musical instrument.

"After you'd left," she said weakly.

"Good god," Deborah shrieked. "Louder, or else they won't be able to hear you beyond row C. We don't have microphones for this production thank you very much."

"After you left," Jess said again, her voice cracking a little. She hoped it came across as the character being affected rather than Jess being unused to projecting.

"How soon after I left?"

Jess twitched again, genuinely. Jonathon's voice boomed with threat right through her.

"Not straight away," she stuttered.

Jonathon pounded the stage behind her, taking up space. In contrast she must have looked part of the set, twisting round to follow his movement. Jess realised she was keeping her spot and staying within camera field of view. She decided to step slowly towards the audience, at the same time making herself smaller as she went.

"Was it when the others returned?"

"No," she said, inching forward, as if bracing herself. "Not even then."

She walked right to the very edge of the stage, as far away from Jonathon as she could, as if protecting herself from her husband. She was more intimate with the audience, confiding in them almost.

"Was it..." Jonathon's voice softened but remained powerful. "When you thought I was dead?"

"No," Jess whispered, with fear. She stopped. "It was when I heard you were coming back."

The theatre was silent.

"What?" He said it with a heart-broken whisper that Jess could tell carried right up to the gods. It was thrilling.

"When I knew you were alive and coming home for good," she said.

"But..."

"I wanted to know what it was like."

"What?"

"Love." Jess hugged herself and leaned over the edge of the stage. She felt Jonathon follow and loom over her. "I wanted to know what it was like to be touched by someone who cared. I wanted, for one moment, to be loved for who I am, not whose sister or daughter or beneficiary. Just me."

"And now?" His words surrounded her. She saw Deborah twitch at the threat. The atmosphere bristled, even between the three of them, and she caught Deborah leaning in too.

"And now?" Jonathon repeated louder.

"I wish I'd never known," Jess said, closing her eyes in despair.

There was silence again and Jess had the sense of being cocooned in a moment of magical tension that all three of them inhabited.

Then Deborah's chair creaked and the whole room switched back to reality.

Jess looked up to find the director shuffling in her seat and contrition squirming across her face.

Jonathon grabbed her hand and grinned. "Liked that. Liked that a lot. Injects real pathos into an otherwise unsympathetic character."

Jess beamed, all the time watching Deborah.

Deborah narrowed her eyes and said, "Do it again." That was it.

Jess wondered if this was a challenge but she was more than up to it. She'd had to repeat a scene fifty times, every time perfectly, while others corpsed or otherwise ruined the take.

After five more times, each experimenting with suggestions, Deborah waved her hand and said, "Thank you, Jonathon. Take a break before the matinee."

After he left, shaking Jess's hand and showering her with encouragement, Deborah busied herself with the script for the whole of five minutes while Jess kicked her feet on the edge of the stage.

"Well," Deborah said, deigning to speak at last. She removed her glasses. "Your projection is appalling."

Jess couldn't fault her for that. The difference between her and Jonathon was vast.

"But..."

There was a but. At least there was a but and Jess's heart skipped a beat.

Deborah fixed her with a scrutinising gaze. "You have a naturally strong voice and good range. And after a very shaky start where I feared you'd actually glued yourself to the floor, you have a stage presence which is," she breathed in deeply, "emerging, if I'm being generous."

Jess tried very hard to keep her eyebrow from twitching but must have failed.

"Ms Lambert," the director snapped. "People pay over a hundred pounds to see this play. They won't take kindly to a substandard performance and neither should they."

"A hundred quid?" Jess said, surprised.

The director leaned back in her seat. "That might be a pittance to you, but it's a much anticipated treat for people although it's the better off who are more likely to crucify you in reviews."

"That's not a pittance to me." Jess shook her head. "I think I can count on my fingers the number of my possessions that cost that much."

"Really?" The director tutted.

"My phone. Shoes. Winter coat." Jess thought hard. "My suitcase, but that was a gift. Outfits are hired for me for public events, when fashion houses don't want me to model their clothes. Otherwise, there's not much else apart from what you see. Music, books, all on my phone. I live out of a suitcase and I don't want it to be a large one." She shrugged.

The director was still considering Jess over her glasses.

"Ms Lambert," the director sighed, "your frugality is commendable, but I'm sure you are comfortable after your blockbuster series and other lucrative roles."

"Jess. Please call me Jess."

Deborah hesitated again. Jess smiled, realising she was wearing down the director by a process of congenial attrition.

"Jess," the director sighed. "As you can see I'm not sure what to make of you. But..."

Jess held her breath.

"With some specialist help and a lot of work, I believe we can make something...passable."

And Jess couldn't help laughing out loud.

28

Jess could see Anna. She could see her every single day if they wanted. Jess was hurrying up town, her heart in her mouth and the kind of smile that made her feel stupid with happiness lifting her face.

Jess couldn't remember being this excited about anything since the first *Atlassia* film and this meant something deeper. She was jangling with nerves from the audition and trepidation about performing professional theatre, but none of this compared to the anticipation of seeing Anna again. And properly this time. There was an opportunity to get to know each other now that she had weeks rather than hours in London.

She paused to get her bearings. She'd wiggled her way through the small streets of Soho without even thinking and she pulled out her glasses and hat as she noticed people staring from cafés. She picked a long narrow street towards Regent's Park and put her head down, the smile creeping across her face again.

What would she say? Jess mulled it over. "I've got a role. In London. I can stay." She imagined Anna happy and cupping her face and gracing her with another of those heavenly kisses. It would be wonderful.

But then, Jess's heart fluttered, she would have to sit her down. "I'm an actress, some would say movie star. In fact, almost everyone calls me a movie star, apart from me." Jess shivered with nerves at the thought of telling Anna. How would she take it? Would Anna change? Would her face be overcome with avarice like Jess had seen many times, with hunger for all that Jess's fame could do for her. Jess couldn't imagine it. Of all the expressions on Anna's face that she'd seen, and Jess appreciated again exactly how expressive it was, she couldn't imagine that. Greed for money, fame and attention? No, Jess shook her head, that wouldn't be Anna. Jess sometimes got people horribly wrong, but knew Anna well enough for that surely.

In fact, wasn't disappointment more likely? Despite Anna being more confident and outgoing than Jess, she was still reclusive and her reticence showed a private person in many ways. Would Jess's noisy fame be intrusive and daunting? Would it be an aspect, no matter how unwelcome Jess made it and avoided it, that was too much for Anna? Jess hesitated at a road as her heart skipped a beat. This scenario was much more likely and for a moment all her hopes dropped down a chasm of anxiety. She stared at the road ahead of her, fearful that her confession would ruin her future with that exceptional woman.

She had to do this. Jess shook her head and walked on. No matter the outcome, Anna had to know. If this was going to be more than an encounter with a kind stranger and a night of passion, and it already felt like so much more, then Anna needed to know and Jess broke into a jog, eager to see her.

As she turned up the street past Zehra's towards the flat, she was early again. She must have run most of the way across town and arrived an hour ahead of when she'd said. She reached for the buzzer, hopeful that Anna was ready to see her in any case.

She pushed the button and the door clicked unlocked without Anna querying and Jess dashed up the steps taking them two at a time. The flat door was already ajar when she reached the top floor and she burst in.

"You were quick. Did you come back for your keys?" said a voice, which in retrospect didn't sound anything like Anna's. In fact it had an Irish lilt to it if Jess had stopped to think about it. And when she saw the short, full-figured woman, with flaming red curls, it did in fact sink in.

"Holy shitting fuck. Who the hell are you?" said the flaming woman.

"Whoa!"

"Jesus."

"Where's Anna?"

"You're not Anna."

"Shit."

"What the hell?"

"I'm really sorry, I thought Anna was here."

"This is Anna's flat."

They both seemed to take a breath at the same time and the room descended into silence as they stared wide-eyed at each other. The impasse was broken by a loud, but at the same time diminutive, belch and they both shot glances to the sitting area where a small child was sat cross-legged on the rug, glugging a large sippy cup of orange juice.

"What do we say?" the red-head said.

"Pardon," replied the toddler.

Jess returned her wide-eyed gaze to the effervescent woman with larger still eyes.

"I...I...I've come to see Anna." Jess suffered a second's worth of absurd panic thinking she had the wrong building and walked into an entirely random flat. But this was Anna's. And the red-head did look familiar. In fact Jess had an image of her happily inebriated and hoisting two Champagne bottles in the air.

"Penny?" she offered.

"Oh Christ, are you Jess?"

"Yes."

"Jesus. You're early."

"Sorry, I..." Jess patted awkwardly for her hat, for reassurance that it was on her head. Nothing about Penny's reaction hinted at recognition, in fact so far it was plain hysteria at an anonymous intruder.

"Anna's going to be livid. Well you know, decorously miffed, being Anna. She said I had to scarper before you arrived. Haven't you heard of calling or something? You frightened the living shit out of me."

"The.... Baby..."

"The baby's mine, aren't you Bibs darling?"

"I mean..." Jess had been worried about the onslaught of expletives. The child, Bibs it turns out, looked unperturbed. "I'm sorry," Jess managed.

"Well, now that my heart rate is climbing down from way-too-frigging-high, it's a pleasure to meet you." Penny stepped forward with a naughty grin on her face and a pale freckled hand thrust forward. "I kind of wanted to see you," she said with a giggle. "Who am I kidding? I was desperate to meet you. Anna's told me so much about you."

When did that ever put anyone at ease, Jess wondered.

"You have definitely put a smile on Anna's face," Penny continued.

Jess's jaw dropped in response.

"Keep your knickers on. She hasn't dished the dirt," Penny said, arm still outstretched. "She didn't need to. That kind of smile says it all."

That wasn't in any way reassuring.

"Anna's going to kill me." Penny sniggered. "But I think it's wonderful that she's been having a fling." And at last she stood directly in front of Jess.

Jess gulped and lifted her hand to Penny's, the greeting unavoidable. Penny grabbed Jess's hand and gave it a vigorous squeeze.

"Pleasure to meet you Jess...?" Penny raised her eyebrows in question.

Jess raised hers, also in question. "Oh," Jess said, realising Penny was querying her surname.

"Oh," Penny repeated. "Jess Oh. Penny MacFarlane." And Penny squeezed Jess's hand doubly hard.

"No, I mean," this wasn't going to plan in any conceivable way, "that's not my surname."

"Oh?"

"No it's not Oh."

"Oh."

"Oh god."

"What is it then?"

Jess stared, her desperation no doubt wearing itself plainly on her face. She wasn't the best at hiding her feelings at any time and Jess hadn't had time to think through the ultimate way to reveal her movie star persona to Anna, but she was pretty sure telling her best friend first was not the perfect scenario.

She kept staring. And Penny's eyebrows kept rising. And Jess stared some more. And Penny tilted her head. All until a penny seemed to drop for Penny and her expression plummeted in a frown. She studied Jess and leant closer, a fraction at a time, so that she loomed.

"Have we...? Do I know....?"

It felt like the walls were drawing in. Penny tugged her imperceptibly nearer while peering through Jess's glasses, closer and closer. The room froze and Penny stood like a statue, except her eyes which were now growing and growing, wider and wider. And her mouth. Oh this was going to be loud. Her mouth was widening into a gaping tunnel. Jess's shoulders started to rise, in a ludicrous attempt to cover her ears, but here it came. Oh no. Oh no no no.

"Sweet Mary and Joseph and Christ on a bike. You're.... You're..."

Oh god.

"You're Jessica fucking Lambert!"

Shit.

"Jessica Lambert! Anna never said... I'm holding hands with Jessica fucking Lambert!"

"Hi," Jess grinned, or more bared her teeth and tried not to exude extreme stress. "Nice to meet you."

"Holy mother of...." Penny was gripping her hand hard. "Wow. You look really...Wow. Honestly. I wondered if it was all the makeup and everything they do in post-production these days, but you look sensational." Penny, very unsubtly, checked Jess up and down and from side to side at chest level.

"Wow," Penny said again.

Jess tried to keep a grip on Penny's hand that shook up and down with great gusto.

"But, Anna never said. I mean," Penny prattled on. "Was it a secret? How on earth did you two meet? I can't believe it. I'm such a mega fan of the films. Seriously, I'm sure Anna's said. But...." Penny frowned. "I'd never thought in a million years she'd go for someone–"

"I'm sorry to interrupt, but where is Anna?" Jess said, her shoulders around her ears.

"She had to pop out a sec. She left her keys so I just buzzed you in. But, Jessica Lambert!"

"Please," Jess begged in a whisper, "Could you speak a little quieter?"

"What?" Pen said, not at all quieter.

"Could you perhaps, you know, stop shouting my name?"

"Of course. But, sorry. Jessica Lambert! This is so exciting," Pen said in a whisper so loud Jess considered calling the *Guinness Book of Records*. "I can't believe Anna's done this. Although I'm going to kick her arse for keeping it a secret, or at least take the piss out of her for forever."

Jess's arm distinctly ached and she grabbed the hands that had been in motion a good minute now and firmly brought them to rest.

"Could you perhaps," Jess grinned painfully, "could you perhaps stop saying my name altogether?"

"Of course. Sorry. I bet you get exited fans doing this all the time."

"Yeah, no, indeed, but–"

"Of all the people." Pen shook her head. "Anna's a lot further along than I realised. This is so healthy of her."

Jess wrinkled her nose, losing Pen again, but shook her head to refocus. "I need to ask a favour," she said, her insides tying up in guilty knots.

"Anything!" Pen said with the enthusiasm of a child tempted with a supply of chocolate for life.

"Could you perhaps not say my name, or mention that you know who I am, in any way whatsoever when Anna gets back?"

"Excuse me?"

Jess's heart sank. "Could you not tell her who I am?"

It was another heart-stopping moment of tension, Penny frozen with her ear cocked to the side, Jess holding Pen's hand in prayer and plea.

"She doesn't know who you are?"

"....no." And Jess had never felt so small.

"As in, you haven't told her?"

Jess shrank some more. "No."

It was rare that Jess had seen someone visibly fill with anger, but that is what happened with Pen. It was as if the small woman grew several inches and darkened several shades of red. Jess braced herself.

"You mean," Penny spat, "she has no idea who you are!?"

29

"I can explain," Jess stuttered.

"What the hell kind of game are you playing at?"

"There's no game," Jess pleaded. "She didn't recognise me at first, so I didn't tell her and–"

Pen puffed out several inches more. "She's a fucking recluse, of course she didn't recognise you."

Oh god.

"She's been hiding from everything," Penny spat, "because she doesn't trust people and you think it's OK to hide who you are?"

Jess flinched. The guilt was hitting her like a hammer. "I know, I know, but I didn't realise that to start with."

"Is this a joke to you?" Pen's hands were knuckled into her hips.

"Not at all. Please." Jess put up her hands. "Let me explain."

"You'd better. Much as though I'm a little bit star-struck with you right now," Pen gave Jess another barely disguised look up and down, "and I bet you have a girl in every city, but if you mess around with Anna you will be in deep shit with me."

Jess was a little afraid, a little amused, but heartened that Anna had a friend in Pen. What she would give for a mini Rottweiler with a devoted heart like this.

"It's not like that and I'm not like that. A girl in every city couldn't be further from the truth." Jess took a deep breath. "I was in trouble, cracking up, and Anna let me stay."

"Well," Penny relented the tiniest amount. "That's Anna for you. She was always the grownup, the one who was there to pick everyone else up off the floor."

"Really?" Jess said, her heart flooding for Anna. "That's what she did with me. I was freaking out and in meltdown when I got to London. I couldn't turn a corner without someone recognising me. I was exhausted and needed a break, five minutes even, and there was Anna. It seemed the only person in the world who didn't know who I was, and the only one to treat me like a human being."

Pen listened.

"I never meant for anything to happen. I had no idea anything would." Jess wanted to cry, this was going so wrong.

Pen glared some more.

"I kept meaning to leave and saying good bye, but it was like neither of us wanted that. I thought we'd never see each other again, then I stayed longer and we became closer. I didn't think I would be back in London to see her. And the funny thing is, I'm more like myself than I have been in years. Far from not knowing who I am, it's as if she's one of the few people who really knows me, and now...."

Jess had been seduced by small turns, and rationalised other steps, until she found herself trapped by what she abhorred most of all, a plain lie.

Penny's face was neutral, then she said, "You're smitten aren't you?"

"Sorry?"

"You've fallen for her."

"I..." Jess was compelled to deny it, but why? Penny was right. That was the reason Jess was standing there so afraid of hurting and losing Anna. "Yes," she said. "I'm smitten."

"What a mess," Pen said, deflating back to her normal size.

"I was going to tell her today," Jess said, with a tiny ray of hope. "I've got a role in the West End. I can stay in London two or three months. I'm going to tell her everything."

Penny looked at her with uncharacteristic thoughtfulness.

"I will make it OK," Jess tried to reassure her. "I will make everything better and apologise and I hope to god Anna will understand."

"But you can't make it right," Pen said quietly.

"I should have said something earlier, I know that now, but I had no idea any of this would happen. I was enjoying getting to know someone as me, not the character, not a movie star, just Jess. I never have that chance."

"It doesn't work like that though."

"Why?"

"Because that's a part of you, and a part that makes you the last person on Earth that Anna would want."

The air seemed to disappear from Jess's body. "What do you mean?"

Penny narrowed her eyes at Jess, perhaps searching for an inkling that Jess knew what she meant, perhaps wondering whether it was her place to say. She deflated a little, her shoulders sagging.

"She was an actress," Penny said at last, "a good one too."

"What?"

"Does the name Anna Mayhew ring any bells?"

"No. I…I didn't know her surname."

Penny raised her eyebrows.

"It didn't come up." Jess shrugged. "And, no, I don't recognise the name."

"She was best known for her theatre work, particularly with the Royal Shakespeare Company?"

"I'm not a big theatre goer, so…"

What separate worlds people lived in, all inhabiting the same space but never noticing each other. Jess had no idea what shows and actors were hits in the West End just as another thespian would have no idea what Jess's films drew at the box office. But Jess had the impression that Penny was further underwhelmed by her admission, so left it there.

"Well, she was," Penny said, "and by her mid-twenties she was never out of work with productions in the West End and nationally. By her thirties, she was breaking into high-profile films."

Jess breathed in sharply. "Then a man started following her."

"Yes," Penny said, and she looked devastated by it as if her world was collapsing. She clasped her hands in front of her. "It changed everything."

Jess realised Penny's life must have been turned upside down too.

"Not at first," Penny continued. "It was unnerving, yes, but she carried on with most of her life. I remember how she avoided the odd party invite, but by the end she lost her confidence completely and she was a different woman. It was horrible to see. It was little by little. Some days huge setbacks would occur, then she didn't want to go out at all let alone perform on stage. Then she didn't want to talk about acting anymore. Now she won't even listen to a review program on the radio if it mentions film or theatre."

Penny looked up at Jess, tears threatening. "I was an actor too, still am, although we don't talk about it much."

"Really?"

"Commercials and the odd comedy," Pen said. "You wouldn't have heard of me, unless you're a fan of Maltesers and watch the ad on repeat."

"No," Jess said, "I'm sorry, I hadn't."

"Anyway." Penny drew herself up and took a lungful of air, perhaps to purge the sadness. "It was a huge part of Anna's life, from a young girl right up to five years ago. Acting meant everything to her. Now she won't watch a film with me and, I'm afraid, you represent everything she's lost."

"What am I going to do?" Jess murmured.

Penny smiled at first then became serious. "Where are you going with this?"

"How do you mean?"

"Miss global movie star? Miss not quite a girl in every port but I imagine there's an awful lot of interest?"

"I'm not like that."

"Regardless of Anna's reaction when you tell her, you're not going to be hanging round for long are you."

"I don't know. I've auditioned for a role until Christmas and was hoping to spend weeks with Anna."

"Don't break her heart," Penny said.

"I have no intention of doing that, but I still can't say where I'll be next year. But I do want to be with her. I want to be with her every second of the day. I met her one night and haven't been able to stay away since."

Penny pursed her lips. "Anna used to be such a confident woman, I mean without being a total arse about it. She was the one we all relied on to be the grownup and sort us out. And sexy. Without fail, she always had a hot date."

"She's still sexy," Jess said without reservation, "and confident too. When I'm with her I have a sense of calm. Everything feels like it's going to be OK."

Penny gave her an indulgent smile. "You really are smitten, aren't you?"

"Yeah," Jess lowered her gaze, "completely."

Penny seemed to ponder. "The difference is you're young and free to travel the world."

"You make Anna sound like a geriatric. She's only nearing forty, immensely capable and independent, so much so that she helps lost actors on the Underground."

Penny's mouth pinched in the corner. "True, but do you know what it's like when she has to trespass beyond her usual routine?"

Jess was about to counter but realised that, no, she hadn't.

"You have to be careful," Penny said. "You have the potential to hurt her in so many ways."

The buzzer rudely cut into their conversation and jarred Jess from her torment.

"That'll be Anna," Pen said quietly, and she pressed the door release. They both stood back and waited, hearing the front door open and shut, the footsteps dull on the first flight of stairs, then louder on the second until Anna emerged from the stairwell.

"It's getting late," Anna said, her head down, concentrating on the steps. "You and Bibs better get....Oh."

And there she was, beautiful Anna Mayhew standing before them, a look of surprise on her face turning to delight as she caught Jess.

Jess could suddenly imagine her on the stage, full of grace and poise and magnetic to the eye. And that voice, Jess bet it had seduced whole audiences.

"Oh dear," Anna said with an elated smile. "Too late. You've met Penny, the biggest gossip in North London. I hope you haven't told her all your secrets."

And Jess wanted to bury herself in the ground.

"Hi," Jess said, her heart both heavy and light with eagerness to see Anna again. She wanted to rush over and hold her in her arms and at the same time she was struck rigid by Penny's presence and everything she'd told her.

It seemed Anna only had the former compulsion and came forward, cupping Jess's face in her hands and placing the sweetest kiss on her lips. "It's good to see you," she murmured.

"I couldn't wait," Jess said, closing her eyes to hide all the fears that swirled inside.

Anna slipped her arm around her waist.

"I hope you haven't been giving her a hard time," she said to Penny.

"Me?" Penny shrieked, and a veneer of bubbly carefree persona swept over her. Jess could imagine her vividly in a comedy series.

"Well," Penny feigned mortification. "I know when I'm not welcome. Come on Bibs, love of my life, we need to vacate the love nest. Adult only time here I think."

Anna laughed and Jess wanted to die.

30

"Coffee?" Anna offered as soon as Bibs and Penny had bundled out of the door with so much noise and commotion it was as if a whole party had left.

"Please," Jess murmured, still in shock.

"She's like a whirlwind," Anna said over her shoulder as she filled the kettle and pulled out a cafetière. "Appallingly nosy and a gargantuan gossip, but with a big heart that's always in the right place."

"Yes," Jess managed.

Anna set about making the coffee and Jess remained where she stood, paralysed by indecision and heartache. The silence beyond the clatter of the mug and the ring of a teaspoon was oppressive.

"I hope she kept you entertained," Anna said, faced away. Jess could hear the hesitation creeping into her voice.

"Yes," she said.

Anna stopped and waited for the kettle, hands resting on the top, all the while facing away. The kettle gurgled and rattled on its base, the steam billowing into the air, and when it seemed as if it might explode the switch clicked off and it settled almost with a sigh of relief into silence. Anna didn't move, except for the slight slump in her shoulders.

"Penny told you didn't she?"

"Yes, she did," Jess replied. "It came up. She wasn't gossiping."

"Oh." And the disappointment hung like a weight around Anna. Jess could see her trying to heave it off before she turned around and leant back against the surface, attempting a smile to lighten the moment. "I wondered if she had."

Jess couldn't move. If she'd doubted Penny's story and the impact it'd had on Anna, here was evidence enough. Anna was the picture of someone changed.

"She said you didn't want to act anymore," Jess offered.

"Couldn't is more accurate," Anna said gently. "Stage fright. It sounds so simple and little doesn't it – being a bit scared of going on stage – but I physically wasn't able to act anymore."

"Was it because of…him?" Jess realised Anna had never mentioned her stalker's name, in fact how little Anna had told her about this, as if she wanted it kept in the past and to move on but couldn't.

Anna nodded. "It's mind altering, having someone pursue you," she said. "You question your own sanity after a while. I told him plainly many times that I wasn't interested and plainer still to stop contacting me. Every time he would invent another excuse. He told me that I wasn't being fair and that I needed to listen to his side of the story, that I owed him that. How dare I ignore him. Who did I think I was.

"Every confrontation, I thought that I'd finally got through to him and he would stop calling or leaving messages. I believed he understood at last, that I wasn't the person he thought I was and we shared the same reality at last. But then he'd appear at the corner shop near the theatre. He'd say it was by chance, but that was the thing, I'd told him not to talk to me ever again. Then perhaps that would stop, and he'd send a letter on behalf of someone else. He established a fanclub with others and made an utter fool of me when I freaked out in front of them all after a performance. He'd promised them that we were friends. It was relentless, like a bad dream that won't stop." She took a breath. "I began to think that nothing would get through to him and he would never ever stop."

She peeped up, perhaps to see if Jess followed.

"It's the unrelenting pressure of someone hounding you and inventing new ways to contact you and surprise you. You lose faith in your understanding of the world and your own perception. It's profoundly disorienting and undermining. I still fear losing faith in my own judgement like that and trust in people's behaviour."

That hit Jess hard. How was she going to explain?

"Have you ever had that?" Anna said. "When you think so differently to someone else and they cannot entertain the possibility of divergence and insist on forcing their reality on you to your detriment."

Jess had, often.

"Eventually I secured a restraining order," Anna said, "but his behaviour deteriorated. Gone was any pretence of passing by or excuses to see me. Someone pinched me, hard, here," she indicated the soft flesh at the side of her tummy. "I was on a packed Tube carriage. It was like a nasty prank, a stupid and childish thing to do. It sounds ridiculous doesn't it, but it was him. I saw him as the train pulled away from the next stop, staring at me with glee and gloating as if challenging me to prove that it had been him. And that was just the start of another phase of escalation."

She hesitated, and Jess's heart heaved at Anna's face so full of dread at her recollection of details left unsaid.

"So," Anna said, shuffling. "It didn't stop until he was imprisoned."

"And the stage fright?" Jess gently encouraged.

"Well, I thought it was all over." Anna raised her eyebrows. "Time to be free again and not live in the prison of his making. Not having to think about him every second of the day. Where he could be. What he'd do next. What new way he'd find to contact me. I thought all that was behind me. Then I froze on stage. Like I say, it sounds so little doesn't it – a bit frightened of appearing before an audience – but I couldn't move. It was completely debilitating. I thought I was going to have a heart attack it was such an overpowering physical experience. It wasn't even at the opening act of the play. I was into the second half and someone had coughed. I'm not sure if it sounded like him, but my mind was already convinced – I would never be safe, he would always come back, he was relentless and I froze."

Anna shook her shoulders and stood up straighter. "So," she said. "I took a break, but then I was seen as demanding, an awkward precious diva. I felt ridiculous having stage fright after all my experience and years of treading the boards. I tried work in smaller theatres but eventually no-one would take a chance on me. My current business partner was the one to suggest voice coaching. Therapy helped. It gave me enough coping skills to leave the flat and enough confidence for coaching work and to meet new clients in a single location, but that was the end of my acting career."

Her words trailed off and her face fell into forlorn desolation as she stared at the ground. The loss was obvious and more profound to Jess because she could empathise so deeply.

Jess took a step toward her. "You must have been devastated, losing that on top of everything else." And Jess couldn't keep the sympathy from her voice.

Anna nodded but turned away, not inviting Jess's consolation. She sighed, hard. "Sorry, I'm not used to talking about this, even after all these years. Honestly, I feel foolish about it sometimes, knowing rationally that he's gone but avoiding the life I had. I think if I dwell on the past it might set me back further, and other people...well, no-one wants to hear anymore. They're impatient and think I should be well, even Penny, although she's kinder about it. They want me to be my old self."

Jess opened her mouth and was about to step forward but Anna stopped her with, "Let me get us a coffee and we'll sit down." And Jess nodded, giving her space.

They sat at the island, steaming cups in front of them, and some of Anna's usual cheer seemed to revive.

"Look, I hope Pen didn't exaggerate," Anna continued, more upbeat, "about the loss of my career, but acting did mean an enormous amount to me. Had you heard of me?" she added as if the thought had only that second occurred to her.

Jess shook her head. "No, I'm sorry."

"Don't be. I mainly enjoyed theatre work. I wasn't a huge household name."

Anna took a sip then rested the mug on a mat, her fingers wrapped around its entirety.

"Did she tell you about my family?" Anna asked.

"No."

"Ah, small mercy then," Anna said with something approaching sarcasm. "Sorry," she added, again trying to cast off the seriousness. "They were never supportive of my going into the profession. I wonder sometimes if that's why acting is so closely bound up with my identity and why my failure is so," she took a deep breath, "debilitating in a way."

Jess made a noise to show she was listening.

"Does this all sound rather precious to you?"

"Nothing of the sort," Jess blurted out. "I can imagine how much acting meant to you." And Jess had to stop herself from telling her everything.

"Good, because I don't want to exaggerate about my background. My parents were nothing like abusive or negligent, but I couldn't describe them as nurturing or accepting either."

"That can still hurt," Jess said, not for the first time grateful for her family, who muddled through every eventuality with love and best intentions.

"They are a traditional conservative family in general," Anna continued. "My father's a barrister and my brother and sister have worked in the City. I'm the odd one out – the actor and the bisexual of course." She squeezed her coffee mug. "I think that's why I loved acting from such an early age. I knew I was different to the rest of the family and I was always drawn to 'deviant' roles." She grinned at the word. "I always leapt at the chance to play the character with the subtext: the girl who dressed as a boy, the woman who led, the woman who fell in love with someone of an unacceptable gender. It helped me discover who I was. I always find that ironic, that I discovered who I was by pretending to be someone else. But it's true, I think, for many actors."

Jess's heart thudded in her chest. She knew exactly what Anna meant. She could feel the truth of it in her bones. How much confidence had the character of Kalemdra given her as a teen when she played with her friends, and how much more so now that she shaped the role herself.

"My parents have always been dismissive of my 'little career'."

"Why though?" Jess couldn't help saying. "Don't they watch films, the TV?"

"All the time."

"Have they ever gone a week without being entertained or informed by a radio play, or listened to a story read by a narrator who brought it to life?"

"They live for all of those."

"Then why don't they respect your choice?"

"Odd isn't it," Anna smiled, "how people dismiss the arts while elevating them at the same time. They'll celebrate excellence and notoriety but dismiss aspirant actors as ridiculous. I always found that perplexing."

"What about when you performed for the RSC?"

"That was the first time my family came to see any of my work. I was in my mid-twenties and after I received a rave review in *The Times*."

"Wow," Jess let out. "You had to do all that first?"

Anna pinched her lips together. "I say all this to explain how much that world meant to me, not to berate my parents. I admit I feel silly for how it has affected me sometimes, when things could have been so much worse, but at the same time it was what made me tick. It was always the high." Her eyes sparkled as she recalled. "Appearing on stage, there's nothing like it for me. When you have an audience's heart and mind and they are consumed in the moment as intensely as you are, engulfed in the emotions of the character and situation, their suspension of disbelief complete, the trust between audience and actor unwavering and the moment so vivid it's more powerful than any reality. That kind of experience is a potent drug." Anna paused in thought. "Penny understands. She's an actor too. I didn't want you to think—"

"I understand." Jess understood painfully well and she wished Anna wouldn't apologise.

"I don't think my parents ever did. I'm not sure they really understand the power of stories and performance." A sad smile overtook Anna's features. "I know what it means to others though. There was a woman once who came every week for an entire run of a play. I was cast as a mother who'd lost her child. It was an exhausting role. Every evening I had to fall apart on stage, broken into a thousand pieces and shattered by the death of her girl. It was a brutal experience.

"Then one evening, the audience member requested to meet me. She'd clearly been crying, her face all raw and glistening with tears. She said she'd found it cathartic. She'd lost a child of her own and couldn't let herself fall apart for the sake of the rest of the family. She thought she'd never be able to put herself back together again. When she watched the play and another woman suffering the same way, it gave her permission to let go. She'd gone home and fallen apart. When she woke the next morning, she was in pieces but knew she couldn't break anymore. All the fracture lines were excruciating, but she knew where they were now and how to take care of them, and that alone made her feel stronger."

Anna looked up at Jess, "That woman thanked me as if I'd saved her life, in fact she said I probably had. With that play, that story and that cathartic performance, I realised I'd done something more important and more enriching for my life and that woman's than anything my family had planned for me."

Anna drew herself up. "Sorry. I didn't mean to get quite so heavy. I was trying to lighten the mood by telling you what I loved. I only wanted you to know what it meant, what I was, what I still miss," she paused, "so you understand why I avoid the subject."

And Jess was crushed.

"Did you ever try acting again?" she asked. "Film? TV? Something away from the stage?"

"I had my chance once, but I'd already hit that point for women where roles rapidly dry up and, well, my reputation had changed from one of consummate professional to flake."

"But..." Jess racked her brain for ways Anna could come back. "Is there anything you've wanted to try? Anything related. Radio work?"

"Do you mind if we talk about something else," Anna said quietly, and the fatigue showed in her every muscle.

But there was so much more to say. Any semblance of a plan for how to break Jess's fame to Anna had flown out the window and Jess never regretted her inability to think on her feet as much as she did now.

The issue seemed colossal and Jess's brain stalled, contemplating how Anna would take the news. She couldn't think of a single way to approach it without stamping over sensitive ground and yet she didn't want to blunder her way through for the sake of getting it out in the open.

"Do you want me to go? Do you need to be alone?" Jess asked.

Anna was sagging with tiredness, but she tried to smile when Jess spoke. "No," she said. "I'd like you to stay."

"Of course." Jess leapt off her seat and surrounded Anna, pulling her in as close as possible.

The evening was quiet and they went to bed early, Jess cradling Anna, who fell into a silent slumber. Jess held on tight, her mind racing and too fraught to manage any sleep until the early hours, then waking with a start and finding Anna again, acutely aware that this may be the last time they shared a moment like this.

31

Jess's morning disappeared in a blur. Anna left early for a training session and Jess attended her first rehearsal. Her thoughts were a mess, attempting to get to grips with new stage direction, meeting the cast, the intensive session before the rest of the crew performed the matinee, all the while Jess trying to conjure a way to tell Anna.

It was with tearful relief that she met Matt after rehearsals at a little patisserie in Soho. Jess sat in the window, a cup of coffee on the marble-top table, fidgeting with her beads and staring at the coffee swirled in the milky froth, still unable to magic up an explanation that would fix everything. The small vivacious character of Matt, best friend and producer, appeared through the window, nose pressed up against the glass, deep brown eyes crossed and mouth wide open.

Jess burst out laughing and at the same time tears rolled as he bounded inside and threw his arms around her shoulders. She squeezed him within an inch of his life, lifting the scrap of a man off his feet.

"Holy crap, Jess," he squeaked with what little breath remained in his body.

"It's so good to see you, mate," Jess said.

"Well don't kill me and you'll be able to see me again."

Jess dropped and let him go and wiped her nose in a sniff. "You are a sight for sore eyes."

"Been too long, hasn't it," he said, pinching his mouth in the corner. "Let me get a drink and some scoff then we'll do some serious catching up. And we have business to discuss," he called over his shoulder as he jogged to the ornate counter of sweet pastry delights.

Jess rolled her eyes as Matt chatted and flirted with the male and female assistants behind the counter, dancing back and forth as he pointed out various temptations and considered recommendations. He returned with a large mug of his habitual mocha with a mountain of whipped cream and some choux pastries filled with much more of the same. She didn't have to wonder at where all the energy went that he consumed. The man never stopped thinking, moving or talking.

"First," he said, sweeping aside his floppy fringe of dark hair, "I have to thank you for braving the Menace of Shaftesbury Avenue and agreeing to do that play."

"The menace?"

"The director."

"She's not that bad."

"Ha!" he snorted. "Not that bad? She's reduces action heroes to tears."

"Well," Jess mused. "I suppose that's one advantage of being a little slow off the mark. By the time I realise someone's made a cutting comment the moment's gone and I have to shrug my shoulders."

"You are anything but slow," Matt said, taking an enormous bite of pastry, squirting whipped cream from either side of his mouth. He poked it in with his fingers then noisily licked them clean. "Out of everyone I know, you're always the one who cuts to the chase quickest."

"It doesn't feel that way."

"I mean, you're bollocks at chit chat, but I always trust your gut instincts. If in doubt about someone, I always look to you. I can tell in a second from the expression on your face exactly how you feel about someone even if you can't articulate it straight away."

"Great," Jess said, not particularly comfortable at being so transparent.

"It's a rare gift, especially in this business. Don't ever try to hide it."

"Not much choice about that," Jess grumbled.

"But in any case, are you getting along with Deborah Warwick?"

"Actually, yes. She's demanding but so she should be. I need to be word and position perfect in two weeks."

"Good, good," he said and he slurped his mocha coffee so that its volume halved. "We're leaving the studio."

"What?"

"We're leaving Apex. Finished. No more *Atlassia* with that company."

"But... So that's it.... I mean I knew something was up, but–"

"There you are, your gut feeling. You always know when something is wrong and no-one can ever charm you out of it with anything other than genuine substance."

"I didn't see anything like this coming." Jess shook her head in disbelief. "So that's really it?"

Matt regarded her out of the corner of his eye with a smirk on this lips. "It's just the beginning," he teased.

"Oh bugger off. Tell me what's going on."

Matt threw his head back with laughter and turned towards her fully. "So," he said, clapping his hands together. "We've been unhappy with the interference from the studio all along. Right from the start, they had too much say in the story – an ensemble film with more focus on the male characters than was ever there in the novels for a start."

"Hmm," Jess shrugged. "I assumed you were happy with that."

"Never was," Matt said, "and neither was Kuniko or Jacob or any of the writing team for that matter. And now the studio has taken umbrage with the direction the fourth series of novels."

"Oh?"

"In particular, Kalemdra's friendship with a new character – the Queen of the Northern Territories."

"Friendship?" He'd said the word with such salacious innuendo she couldn't not pick up on it.

"Exactly. They want to change the character to a king and Kuniko and Jacob are livid and ready to walk away."

"I'm…." Stunned. Jess's already aching brain seized further with the news. "So that's the end of it?"

"Well…." Matt's knees were bouncing up and down. "This is what I've been working on, you see. I always thought the novels were much better suited to a television series, but that's not where the industry was several years ago. Big investment, high production quality series were seen as risky whereas now it's the mainstay of everyone's viewing and we have a chance to dramatise the books as they always should have been."

"How do you mean?"

"We're thinking: feature-length episode to introduce new viewers to the characters, concentrating on Kalemdra's point of view as it always should have been, then Kuniko and Jacob think we should skip into series four and proceed where the films left off."

Jess could imagine it. She knew the stories inside out. Besides, she had faith in Matt, Kuniko and Jacob.

"So, a series?" she said.

"Yes. Several series, hopefully."

"On subscription TV?"

"Yes."

"And," Jess exhaled noisily, "what kind of shooting schedule would that need?"

"Busy," Matt said with a laugh.

"Oh."

Matt picked up her hand and held it. "This is all dependent on your availability and willingness to sign up, but I'd kind of assumed...."

"What?"

"That you'd jump at the chance?" He slowed for the first time since his arrival and became pensive, watching her like a hawk.

Jess's brain was overwhelmed and a wave of fatigue washed over her. "You know how much I love *Atlassia*," she said, her eyes heavy as she attempted to catch his gaze. "But I'm tired."

"I know," he said gently. "I'd noticed and I've been talking to Femi."

"Oh," Jess replied.

"And Celia."

"Oh," she said again.

"Which is why I assumed that regular work, based in the UK, might suit you." He lifted an eyebrow and wiggled it.

"Really? Here?"

"Yeah. Studios in West London, locations around the country. Basically, a large part of the initial funding is from the UK so with the pound in the doldrums we can't afford mainland Europe, and we're getting a cut rate at the production company because they're new and trying to establish themselves and the CEO is–"

"On the board of the theatre which is why I'm doing you all a favour and doing a play where I'm out of my depth and bricking it."

"Got it." Matt grinned.

The whole thing made Jess's head ache. But somewhere under all that scheming politics and whirling chaos of contracts, funding, studios and networks, Jess realised, "I could be based in the UK for years."

"Yes. I mean there would be opportunities for short periods away for film work. But, yes. This is a long-term project."

Jess didn't know whether to laugh or cry. The weight of the situation with Anna and also the possibility of more with filming in London was overwhelming. So much to gain and also everything to lose.

Matt leant back and slurped his mocha, his bright eyes not leaving Jess for a second.

"Can you manage it?" he said. "Are we asking too much of you?"

Jess laughed with despair. "I honestly don't know."

She sipped her coffee absently and stared out of the window, aware that Matt watched her. She distracted herself from one whirlwind of indecision and complexity to another.

"You don't know an actress called Anna Mayhew do you?"

"Anna Mayhew?" The lift of his eyebrow said so much – yes, he knew her and he already had a suspicion about why Jess asked. "What?

Queer, gorgeous, honey-voiced Anna Mayhew?" He definitely had thoughts about why Jess asked.

"Yes," Jess said, smiling despite herself.

"Might do." Matt sniggered. "Why?"

"Stop it."

"What?" he said, all innocence.

"I met her recently and didn't know she was an actress."

"She's theatre mainly. Did you meet at an audition?"

"No, nothing like it. She hasn't worked for several years, in theatre I mean."

"Oh, why? She was spectacular. I can't imagine it was because of a shortage of roles."

"No, she's suffered from severe stage fright after trouble with a stalker. She won't even think about theatre these days."

"Shit, I had no idea. What an absolute fucker, someone totalling your career like that." Matt put his mug down and leant forward. "When?"

"Five years ago."

"Christ, five years? How quickly we forget people in this business. Come to think of it, I heard a rumour she'd become difficult to work with, demanding, which I found surprising. Other than that I don't think I've thought of her in all that time, but I was a huge fan. I saw her in Stratford and at the Globe several times. Really gifted. Consumed an audience like none other. And," he looked excited now, "she had that rare gift of transferring that intensity on to the screen. People forget you sometimes have to be quieter to be louder on screen, but not Anna." He looked up at Jess. "She was a bright light at the RSC for years."

"You're such a Shakespeare nut," Jess said with a smile.

"Drama of epic proportions? Personal demons and battles in the microcosm reflected in the macrocosm? Right up my fantasy street. And if you want to pull off epic and grandiose, there's no better example. Sometimes a fantasy film needs that touch of theatre."

"I know. Ian McKellen as Gandalf." It was always Matt's stock example.

"Exactly." He grinned. "Besides, did you ever see her in *Beyond Turbulence*?"

"What? She was in *Beyond Turbulence*?" Jess had heard of the film. In fact she knew her brother and father were fans.

Matt snatched out his phone from his jeans pocket and tapped and swiped until, "Here. There's a showing this afternoon at a little independent cinema down the road. Want to go and admire the ethereal Anna Mayhew?"

Jess found herself in a small cinema with Matt, popcorn and a handful of other audience members and Anna several times life size on the screen. Jess could have watched her all day. It was a slightly younger version of the woman she'd fallen for, in some ways foreign with softer, plumper features, in other ways so strikingly familiar it struck Jess painfully in the chest.

Anna was captivating, beautiful. It was the way she held the attention and gazed at the object of her affection on screen that made her utterly compelling – the flicker of emotions and death of love in her eyes when she was betrayed. And Jess had seen that intensity in real life.

32

Anna's mother was in town. This was a four-weekly event which Anna cherished about as much as other monthly visits.

As was her mother's habit, she'd arranged to meet Anna at a restaurant for lunch, despite Anna's protest about cost. "Don't be silly. I come to London to treat myself. I spend all my time attending functions for your father and managing the family. Don't spoil my bit of fun. Of course I'll treat you if your job isn't paying enough."

Anna wondered if she would today, especially as she'd chosen a restaurant in Knightsbridge with two Michelin stars. As was also her mother's habit, she'd chosen a new restaurant, it would seem not to allow Anna any comfort of the familiar. After mentally running through the journey there – an unfamiliar Tube ride and unfamiliar station, confounding at the best of times – Anna opted for a taxi to drop her outside, which was another expense. And her outfit of course. There wasn't usually a dress code as such for the places her mother chose, except there was always a level of expectation, which could be more expense. This time Anna had chosen a tailored dress and jacket she sometimes used for work and she readied herself for a comment from her mother along the lines of "That's very functional, darling."

The driver, a talkative young man called Adam from Poland, whom she'd booked regularly over the last few years, told her a little more of his life's story while they crawled through traffic around Hyde Park. She was always grateful for it, distracting her from stressing about the impending unfamiliar environment under decidedly unfriendly fire from her mother. She was inattentive today though, gazing across the expanse of park, wondering if she could explore sometime with Jess. Perhaps they could visit the Serpentine Gallery? They could amble past the Albert Hall, take in a museum, then dine out somewhere quiet and unfussy.

She noticed the silence suddenly and realised Adam had stopped talking. He was peeping up at her in the mirror.

"Sorry, what did you say?" she said, coming to.

"I only mentioned that you were more relaxed today." His eyes crinkled in a smile.

"Oh." Indeed she was. She'd been dreaming of wandering arm in arm with Jess, taking it as easy and as far as Anna liked, simply enjoying the woman's company with no pressure.

"Actually, yes I am," Anna smiled at him, "for the first time in a long while."

"Suits you," he said. "You look radiant and happy."

"Thank you."

When they drew up to the kerb, she peeped outside. It was a gloomy day and she was surrounded by tall buildings, also grey and featureless in the subdued light. It was busy, the pavement bustling with pedestrians, and her heart rate rocketed for a moment.

"Would you like me to accompany you inside?" Adam asked. He had done so on several occasions.

"I'm," she took a deep breath, "I'm OK today, thank you." And she left her usual generous tip and readied herself for the short distance to the restaurant and the forbidding company of her mother.

From Anna's point of view, her mother had changed little in the last five years. She had the same sculpted hair style, swept around the sides. Still dyed. She wore smart clothing as if attending a function, even if taking a walk around a garden. What had changed was that Anna, unlike her siblings, could no longer compliment her on her appearance with confidence. She didn't keep up with fashion or frequent the couture shops she used to. She'd hazard the odd comment about a new brooch her mother sported here or a jacket there, but her mother would dismiss her judgement and Anna had given up offering an opinion, which was apparently also the wrong thing to do. At least her siblings weren't here today to engage in compliment one-upmanship.

Her mother rose from her seat in the middle of the restaurant as Anna approached with the guidance of the maître d'.

"Well, you made it." Her mother made it sound like she was expecting Anna to fail while at the same time not comprehending how difficult it had been for Anna to meet her. The phrase was accompanied with a look up and down of appraisal and a nod to the head waiter.

"Oh, you shouldn't have," her mother said to the maître d'.

"Pleasure, madam," he said, and he clicked his heels and left Anna to her mother.

Anna sloughed off her jacket onto the back of the chair. "He insisted," she said, defensively.

"Indeed," her mother replied. "I'm sure you're brave enough to make you own way across a dining room." Her mother laughed at her own joke, although it didn't sound pleasurable, and she sat in a way that appeared decorous if not comfortable.

"Well, you look beautiful," her mother said, which would have been heart-warming if it wasn't for the follow up, and there always was one, "even in an old outfit."

"Thank you," Anna said, taking the comment for what it was.

"It shows your lovely arms," her mother said, and she reached out and stroked along Anna's limbs. "Just like mine. Not a drop of Daddy in your appearance is there? Although god knows where you got your spirit from."

The word "spirit" covered all manner of sins, as far as her mother was concerned.

"I always think I take after Aunt Sophie," Anna offered, and she kicked herself. It was unnecessary, but also satisfying. Her mother's sister had been an actress and would never have called herself queer but loudly proclaimed she fell for someone's soul rather than their vessel.

"Yes, well," her mother said, and she flicked up the menu card. "Shall we order then we can catch up?" And the subject of Anna's aunt was firmly closed. "I'm tempted by the Galloway beef. Do you want the same, save you having to read the whole menu?"

"Actually I fancied something lighter."

"Do you mean cheaper?"

Anna opened her mouth.

"Because it's a set menu," her mother continued. "It's over a hundred pounds whatever you choose."

Anna closed her mouth.

"Oh, don't look like that darling. I said I would treat you."

"Thank you," Anna said, indebted, embarrassed and all the while wishing she had the hundred-plus pounds to spend on something else.

"I'll order two beef then," her mother said, putting the menu aside. "You should sell that flat darling and move back to Edinburgh. You'd make a killing and you could eat out with us all the time."

This was one of the most confusing aspects of her mother. She would belittle Anna, borderline despise her, then imply she should move nearer to see them more often. Anna had never been able to wrap her head around her mother's thought processes. Maybe she hoped Anna would change if she moved home.

"So, how are you?" her mother said. She waited less than fraction of a second before moving on with, "I saw Cameron the other day. He asked to be remembered to you."

Ah. That was it.

"Did he?" Anna said, failing to hide her irritation.

"He said he'd emailed."

"He did."

"He's single now, you know?"

"Yes, he mentioned that in his email."

"Next time you're home you should meet up. He's a catch."

Anna thought she'd like to catch Cameron about as much as she'd like to catch herpes. She could hear Pen cackle as she thought it.

"He's dying to get reacquainted," her mother continued. "I mean, I told him about your trouble, but he's still keen."

"How lovely."

"I would jump at the chance if I were you."

A waiter took their order, or at least Anna's mother's order for them both.

Without blinking, her mother continued. "It's not like beggars can be choosers, Anna. Life is passing you by." Her eyes flickered, regarding Anna up and down again. "You haven't even ventured out for new clothes in years. You might be oblivious to changes in the world, but I'm not. Yes, he does have dependents, you would have to put up with the two children staying sometimes, but he's considered a decent catch."

It was to her mother's credit that she'd seamlessly skipped ahead into cohabitation and mapping out Anna's future in Edinburgh without so much as blinking and made it seem natural and inevitable. Anna saw herself in a Georgian home, stuck inside during the day, Cameron returning with a briefcase at night, all very presentable, but another kind of prison. She'd had enough of those.

"Mother, Cameron might not be looking for someone. He said in his email they'd only recently decided on divorce."

"Don't be silly. A busy man like Cameron is lost without a wife, of course he'll be looking. And what's better than settling down with a friend."

"We were twelve when we were friends."

"I know." Her mother appeared to be smiling. "Your first boyfriend."

But not her first kiss. That had been with Daisy Miller and had been a much better introduction to romance than Cameron later offered. Anna was tempted to remind her mother loudly but decided to be braver and said, "I'm seeing someone anyway."

The waiter arrived with a bottle of wine as cool as her mother's reaction and poured a taster for them both.

"I'm sure it's fine," Anna said. "A small glass please."

It sounded like her mother was choking slightly on her sip.

"Thank you," her mother told the waiter icily. "So?" she added when the waiter had gone. "Tell me about him. It's been a long time since you've dated, hasn't it."

Despite the majority of her partners having been women, her mother always assumed a man.

"She's called Jess," Anna said.

"Oh?" her mother said. Such a small word, and yet it carried so much disapproval."

"We've just started seeing each other, but I like her very much."

"And what does this Jess do?"

It was funny how some people fixated on people's professions. Perhaps because her job was a source of ambivalence for Anna she shied away from talking about it.

"She works in publicity and has to travel around Europe, although she's hoping to be based in London for a little while."

"Hmm," her mother said, taking another sip of wine. "Publicity."

It wasn't law, medicine or politics. But at least it wasn't acting, so her mother seemed happy to remain silent on the matter.

"And," her mother swirled her glass around, "this Jess is OK with you being a hermit?"

A flush of annoyance warmed Anna's cheeks. "I'm not a hermit." She couldn't help saying it between gritted teeth. "I work. I have friends."

"Well, I suppose you're not quite that bad now. Is she aware of how restricted you are though? How much support you needed?"

"When did I trouble people?" Anna said, indignant. "I've been independent throughout all this."

"Oh, my dear, the number of times you've had to call on dear Penny."

"I return the favour many times over."

And it was galling how "that Penny" had become "dear Penny" ever since she'd procreated.

Anna paused and called up a version of herself who could handle her mother better, an armour.

"Jess is a wonderful woman," she said clearly, using all her training to keep her voice even. "I think the reason that I've fallen for her is because she realises people are different. What is difficult for her might be easy for someone else and vice versa, and I don't feel inadequate with her. She acts as if the to and fro of helping one another is part of life, rather than charity."

"Lower your voice, Anna," her mother growled. "We're not in the theatre now."

And with a simple phrase her mother pierced her armour in one.

Anna's rage was building. "I need the loo," she said, standing. "Could you tell me where they are please?"

"Not a clue dear. I'm sure you'll find them, being so independent that is."

And another blow. She must have visibly flinched.

"Good god, Anna," her mother tutted. "They're over there." Her mother pointed.

Anna slammed the cubicle door behind her, leant back and closed her eyes. It had deteriorated rapidly today. There was always some source of contention and lunch was often fraught, but this was special today and for once Anna was unwilling to let it go.

Perhaps it was because she'd had a glimpse of what it was like to trust and love again and be filled right up with the self-confidence that brings. To feel like a special, whole and desired human being. To be touched. Craved. Her heart leapt as she remembered her outburst to Jess on their walk along the canal, when Anna had let out a desperate plea that she wanted to be touched again, and Jess had caught her and desired her and lavished her with passion and kindness. Anna had stepped beyond her safe world and the rewards had been heavenly.

She took a deep breath, realising what a source of comfort and strength meeting Jess had become. She thought of Jess wrapped around her in bed last night and although only imagined Jess was a soothing presence.

Anna resorted to vocal exercises to reassure herself that her voice would remain even and when she returned, her mother sat bolt upright at the table, as relaxed or uptight as she always was. Anna was guessing a modicum of contrition though, and she guessed correctly.

"Anna, darling," her mother said, quietly. "I'm sorry we're arguing like this. Please sit down."

Anna could feel eyes on them and obliged.

"I know you haven't found it easy, but it's frustrating to see you struggle and working so hard. You would have it much easier if you came home. We could help you. All any parent wants is to see their child safe and thriving."

But it would take Anna away from everything she loved.

"Why do you insist on living here?" her mother continued. "You obviously can't act anymore and being near the West End is no longer an advantage." She reached across the table to hold Anna's arm. It felt cool and foreign.

"You need to live in the real world. You've hidden away although John Boyd is dead. It's ludicrous. It's time to stop locking yourself away in the fantasy of acting, or a book, or literally in your aunt's flat. Life is passing you by and you're oblivious. Did you even know your sister was trying to get pregnant again?" Her mother looked at her as if it was all obvious. "If you can't cope with London, come back to Edinburgh where we can help you."

The most annoying thing was that her mother was right. Life had been passing her by and Anna did feel older and out of touch and oblivious. And it hurt.

But leave London? That would be giving up on that girl who moved there at eighteen to be the woman she wasn't allowed to become at home. She was so close to giving up. And she silently thanked Jess. Perhaps another time she would have caved and gone back with her tail between her legs. But returning home, marrying someone like Cameron, yes that would be another kind of prison, only one her mother approved of.

"I'm not moving. This is my home," Anna said, more tactfully.

33

Anna had been home five minutes when the buzzer went. She nearly didn't hear it above the chatter on the radio. She'd come home, switched on Radio 4, turned up the volume and tried to concentrate on the concerns of a small rural community in a farming programme rather than become preoccupied with her own. The buzzer was insistent and when she peered at the small screen she saw the curls of Penny and smaller blonde head of Bibs and let them in without a word.

Penny put a subdued Bibs down on the rug, leaving her to suck at a small blanket comforter and paw a picture book. She came over to Anna and silently reached up on tip toes and gave her a hug. When she leant back she held Anna's hands and raised her eyebrows in sympathy.

"I knew you were seeing your mother today," Pen said. "Need to download? Have another hug? Punch someone?"

"Thanks, Pen," Anna sighed a laugh. "Could have been worse."

"Oh. One of those."

"What do you mean?"

"That it must have been shit, but you're trying to look on the bright side and not feel too sorry for yourself."

"I have a lot to be grateful for, including you. I don't ever want to lose sight of that." She was in danger of spiralling down and glad Penny had invited herself over. Her friend stretched up and gave her another hug and it was what she needed.

After a good squeeze Pen said, offhand, "Well, if it wasn't so bad, how about you make me a coffee?"

"Trying to keep me occupied?"

"No, just bloody lazy."

Anna let her go. "Fine, you indolent oaf, I'll get you a coffee."

She turned the radio lower so that she could hear Penny speak over the background noise of sheep in the countryside and filled the kettle. When she leant back on the kitchen top to chat she found Penny perched on a stool, her body rigid and a tense expression on her face. Pen was particularly attentive today and Anna wondered why. It seemed silly. Anna had been robust for months and with the treat of meeting Jess recently, she hadn't felt better in years.

"I'm fine," Anna said with a smile.

"You're never fine after seeing your mother and neither should you be. The woman could undermine the pope's confidence and sense of place in the world."

"I'm OK," Anna replied, but at the same time she crossed her arms and wished she didn't feel like someone had minced up her insides and jumped up and down on them while making her watch, utterly pathetic at being able to do nothing about it. "Really," Anna said with a smile at Penny who watched her like a hawk. "I'm good."

Penny's shoulders relaxed, a little. "OK," she sighed, and she shuffled, getting comfortable on her stool. "Go on then. Tell me, how is the vicious old bag?"

"Pen!" Anna tutted out a laugh. "She is still my mother."

"Are you sure though? You could get a DNA test then disown her if the results are favourable."

"I have her arms apparently."

"Well give them back and be done with her."

Anna sniggered. It was one of the things she loved about Penny – she said out loud Anna's worst thoughts so that she didn't have to feel bad about them. It was always her first step to being able to think about her mother with any equanimity.

"Were the ugly sisters there?"

And Anna smiled again at Penny's name for her brother and sister.

"No. Celeste is in Edinburgh more than London these days and Sebastian's time is planned to the minute and full until Christmas."

"That was a blessing at least," Penny snapped.

"Thank you," Anna said.

"For what?"

"Bitching on my behalf."

Penny giggled at last. "That's what friends are for. Now where's my coffee?"

Anna poured two mugs and filled a beaker of milk for Bibs and sliced some apple. She handed the toddler a bowl on the rug. "There you go, lovely," she said, leaning down, and Bibs reached up to hold Anna's cheeks. "Banna," she said, then was distracted by the fruit and began gnawing at a slice.

"She's quiet," Anna said, shuffling onto a stool beside Pen.

"Teething I think. Her cheeks are rosy and she's chewing absolutely bloody everything. I thought having pets was bad, but I've got tiny human teeth marks on the corner of all the books."

Anna smiled, still raw from meeting her mother and grateful for their company.

Penny started talking but Anna was distracted by the radio. The agriculture magazine had finished and the programme had changed to a culture show.

"That's strange," Anna said. "That sounded like Jess."

"What's that?" Penny sat up.

"On the radio."

They both listened a moment. The presenter was talking. "*That was Jessica Lambert at the French premiere of the latest* Atlassia *film...*"

"Oh," Anna said. "I probably just caught the name Jessica."

The presenter continued. "*...an ostensibly superhero series which has been a surprise success in the last few years, gaining popular and critical plaudits. This is what Ms Lambert had to say.*"

"*The parallels between our own world and* Atlassia *and the desperation of the character I think resonate with teens and young adults...*"

"But that sounds exactly like her," Anna said. "How weird."

Penny didn't move.

"Don't you think it sounds like her?"

Anna thought the similarity remarkable with the rich depth of the voice and slips into gentle Birmingham accent. "It could be her, honestly."

"*It certainly chimed with me,*" the voice continued on the radio. "*Dismissing the series as fantasy belittles the anxieties of a generation. Perhaps if the concerns of the young were taken seriously the* Atlassia *phenomenon might be less of a surprise.*"

Anna laughed. "That's exactly how Jess speaks. Isn't that odd, Pen?"

Her friend hadn't moved.

"Penny?"

Anna's body reacted before her brain made the final realisation. A chill settled over her skin and then seeped inside until she froze.

"Penny. What's going on?" she said, nauseous at her suspicions.

Penny had opened her mouth but no words came out.

"I'm thinking all kinds of things right now. Please could you tell me what's going on?" Anna said, clutching her hands together.

At last words came from Penny. "I hoped she'd told you." They were quiet words. Awful words.

"Told me what, Pen?" Anna said, her agitation growing.

"I know why she hasn't. I can understand, but–"

"Just bloody tell me," Anna spat.

Pen drew herself up with a deep breath. "That is her on the radio. She's Jessica Lambert."

"The woman from the *Atlassia* films that you're mad about?"

"Yes."

"An actress?"

"Yes." Penny sank lower with every answer.

Anna sat stunned. The chill had made her body numb. Even her head tingled with creeping dread.

"Are you telling me I've been seeing one of the most high-profile movie stars of the moment?"

"Yes."

"And everyone," her voice broke, "and I mean everyone has known, except me?" Her voice was getting louder, but she couldn't stop.

Penny was looking down. She couldn't meet Anna's gaze. "Yes," she said, almost inaudible.

Anna stood up and turned away, her arms wrapped around her instinctively. Why hadn't Jess told her? Why had she hidden it when she must have known everyone else realised?

"You must think that I'm a colossal idiot," Anna said in one breath before the humiliation and anger in her chest had a chance to erupt.

"No, nothing of the sort." Penny's voice was charged with hurt, but Anna couldn't stop.

"Good god. Did Zehra know? Have you all been laughing behind my back?"

"No, she didn't realise," Penny said quickly. "She had her suspicions but didn't twig who she was so I left it."

"But didn't you think it pertinent to tell me?" Anna swung round, hot tears swelling in her eyes.

Pen flung her hands onto her head. "Oh god. I didn't know what to do. She's seemed like the best thing to happen to you in years."

"What?" Anna spat in disbelief. "Letting me fall for someone who would remind me of everything I've lost? When I find it profoundly difficult to trust anyone, I fall for someone who can't even tell me the truth about who she is. Really? Is that the best thing that's happened to me? Because it's sounds pretty shit at the moment."

Just when she was starting to feel normal again, as if she was re-entering the world to enjoy life, to trust people and be free again.

"Why didn't she tell me? How the hell did I not know?"

Pen looked sheepish.

"Have I become that out of touch?"

"You avoid everything about theatre and film. I've watched you, when we're on the Underground, you never even look at the posters. I burble on about films and TV and hot actresses all the time, but you never really listen."

Ouch.

"Jess said she didn't realise how far things would go," Penny said, an earnest and fearful look on her face. "I believe her. It sounds like she was at the end of her tether and needed a break and you were the only person in London who could help her – as a human, not a superstar. I think she genuinely needed a break, and then–"

"For christ's sake, Pen. I didn't recognise her because I'm a reclusive middle-aged woman who's letting life pass her by and who is oblivious from being too fucking scared to go out and trust anyone."

And the rage that had been building all day flamed through Anna until her face flushed red.

"I know I know I know I know," Penny murmured with her head in her hands. "But I think she's genuine about you. She seems nice, nothing like I'd expected. I assumed she was some lucky brat who'd made it big. I'd never seen her interviewed – avoided it so I wouldn't hate her – but she's lovely."

Anna didn't want to hear it. "I'm a bloody fool."

"Anna you mustn't–"

"I spent days with her, letting her in. I…" Anna hugged herself feeling suddenly more vulnerable. "I slept with her and I had no idea who she was."

"God, I understand, I really do, but please try and see it from her point of view. She didn't realise you'd been an actress and it would be an issue. You hadn't told her that either."

"There's a difference to once having been an actress, which might come up in conversation one day, and being the mega movie star of the moment."

"I know." Penny had her hands up. "But I don't think she meant to hurt you."

Penny talked on, but Anna didn't hear anymore. She replayed meeting Jess over in her head. It made sense now. A hounded superstar. Everyone's attitude on the Tube. Jesus, people must have been taking photos. Anna was probably in several all over the Internet. Already wounded from meeting her mother, she wanted to curl up in a ball and block out how ridiculous she'd been.

"Did you laugh?"

"What?" Penny said, timid.

"When you met her? When I was out of the flat? Did you have a good chuckle when you met your crush and about how I had no idea?"

"Nothing of sort," Penny said desperately. "We both felt god awful about the situation."

"Well, how nice that you had each other for comfort."

"Please, Anna. This isn't like you."

"What isn't?" Anna said, glaring at Penny. "Being stupid. Not being able to inhabit the world you do? Being so oblivious and out of touch that I fail to recognise one of the most famous actresses and fall for her. Tell me, exactly what am I meant to be like? Because, I don't know any more. Who am I now?"

Penny sagged. "I didn't know what to do. Neither of us did."

Anna looked up when she heard a quiet whimper from the other side of the room. It was followed by a louder cry.

"Oh Bibs, darling," Penny said, getting off her seat and rushing to the toddler. "Don't worry sweetheart. Everything's OK."

But it wasn't.

"I'm sorry, Bibs," Anna said, the anger still tight in her voice. "I think you'd better go," she said to Penny, her tone harsh. "I don't want to upset her."

Penny picked up the girl and brought her over. Anna swiped at her eyes and sniffed. She could barely cope with Penny in this close proximity. She wanted her gone.

Anna gritted her teeth. "Sorry, lovely girl," she said as gently as she could. She clasped Bib's small hand and brought it to her lips. "I love you, sweet pea. I'm upset about something but you've done nothing wrong and I'll see you soon."

Anna had to turn away, unable to face her friend.

34

Anna locked the door, pulled down the blinds and curled up on the bed, simultaneously seething and protecting herself from the world. But as the light faded and night fell, a part of her still craved Jess.

She had called and Anna left the phone unanswered, replying later with a curt message of feeling unwell. She used every excuse not to see her the following days, busy at work, emergency with Bibs, all true to an extent. She avoided Penny but babysat Bibs, the handover at the door stiff with unresolved issues.

Anna threw herself into work, accepting a heavier schedule with extra classes at the office and even booking a one-on-one session as a favour to an old RSC pal and director to fill her schedule. Anna didn't want a minute free to think about Jess. Except at the same time she was hungry with curiosity about the mega movie star.

She sat at the kitchen island one evening, the orange beams of the setting sun glowing through the windows. She closed her eyes. It was impossible to reconcile her impression of Jess with the actress that Penny had lustfully regaled for years or the earnest young woman on the radio who been drowned out by a screaming crowd, or the voice that Anna caught on an advert that purred and ended with a coquettish laugh.

Jess had seemed so down to earth. Real. Anna had known more than her fair share of high-paid, high-profile actors and they were a varied bunch, phenomenal egotists to surprisingly ordinary folk, but none had been as vivid as Jess. She could be quiet one moment, then exude life and vivacity the next. Her connection to her family was so wonderfully ordinary and extraordinary at the same time and Anna recalled Jess so completely that it was like she was in the room. Then she evaporated as Anna tried to superimpose the young star who Penny said was currently plastered over every billboard in London.

Anna called up a search on her phone. Jess had apparently been acting from the age of seventeen. That was young. There were plenty of younger child actors who travelled with their parents, but Jess had left school and home to be on set – quite a transition. She read on, of Jess's stratospheric rise to fame over the next seven years and the demon of envy and tantrum-toddler of hurt got the better of her and Anna stopped reading the article.

Besides, it seemed wrong to be researching Jess, without her knowing that Anna could. Then the humiliation would burn through Anna again and she would remember all the time she spent with Jess not knowing who she was and she went to bed, her body in knots.

She had an early start the next morning on a Shaftesbury Avenue that was filled with freezing fog and a theatre she'd frequented many times as an actress and audience member. She hadn't visited since leaving the profession and took a taxi to the front door where she hesitated, wishing she hadn't been so eager to fill her schedule and accept this reminder of her old world.

She stood in front of the building, her breath billowing in the cold air, the theatre exactly the same as she remembered – the grand canopy that circled the building, the row of double doors with brass handles into the foyer, even the weight of the door and the force with which it swung out of her hands and closed behind her. She remembered it all with reverence and a sadness washed over her as she stepped inside. The theatre might be the same, but how changed Anna was since last being here. And for a moment she was unsure of herself in a new way. She'd become accustomed to her fears and limitations and her new identity as voice coach – the Anna who scurried home at night. But here she was, on her old turf, something she would have abhorred not so long ago.

She'd changed and was in flux with Jess's entry into her life, tempted out of her existence but into what? She was floundering with the revelation of Jess's fame but also uncertain of her own place in the world.

"Darling!" came a voice.

It was dark inside the foyer and Anna took a moment for her eyes to adjust and make out the small figure who marched towards her, arms outstretched.

"I am so pleased to see you again," Deborah, the director, said. "It's been far too long."

Anna held on to her shoulder bag with one hand and reached to hug her old friend with the other. When Deborah leant away she clung to Anna's shoulders and gazed at her.

"How are you, my dear?" she said, concern written on the older woman's features.

"I'm well, thank you," Anna said with a smile.

"I feel god awful for not keeping in touch."

"Please don't. I know what it's like. I imagine you've been busy."

"Goodness, yes." Deborah hesitated. "And how've you been, since…?"

"OK," Anna said, nodding. "Busy with coaching," she added, avoiding the obvious.

"Good", Deborah said. "You know, you come highly recommended."

"Really?" Anna didn't need to politely query this. She knew how well received her tuition was.

"And, actually, once your name had been mentioned with your change of career, I remember how much you used to informally tutor on stage. Do you remember that production of *Much Ado* in Stratford? Such fun that play. Almost ruined by that Ryan fellow. I can't believe how many extra rehearsals you did with him, just so the man could wrap his tongue around Shakespeare. I vowed never to work with big film stars after that, but," she sighed, "here we are."

She released Anna's shoulders and took her arm and turned towards to the auditorium.

"I also trust your discretion." Deborah chuckled. "The number of people in this business I think are here solely for the gossip is staggering, but I always remembered your respect for others above everything else."

"I always hoped they would repay the favour," Anna replied.

"Oh, darling, I never had you down as a fool."

Anna flinched. It would have been amusing another day. "I didn't say that I expected it to be true."

"Very wise, dear." They sauntered towards the doors that led into the stalls. "Anyway, I'd like to make use of your coaching skills and your discretion please." Deborah paused. "I've had another damn celluloid wonder foisted on me. Not without talent, but the girl's never been on the professional stage and when this place is packed to the rafters no-one will be able to hear a thing."

"OK," Anna nodded. "Understood."

"At least her voice has some oomph so you have plenty to work with. It's not a hopeless case by any means. But good god she needs some work. But I'd prefer that this remained on the QT please. We need bums on seats and that's the reason she's here."

Anna nodded.

"No doubt you've heard of her. She seems to be everywhere at the moment. Can't say I've seen the films but everyone talks of nothing but Jessica Lambert."

Anna almost tripped.

"Sorry?" Anna stuttered. "Did you say Jessica Lambert?"

"You have heard of her, haven't you? Not been hiding away that much surely?"

"No... I... Yes, I know her."

The warmth had drained from Anna's body and her heart thudded in her chest.

"Would you like to start?" Deborah pointed towards the doors. "She's waiting on stage."

"I..." Anna was reeling from the news. How the hell had this happened? Anna hadn't read anything to suggest that Jess did stage work. What was the film star doing on Shaftesbury Avenue?

"Are you OK?" Deborah said, peering up at Anna.

"Could you give me moment please," Anna said, struggling. "I could do with the loo before we begin."

"Of course. Shall I get you a cup of tea as well?"

"Please," Anna gasped.

She put her hand out for support and her fingertips found the velvet wallpaper that had plastered the interior for decades and she made her way round to the toilets and automatically turned right into the ladies. The room of cubicles was empty and she leant on the long marble top of basins and let her head drop.

She wasn't ready for this. She still didn't know how she felt. There were so many conflicting issues, but the anger was always there and it flamed up again. Why the hell was she in this position?

Then she wanted to go home, lock all the doors, avoid this humiliation, build up the walls and not set foot beyond her carefully controlled world again and pretend she'd never met Jess.

But none of that was fuelled by anxiety. She blushed with anger and embarrassment but it wasn't fear. She shook her head. She wasn't going back in her box again. She was not going to be set back by anyone else ever again.

She glanced up at the mirror and at the image there. Blonde, almost shoulder length hair with a slight wave now she'd let it grow a little, brighter eyes since she'd indulged last week in having her eyelashes and brows tinted. What did Jess want with this woman? The woman Anna was no longer sure of. This woman who looked quite frankly enraged.

Jess had unexpectedly turned up in her life, enticed her beyond her usual boundaries, charmed and filled her heart then loved her body like it had been craving for years, and Jess was on stage a few metres away. Anna could feel the pull of her presence and the warmth that sensation always gave her. She mentally batted the compulsion away. How could she know anything about Jessica Lambert and what she wanted?

Anna looked at the woman in the mirror again. Right now, she didn't even know who she was.

The question was, did she want to find out?

35

Jess milled about the stage, waiting for the director and their morning session. She muttered lines and paced across the stage, trying to keep warm in the old theatre where the ancient heating was shuddering into action and struggling against the frost outside. Deborah had gone to receive a friend who was going to assist in today's training after the director had torn out her hair at Jess's inability to reach the gods.

The door at the back of the stalls whispered open and shushed back and forth several times before it settled shut. A woman in a dark tailored dress and coat had entered and something about the figure's walk immediately alerted Jess. She tried to peer around the columns to the rear of the stalls. Strawberry blonde hair. Careful elegant stride. With every familiar step, Jess's heart sank.

The woman climbed the steps onto the stage, left her shoulder bag on the table set aside for scripts and coffees, removed her gloves, pinching one finger free at a time, and only then did she turn to face Jess, her face pale and eyes icy.

"Anna," Jess whispered.

Jess's whole body was leaden with dread. It was as if the entire building was collapsing upon her.

Anna took several slow deliberate steps forward, each accompanied by a click of her high heel on the stage. She stopped within touching distance but her stance invited no such intimacy – chin tilted up, shoulders rigid, hands beside her hips with a single finger twitching.

"So, you're Jessica Lambert," Anna said, her voice colder than the chilly auditorium.

Anna already knew. With desperate realisation Jess's mouth fell open and all she could do was stare at the striking woman who appraised her with such disdain.

"I…" Jess couldn't get the words out. She'd been practising for days, all kinds of approaches and scenarios, over and over. None had been ideal. No explanation could appease. Every day Anna's excuses gave Jess more time to prepare, while she tried not to agonise over why Anna couldn't see her. But here Anna was, and she already knew, which made it ten times worse.

"I asked to see you alone," Anna said, you could almost see the chill in her breath, "to save embarrassment for us both."

"Anna, I didn't know…I don't know how to…"

"What? What didn't you know?" Anna's fingers curled into fists at her sides.

Jess cursed her brain for seizing. All those scenarios that she'd practised, they jumbled together making no sense and tying her tongue.

"Enlighten me," Anna snapped. Jess twitched at her voice, so saturated with resentment.

"I…" Her head throbbed as if all those jumbled words were pounding inside her skull, trying to get out. If she could just have a moment to untie them all.

"Did it not occur to you to mention the precise nature of your job? Your status? Your obvious fame?" Anna tilted her head to the side, eyes narrowed as she looked down.

Jess opened her mouth, but she couldn't even breathe.

"At what point, exactly, did you think it appropriate to explain what was so obvious to everyone else?" Anna glared at her, waiting. "Do you think that was fair?"

The words and thoughts locked together and no matter how much Jess willed an explanation none would come.

"Say something!" Anna shouted.

"I'm sorry," Jess blurted out. She recoiled at Anna's words.

"For what?"

Jess took another step back. It had taken every effort to vocalise that feeling.

"I'm sorry," she said quietly again. "I'm sorry. I'm sorry. I'm sorry."

"For lying?"

"For…." Jess wished several times over that she'd never been a film star, never been famous. She wished that she'd been on a London Underground carriage for any other reason so that Anna could have taken her in, flirted, walked and loved together with no complication.

"I'm sorry for how this has happened. I wish it could have been another way."

Anna took a step forward and loomed over Jess. "But not sorry for anything else?" She seemed incredulous. "That when I took you to my flat, you didn't explain exactly why someone might be following you or why people were photographing you?"

"I..." Jess wrapped her arms around herself.

"There are photos of us all over the Internet. Apparently there are multiple views of us on the London Underground, you with your face buried in my chest."

"Oh god, no. I didn't know. I've been avoiding social media."

"Perhaps you could have explained the next day, when you'd had a chance to gather your thoughts over a cooked breakfast and enjoyed my hospitality."

The guilt bit hard at that.

"Or perhaps you could have worked it into our chat at the park?"

All those lovely times.

"I didn't realise why."

"Why what?"

"Please," Jess begged. She just needed some time to gather her thoughts into coherent sentences. "I didn't understand why you didn't recognise me. I thought perhaps I wasn't as famous as I feared. I didn't realise," she paused, "you were hiding too."

The contempt on Anna's face relented a little. "At first, I will give you that."

"You didn't explain straight away," Jess said quietly. "Do you think I would have treated you differently if you'd told me?"

"What? That I'm a sorry recluse, a has-been and spectacularly behind the times? Yes, most people do treat me differently when they find out," Anna snapped.

"But I might not have done."

The wind seemed to have abated in Anna's sails. "We'll never know," she said, voice clipped.

"I've been thinking about this," Jess said quietly, "constantly over the last few days. All of it. And," she couldn't help a sob or the warm tear that ran down her cheek, "you're right, I'll never know if you would have treated me the same way, and I've been kicking myself that I didn't give you the chance earlier."

Anna glared at her in challenge.

"Would you have taken me in?" Jess asked. "Would we have flirted and chatted in the same way?" She couldn't help the smile on her lips as she recalled. "Because it was lovely. No-one has treated me like that in years."

Anna's appearance remained stony.

"Haven't you experienced that?" Jess offered. "Didn't you have the same, when people want to be seen with you? When no-one talks to you for your company anymore."

"I was never as ridiculously famous as you. It wasn't a problem."

Ouch. Jess drew breath at the comment but tried to carry on with her thoughts of several days.

"Staying with you was the first time anyone wanted my company for a long while. The first time I relaxed and put aside every mask. It was so refreshing to enjoy company as myself and have that person enjoy me too. That is so rare for me. I'm sorry I indulged." Her throat strangled. "I thought you'd change if I told you, then I was too swept up to stop."

Anna closed her eyes.

How would Anna have changed? Perhaps not in the way Jess had first feared.

"I have worn so many masks over the years, playing a role, trying to fit in," Jess said. "It's always disconcerting to see how people respond to them all, and even more when they find the person I am underneath. You saw me, just Jess, and I was scared you wouldn't see me for who I really am anymore or, worse, wouldn't want to see the real me anymore," Jess said gently.

Anna's eyes snapped open. "A liar? Someone I can't trust? Someone I don't know at all?"

And Jess's head dropped.

Anna seemed to rein in her anger. "I can understand," she said. "A little. I do empathise with wanting a break from people's preconceptions." As ever, Jess admired Anna's articulation and ability to think on her feet. "But christ," Anna said more sharply, "you should have told me before you slept with me." And she folded her arms protectively over her chest.

Jess felt a ton of guilt and regret and closed her eyes, trying to keep her thoughts clear. "I didn't sleep with you, we slept together, and we slept together thinking we might not see each other again. Would it have mattered then?"

"What?"

"When I left? When I didn't think I'd be back in London? A one-night stand. Would it have mattered then?"

Anna was silent.

"I didn't know that you were once an actress," Jess said quietly. "I still don't know everything about you."

Anna looked away over the seating in the auditorium.

"I'm not trying to say what I've done is right," Jess offered. "That I feel so bad about it makes it obvious it wasn't. I didn't plan to mislead you but, at the same time, I doubt I would have met you any other way. And..." she gulped, "I really want to know you more than anything."

Anna snapped her head round. "We'll never know if we would have hit it off any other way."

Jess's shoulders slumped. Anna wasn't listening.

"As soon as I heard I could stay in London I was going to tell you," Jess said desperately.

Anna turned on her heel. "But you didn't," she said loud over her shoulder.

"Penny…" Jess stopped herself. She didn't want to get Anna's friend into trouble.

"Oh, don't worry," Anna said, rifling through her bag on the table. "You're not dropping Penny in it. She was there when I found out. I heard you on the radio, recognised your voice, and I looked like a complete and utter fool."

"I'm sorry," Jess murmured. "I'm so sorry."

She could have screamed. Her brain was still tied in knots of regret and at the same time clinging on to the knowledge that they never would have become involved otherwise.

"All I can say," Jess started, "is that I've been trying to tell you all week. Even though I knew you would be hurt and I risked not seeing you again. I value honesty and truth. In this business I've seen so little and it's worn me down. I hate that I've got into this mess with you, misled you and ended up lying." She was breathing hard. "I hoped you'd understand how it happened. I hoped you would still want to see me when I explained."

Anna stopped, turned and seemed to look right inside her. "Like I said, now we'll never know."

36

Anna could hear her mother's voice in her own and the chilling realisation forced her to retreat. She rattled around in her shoulder bag and checked her phone as an excuse to distance herself from Jess. She hated what she was doing to her; at the same time the humiliation had sharpened her tongue. And that was before she let herself acknowledge the hurt. She had been falling for Jess fast and cutting her away was leaving her sore and resentful.

"Well," she said, turning to Jess. "I've been paid for a job," she carried on, not wanting to acknowledge the pain, "and apparently you are running out of time, so I suggest you take advantage of my expertise."

There was slightest nod from Jess and the younger woman cleared her throat and said, "OK".

Jess's voice was thick with remorse. Anna could tell she was deeply affected. There was truth in every word Jess said and the way she spoke. That was the galling thing. Jess seemed so transparent and honest, with an almost naïve enthusiasm and openness at times, then there had been the moments she'd clammed up. In retrospect, there was an honesty to those too. You knew when she was hiding something, when something caused her too much anxiety to speak, and Jess's plea for Anna to understand how it had all happened made its target at last and Anna felt the simultaneously painful and soothing sense of it hitting home.

But then Anna knew nothing of what Jess left unsaid about her life, this other possible persona. And now Anna was adrift again, not knowing how to reconcile Jess with Jessica Lambert.

"Who are you?" she whispered.

"Sorry?" Jess said, and the warm familiar voice full of heartbreak pulled at Anna's being. The temptation to walk over and throw her arms around Jess and tell her that she understood was enormous. Moments with Jess had made Anna happier than she'd been in years but, and the "but" was so loud, the humiliation was overpowering. It made Anna weak at the knees and any temptation to run to Jess was cut down. Anna steadied herself on the table and the walls went up again.

"So," she said, straightening. "Perhaps we should pick a scene with which you've had difficulty." So professional. Business-like. Cool. "Could you read one for me?" Anna said.

"Erm," Jess wandered to the table and flicked through a script that had been lying there. "Actually, the scene I auditioned with Jonathon is the worst," she said, her movements slow and tentative. "It's silly. I mean, Deborah likes the way I perform it, she thinks the emotion is spot on, but it has the largest vocal range."

"Well, let's start with that to see where the difficulties lie," Anna said, crossing her arms and preparing to listen. "Could you read both parts please?"

Jess handed Anna the open script and took centre stage. She talked through the dialogue and described the stage direction as Anna followed the lines on paper.

"OK," Anna interrupted. "Those few lines are enough to work with." She put the script on the table. "Act it through and I'll supply Jonathon's lines."

"You know the play?" Jess said, her eyes wide with surprise.

"You've read it through. I should have the lines."

"That's fast."

"I was a quick study."

Jess hesitated and Anna could tell her silence was filled with guilt.

They took their positions, Jess wandering downstage towards the audience and Anna hanging back, upstage right.

She breathed down to her belly. "When did it begin?" Anna said it with her full power and menace. She didn't have to dig deep for either.

Jess twitched and looked over her shoulder, her shape silhouetted against a spotlight. "After you'd left," Jess said weakly.

"How soon after?" Anna shot back, her voice both strong and smooth. No matter how much missing acting pained her, she always found using her voice in sessions satisfying, like taking out a beloved old instrument and finding you could still play a sweet tune.

"Not straight away," Jess stuttered.

Anna prowled down stage. "Was it when the others returned?"

"No," Jess said, inching away, bracing herself. "Not even then."

"Was it..." Anna softened her delivery with hope, "when you thought I was dead."

"No," Jess whispered. She paused and the tension that generated even without an audience was astonishing. "It was when I heard you were coming back."

Anna froze. She could feel the emotion radiating from Jess. Her fear, the sense of being cornered, dangerous and all at once ready to break. She was drawn into the scene, into that sublime other world when disbelief was suspended. The thrill of it. Her energy in it. Her awe of Jess's portrayal. It gave Anna goose bumps.

"Let's stop there," Anna said, afraid of what she felt, the simmering admiration and more. Jess turned and waited. Anna didn't catch her expression and didn't want to stare too long in case she gave away her own.

"OK," she said, stroking a ribbon of hair away from her face. "I see what Deborah means. We need to open up your whole body if you're going to be heard."

Jess came forward but didn't speak.

"You don't have much time," Anna warned. "So a trick that will get you a long way is to speak clearly. You will find the audience appreciates it no end."

Jess opened her mouth and hesitated. "I'm not sure I can play the character like that."

"I don't mean to enunciate to within an inch of the queen. Simply make sure you say every word."

Jess put her hands on her hips and looked to the ceiling. Anna didn't think it in animosity, more in consideration. "I'll have to slow her down a little."

"Is that in keeping with the character? Can you see her as someone who speaks carefully? Clearly?"

"Actually yes," Jess nodded enthusiastically.

"OK, see how that flies with Deborah," Anna said. "Now. About getting more power. What warm up exercises and training do you do?"

Jess hesitated. "Not much to be honest."

"Do you mean none?" Anna snapped.

"I've picked up the odd exercise over the years but lately," she shrugged, "I do several read-throughs out loud in my trailer before we shoot so I'm used to the right words coming out. That's about it."

"That's not going to cut it here," Anna said, too sharp. "You're battling with an old auditorium where the acoustics are variable, with an audience shuffling and sometimes the noise of traffic will intrude."

"I realise that now," Jess said, in a voice so little, Anna silently reprimanded herself. Jess seemed woefully unprepared for a role in theatre.

"Then start," Anna said. "You will feel some of the benefits straight away, so don't put it off any longer."

Jess nodded.

"Right, let's loosen you up and remind your muscles that you don't just talk with your mouth but your whole body."

Anna took off her coat and slung it over the back of a chair by the table and took centre stage. "Follow me," she said facing Jess, before modelling some exercises to stretch the ribcage and loosen up the facial muscles.

"Say your name," Anna ordered as they faced each other and Jess complied.

"Louder this time. Breath in and use your chest."

Jess replied with more clarity.

"Good," Anna said. "Now breathe in using your stomach. Lower the diaphragm and let the air fill your whole body. Say your name."

Jess attempted to inhale down low, Anna could tell, but it lacked strength when she uttered her name.

"No," Anna snapped. "You're not getting the air down deep enough." She stepped forward. "Don't open your ribs. Push that stomach out."

Jess tried again, but Anna could hear the lack of power.

"Here," she said exasperated, and she placed her palm on Jess's stomach. It was almost as if it burned, the sudden touch on her lover's body. She snatched her hand away, irritated at the reminder of that heated touch. "Breath to there," she said loudly, stepping away annoyed.

"Jess!" came out loud and strong.

"Good," Anna said. "You have a great voice, naturally very strong and smooth, but these exercises will remind you that you have many ways to speak in your repertoire. They're all at your disposal. Use them appropriately." Anna said it all quickly, the compliment and advice, as if she couldn't stand to spend any more time talking to Jess in case she soften, or break, or rage. She didn't know which would come. "Now turn to the audience. We're going to work on projecting to every single person and throwing that voice out there." Anna stormed down stage, Jess's lack of preparation and that heated touch aggravating her.

"OK," she spat, every ounce of irritation evident. "Lift your arms, open your lungs with a deep breath," Anna breathed in too, "and throw out your arms and your name to the stalls."

Jess's effort was pitiful. She hadn't given anything like her full effort. The arms flicked forwards with the resolve of a piece of limp seaweed.

"Good god," Anna said. "What the hell was that?"

It was like Jess had become smaller beside her.

"You don't have time for half-hearted efforts," Anna said. "Try again."

If anything, Jess's second attempt was poorer.

Anna put a hand to her hip and gestured to the balconies with her other. "This place is going to be packed with hundreds of people out there all paying to see you. How on earth is someone in the stalls let alone the gods going to hear you with that?"

Jess lifted her arms half height and seemed to freeze. Anna could hear her breathing. It became more rapid, rasping short breaths, then deeper as if Jess was on the verge of panicking.

"OK, stop," Anna said, half irritated, half concerned. "Is there something I need to know?"

Jess didn't say anything, but her hyperventilation abated at least.

"What's wrong?" Anna said, quieter but her tone still unsympathetic.

"I…" Jess had to stop and take a deep lungful of air. "I'm scared."

"What?"

"I'm petrified."

"Why?"

"The audience," Jess said, her words clipped as she tried to breathe.

"What the…? You get stage fright?" Anna said, stepping back in disbelief.

"It's why I haven't done much theatre, only film."

"But…? Why?"

"The thought of all those people." Jess looked up at her, those big brown eyes full of trepidation. "Real life people. Unpredictable people."

Was she trembling?

"All of them watching," Jess continued. "Anything could happen and I wouldn't get a second take. They could laugh, shout, or storm the stage. I'm terrified," she said in a gasp.

Anna was struck quiet. The remembrance of her own stage fright filled her body with an empathetic shiver. She would be the last one to belittle and dismiss Jess's fear and although she couldn't trust Jess right now, she believed this.

"Then, why on earth are you doing this?" Anna whispered.

Jess was silent.

"You've got Deborah tearing her hair out, a lot of money riding on your performance and yet you're hating every minute of it?"

"I love it too," Jess said. "It's like the most intense reality. And afterwards I will be on a high for hours, days. But, sometimes, often, most times, I'm scared stiff."

Anna stepped closer. She could see that Jess was shaking. "Why on earth put yourself through this? You're not short of screen work, I imagine."

"No," Jess replied, her voice so small. Anna waited, watched Jess breathe so deep her body expanded with the effort. "I wanted a break,"

Jess said quietly. "I wanted to stay in London a while. My agent found this role and said it would help production of the films too and I didn't hesitate."

"So you could see your family?" Anna tried to say more gently.

"Yes." Jess peeked up. "That was part of it, but mainly because I met someone."

Anna flinched.

"I met someone amazing," Jess said. "Someone I wanted to spend every minute of the day with."

Anna couldn't speak at first. "Do you mean for me?" she said, her voice weakened and devoid of any anger.

"I was tired when I met you," Jess said, "exhausted from running around from location to location, from publicity event to interviews. I was sick of living on junk food. I was followed and photographed everywhere I went. I once left a serviette I'd wiped pasta sauce from my mouth at a restaurant and the next week it was on eBay. I've been photographed in toilets. I couldn't buy tampons from a nightclub machine in the loo without it appearing on social media. Every new friend I made was an aspiring actor, or wanted a book endorsing, or an Instagram feed sharing. And I'm just a geeky girl from the Midlands, who likes to sit and eat crisps in front of a film with a good mate or two then disappear into music on my headphones."

Anna was silent.

"Then I met you, a kind, elegant, beautiful woman, and I was smitten from your first words. When you brought me in, when you took a stranger in who was having a meltdown, it was the most normal, human, lovely thing that had happened to me in years, and I didn't want it to end." Jess dipped her head, in exhaustion or in shame, Anna couldn't tell which. "I didn't know how I was going to make it work, or if you'd want to try after I explained who I was, or what would happen months from now, but I jumped at the chance to see you."

Jess finished and they both stood unmoving, Anna in turmoil.

37

For a moment, Jess thought she'd got through to Anna. She hung by her side, frozen perhaps with indecision, though Jess dared not look at her. The compulsion to reach out for her hand and tentatively curl her fingers around Anna's was potent.

"Perfecting your role will help with stage fright," Anna said quietly. "Also imagine what you would do in the event of all your fears. If an audience member came on stage for example, security would intervene. Visualise that and what action you could take. The preparation will ground you." She hesitated as if she were both reluctant and tempted to help more. Finally she settled on, "We're running out of time," and turned and walked upstage.

Jess's heart and hopes plunged through the floor.

"Now," Anna said, her voice filling the stage. "We will run through the scene, ensuring every word is clear and I want you to over-project, whether up to the ceiling or to the first row or the character talking to herself. It will feel forced, but I want you to throw your voice out, peppering the walls of this auditorium with your words."

Jess didn't move. The weight of the world seemed to pin her down.

"Then," Anna said, "we will rein it in slightly with another run through, and you should find that the volume and clarity is good for the audience while feeling more natural to you."

"OK," Jess said. She breathed in, as if trying to fill her soul with the character so that she could cope with Anna, despite the disappointment.

She used her entire body, speaking from deep down, using her arms as Anna suggested to power out the lines. It was cleansing, as if she were shouting out her grief, and she could hear her voice at last carrying to every corner of the theatre.

"Brilliant," Anna said behind her, brief but full of encouragement. "Again, but this time turn it down a little, full character, but keep that power and clarity in her voice."

Anna retreated up stage. "Ready?" she said, and this time Jess wasn't overawed by Anna's voice. She could match it at last and she nodded.

"When did it begin?" Anna said with a quiet growl simmering with rage and jealousy.

"After you'd left," Jess said, and this time fear came resonating from her body.

"How soon after?"

"Not straight away." Jess's fear was real but she could send it all the way to the back of the stalls.

"Was it when the others returned?" Anna prowled closer.

"No."

"Was it, when you thought I was dead?"

And there was something about Anna's presence that thrilled and made Jess respond. Jonathon had terrific control of the role but Anna brought another dimension to it. She gave it a menace but also fragility and possibilities that Jonathon's rendition couldn't promise. Jess's whole being came alive, sensual with memory, prickling in goose bumps with fear and her mind on fire. The tension alone filled the auditorium.

"No," Jess moaned from her throat so that a sonorous note rang out.

"What?" Anna gasped.

"When I knew you were alive and coming home for good."

"But…"

"I wanted to know what it was like." And as she said the words, their poignancy hit home.

"What?"

"Love," Jess said with despair. The connection to her character pulsed through her. "I wanted to know what it was like to be touched by someone who cared." And she closed her eyes, to hold back the tears. "I wanted, for one moment, to be loved for who I am, not whose sister or daughter or whose beneficiary. Just me. Who I really am."

And the parallel between her character and herself rang painfully true.

Anna stood behind her. Jess could feel her warmth and also the chill of the threat. "And now?" Anna gulped, as if realising the irony too.

"I wish I'd never known," Jess murmured, and a warm tear escaped and ran down her cheek.

The whole auditorium was centred on Jess, the weight of it, the drama, the desolation, Anna drawn in behind her. It was as if gravity was consuming the entire building and pulling everything into Jess's imploding body.

Anna moved a fraction towards Jess, her warmth soothing suddenly. Jess felt enveloped by her. She could hear Anna's breathing, deep, quick and clearly affected. It was like Anna had already put her arms around her and Jess willed her to come closer.

"That was fucking amazing!"

Jess snapped out of her reverie. The voice, a familiar one, had come from the entrance to the auditorium. It was a sharp slap in the face and snapped her back to reality.

"Matt," she groaned.

Her best-friend and producer ran out of the shadows of the stalls and bounded up the steps onto the stage.

"Seriously, fucking incredible," he said, walking straight up to them.

Anna stiffened beside her and when Jess turned round the iciness had descended again, Anna's face pale and stony and arms rigid by her sides.

"Matt Abramson," he said, reaching out a hand to Anna. She took it as gracefully as ever, but Jess could see all the defences being built right before her eyes.

"I'm the producer of the *Atlassia* films," Matt continued, seeming to disregard any frostiness. He could be insensitive at times, perhaps his enthusiasm getting the better of him here. He shook Anna's hand with too much vigour. "I came in a couple of minutes ago and didn't want to interrupt your flow," he chatted on.

Jess feared how Anna would respond to that clandestine observation. She wouldn't appreciate it at all, having someone watch her from the shadows.

"Anna Mayhew," Anna said at last.

"Oh, you need no introduction," Matt countered. "I have been a fan of yours for years. I mean years. I'm a regular in the audience at Stratford for a start."

"Thank you," she said graciously, remaining poised.

"God," Matt said, holding Anna's hand. "What a treat to see you on stage again. You still have that presence in spades. Jesus, you two," he said and he glanced from Anna to Jess. "The energy of that performance. Anna here, I could never take my eyes off her. You could always hear a pin drop when she was on stage."

Anna smiled and nodded her head.

Perhaps Matt couldn't see it, but Jess could. The stiffness in Anna's demeanour, the polite and forced smile.

"But fuck, Jess!" Matt laughed. He at last released Anna's hand. He stepped beside Jess and put an arm around her shoulder, pulling her in with playful force. "That was fucking awesome."

Jess wanted to die.

"I can't believe that was you up there. Deborah said you were having trouble making the transition to stage. The woman's talking out of her arse."

"No, she's not," Jess said. "I've been struggling, and Anna...." Oh god. "Anna's made a huge difference this morning." Jess had hurt this woman, but she'd stayed and carried on with her job.

"I've simply reminded your body of what it can do," Anna said, evenly, and she didn't attempt any kind of eye contact.

Matt remained at Jess's side, his arm around her shoulders, and no matter how much she willed it away, there it remained. He buzzed beside her, full of excitement, the hug one of friendship and congratulation, but it divided them from Anna, and the gap between them seemed to grow and become colder.

"Sorry," Matt said. "I'll leave you in peace. I wandered in looking for Deborah and Jess. I'll catch up with you at the end of the session."

"No need," Anna said coolly. "We're done here."

Jess wanted to cry out.

Anna retreated to the table and her coat hanging over the chair. She threw it round her shoulders as if she couldn't escape quickly enough.

"But that was the first time I was anywhere near good enough," Jess said, desperate to say something to make Anna stay. "Is your time really up?"

"You've made significant progress this morning. I will report back to Deborah in the remaining time and she can remind you of the points you need to improve upon."

The formality of her words drained any hope from Jess. They couldn't have been less personal.

Anna retrieved her bag and clutched it in her hands.

"You're a good actress," she said, all the life gone from her eyes, only a notional tilt of the head towards Jess. "Goodbye, Mr Abramson," she said. And for a moment Anna paused, and her cold demeanour slipped.

Then, "Good luck with the play, Ms Lambert," and she left the building.

The farewell couldn't have been colder.

38

"I was mean to her," Anna said, leaning on the top of the bookcase and staring from her flat window.

"I'm sure you weren't," Penny said. She stood beside Anna, elbow to elbow and upper arm pressed against her for comfort. "You don't do –"

"I was horrid," Anna said bluntly, not wishing Penny to credit her with more kindness than she deserved. She rested her forehead on the cold glass and rivulets of rain running down the windows blurred in her vision. The day was overcast with iron grey clouds and lights from the street and early Christmas decorations on the house opposite twinkled in watery blooms through the raindrops.

"I kept needling her," she admitted. "I outright shouted at her and I know that she clams up when she's anxious." Anna blew out her breath, as if to rid herself of her unease. "I didn't want to hear her side of the story. I just wanted to yell."

Pen leant in, her arm gently nudging Anna with reassurance. "That's understandable."

Anna shook her head. "It was like she was seizing up inside, unable to get the words out, but I couldn't stop haranguing her."

"I'm sure you weren't that extreme. It's not like you."

"But that's the trouble," Anna whispered. "What am I like, Pen?" She turned her head towards her friend. "Who am I now? I'd come to terms with how my life had changed. I'm independent. I have my job and my flat, but now I'm so at sea. It's like I'm in a tiny life boat, safe with all my supplies, but not really knowing where the hell I'm going."

Penny stayed close but was quiet.

"I'd forgotten what it was like to have something make me feel incredible, and I miss those times, when I used to act and," she inhaled sharply at the thought of her admission, "when I had someone to love." That human contact and fulfilment.

Penny nodded with understanding.

"Jess," Anna had to steady herself again, "felt special."

"I know," Penny said. "I could see it in you."

"I don't know how to feel about her." Anna stood up straight and twitched her shoulders, uncomfortable in herself. "I haven't been involved with anyone for years and I'm not who I remember. I'm suddenly middle-aged, withdrawn and reticent. I've been hurt and I don't recognise myself."

"That's not you." Penny murmured beside her, distress in her voice. "You're still the Anna I've always known." And she looped her arm through Anna's and cuddled up. "You're my bestest friend in the world. You're like another mother to Bibs and with me through thick and thin, cheering me on when I do well, being super classy but still letting it go when I say things like 'bestest'."

Anna let out a chuckle and clasped Penny's arm.

"I realise your job isn't special to you like acting was," Penny continued, "but you are good at it. The number of people I hear saying you've worked wonders with them. You go above and beyond to help them."

Anna looked down at her friend. "Really?"

"Of course," Pen said.

Anna pursed her lips together. "Don't ever think I don't appreciate you or Bibs please. I know I'm moaning about being at sea, but you and Bibs are the lifeboat."

"There," Pen said. "That's my Anna. That's the grownup who looked after us all when we tumbled through our twenties."

Anna smiled and Penny squeezed her back.

"And besides," Pen continued, "I'm not going to feel sorry for someone who's just shagged the most beautiful woman on the planet."

Anna burst out laughing, a tear falling at the same time.

"Honestly," Pen said, "get a grip."

"Stop it," Anna said, pinching her lips together, reluctant for Penny to lighten her mood.

"Seriously," Penny chided, "if she'd picked me you'd be standing here covered in dust and holding my abandoned child."

Anna laughed out loud and they both peered over their shoulders to check on Bibs who was stacking old boxes of cereal and tea in the middle of the lounge area.

"I'm not even joking," Pen added which made Anna laugh more.

"Well, if you ever meet the lust of your life, I will gladly take Bibs in."

"I'm depending on it," Penny said, and there was a hint of seriousness that surprised Anna. She didn't doubt that Penny joked about abandoning

Bibs. For all her light-heartedness she was ferociously attached. Something was up though, but Anna didn't feel she should push.

They both stared through the window.

"What am I going to do?" Anna muttered.

"Call her."

It was exactly what she wanted to do. To say she could understand how this had happened. To invite Jess to the flat, hold her and kiss her all night long. And yet, when Anna recalled Matt bursting into applause and bounding up onto the stage it was like he'd torn her reality apart and snapped her into another world. For a magical minute during their session, Anna understood the two sides of Jess's character – the actress and the person – in that electric moment on stage where Anna was empowered beside her.

Then this unfamiliar man, who was clearly a large part of Jess's life, had walked up and claimed Jess and a cold disconnect had crystallised between the Jess she knew and the movie star Jessica Lambert. The terror at being watched when she was unaware of an audience made her shiver again and compounded the humiliation at not realising Jess's identity. The warm sense of Jess disappeared and Anna felt the cold isolation all over again.

The Christmas lights blinking across the street drew her back.

"Christmas soon," she sighed. She'd meant it as something to look forward to but the truth was outed in her tone and Pen deflated beside her too.

"What are your plans?" Anna tried to say lightly. "Ireland or Lana's parents?"

"Lana's." Penny said. "For old time's sake."

"What do you mean?"

"I think we're going to split up."

Anna opened her mouth to say something reassuring but Penny quickly continued. "I know she and I have talked about it before but this time... It's all we've talked about recently."

"Oh, Pen." Anna felt a horrible weight of loss for her friend. She could hear it was different this time and skipped the platitudes. Penny's lips twitched down and her eyes watered and Anna flung her arm around her friend's shoulder and drew her in. "Shit, I'm sorry Pen." Penny snuggled under her arm and rested her face above Anna's bosom. She sniffed and her weight sagged in Anna's arms. "I'm really sorry," Anna repeated, not knowing anything that would help. All reassurances seemed empty.

Pen held on tight. "It's been coming a while," she said, her words strained and punctuated by snotty inhalations.

"I know."

"You always had your reservations," Penny hiccupped.

"Oh don't," Anna said and she squeezed her tighter.

"You didn't say anything, but I knew you thought I was making a mistake."

"That's not…" Anna sighed with frustration that she'd been right and for her friend's hurt. "I could easily have been wrong. There were plenty of good things going for you two."

Penny succumbed to a sob. "Don't let Bibs see," she whispered.

"OK," Anna said and she kissed the top of Penny's head, the mass of soft curls pressed into her cheeks.

"Oh…." Anna started, at a loss for words and full of frustration.

"…bollocks," Penny finished.

Anna laughed through her nose and brushed away a tear.

Penny sniffed then wiped her nose on Anna's shirt. "Do you want to get shitfaced?" she said, muffled in Anna's chest.

Anna smiled. "Might need a baby sitter first."

"Bibs will be all right. Is she old enough to pop out and get us a bottle yet?"

"Another sixteen years I'm afraid."

"Arse."

And they stood facing the window, hiding their tears.

39

Christmas, and Anna still hadn't picked up the phone to call Jess, despite every night wishing she were there.

Anna felt her absence as she slipped into bed, cold between the duvet and sheet. She had slept alone for years but after a taste of company her longing for human touch flooded back and her bed seemed all the more empty. No comfort of someone lying beside her. No intermittent shuffle and gentle movement. No quiet rhythmic breathing of someone asleep. The silence. The lack of her. And Anna hated it.

She heard news of the play on the radio. Deborah's voice in an interview caught her ear and she recognised the director's understated admiration for Jess as she talked about the recent performances and reception of the play. Anna tentatively read a review in *The Guardian* which raved about Jess's performance – a revelation, such impressive range, a layered performance. Anna's heart tumbled about, elated for Jess, but also with trepidation. This was about Jessica, who she didn't know.

Jess hadn't called but Anna could imagine why – her hectic schedule, travel to other obligations – but most of all because it was Anna who should call. Jess had apologised and Anna had walked out. It was up to her to walk back again.

She wondered where Jess was and pictured her each night at the theatre for the evening performance, at the same time resisting the temptation to search the gossip columns which would have told her every other detail.

December flew by and it gnawed at Anna that Jess's run at the theatre would be coming to an end and with it Anna's chance to see her. She could have called round at the theatre and asked for Jess, but every time Anna feared who she would find and it risked further humiliation. What if Jessica Lambert wouldn't see her or met her with disinterest? It was an unbearable prospect.

On the morning of Christmas Eve, Anna readied herself for a challenge to put Jess from her mind – a train journey home to Edinburgh by herself. A Tube ride, a walk to the station, a frantic squeeze between passengers loaded with suitcases for the holiday and a frazzled but elated Anna found herself on a train speeding smoothly through countryside with a scrap of an old woman next to her for company. She must have smiled the entire way, relieved she hadn't fallen into old ways and that she was continuing to strike out. She was mesmerised by the continual new view outside. She stared at the unfolding bleak and beautiful countryside of Northumberland and tried to ignore the sense of leaving Jess in London for her final performance and Anna's chances slipping away.

With a lift from her sister Celeste from the station, the perfection of her parents' Georgian home in Edinburgh welcomed her – an airy three-storey sandstone townhouse with all its classic features highlighted in tasteful heritage colours.

The front room was a blaze of traditional Christmas, her mother's insistence for decades. The cast-iron fireplace was decorated with holly. Large candles glowed on the mantelpiece, a glimmer of genuine warmth in the room. Anna sat in one of the sofas by the fireplace and reached out for the Christmas tree, always displayed to full advantage in the large window.

"To cheer everyone as they pass by in the street," she could hear her mother say from when Anna was a girl. As a woman she'd begun to suspect it was more her mother showing off.

Nordmann fir, Anna guessed from the flat needles she stroked. They usually chose one of those. She reached for a large red bow and let the sleek texture of silk run between her fingers. She tapped a bauble with the tip of her fingernail. It rang quietly and swung with the heaviness of one of her mother's old glass ornaments.

"Be careful, darling," her mother's voice came into the room accompanied by clipped footsteps. "Those baubles are considered antique now."

Her mother's comment was off hand, as if dismissing a child. It needled.

"Hello, Mother," Anna said, not letting her irritation ripple at her surface. There was little point in taking offence, considering the likely onslaught of comments to come.

Her mother kissed the top of her head and sat beside her. "I've had Harry put your bags in your room. How was your trip? How did you cope?"

There was nothing that took the shine off a success like her mother's complicated interest.

"It was a beautiful journey," Anna said honestly but having to force levity in the shadow of her mother. "It was refreshing to have a change of view."

"Good for you," her mother said with a tight smile. "I told Celeste not to bother herself getting you from the station. I knew you'd manage perfectly well."

"It was much appreciated," Anna said. "I don't get much of a chance to speak to her alone."

"Indeed, she's far too busy with the children, which is why I told her not to bother."

"How thoughtful," Anna said, grinding her teeth a little. "In any case, I was quite tired," actually she'd been exhausted, "by the end of the journey so I was very grateful."

"Oh, what a shame," her mother said, with exaggerated concern. She stroked her fingernails through Anna's hair. "Why didn't you wait a day, like I said in the first place? You could have come up with Sebastian and Helen. There's plenty of room in that SUV thing that they have."

Anna blinked at the contrary conversation. She could tie her mind in knots trying to follow her mother's logic and why a lift from her brother Sebastian at her mother's suggestion was acceptable but Celeste volunteering to fetch Anna from the local station was not.

Anna was about to comment on the matter, in not too friendly a way, when her mood was improved by two small children barrelling into the room. Her niece and nephew, four and five years old, pushed past their grandmother and leapt onto Anna's knee accompanied by a drawn out squeal of "Auntieeeeee". Their heavy landing was a reminder of how much bigger they were since she'd last seen them in London. She was pushed back in her seat and two warm squirming children covered her with flailing arms and cuddles. They were at an age where a few months absence no longer erased her impression in their memories and they showed no shyness at her arrival.

"Careful you two," Anna's mother snapped. "Celeste!" she called. "For god's sake control these two."

Anna's sister didn't appear and Anna grinned naughtily while her mother tried to wrestle the children from her knee.

"Auntie Anna," her niece Katie said, "come and play hide and seek. Come and find us."

Anna's mother tutted. "I thought I told Celeste to explain that Auntie Anna will be exhausted from her journey. She can't come and play hide and seek."

"Awww," Katie complained.

Anna had spent hours with them last time, the kids giving her clues of their hiding places with coughs and giggles while Anna crawled around pretending to be a wolf, commentating as she went at the impossibility of finding them.

"It's OK," Anna said. "I can play."

"Don't be ridiculous. You've only just arrived."

Anna suppressed the annoyance that began to simmer inside. She had a lower reserve of patience than usual.

"Come on you two. Let's not crowd Auntie Anna," her mother chided and she hauled the lovely bundles away from her. The two young children scampered away laughing and Anna had the strong urge to do the same.

"Now," her mother said. "Would you like a cup of tea? Let's get you refreshed. I've invited a few people over early evening for a little get together."

Anna was starting to get whiplash from her mother's contrariness. Too tired to play with the kids but not so tired as to endure a surprise party.

"Oh, don't worry darling," her mother said, letting her hand rest icily on her knee. "Just a few people for a last get together before Christmas. The McAdams next door, the partners from your father's practice, my friends from the club, Cameron–"

"Mum!" Anna stood up. The reaction had been instant and she couldn't have fought it.

"Whatever's the matter?"

"Stop pushing Cameron on me."

"He's a family friend darling." Her mother looked affronted and feigned innocence. "He's good company. I don't know why you can object. I," she emphasised the word, "wanted to invite him."

That was about as likely as her mother shopping in Aldi.

The last thing Anna wanted was her mother pushing a suitor on her. It was as if the walls were closing in already, the prison taking shape around her and her confidence steadily eroding. She took a deep breath. "I don't want to see Cameron."

"But they'll be here in a couple of hours."

Anna was lost for words. "I'm going to my room," she said at last and she hated how childish that sounded.

She tried to convince herself that every stamp up the steps was to make sure of her footing, but she could feel the heat of anger in her cheeks. A few minutes. She'd been there a few minutes and she'd already walked out on her mother. This was imploding at record pace.

Her old room was first at the top of the curving stairs and she was grateful to find the glowing white room quiet. She shut the door, slumped onto the single bed and closed her eyes. She was trapped at her parents' for the whole of Christmas and this was only the start of a hectic few days and her confidence was already fracturing.

She wished she was home in her flat with Penny and Bibs and she realised, more and more, with Jess. Her anger at their situation had burned out and now that it had time to subside all that was left was a glowing yearning for Jess's company. What a contrast it was, full of good will and accommodation. It was soothing just to think about it.

There was a light knock the door, too tentative for her mother.

"What is it?" Anna called out.

"Can I come in?" It was her sister Celeste.

"Yes, of course," Anna said. Although her sister was brusque at times it was more due to fatigue and looking after young children rather than like her mother's ingrained hostility.

Her sister poked her head round the door, long blonde hair hanging down. "You OK?" she said gently.

"I'm…." Anna paused, "simmering," was the best she could manage.

Celeste came in, a sympathetic smile on her face, and sat beside her on the bed. She picked up Anna's hand and held it. It was funny being comforted by her younger sister. Celeste was a mother of two and responsible for the lives of young things, but it was difficult to shake the sense that Anna should be looking out for her.

Her sister squeezed her hand. "I hope you brought a yoga mat to meditate and unwind. You look like you could do with a few breathing exercises."

"It's certainly going to take more than downward dog to get through this bitch of a day."

Her sister laughed. "Anna!"

"Sorry."

"I can hear Penny in that."

"I was just thinking of her. Oh," Anna tutted. "I'm sorry. She always manages to needle her way in." Anna didn't need to clarify who she meant.

Anna could feel herself unravelling. Families, her mother in particular, did that – tearing away at the person you'd become until they dug down to the one they knew. But not everybody wanted to be that person anymore.

"She still calls this 'Anna's room' you know," Celeste said.

"I'm sure she calls your and Sebastian's rooms by your names too."

"No. They're guest rooms. This is yours in her mind."

It surprised Anna. Her old room, light and airy with minimal tasteful furniture, had been stripped of any traces of her long ago in a fit of her mother's fury when Anna insisted on going to drama school in London.

"You were always the favourite," Celeste said, her tone full of resignation more than jealousy.

"Me?!"

Celeste nodded.

"No, I was the disappointment." Anna laughed though not with pleasure. "I was the queer. The actor. I refused to plan for 2.4 kids from the age of five. I'm pretty sure I'm last on the list, especially with both you and Sebastian having families."

"We were never going to match up."

"Why?" Anna laughed in disbelief.

"Because you are her."

"What?"

"You were the only one as beautiful and elegant and gifted. None of us came close." And the disappointment that hung on Celeste's face was enough to convince Anna of her truthfulness.

"But…"

"We all took after Dad," Celeste smiled, her eyes mourning. "And although we always said the right words, wanted the right things, Sebastian too, she was never as proud. She never looked at us with that awe and intoxicated love and pride that she did with you."

Anna didn't know what to say. It was almost perverse but rang horribly true.

"She was craving what she couldn't have," Anna said, a bitter taste in her mouth. "What she couldn't control when it disagreed with her."

"Perhaps," Celeste said, though it didn't lift her tone. "She used to come and sit in here when you were gone."

"Really? But she had the room stripped bare as soon as I left."

Her sister shrugged. "She regretted it, I think. I saw her salvage a strip of your wallpaper from the skip after the decorators had cleared the room."

"I didn't know that," Anna said. "I'm sorry."

"What for?"

"Letting mother get under my skin and for any time you felt undervalued."

Celeste squeezed her hand. "Party's at seven," she said, getting up. "We're doing black tie."

"Mother's idea."

"Who else." Celeste rolled her eyes. "Do you need a hand? Mum said you might need to borrow some clothes."

"No," Anna said sharply. Then when she realised her anger was at her mother not her sister's offer, she softened it to, "No, thank you."

The woman had been mothering Anna more these last years, goading her like she was a teen, then wanting to coddle her one minute and wishing her gone the next with crushing disapproval. Her mother seemed to go out of her way to make Anna's life awkward, the bits she disapproved of anyway. Anna wondered if her mother was aware of it. Was it the result of scheming or so innate she was oblivious?

"She will have to take me as I am," Anna said at last, sending an apologetic glance which her sister received with knowing.

Celeste closed the door quietly and Anna was left in the small room alone, the setting sun turning the walls golden. The day was running out. The last matinee performance would be over at the theatre in London before closing for Christmas. She thought of Penny packed up with Bibs, bickering in the car with Lana on their way for the holidays and, she couldn't avoid it, Jess. She would be leaving the theatre soon. For where? What were her plans? Anna couldn't picture her anymore. She could be moving to another country for a film, a tour for publicity, any number of things and places.

Anna snatched up her phone from the bed and swiped to Jess's number. It lit up and Anna watched the circle of red as it dialled the number. She put her ear to the phone and waited.

She didn't know what she was going to say, it struck her suddenly. Not a clue. She should apologise. She didn't know how. She should say that she was still hurt and that it would take time, so please don't go without seeing her.

The phone beeped in Anna's ear and an automated voice message began in monotone, "The number you have called is no longer in service."

Anna stared, frozen with the phone at her ear. "Oh," she said out loud, then flushed embarrassed that she'd tried calling.

She dropped the phone in her lap.

So Jess's number had changed. Anna's hadn't though and neither had her address. Jess had ample opportunity to keep in touch and send her a new number.

"OK," Anna said quietly.

So Anna wasn't on Jess's list any more.

She tapped and swiped to her contacts list, hesitated with her finger over Jess's entry, then deleted it from her phone.

She remained sitting on the bed.

40

"Is that Anna Mayhew?" the woman asked on the other end of the phone. The cut-glass accent and timbre suggested a mature individual.

The phone had rung on Anna's bedside table at the flat three times before she'd answered, the number unknown but the caller clearly persistent.

"Yes?" Anna replied, leaning up on her pillow. It was Monday morning but she was indulging in a lie-in. Her schedule was still quiet at the beginning of the year although, she reminded herself, they were already into February.

"This is Celia Hartingham." The woman announced it with such confidence that Anna struggled for a moment, assuming she should know her. "Oh," she said at last. "The agent?"

"That's right."

"Well," Anna said, flummoxed. "Hello."

Celia was a high-profile agent who represented a number of actors, but out of context Anna had struggled to place the name. She hadn't the foggiest idea why she would be calling.

"I understand you don't have representation at the moment," Celia continued.

"That's right?" Anna replied, wondering where the conversation was heading. "I stopped acting a few years ago."

"*A Midsummer Night's Dream* at the Globe was your last performance, I believe."

"Yes."

"Five years ago."

"Yes."

"And you didn't renew your contract with your former agent?"

"No…I…." Anna frowned and rubbed her eyes, not quite fully awake. "Could I ask what this is about?"

"I wanted to offer my services, dear."

"Oh," Anna laughed. "I'm afraid I haven't done any creative work in that time and I'm not looking to."

"I know, but there's a new role with your name on it."

"I'm sorry," Anna said. "I'm no longer acting." She said it by rote, but the disappointment still gripped and her spirits sank. "I'm not interested in auditioning," she said quietly.

"No audition," Celia batted back. "The producer has you specifically in mind. He would like to discuss the role."

Anna was torn between curiosity and wanting to end the conversation, the offer a cruel reminder of what she missed. She chose the latter. "I'm sorry. Please pass on my gratitude but I'm unable to pursue the role."

"He warned me that you might be reluctant, so he suggested a screen test to alleviate any concerns either way, yours and his."

"Screen test? This isn't for theatre?"

"No, television series."

"Oh." It was so out of the blue that Anna didn't know what to think or feel. "I haven't done any studio work in a long time."

Celia persisted. "That is as may be, but he's convinced of your suitability for the role after seeing you on stage recently."

"Sorry?" Anna sat up in bed and drew up her knees. "I think you must have me confused with someone else."

"I don't think so. Matt Abramson was very clear."

"Matt Abramson?"

"Yes, you have heard of the *Atlassia* phenomenon?"

Anna paused, her mouth open. Her heart beat a little faster in her chest at the same time her stomach dropped, making a hollow. "Yes, of course."

"The producer wants to cast you in the new series they're shooting at studios outside London."

"A new series of *Atlassia*?"

"Yes."

"Starring Jessica Lambert?"

"The very same."

Then surely Jess knew about this. Matt wouldn't have approached Anna without Jess's knowledge, would he? Did that mean, if indeed she did know, that she was amenable to working with Anna? How quickly her mind had gone there.

"Ms Mayhew...?"

"Sorry." It was so unexpected that Anna genuinely had no idea how to react. "I'm flattered," she said. Her body fluttered with nerves. "I..." She'd not even allowed herself to dream of performing again. "I'm not sure I could manage even a small role."

Could she? Could she perform in front of people – a small group of trusted cast and crew in a studio not open to the public? Her heart rate rocketed at the thought.

"It's best if you take up those concerns with Mr Abramson. He's quite convinced of your suitability after what he saw. If you want to talk yourself out of a role, by all means take that up with him, but are you happy for me to represent you come what may?"

"Yes, I suppose so." And Anna felt a bit silly.

"Are you available this afternoon?"

Oh god this was moving fast. "Yes. My schedule's quiet this time of year."

"Good. The studio will send a car for you at one o'clock."

And Celia rang off.

What had just happened? What on earth did she think she was doing? Anna had dismissed the notion of acting so long ago that the offer had caught her unaware and she'd stumbled through the conversation chivvied along by Celia. She had the feeling that, should she need it, Celia's representation would be effective.

So, acting? A series? It hadn't been her first love, that would always be theatre, but she wondered if she could pull off a role on camera. Her confidence crashed as she imagined being the focus on set, even as a co-star, eyes all on her. She almost called Celia straight back to refuse the role.

Anna shivered but it wasn't a chill. She was overwhelmed with nerves and excitement. The prospect made her nauseous. The chance to act again, that made her heart sing, but what if she was terrible? She was woefully out of practice and she shivered again.

And yet, she didn't pick up the phone.

Was this to see Jess? Was that tempting her out of her comfort zone again? She was afraid to acknowledge it and didn't want to examine her hurt feelings too closely. Besides, this offer said nothing about Jess's desires. She'd made no attempt to contact Anna, had made a step to avoid her in fact, and Anna suddenly regretted agreeing to the meeting.

But, with the time approaching one o'clock, she hadn't cancelled.

"A small role," she murmured to herself. "A bit part for old time's sake."

And a chance to see Jess. She'd said it loud and clear in her mind and she closed her eyes as if hiding from that admission.

She readied herself for an afternoon of, well, what exactly? A screen test? A meeting with Matt? She hadn't even asked where the studios were and she slumped on the bed as her breathing threatened to accelerate into hyperventilation.

There was a driver, right to the door. She could always tell them to turn around and take her home. This was really stepping into the unknown and she felt unprepared.

She dressed comfortably – jeans, loose T-shirt and jumper – then unable to overcome her upbringing she chose her long woollen overcoat to make herself more presentable.

Telephone. She patted her pocket several times. That was her lifeline.

Glasses. Dark glasses. A comfort sometimes when she wanted to hide.

Bag. She shouldered it. That had everything else from paracetamol to Valium. She was sorely tempted by one now. God, she felt like she was going on an expedition.

She smiled at last.

Anna Mayhew, pushing middle age, a bag of nerves and anxiety, was going for a role.

41

A young woman, who introduced herself as Angelina, opened the car door for Anna. When the catch hiding between the seats eluded Anna, Angelina assisted with the seatbelt in a well-practiced manoeuvre. In one fluid movement, she stretched the seatbelt around without touching Anna, clicked it into place without so much as an exploratory rattle and gently let the belt settle across Anna's chest before she could even think about being anxious of the intimacy of it all.

"Happy?" Angelina said.

"Yes," Anna laughed.

In another blur of activity, the young woman settled in the driver's seat and started the car and they were silently rolling down the incline and into the traffic of the main road.

"Oh," Anna exclaimed at the car's quietness. "Electric."

"First time?"

"Actually, yes," Anna replied.

"It's a bit unnerving, isn't it." Angelina replied, tilting her head up to the rear-view mirror, her eyes creasing in a smile. "Feels like someone's knocked the handbrake off, but you'll get used to it. The whole studio fleet has gone electric as a special requirement of the series."

"Really?"

"Yeah, yeah. The *Atlassia* production has always aimed to be low carbon, what with the apocalyptic storyline you'd see why."

"I suppose, yes." Anna blushed a little. She hadn't read up on the films since she'd realised who Jess was. It felt intrusive.

"I think it's one of the things that make it so popular," Angelina continued. "You know, with Jessica Lambert's credentials as well."

Anna twitched at the mention of Jess's name and the beat of her heart made itself known in her chest. She stared from the window to avert her face and regain her composure. She was going to have to get used to this.

"How so?" Anna said evenly.

Angelina tilted her head up to the mirror again. "She and the creators pushed for it from the start. And she doesn't just talk the talk either. She's not one of those celebrities who bangs on about climate change then travels by private jet everywhere. She refuses to sign up to any contract with a schedule that would have her travel by air."

"Oh," Anna said, unsure she was managing the balancing act between intense interest and a level that would be polite. "I had no idea."

"That's what I love about her. She's principled."

Anna didn't know about Jessica Lambert, but it was something she could imagine of Jess.

"That and being smoking hot," Angelina said, with a huge grin reflected in the mirror.

Anna blushed. In fact it was so intense Anna broke into a sweat. This wasn't like her. Mayhews were meant to be composed at all times. But the combination of a possible acting job, the prospect of bumping into Jess and being superstar Jessica Lambert's ex secret fling was quite testing.

Angelina added, "Sorry, I read you were bi. Thought you might also appreciate her."

That was an understatement.

"Oh," Anna said. "Yes. You're right. Smoking hot."

This was strange, talking about your ex as if she were public property. That and being an open book too.

"I'll shut up," Angelina chuckled. "Not long to the studio."

"Which one are we heading to?" Anna asked, grateful for the change in subject.

"Richmond Film Studios."

"I thought they went into liquidation?" Anna remembered hearing a headline on the radio a year ago, but hadn't pursued it: part of her avoidance of as many things associated with acting as possible.

"New owner apparently. He's taken over the whole complex. Some of the small companies are still based there, but the rest's been reserved for *Atlassia*."

"Right," Anna said.

She was out of the loop about almost everything. She hadn't acted for years, had no idea how things had moved on, and that was before trying to unravel the enigma of Jessica Lambert. A rising sense of panic threatened to send her yelling at the driver to turn round.

Anna closed her eyes and listened to the quiet whirring of the car over the road through the west of London and when she opened them again the city had opened up to waves of trees and parkland and the buildings were morphing into the Georgian architecture of Richmond.

"We're coming up to the gates."

"Oh." God. They were already there.

The familiar imposing frontispiece of the grand studio building loomed overhead, the great white façade glowing in the winter sun. She'd been involved in a couple of productions here, a film and TV series. Perhaps some of it would be the same.

Angelina pulled up in front of the main building and leapt out, releasing Anna with a slick movement as before.

"Wow. The producer's coming over to greet you," she whispered. "I was kind of hoping for Jessica Lambert," she said conspiratorially. "I never get to drive her."

And Anna's face burned again. She was grateful it wasn't Jess. She didn't want to be this ruffled and unprepared when they met for the first time and it would preferably be without an audience too.

"Anna!" The slight form of Matt was bounding over to them. She was barely out of the car before he grabbed her hand and gave it an enthusiastic shake. "I am so pleased you've decided to sign up."

"I think we need to talk about that first, Mr Abramson."

"Matt, please."

"Matt," she confirmed. "I have a lot of questions, and you should of me too."

"Of course," he said, his enthusiasm undiminished. "Shall we?"

Before Anna followed, she turned to Angelina. "Thank you for driving me," she said.

Angelina saluted with a big grin and skipped away around the car. The vehicle silently pulled away, the only sound being the grit beneath the wheels, and she was gone. It was as if Anna lived at a different pace to those she encountered today.

She took a deep breath and steadily walked beside Matt. She deliberately set a moderate controlled speed – if she didn't regain her poise now, she never would.

"Thank you, Matt," she said, a little more at ease with herself.

He led on, twitching with energy at every step.

"I can't tell you how excited I am about this," he continued. "We're wrapping up the feature-length series opener and going into post-production then working on sets for the series. All this building," he waved his arm over the long 1930s warehouse that housed the original studios, "is dedicated to post-production and in-situ companies. We're over there in the new complex." He threw his arm to point beyond.

Anna had to smile. His enthusiasm was infectious.

"I think that must have been built since I was last here," she said.

"Of course, *Beyond Turbulence* was shot here wasn't it?"

"That's right." It was flattering that he'd followed her career. Anxiety gnawed at her though. Did he have an inflated opinion of her acting abilities, perhaps based on her old performances? She didn't know what she was capable of now.

They passed a square Georgian house, which would have stood alone in the countryside alongside its manor when built. It was a studio café now and the path took them through the old walled garden behind, tables and chairs outside occupied by studio staff in thick coats and no doubt the odd star. Anna tried not to look for Jess but she scanned around anyway. Beyond was a lawn and a small wood of trees, bare of leaves this time of year, but Anna remembered them fondly from summers past, then the new complex opened up before them and Anna found herself staring up at a colossal building.

"Four sound stages." Matt beamed. "All of them ours. Dressing rooms, hair and makeup, offices right by the stages. It's luxury. The roof has solar panels the entire length and we even generate enough electricity to pass back to the grid."

As Matt led her into the building, through corridors that opened into cavernous stage areas, Anna half listened with excitement and was fearful of catching a glimpse of Jess.

"These sets are in place for shooting the entire series," he said, waving his arm towards a snow-covered cliff and ravine, unconvincing in the flesh, but Anna knew what the magic of lighting and post-production could achieve.

"You'll get to know them well over the next few months."

"The next few months?" Anna said, her complete attention switching to Matt.

"Yes."

"I thought this was a bit part? Are the appearances spread out?"

"This is no bit part. Your role is Kalemdra's main adversary this season."

"I'm sorry? I thought, maybe I'd assumed, that Celia said this was a minor role."

"Not at all."

Anna's heart tripped over. "Mr Abramson—"

"Matt."

"I haven't acted in a long time. I'm not sure I can pull off a minor appearance let alone a main role. This is risky, for all of us."

"We'll accommodate you." He shrugged.

"It's not impossible that I might freeze in front of a large cast and crew."

"We can keep the crew minimal on those days with a closed set."

This man was indefatigable, undeterred and exuded boundless energy.

"Also," Anna persisted, "as far as I know, *Atlassia* is a dynamic and physical kind of film and I'm not at my fittest."

"That's why we have stunt doubles."

"There is also the matter of starring with Jessica Lambert."

There. She'd said it. The issue that had been nagging at her most loudly and had been on her mind constantly. Anna had to dig deep to keep her composure.

"Is she comfortable with my appearance?"

Here Matt hesitated and Anna's insides sank. So there was an issue and her spirits fell lower at the thought that Jess might not be as keen to see her as this man was.

"Does Jess know you're offering the role to me?" she asked quietly.

"Yes," he said.

"And she's OK with that?"

He paused. "You have to understand that Jess is above all fair."

That was no answer at all and Anna's hopes plunged another league.

"She can understand some of my reasons for wanting to cast you – and the other reasons, she doesn't have to know about." Matt laughed. He gestured for them to continue. "Jess is the most fair-minded person I've ever met. She wouldn't stand in the way of anyone. Up to a point. You see, she is also one of the most forgiving people I've ever met too, something I've taken advantage of, I imagine, far too often. You can expect Jess to be patient, is what I can tell you, but there is a line."

Anna looked at Matt and decoded his speech. She'd always been comfortable at reading in between the lines. It was a reassurance but also a warning, protective on his part too, which Anna admired.

"I think I understand, Mr Abramson." She didn't qualify it with Matt. "And I think I can work with that acceptably. Would there be much screen time with…Jessica?" She still had trouble saying the name. It seemed cumbersome and foreign compared with her familiar "Jess".

"You'll have appearances all season. Your relationship is one of the main threads this series."

"Relationship?"

"Yes, the whole series focusses on Kalemdra making allies in the Northern lands and your forest domain, and your interaction is by far the most intriguing. The last studio hated the Sapphic slant."

Anna paused, her heart thudding. "Just how Sapphic are we talking?"

Matt narrowed his eyes and smiled. "Meaningful looks, simmering desire, I want the chemistry to sizzle on screen."

Oh.

"Suggestive rather than explicit is what we're going for," he lightened. "This is a series that's aimed at a large age range so we're not talking full-on sex scenes."

"I want that in writing," Anna said, more sharply than she intended. "I want a no-nudity clause and that is non-negotiable."

"Of course," Matt said.

"And Jessica is all right with this level of intimacy too?" She held her breath and felt the blood threatening to fill her cheeks.

"Jess is a pro," Matt said.

And the answer killed her hopes as much as it reassured her.

42

"This," Matt said grandly, his arms wide, "is your castle."

They'd entered the largest stage. The black walls were almost bare and the set had been built in a raised, self-contained box in the middle. He guided her up the wooden steps into a still huge space with twisting walls inside.

"It's a living castle. The walls are roots, branches, tendrils and there," he pointed to a raised area, "is your throne."

He led her forward, stepping over cables taped to the floor, past two large cameras and a woman setting up.

"One of the scenes I'm most looking forward to is when Kalemdra finds your palace. She doesn't see you at first, you're dormant within your resting place." His eyes had gone wide, and his hands expressive. "Then, sensing the intrusion, you rise up from your throne, twisting out of it as if you're part of the forest, limbs indistinguishable from branches and face blazing with indignation and menace." He thrust his hands skywards.

Anna considered the set, trying to imagine it. It could be impressive.

"Want to give it a go?" Matt said, a grin on his face.

"Now?"

"Yeah. As a screen test?"

"Well..." Her legs had turned to jelly, but she matched his smile. "OK," she said.

Matt shouted over to the camerawoman and showed Anna towards the throne. There was a slight scramble over roots and Anna found herself exposed at the peak of the royal seat. She had to breathe out to calm herself at being so prominent and visible, a touch of vertigo making her head spin.

"You OK?" Matt checked.

She nodded and watched him retreat to the camera operator.

"OK, roll camera."

Anna crouched down, twisting her arm around her body. She wished she'd warmed up with yoga exercises first, but slowly she made her body relax and she stretched it a little further, coiling up like a spring.

"And here Kalemdra will enter to where I stand," Matt shouted. "So, action!"

Anna blew every scrap of air from her lungs to compress her body further then in a slow, fluid movement stood uncoiling her body. She stretched out her arms and inhaled until her chest was full, making her impact as large as possible. She narrowed her eyes and threw daggers at Matt, and hung there, threatening and chest heaving as if burning with defiance.

"And cut!"

Anna had to crouch down and take a rest, fearing she might topple. Matt came running over and she put up her hand. "I'm fine. Just a bit light headed."

He scrambled up the roots and grabbed her arm.

"You sure you're OK?"

"Yes, give me a moment to recover and I can do it again."

"Good." His face broke out into its most expansive yet. "Because that was fucking fantastic."

"Really?"

She filled with adrenaline at his enthusiasm, which made her head swim more.

"That movement," he said, shaking his head, "was inhuman. I bloody loved it."

She was grinning. She couldn't help herself. Actually she wasn't sure if she was going to cry or not, the elation and relief was so profound.

"Do you," she stuttered. "Do you need me to do it again?"

"Want to shoot it for real?" he said, full of conspiratorial excitement.

"You know," she said, "I do."

The man was genuine with his enthusiasm and it was hard not to at least give it a chance. Besides, the bug was biting hard.

"Great," he said. "Let's get you into the CGI suit, do makeup and I'll get the crew and Jess."

And Anna wasn't sure if she was going to have a heart attack.

—

Every ounce of professional training and stultifying upbringing came into play to keep Anna in the makeup seat while her insides tumbled over with nerves.

Jess. Would she be hurt? Would she be cold and distant? Worse, flippant and moved on. The movie star could already be associated with who knows how many lovers. Perhaps that was better. Better that she was over Anna and it was only Anna who was sore.

"You probably don't remember me."

Anna snapped her gaze up to the makeup artist. She took a moment to take in the middle-aged woman.

"We've worked together before, haven't we?" Anna said.

"That's right. On *Beyond Turbulence*."

"Oh," Anna burst into a smile. "Babs?" she offered, recognising the voice and East London accent.

"Hey, you do remember. Just a makeup artist back then, but I do the design stages and train up the team here." She paused. "Course, I haven't aged as well as you. Don't blame you for not recognising me."

"It's not that. I'm distracted." Anna lifted her hands to shrug. "Actually, I'm having a bit of a panic. I haven't done this for a while."

The woman squeezed her arm. "I had heard, now you mention it. Stage fright?"

Anna nodded.

"People underestimate that don't they," Babs said kindly. "Seen it kill a few careers."

Anna flinched.

"You're with good people here though," Babs added. "If anyone can get you on track it's this bunch. Down to earth this lot are. Matt the producer, the actors–"

"Jessica Lambert?" It tumbled out, exactly what was on Anna's mind. It was embarrassing. She prayed her interest came across as the natural curiosity about a new co-star.

"Yeah. You met her yet?"

"Not...not at the studio."

"She's a great girl. I love her. Not what you'd expect from the media. They don't half write some bollocks about her."

"Really? I thought she was very popular."

"Young 'uns love her. Lots of us oldies too." Babs winked. "But it's predictable isn't it. A cute, queer, mixed-race girl like that. You can imagine how her success winds some of them up. Gets those male columnists frothing at the mouth."

"Oh."

Anna hadn't thought of that aspect and her heart sank, imagining the vitriol Jess faced, and she wondered if that was one of the pressures that had thrown Jess into the state of anxiety in which Anna had found her.

She imagined it all contributed. Anna was beginning to appreciate over time the full picture of Jess and Jessica Lambert.

"See, she's the genuine article," Babs carried on. "Real lovely girl that one. Quietly gets on with everyone. There ain't no superstar arrogance with her. She respects what everyone does on set. You wouldn't imagine it would you. She's made those films the hit they are, but she always insists on crediting the creators, writers, her mate Matt the producer. She's always honouring the skills of others, things that she can't do but others can. Like makeup, says she looks like a Picasso painting if she does it herself."

Anna smiled. She could hear Jess saying that and it filled her with a tickle of affection.

"My team even got a mention at the Sci-fi awards," Babs said, "when she accepted her best actress award. She stands up for what she believes in too. That really drives those columnists wild."

Anna wondered how stressful that all was for the quiet, sensitive Jess that she knew. She suddenly shuddered and screwed her eyes tight as Babs rubbed makeup close to her eyes.

"Sorry," Anna said, holding up her hand. "I'm not used to others applying my makeup. Out of practice. It feels strange around my eyes."

Babs stood back but squeezed her arm. "Course love. Let's have a think. If I use this," she held up a thin tapering brush, "it paints on lightly and the remover wipes it off in a single sweep. Would that be all right?"

"Let's try it," Anna said, taking a breath.

And as Babs adapted, took pictures for her team and continuity, and noted down the makeup used, she could see why Jess would thank the woman.

The butterflies fluttered in Anna's stomach. Not long now, and she would be meeting Jessica Lambert. Jess.

43

"That's a wrap," Shawna, the director called, her voice growling with satisfaction then following it with a deep chuckle that always made Jess smile. Jess leant up on her elbows from the crash mat, thankfully for the last time.

She'd leaped through the air, arms cartwheeling, the clapboard said twenty times that day and, though the scene they'd been shooting of Jess's escape from a cliff was invigorating, she was beginning to feel a bit sore.

"We've got every conceivable angle," Shawna said, coming to pull Jess from the mat, her round figure and head of generous black curls blocking out a spotlight. "I promise."

They'd been retaking a scene for the feature length episode that had been bodged in the original shoot, Jess's hair style and the state of her suit too incongruous for continuity.

Matt came running up too.

"Can I keep you two around?" he said. "I want to get a couple of shots for the season preview.

Shawna nodded and sauntered off to the camera operators. Matt conspiratorially took Jess's arm.

"What's up?" Jess said, absent-mindedly rubbing at her thigh. The muscle twinged. She'd have to go easy at the studio gym for a couple of days.

Matt led her aside, away from the crashing noises of the crew clearing up around them.

"I need to talk to you about Anna."

Jess deflated with a frustrated sigh. They'd been having this conversation for weeks. Ever since Matt had glimpsed Anna on stage he'd become obsessed with the idea of Anna returning to the profession and taking the role of Queen of the Northern Territories. It's something they had in common, becoming fixated on an idea once enthused, but it was bloody irritating when you were on the other end of it and could say nothing to dissuade. She could predict how this conversation would go.

"Matt," she said. "Drop it. She won't be interested." Jess hadn't admitted the details of their falling out, but she didn't need to. He could tell enough. "Besides, her confidence is shot to pieces. It would be a huge step returning to acting."

"That was a woman in full command on the stage with you, whether she knows it or not."

"We can see she's astonishing, but she's lost her stage confidence and that's not something you tell someone to snap back into."

Then the guilt cut sharp inside. Did Jess contribute to keeping that confidence low? Was she another reason to lose faith in acting?

"Performing was intrinsic to her," she said quietly, avoiding Matt's gaze. "It was a part of her. It would be a massive challenge to try again. Imagine trying but failing in front of us all." And the possibility panged inside.

"I understand if you don't want her to join the cast. You're my priority."

"It's not that," she said, again avoiding his gaze.

Although that was something Jess had dwelt on. She remembered vividly the fury with which Anna had confronted her and guilt descended all over again – all the things Jess should have said earlier. The squirming inside made Jess shiver with discomfort at her deception. Her Nan had always said her reactions were extreme, called her a sensitive girl, but she'd not grown out of it. She was overwhelmed with dread when she'd done something wrong.

"She should have the chance," Jess said, "if she wants it, but I doubt she does with this series." With Jess.

"Rubbish," Matt said with a grin. "She still has the hunger." And the lasciviousness of tone was in no way subtle. There was no mistaking his insinuation, but she didn't want to acknowledge it. He knew something intimate had happened between them. He read people in a way she envied. Did he really have to hear it plainly, that there was no way that Anna Mayhew would be seen dead anywhere near her?

"You are running out of time," she said. "For christ sake, cast another actor."

"She's here."

"Who?"

"Anna. She's here."

Jess stared, immobile. "But…." That was impossible. This should be the last place Anna would be. Acting? With Jess? At least Matt had the good grace and knew her well enough to give her a moment to let it sink in. She still wasn't processing it though.

"Now?" she said, feebly.

"Yes."

"For the role?"

"Yes." He was pretty much dancing on the spot.

"Why?" she almost said aloud. "Oh," came out instead.

"Told you she'd come," Matt said, with the lewdest grin she'd ever seen.

That man. He had an intuition and read people like a book, especially her.

"I'm surprised," she as evenly as she could.

"I'm not," he said, and he wriggled his eyebrows suggestively.

"Has she accepted the role?"

"We're shooting a scene to reassure her that she's convincing. There've been no jitters so far. Believe me, she's hooked."

"What if she freezes? What if she freaks out some days? Don't promise her a role then fail to support her."

"I will listen," he said with a solemn face. Then he burst into a grin. "But after you both finish the scene."

"What?"

"I want you to shoot a scene, then you will see. You will see what I can imagine and it's going to be TV that drips with hormones."

Jesus. That made her freeze again.

—

Jess cautiously entered the largest stage in the studio, the new set of the forest palace a hive of activity. Everyone seemed to have been pulled in. Matt and the lead writer were climbing the steps into the set, the episode director, assistants, camera crew, sound crew already assembled inside.

Jess crossed her arms. She felt unprepared. This was usually her domain, free of anxiety, except that necessary only for the thrill of filming and performing. She was familiar with the people, trusted them now, some having worked on the films for years, others new acquaintances and casual friends. One or two she counted as genuine friends including the outgoing and fellow Brummie, Shawna, responsible for enticing her out on occasion the last few weeks when all she wanted to do was curl up in bed after work.

But now, Jess was terrified.

Would Anna greet her with the same disdain with which she had left her on the stage in Shaftesbury Avenue? Jess gasped at the prospect and gripped her arms tighter around her. Not a day had gone by without Jess reliving that moment.

"Jess?"

She stopped. The voice was unmistakable. Smooth as honey. Soft as velvet. It was disarming and Jess's arms dropped. The words were like a caress through her whole body, comforting and seductive all at the same time. It was as if Anna had stroked her cheek, traced around her neck and trailed a delicate finger down her cleavage.

Jess turned. "Anna?"

She wasn't quite as Jess had expected. Anna glided towards her, her slim figure svelte in a CGI suit. If Jess hadn't appreciated the curve of her breast and line of her hips before she couldn't help it now.

Anna's face was made eerily striking into that of her character queen, her blonde hair coloured ash grey and swept back into tendrils. But the forbidding character was at odds with Anna's familiar movement and the expression on her face – her careful elegant stride and a smile that was at once trepidatious and keen and above all genuine.

"Hi," Jess said, not much more than a whisper.

"Hello," Anna said gently.

They stood apart, the past and conversations hanging in the air suddenly. The warmth of her company, the desire to be with her, the hurt of their fall out, all hung over them and Jess didn't know where to start.

"I look a little different than last time I saw you," Anna joked.

Jess smiled surprised at Anna's levity. She'd been expecting a cold rebuttal.

"I feel a bit silly," Anna said, sounding tentative and reaching out, while clearly still sore at what had happened.

"You look incredible," Jess said, and she rolled her eyes at herself. But she did. The figure-hugging CGI suit showed Anna's slender figure to full advantage and the makeup was striking.

Anna's face flickered with surprise. "It's, um, unnerving."

Jess recognised Anna's anxiety, perhaps at her appearance and the unfamiliar surroundings.

"The makeup's amazing," Jess said, stepping closer. "Babs has done a great job, using the natural contours of your cheek bones and accentuating your eyes, always a striking feature."

Jess couldn't have worn her admiration on her sleeve more blatantly if she'd tried. And that was the thing. She couldn't help her honesty and it was why her deception with Anna had struck her so badly. She'd been swept along on a wave of desperation then been seduced by the sanctuary of Anna's company so sweetly she hadn't realised how far out to sea she'd been.

She swallowed, wanting to say all that, but remained tongue tied. Anna looked away.

"Nervous?" Jess ventured, desperate to keep their conversation going.

"Terrified," Anna admitted with a laugh, and she turned towards Jess in camaraderie, the warmth of the movement as Anna stood closer and the familiarity lifting Jess.

"Everyone on set please!" Shawna shouted from the entrance to the palace, and they both twitched to attention. The call jarred, Jess wanting so much more with Anna, and they wandered across to the set.

Anna stopped and held Jess's arm before they reached the steps.

"I just wanted to say thank you," Anna said, her blue eyes intent on Jess's, many feelings running through their depths. "Thank you for letting me join the cast."

"Oh. Well. Of course, it's Matt's decision."

"I know, but if you'd put your foot down and said you couldn't act with me, he would have respected that."

Jess couldn't think clearly. The gentle touch of Anna's fingers on her arm had been so unexpected, with its intimacy, vulnerability and trust. Its familiarity too and Jess could imagine those warm fingers holding her and exploring her. It did all kinds of confusing things to Jess inside and she had to wait for the swell to subside.

"That wouldn't have been fair to you though," she said at last. "I'm...I'm glad you've got this opportunity to get back into acting. I know how much it means to you."

That elicited a frown and an intensity to Anna's gaze that tugged at Jess's heart.

"This," Anna emphasised. "This means a lot." She squeezed Jess's arm and let her hand drop. Anna headed up the wooden steps and Jess followed, irresistibly drawn after her.

Jess stood on her mark. She'd seen the storyboard for this scene. She was impressed at the set design and how Babs has translated Anna's character mock-up so closely into reality.

The assistant director was helping Anna into position on her throne and the two were conferring about the scene. Shawna set Jess into her stance and pointed to where she wanted Jess to look. Two cameras would be rolling and there would be multiple takes.

Then the main lights turned low and gradually several spotlights blended so that the set became eerily alive. The peak of the throne was highlighted and Jess was prominent in another beam.

"Final touches," the assistant director called, and Jess readied herself, her limbs eager with excitement, regretting the scene wasn't more physical, and that all she had to do was watch the emergence of the queen.

"Action!"

Jess's attention shot to the organic throne into which Anna seemed to have merged. She could hardly make out Anna's winding limbs from the tendrils of the set at first. Then Anna grew before everyone's eyes. A slender arm unnaturally bent. Then the curve of her neck, the line perfect with her extending hair. An angular hip jutted out and her body extended. She twisted to the side in a disconcerting twitch, and with every expansion of her movements her presence grew. The transformation was spectacular and everyone gawped.

Jess was spellbound by Anna's agile twisting from the roots of the castle. She stared as Anna reached the pinnacle of her performance and lifted her head so that it dazzled in the spotlight. Her face was filled with ferocious threat, her eyes piercing, and she threw out her arms and fingers as rigid as claws.

Jess stood, petrified and overawed by the transformation of Anna twisting and writhing into her formidable character, every ounce of strength and determination of Jess's character gone.

"Cut!"

"Wha…?" She'd forgotten to act.

"Brilliant reaction, Jess."

"Yeah…" Fuck.

She'd been caught out, completely. Anna was electric and Jess embarrassingly enraptured by her. She could see what Matt meant by her being captivating. She drew every single person's attention.

"Let's try again from above on camera three," Shawna shouted.

And every single time, Jess was stunned. Anna transformed into a different persona and Jess shuddered with a chill of fear and a frisson of something else.

Matt was buzzing around. "Come here," he shouted, beckoning her over. Anna was already by his side, nerves and elation playing out on her face.

"Let's see a quick mock-up on the computer," Matt said.

They were standing behind one of the post-production crew and a large screen and Jess peeped over their shoulders.

"We've started to load up the background effects." Matt said to Anna. "The details on the suit and where it'll meld into the throne is trickier, but this should give you a good idea of how it will look."

The screen showed footage from camera one of Anna extending from her throne. It gave Jess chills all over again.

"Oh good. I wanted to check the movement," Anna said, peering at the screen. "That looks like it works to me."

"It's bloody incredible," Matt replied. "Gave me goose bumps."

Then camera two footage, focussed on Jess, started to play. She saw her features switch to attention as action was called. Then all the blood drained from her body as she watched herself bewitched on screen. Awe that was both fearful and carnal overtook her expression. Adulation was written all over her face. Was there any chance that Anna wouldn't notice it? Jess's spellbound expression continued undiminished on film. She stood there, undone by Anna's performance that did indeed drip with charisma and sexual power. Jess bet everyone could see it.

Matt turned to her and wiggled his eyebrows. She could have killed him.

"Can I see it again?" Anna said, drawing Matt's attention.

More of the crew had gathered in admiration around the screen. Jess could see Anna's confidence growing as she watched herself act again. How fluently she talked to everyone, surrounded by quite a group now. She was at the centre, completely at ease, indulging in small physical touches of familiarity to draw people in. Jess envied that. Jess never had that kind of comfort with new acquaintances or in a large group. It could take months, years even, to accomplish that, unless she had a strong common bond with an individual. Jess imagined this is what Anna had been like of old.

If pushed, Jess would confess she'd seen more than one of Anna's films by now, and old interviews and a video of plays. She was a little embarrassed she hadn't realised what theatre royalty Anna had been. Anna had the same presence on screen that she had in real life too: the calm poise, the captivating and easy physical presence.

Jess felt a prod in her back and turned round to see Shawna grinning at her. "Want to get a coffee, bab?"

Shawna had a twinkle in her eye which meant she wanted to gossip. And judging by the tug on her arm Shawna wasn't going to take no for an answer.

Jess opened her mouth wanting to say something to Anna, she had no idea what, but Anna was engrossed in conversation with Matt and Jess reluctantly let Shawna pull her away, acutely aware of the draw of Anna's presence tugging at her as she walked away.

"Want to go celebrate getting the first shot of the series under our belt?" Shawna said.

"Hmm?" Jess said.

Shawna rumbled another laugh out loud and rolled her eyes. "Let's go have a drink." She put her arm round Jess and pulled her close. "Then you can tell me about this big crush you have on your co-star."

Shit.

44

When Anna returned to her flat she was in no way calmer than when she'd left, if anything she was on a nervous high. She paced her small abode, not knowing what to do with herself. In days gone by, she'd have gone down to the pub to drink generously and to success. But her old group of friends had moved on and she was not quite herself enough to invite her new acquaintances from the cast to celebrate.

She stopped and peered out of the window across a glowing London night view and put her hands on her hips. It had been a phenomenal day. She was grinning like a woman possessed. She'd surprised herself and even Matt, despite his expectations being high.

She brought up her hands. They were trembling from pure excitement of the day and the nervous prospect that Anna could do this. For the first time in years, she believed there was a way back to herself.

Anna didn't want to sleep in case it jinxed her progress. She didn't want to wake up that anxious woman again, the one who didn't dare step outside or who couldn't throw herself into her creative work. Sleep was beyond her anyway. She'd be tossing and turning all night, reliving the day with her stomach in knots, not quite daring to believe how well it had gone.

Her eyes alighted on a pile of DVDs on the kitchen island. Matt had sent her away with the first *Atlassia* films. She'd avoided drama on TV or at the cinema stubbornly these last few years, but curiosity gnawed at her. What was she a part of now? What was the reason for the staggering success of this series?

She pulled forward her neglected DVD player from under the TV shelf, slotted in the first film and sank into the sofa, crossing her legs and clutching her hands in her lap.

It was a very much younger Jess who appeared on the screen. She must have been eighteen by the time it had finished filming. You could tell around the eyes, more fleshy with puppy fat and those phenomenal cheek bones not so well defined yet.

But Jess's performance was not in the least bit immature. Immediately there was an intensity about her, even in that first *Atlassia* film. Anna couldn't stop watching. She would glance at the other characters in the scene, but then she sought Jess again.

Jess had that quiet quality some actors have, when they look full to the brim with the person they are playing and every small flicker, every slight smile, every tiny gesture is a teasing clue to the person within, as if they aren't acting at all, simply existing as the character. The credits rolled and Anna sat up, shocked that she'd been so engrossed in the film that she hadn't noticed the hours go by.

She skipped forward to the latest film and an older version of Jessica Lambert who she recognised. Anna watched until gone midnight, equally as absorbed and fascinated by the woman who'd slept in her bed.

The floodgates had opened. Anna was insatiable. She searched for a clip of Jess's Bond appearance and found herself staring at an altogether different character. Jessica was undeniably a woman in this, her eyes more expressive and distinct, her costume low cut over her cleavage, tight around her generous breasts, long shapely legs bare, and Anna blushed at how much she admired Jess's athletic body on show in the film. Although a different character, she had the same sense of being a real living person rather than an actor. The camera, and clearly the director of photography, loved the way she moved, and Jess's body was celebrated as a thing of athletic beauty. Then Anna blushed again at how much she was reacting to Jess on screen.

Anna was humbled. Jess very much deserved her star status and Anna appreciated the generosity of her letting Anna join the cast.

Their meeting had gone surprisingly well. Jess seemed a bag of nerves, like Anna in fact. And the warmth between them, Anna thought she'd felt that once more. Not to mention the chemistry in the scene – it couldn't have been only her who noticed it. But when Anna had turned round from checking the rough cut, high on the thrill of performing again and the instant feedback, Jess had been walking away. Anna had watched Jess's retreating figure and that of the director, whose arm was around Jess and pulling her closer. Of course they could be friends. Equally, what looked like a kiss on the cheek could have been a whisper in the ear. But it was still like a punch in the stomach for Anna.

She tried to focus only on her work the next time she went into the studio and Jess's absence for a few days at least made that easier. Anna attended rehearsals with several of the cast while sets for the series were completed and they shot the odd test scene. Every day, she'd been ready and waiting for the studio car, eager to get to work.

Anna was invigorated. She felt alive. With adrenaline pumping through her veins, she was determined to push through this introduction back into acting before her confidence and fears had a chance to derail it.

She waited another two weeks before she dared break it to Penny, having to cancel seeing her often for "work" and old coaching obligations, and not wanting to admit the nature of the new commitments until she was more sure. But it was time.

"I've got a gig," Anna said.

"Sorry, what did you say," Penny said without looking up. They were sat in Zehra's café, Anna, Penny and Bibs, Pen wiping scrambled egg from her chest. She'd claim it was from trying to feed Bibs but a great deal was owed to Pen's distraction, issues with Lana on her mind. It was one of the reasons why Anna hadn't told her immediately about *Atlassia*.

"I've got an acting job." Anna tried to say it evenly and sipped at her coffee to stop herself from grinning like a maniac, that or breaking down into tears that she'd bitten off more than she could chew, and generally being in turmoil about seeing Jess again. She sipped again at her coffee, a picture of poise and a mess of feeling.

"Whoa, what?" Penny's eyes went large.

"I've got a role on the new *Atlassia* series."

Penny's eyes remained wide and her mouth dropped open to join it.

"You're shitting me," Pen said.

"No," Anna said. She held her breath, waiting for the news to sink in.

"An actual role?" Pen said, eyes still like saucers.

"Yes." Anna stared at her friend who remained alarmingly catatonic. "Pen?"

"You're acting?"

"I know," Anna laughed. "It's taken me by surprise too."

"Seriously?" Pen said, her expression had collapsed into a frown. Anna had always loved that about her friend, her wonderful expressive face. Anna nodded, unable to hold back her smile or a tear that couldn't work out whether it was happy or fraught.

"But...." Pen thought for a moment, then leant forward and squeezed Anna's knee. "Does that mean you've seen Jess again?"

Anna laughed out loud. Straight for the gossip. That was Pen.

"Yes, I have. We've done a scene together. Just the one."

"Well how was she?" Penny gave her full attention and placed two hands on Anna's knees. "Was she glad to see you? Did she look completely gorgeous? Is she still single? Have you been out? Did-"

"Pen, slow down," Anna said. Penny was getting way ahead and the fact that Pen thought this possible when Anna was so much less sure made her heart sink.

"She was perfectly polite," Anna said. "More than that, she was pleasant to me."

"And?" Penny shot back.

"She was very professional. I hadn't seen her in her suit before and she seemed the hero even in real life."

"And?"

"The scene went very well as far as I could make out. They showed the rushes with some effects."

"And?"

Then Jess had walked away arm in arm with her director friend and Anna's heart sank just as much as it had the first time she'd recalled it.

"That's it really," she said. "I haven't seen her a great deal yet."

"Oh," Penny said, sitting back.

And Anna shared that sentiment. She had the strong sense of having missed her chance with Jess, if it had been a real chance at all, and she felt the keen disappointment all over again.

"But fuck! You've taken an acting job!" Penny enthused.

"I know."

"On *Atlassia*!"

"I know!"

"Well how's it going?" Penny said, fizzing with excitement again.

"It's....OK. I think," Anna added, grinning again now. Oh dear. She was all over the place.

"Get me into the wrap party. I want serious on-set privileges."

Anna laughed. "Well, the feature length opener won't stream yet, but there's a ticketed pre-screening and Q&A with the cast. It's for critics, journalists, top fans and anyone else who can get a ticket. I have a VIP pass, plus one for a guest."

She could hear Pen's deep intake of breath. "No!" Pen said.

"Yup."

"You're kidding?"

"Nope. Do you want to come?" Anna beamed.

"Does the pope shit in the woods?"

Anna glanced at Bibs who was picking bits of scrambled egg off her mother and eating it. She seemed unperturbed. "No, Pen," Anna said quietly. "The pope does not shit in the woods."

"Bet he fucking does," Pen said. "Course I bloody want to see it."

45

It was mayhem. Anna had expected a preview screening at a cinema, perhaps within the studio, but it turned out there was enough demand to fill a small stadium. The car driving Anna was mobbed at the gates. She was twitchy and anxious at the prospect of her own part in the evening and at the zeal of *Atlassia* fans.

"This is bonkers," Penny exclaimed, as hands thudded against the car and faces appeared pressed against the rear window. Anna blinked as phones and cameras blotched her vision.

"All these girls and boys peering in," Penny gasped.

"They'll be wanting to catch a glimpse of Chris and Jess," Anna realised.

"There's all sorts in the crowd," Penny said.

You could hear the frenzy. Anna had attracted fans when she was younger, but nothing like this. People clamoured for Jess. There was a woman screaming her name and now Anna had sampled Jess's films she'd had a chance to see what all the fuss was about. She blushed, recalling her physical reaction to Jess on screen. She could understand the allure and what sparked the devotion of these fans now hammering on the car. Jess was desired, a pinup.

What on earth had the young star ever seen in Anna? It's not like Anna had been an easy fling. There were possibly hundreds of people outside this car who would have jumped at the opportunity. No wonder Jess hadn't given her a second chance. What were the attentions of a middle-aged actress compared with this adulation?

Inside the stadium, together with the rest of the cast and guests, Anna and Penny took their seats in a box high up near the stage and an enormous screen. The lights went low except for the stage and the several-thousand strong audience rose up in a roar as Jess and Chris appeared on stage to introduce the film. Jess waved to all corners of the stadium and her voice rang clear and strong as she welcomed the crowd.

The energy in the stadium was palpable. It nearly lifted Anna from her seat.

"Enjoy the show!" Jess and Chris shouted and the whole stadium plunged into darkness and the familiar soundtrack began.

The film was overwhelming in so many ways. Anna's stomach was in knots waiting for her time on stage after the screening, but she couldn't help surf the wave of enthusiasm from the audience at the action and drama on the screen. She was absorbed yet again by the intensity of Jess's performance and it was amplified on a large screen this time.

A close-up of Jess's features in one quiet moment filled the stadium, the camera lingering on her thoughtful face, her beautiful cheeks perfect in the soft glow of firelight, her brown eyes capturing everyone's vision and inky long eyelashes blinking over those soulful pools. Anna could almost feel the whole auditorium leaning forward and drowning in those eyes.

Then action again and the audience was carried away to the thunderous climax of the film until they rose as one from their seats when the end credits rolled.

A guide quietly took Anna backstage ready for her part in the event, the part she'd been trying to ignore the whole evening. She waited in the wings alongside Jess and Chris while the crew wired them up with earpieces and microphones.

Jess seemed smaller.

"Hey," she said, looking over her shoulder.

"Hi," Anna replied.

"You'll be OK?" Jess said. Anna may have nodded, but Jess paid her no more attention and turned back to look onto the stage.

Jess hunched her shoulders and clenched her hands, more like the woman Anna had first met, running from everyone that night. Chris by contrast was already in a power pose, feet apart, hands on hips. As their names were announced over the speakers, Jess lifted her chin and before Anna could wish her good luck she'd jogged onto the stage and the two co-stars were leaping around and waving to the crowd again.

The reception for Jess was astonishing. Even when the two actors took questions from the audience, Jess was the focus. Although she didn't strut or bask in the attention, not like living the dream as Jessica Lambert, she spoke fluidly and with authority and Anna realised genuine enthusiasm. Penny had told her once that Jess had been addicted to the graphic novels that had inspired the series and realised Jess talked from the perspective of a fan. That enthusiasm was winning the audience hands down and Anna could see Jess's confidence thriving on it all. This was her subject and obsession, this was her domain, and Jess hosted the event with an authentic charisma.

"How we doing?" Matt appeared at Anna's arm, which he gently took it in his, and looked at her with quiet concern.

"I'm not sure," she said, honestly. The creeping sense of freezing, the rising nausea, the paralysing nerves, they weren't there yet. Yes, she was jittery with adrenaline, but the terror hadn't claimed her. But christ, this was going to be a challenge.

"Remember," Matt murmured. "You don't have to go on. Jess and Chris are primed for any eventuality."

She closed her eyes and nodded.

"If you walk on," Matt said, "and simply wave, then amazing. Any more than that would be exceptional."

Anna kept her eyes shut, Matt's arm steadying her.

What was the worst that could happen? She could freeze, break down and collapse. She'd done that before. Would this be any worse? Strangely she felt it wouldn't. Matt, Jess and Chris knew it was a possibility and it wouldn't be the universal shock that it had been five years ago. It was still pretty fucking awful though.

"And as a special treat," Anna heard Jess say over the speakers that rang out over the stadium, "we have a short clip from the next series, not seen anywhere before. Your first glimpse of the Queen of the Northern Territories!"

The crowd's enthusiasm was terrifying. That blast from the audience seemed to knock Anna back. The clip blazed onto the screen and she peeked around to make out her own form, growing from the forest palace transformed by slick post-production effects into something otherworldly on the giant screen. As the clip ended and the stage lights came on, the crowd's applause and chanting were no lessened. Anna had never experienced anything like this in her life.

"Good god," she gasped. She trembled. Why had she agreed to this? This was a step way too far. How was she meant to go on stage and live up to that reception? She felt ancient suddenly in contrast to the two dynamic actors and the youthful audience. She put her hand to her chest, regretting letting the studio dress her with a more revealing gown than she was now accustomed to. She was physically shaking.

"Anna?" Matt said gently.

But it was to Jess on stage that she looked and found her eyes on hers. Jess's face only showed bubbling enthusiasm, kindness and generosity. Anna realised with a sense of calm, which washed over her, that little of the focus would be on her. The crowd was here for Jess. Anna was free of expectation in front of this audience. She'd be surprised if many had heard of her at all. All the pressure was on Jess, none on her, and the realisation channelled her nerves into excitement and the terror into opportunity. She had a job to do, a job she loved, and that was to support the star – Jess.

Anna breathed out, long and slow until her lungs were empty. This was another stage, another audience. She had a role to play – Anna Mayhew, RSC actress, consummate professional, red carpet regular – her body, personality, voice all part of the act.

She wasn't youthful. She couldn't bound onto the stage. But she had a lifetime of listening to audiences, feeling as well as seeing their reactions. She was a seasoned actor and she'd commanded stages from London to New York. The costume department had given her just that – a costume for this role. She could do this. This is what she was born to do. She let go of Matt and reached out for the rail and climbed the steps onto the stage.

46

Jess clapped to welcome Anna on stage, the crowd thundering in her ears. Her heart was pumping, her body primed with excitement from the reception of the feature. The night had been an unbelievable success. If Anna could make it on stage that would be the icing on the cake. If all she did was wave that would treat the crowd and be a monumental step for the actor's confidence. But as Anna walked on Jess slowed her clap.

Jess's reception had been uproarious but, when Anna walked on, it was as if the night was stolen by a star. Jess gawped, she didn't realise she'd stopped clapping, so taken was she by the woman who appeared on stage. Golden gown flowing with easy grace and a fluid stride of long elegant legs. You would have to be dead not to notice the plunging neckline and pale flawless cleavage. But it was the way she walked on stage: slow, deliberate, like she belonged. Anna Mayhew was here.

Jess could feel that every face was turned, entranced by their new co-star. Anna came to a stop beside her and dropped a hand to her hip in a seductive pose. She tilted up her chin, the line of her neck exquisite, and the smile she gave of pleasure and purpose silenced the crowd into obedience as she scanned every corner of the auditorium.

"Good evening," Anna purred. And did that just make several thousand people go weak at the knees? Its seductive power had completely incapacitated Jess. There was a besotted sigh from the crowd.

"I believe," Anna paused, "you have questions."

And Jess, Chris and the audience laughed out loud in appreciation at her introduction that dripped with insinuation.

Jess found herself beaming and clapping hard. Anna had brought her fearless character to the stage in all but costume, together with decades of experience of captivating an audience. Jess could never do that and she was in ecstatic awe of Anna's ability. And her confidence. She didn't tremble a bit. Anna stood, commanding, her leg provocatively peeping through a slit in her dress without a hint of vulnerability. Jess didn't know whether she was more pleased for the audience, the whole production or Anna. This was a spectacular step for the actress.

Beaming so much that her cheeks ached, Jess took charge of hosting, picking audience members from the crowd, an overhead microphone panning over to chosen questioners. They ranged from young fans wanting to talk about favourite characters in the *Atlassia* books, to critics asking about the creative direction the show was taking, to someone asking Chris out on a date, all handled with charm by her colleagues.

A woman at the front with a tablet, who'd looked irritable at the questions so far, shouted out her name.

"Question for Jessica Lambert!" she repeated, and the microphone swung over her head.

"Yes?" Jess said, smiling.

"How are you coping with the schedule after suffering from exhaustion and going into hiding last year?"

Jess twitched. It caught her completely off guard. The evening had been so dominated by questions from ardent fans, that the intrusive line tripped her. Lulled into comfort by the warmth of the audience, with simple questions rewarded by honest answers, the reminder of people with confusing and destructive motives floored her. Why would a person do this?

Her disappearance had been reported in the media but Femi, her manager, had shielded her from most of it. He'd dismissed it as indistinguishable from gossip and the fiction they usually posted. She'd avoided much of the fallout from that and the change in studio, but these things never went away, not while journalists could smell blood.

"I'm..." Her brain was seizing. "I'm enjoying filming the series at Richmond very much," she said, hearing that her voice was dropping into monotone but able to do little about it. "We're all relieved that *Atlassia* has a new home in London," she pressed on.

"Is it true you're involved with Anna Mayhew?"

What? Where had that come from?

"Sorry?" she said, without thinking.

"You and Anna were photographed on the Tube last year. You looked cosy."

Her mind was contracting with panic now. Questions about the film from fans she could answer all night, but this was personal and like a knife thrust into her body.

"I...." It was personal and about a time she'd nearly broken down. She wasn't sure her parents realised how close she'd come, if it hadn't been for Anna.

"I..."

Then she'd lied to Anna, taken advantage and hurt her.

The lights seemed so bright suddenly. She was exposed on the stage, in the spotlight, in front of thousands of people. This was her worst nightmare – everything she feared about fame and people. Not even her run on Shaftesbury Avenue had prepared her for this kind of exposure.

"Ms?" It was Anna's voice, close by. She'd approached Jess and now that Jess looked up she realised Chris had closed in too.

"Cass Johnstone."

"From?" Anna said, her tone icy.

"*The Express.*"

"Well, Ms Johnstone from *The Express,* Jess and I do know each other, so it should be no surprise that we've been seen together from time to time. In fact Jess introduced me to the producer of the show for which I'm very grateful. She's a phenomenal actress and I'm proud to call her my colleague and friend."

"You haven't answered my question," the journalist snapped.

"I think you've asked enough questions." Anna's reply was final and deadly. "Let's open it back up to the audience shall we?"

Anna's hand pressed lightly on Jess's back, reassuring her and pulling her in.

"What can we expect to see this series?" Anna repeated the question from another audience member. "Chris, would you like to take that one?"

Slowly Jess started to see again, the glare of the lights less blinding, but her heart thudding. She struggled through a few questions, heavily filtered by Anna who steered every question to the story and safer ground for Jess. By the time the event organiser was calling for them to wind up, Jess could look people in the eye again.

Held by Anna on one side and Chris on the other, she hoped her cheery wave to the crowd was convincing and she walked off stage with her co-stars rather than collapsing, which had been a possibility halfway through.

She was fried. She could barely think and struggled to speak. She was half aware of Anna approaching and holding her hand.

"Sorry," Jess muttered, struggling to get the words out. "I'm sorry that came up."

Anna's hand was vivid and soft. Her reassuring presence calmed Jess like it had last year. The world seemed to stop spinning when Anna was around. She looked up into Anna's face and saw the kind concern she'd seen last year, a kindness she'd taken advantage of, which had hurt Anna in a way that still summoned stomach-churning guilt in Jess.

"I'm sorry," Jess repeated.

Before she could say any more, an assistant took her away. Jess was bundled into a car and Anna into another. They were whisked away from the stadium under cover of darkness before the crowds could exit. Jess let her head drop into her hands, exhausted and at least given a reprieve from fans peering into the car and the incessant flashes of phones and cameras.

She hardly noticed the journey to Richmond, where the after-party was held in a grand Georgian river-front bar. The car delivered her into the privacy of the rear of the building and she was escorted through hallways, up a twisting staircase, to a private function room, all sleek with wooden floors and harsh noise. She grabbed a glass of Champagne from a waiter's tray, drinking it almost in one gulp, and headed through the throngs of guests, cast and crew to the quietest corner of the room, then out onto a balcony and solitude.

It was like she could breathe again, surrounded by the cool night air and anonymous in the dark, the only light reaching the balcony from the doorways to the room and the occasional outside lamp. There was space and the wide open world out here, the balcony overlooking the river and the stone arched bridge beyond. Orange light from the vintage street lamps glistened on the water, boats swayed in the swell of the river and the shape of trees in the dusk softened the view. The occasional sound of chatter from people walking along the river was removed and soothing. Jess closed her eyes, enjoying the peace, and slowly decompressed.

"I wondered if I'd find you here."

Jess opened her eyes. Anna.

"I thought you'd seek a quiet corner," Anna said, moving beside her. She leant on the stone balcony wall, a glass of Champagne in her hand, a picture of ease. "Would you like company or do you need more time alone?"

"Yes," Jess said, then realised that wasn't helpful. "I'd like company, if it's yours." And she was too tired for embarrassment at her honesty.

Anna sipped at her glass and gazed at the scenery, giving Jess time to recover, her ease infectious and soothing.

"It's beautiful up here," Anna said. "The way the lights on the water blend in the flow is very pleasing," she said in a sigh.

Jess leant on the balustrade close to Anna. She twirled the empty glass between her finger and thumb, not wishing to refill it and drink too fast.

"Cold?" Jess asked, wondering if Anna's coat slung around her shoulders was enough to make up for her revealing dress.

"I'm fine," she said, although Anna smiled and snuggled closer at the excuse, their bodies touching from shoulder to hip. The warm intimacy soothed deeper still.

"I didn't appreciate, until recently," Anna said gently, "quite the impact *Atlassia* has had and the pressure you've been under, and also its particular effect on you and your personality. I'm sorry I didn't try to understand earlier. I'm beginning to now."

It wasn't what Jess had expected her to say and she couldn't speak.

"I had a taster this evening," Anna continued, "and frankly it was terrifying. I think I would have struggled even at my most confident if I'd been the focus and I'm a person who used to, and is beginning to again, thrive on attention. I've had years on stage, but that was nothing like anything I've experienced before." Anna looked at her, eyes casting around Jess's and the river sparkling in their reflection. "And that's before any of the relentless attention and bigotry on social media."

Jess breathed out. "I've turned it off. I can't cope with social media anymore. Femi," Jess blinked, her brain still sluggish, "that's my manager, he has an assistant who posts on my behalf. Any news about my work, environmental causes I support, charities I fund, that's done for me. I have to stay away now."

"Is it helping?"

Jess nodded. "Being home's made a difference too. I stay at my folks' the weekends I'm free."

"Oh good." Anna grinned and reached out to squeeze her arm. "They sound wonderful. I'd love to meet them." Then she stopped herself, perhaps realising the implication. "You know what I mean," she said. "If they're ever around."

Jess carried on quickly, not wanting Anna to feel awkward. "It's been brilliant actually. I left home when I was seventeen and missed my little brother growing up. We've been catching up."

Anna smiled and held her arm.

"You..." Jess's heart was beating hard, the swell of loss and longing rising inside. "You nudged me in the right direction, when we met."

Anna twitched but her hand remained resting on Jess's arm.

"You made me come home. I wasn't sure what to do, or was perhaps too afraid to admit it. So many people thrive on the kind of lifestyle I've had, but not me. Familiarity and routine is what I needed," Jess said, and she had to gulp away feelings and thoughts that were so intertwined about the woman who stood next to her that she was afraid of what they'd all mean if she ever unpicked them all.

They stared over the river, perhaps both too affected to continue that conversation.

"Why do you act?" Anna said suddenly. "Why carry on when it takes such a toll on you?"

"Oh," Jess said, caught off guard but also grateful for the change in subject. She smiled. "I always loved stories growing up, making up my own with friends at school or reading them. You could do anything with stories – make a world to live in when your own wasn't welcoming or find a character like you when no-one else was. Acting seemed a natural extension for me."

Anna nodded, attentive.

Jess hesitated, wondering if she should explain further or if Anna already understood this about her. She might be beginning to. "I don't always understand people very well. Reading between the lines, duplicity, subtleties of social group dynamics. It's all so complicated and doesn't always lead to anything good. At the same time, I'm very sensitive to people's feelings, crave good company and love having trusted friends. It's…" she searched for the right word.

"Challenging?" Anna suggested with a smile.

"Yeah." Jess laughed. "I was a bit of a mimic when I was a kid. I copied other girls' behaviour to try and fit in. I think that's where I perfected other people's accents and mannerisms, and that's probably why acting became my thing. At the same time, I didn't get the real-life script everyone else seemed to be born with. I played with a mix of boys and girls who didn't care about being different and I found stories. I loved acting those out because they made sense and I knew the outcome. Real life was too fast and unpredictable with too many people behaving in ways I didn't always comprehend straight away."

She turned to Anna to see if she was explaining it clearly enough. "It's like perfect living," Jess said. "You can practise it. Real life happens too fast for me to take in sometimes, like I only appreciate it after the moment's passed. Acting lets me experience it again, properly. Lets me make sense of it all."

"I can see that – getting to relive those intense moments." Anna grinned and Jess could see the light come on in her eyes, that sparkle when a human is lit up inside with something that makes existence special for them. "Except I always craved an audience too. I'm always after that high from the intensity of experience when you draw in an entire crowd. Sometimes I suspect I just like showing off."

And they both laughed.

Jess was comforted that Anna had listened and not walked away. She looked at the beautiful woman, both an enigma but at the same time they had so much in common that she found her easy to understand too.

"Is that why you came back?" Jess asked quietly. "Is that how Matt managed to persuade you to take this role?"

Anna hesitated, considering her answer. "That played a part, yes."

"How's it been?"

"Exhilarating. Terrifying. I'm not sure I've come down from that first high of shooting a scene. I think I'm running on nervous energy. I hope I don't crash too badly."

Jess wanted to say she'd be there for her, but wondered if Anna would welcome it. "Anything I can do, please ask," Jess said.

"Thank you," Anna replied, seeming to accept the offer. "Is it worth it for you? Acting? When it has such a high price?"

"Honestly?" Jess pondered. "I don't know. The fame and money, that's not why I wanted to act. And the publicity and high-profile side of it, I'm rubbish at that. I'm still that quiet kid who likes reading books and watching films with my mates, and who likes to act someone else for a while, and use their words and feel the thrill of performing while safely choreographed. But small talk with others? Networking? Interviews? I'm not a great entertainer, not like you."

"You were a very accomplished host this evening."

"That's me on my pet subject. I can talk all day about the *Atlassia* stories." Jess grinned.

"You seem at ease to me, playful and funny. I find you wonderful company."

Jess's breath caught. "With you," Jess said, unable to hold back the sincerity.

"But you are entertaining and intelligent," Anna said, with a frown as if not quite puzzling her out yet.

"With people I know well. Small trusted groups. When I can relax."

"But interviews," Anna offered, "and being visible in public? You hate those?"

"That's the problem, like you saw tonight. I went to pieces as soon as that journalist asked a personal question. People have expectations of what I should be like, this movie star, an outgoing party girl who wants to be the centre of attention, and I'm not."

Anna was thoughtful a moment. "I used to play another role in public to deflect that kind of intrusion. I played a part tonight to get myself on stage."

"For some reason I don't do that," Jess said. "Even though I'm an actor, I feel like I should be myself when asked a question. Others might shrug it off or blag an answer, but I feel like I'm lying, and I hate that."

Anna looked at her. "You can always say 'no' though."

"To what?"

"When an interviewer asks a question that makes you uncomfortable, say, 'I'm not going to answer that'. It's a very useful defence which is honest and surprisingly strong. It sets a boundary and although they may try to shame you into lowering it, people usually realise they are in the wrong. You don't owe them your whole life. You don't owe anyone your deepest thoughts, unless you want to tell them."

"Makes sense," Jess nodded, and she felt a gulf between their experiences. "I feel naïve next to you, especially after your performance on stage tonight."

Anna snapped her gaze round, her face full of genuine surprise. "Nonsense, you've been acting for eight years and look at your resume. You've done more than many actors have in twenty. If I'd had half your athleticism, power of delivery, focus and empathy I would have been very happy indeed."

Jess felt all the force of the compliment as she stared at the beautiful actress who'd this evening delivered a performance that had given Jess goose bumps. "People are different," Jess said. "Everyone brings something to the table."

"Yes, they do," Anna said, and she gazed into Jess's eyes.

Jess was filled with longing. It made sense then, why they'd fallen for each other so quickly. There was the commonality but also the differences, age, experience, personality, and they fitted together in a way so pleasing as to make a bigger picture. And beyond that, they appreciated more and more where the other struggled and stepped up to help. Jess was flooded with yearning for this woman, realising how good they could be for each other.

She was about to ask her. What? To hang out sometime? To please let Jess earn her trust and friendship? But Anna seemed to withdraw a little.

"I should go and mingle," Anna said. "Besides, I left Penny with a bottle of Champagne. I should find her before she drinks the lot."

"Can I say hello?" Jess said quickly, not wanting to lose Anna's company.

"To Penny?"

"Please. I like her," Jess said with a smile.

"Of course. Don't let her ogle you though. Please remind her you're a real person."

Jess laughed.

Anna offered her arm. "Fancy introducing me to everyone whose name I've forgotten or don't recognise? In turn I'll do the onerous small talk."

Jess grinned and took her arm. "That's a deal."

They joined the party, Anna with so much ease she appeared its elegant hostess. She gracefully circulated and chatted with everyone they encountered, and Jess started to enjoy the evening. A weight had lifted. They'd cleared the air. The tension and guilt had been relieved at last.

Jess was left glowing, the only shadow cast on the evening her complete and utter inability to hide how besotted she was.

47

It was an unseasonably warm spell. The bare winter trees had burst into pink and white blossom in the studio walled-garden and Anna had been sat on the lawns with cast and crew for lunch. They'd all cleared away and Anna was about to get up herself when Jess bounded over.

"Hey," she said, looking down at Anna, a tray of sandwiches and a mug of tea in her hands. That great big smile was back, the one that lifted her face and made her eyes sparkle. Anna hadn't seen it since before that horrible morning on Shaftesbury Avenue in the theatre, an encounter Anna much regretted now. It was a relief to see that smile return, and those beautiful brown eyes twinkling perhaps with mischief. Actually it made Anna a little giddy inside.

"You off or can I join you?" Jess said.

"I've finished," Anna replied. "But I'm in no rush. Please." And she indicated for Jess to sit down.

The young woman seemed to concertina down into a cross-legged position on the grass. Even Anna, supple from yoga, envied the movement.

They'd seen a little of each other since the premiere, shooting the odd scene, and their interaction had taken on a tentative and tender quality. Anna wondered if Jess had noticed too. At the moment though, she was too focussed on her sandwich and Anna smiled as Jess tucked in.

"Busy morning?" Anna asked.

"Yeah," Jess said in between large mouthfuls. "I've been on the phone to my agent. She wanted to talk over a few contracts. Actually," Jess paused, "is she your agent now too?"

"Celia Hartingham is indeed my agent."

"Does she scare the bejeezus out of you?"

Anna laughed. "No, she doesn't."

"How?"

Anna shrugged. "What is there to fear? Once you realise she's concerned about her income but also the long-term welfare of her client, then she's quite straightforward..."

Jess's eyes were wide with shock.

"...if a little forthright."

Jess chuckled. "Maybe it's just me. She's always several steps ahead of me. Makes me laugh though."

"So not so scared?"

"Maybe not," Jess grinned. "She is just human after all."

A group of regular extras passed by, several young women and a couple of men. One, a young woman, with golden flowing hair, who quickly flicked it behind her ear to show her face to advantage, cried, "Hey Jess," accompanied by the kind of smile that had intentions.

Jess looked up a moment, swallowing some food. She appeared surprised that someone had called her name. Anna wondered if Jess would ever get used to being the centre of attention.

"Oh, hi Chloe," Jess said. She returned the wave then immediately tucked back into her sandwich. "She's brilliant at watching your back. You couldn't have hired anyone better."

Jess meant Celia, Anna realised, and she wondered if Jess had registered the interest of the attractive extra at all. Jess sat, unperturbed and likely oblivious, in tight black jeans, black T-shirt and padded jacket not dissimilar to that she wore most days. She ate the same sandwich that Anna had seen her eat the day before with Shawna, and with Matt the day before that.

"You like routine, don't you?" Anna said, with only affection.

"Hmm?"

"You like the same food, same style clothes. Do you listen to the same music at the end of every day?"

"I suppose, yeah. It's more that I don't want to spend energy on choosing sometimes. Once I find comfortable clothes, I'm happy, so why change," Jess said. "With food or music I'm very particular and I have phases, so making a new choice isn't a light decision and could take hours. Besides I really, really like some foods and just want to eat them all the time. I look forward to them. I know they're going to be good and that's like a tick on the way to a good day."

"You like routine."

"I like routine," Jess admitted, laughing. "I suppose I find a lot of things and people unexpected, so it's nice for others to be easy and predictable, like some decent grub. Then I can enjoy the interesting surprises."

"I can understand that," Anna said, mulling it over. "Actually I've done exactly the same."

"The insane order of your flat?"

"Yes," Anna laughed.

"See I'm not tidy. Like not at all. This is one of the reasons I have very few belonging. They just end up in a pile in the corner and I forget about them."

Jess ate on and Anna sipped at the end of her coffee that had gone cool. Jess sat cross-legged, like she had in the park that day when they first met.

"You're very much you," Anna murmured.

Jess lifted her eyebrows and dropped her mouth open, a crumb falling out, before closing it again. "I am with you," she said softly. "And I like that." She said it evenly, without a hint of artifice or embarrassment. She did that often with Anna, said snippets of truth that sounded small and simple but actually meant a great deal.

Jess put her sandwich down and brushed her hands together, her brow crinkling in thought. "I had a meltdown when I first met you. I retreat into my own head sometimes. When I get overloaded I have to stick on headphones and hide away for a while. And you take all that in your stride. I'm very grateful for that."

"It's not like I don't have my own limitations," Anna smiled.

"I know. Many people do. But, thank you."

It took a while for her eyes to settle on Anna's this time, and those brown eyes were full of meaning when they did settle. "I like not having to be anyone else with you."

"Me too," Anna said.

Now that Jess had finished her sandwich, she stretched out her long legs and leant back, arms straight and supporting behind her, her chest thrust forward. She closed her eyes and lifted her face to catch the vague warmth of the winter sun. Anna would have been amiss not to admit, at least to herself, that there were a great many things she liked about Jessica Lambert. And a little bit of Anna twinged inside, appreciating what it had been like to enjoy all those things.

Those soft long legs and the tenderness between Jess's upper thighs. Anna blushed imagining her fingertips once again enjoying the sensitive skin there. Those breasts and the sensation of her nipple pebbling inside Anna's mouth. And that was before Anna remembered the sound of Jess's groan accompanying her enjoyment and before she recalled so vividly Jess's sure touch at Anna's own.

Jess certainly knew her way around Anna's body and her sensitivity was fine-tuned to Anna's enjoyment. Anna could vividly recall that expert touch around where she swelled.

"We'd better get to makeup," Anna said, sitting up straight, her breath catching.

She was coy at her physical reaction that was likely one-sided. Jess had only been friendly and straightforward with Anna. Really, had she shown any more interest in Anna than the gorgeous extra who'd passed by? Was this professional? Was this friendship? Anna didn't know suddenly and she cursed her confidence that ebbed low in this regard. She could immediately tell that the extra had designs on Jess. But Anna's shattered confidence was blinding her to anyone's inclination to her. And what of it? What if she could tell? What if Jess was interested? What then?

"Sure," Jess said lazily, blinking several times. She leapt up and put her hand out to help Anna.

She took Jess's hand, blushing again at the familiar touch of her fingers and the memory of where they'd stroked exquisitely. She underestimated Jess's strength though, and with an energetic pull found herself standing very close indeed to her co-star. Breast to breast close.

"Sorry," Jess smiled, slipping her hand around Anna's back to steady her.

They stood for a moment, their bodies touching, Anna intimate in the shared physical space of someone she trusted and liked. The world dropped away and Anna wished they were back in her flat, sharing that time again of a few months ago, wishing Jessica Lambert could be that woman again.

"We're...we'd better...it's probably starting...you know...late," Jess stuttered.

"Yes," Anna said, all her training modulating her response. "We'd better."

They stepped apart and turned towards the main studios and Anna had to fight the temptation to take Jess's hand all the way.

48

It had been going so well for Anna. Then it wasn't.
The cast together with extras was huge today, and among them was a familiar face – a man her age who'd performed at her last theatre appearance. She couldn't remember his name, but his face conjured horrible memories of five years ago at the Globe. He'd looked startled when he saw her, then shocked when she'd explained her major role. Time had clearly not been kind to him, given that he was an extra, and he didn't seem to view it kindly that she had a larger role.

He'd been there that night, that excruciating night, when she'd frozen mid-performance. She could remember the weight of hundreds of pairs of eyes upon her, confused then disapproving, stoking and escalating her terror. Had he been one of those who'd shouted at her to get back on stage?

Anna was starting to shake at the recollection and rushed to costume and makeup.

Then there had been script changes and extensive ones at that. What made it worse was the sheer number of cast required for the scene and the long tracking shot the director had chosen to increase Jess's isolation. The camera took a sweeping view around the forest castle and the queen's knights, ending with its focus on Anna and Jess, the queen's powerful speech overlaying it all and taken in one seamless shot to end on Jess's defiant face.

"Our forests burn," Anna cried, her arms lifted and her green gown trailing like wings. "The people starve, all for Atlassia, and now you want our help."

"Cut!"

Anna closed her eyes. That was the sixth time she'd messed up.

"Let's take five," Shawna, the director, said and Anna could hear the disgruntled voices of actors and crew. She caught the familiar extra who looked most annoyed out of everyone. She could imagine what he was thinking and the idle chatter he was indulging in with his fellow extras.

Shawna approached. "Nearly there, bab," she said. "But the wording changed on–"

"I know," Anna snapped, putting her hands on her hips. She kicked out the flowing gown to clear it from her feet. She'd tripped over the damned thing twice already that morning. "Sorry," she added. "The fault's entirely mine."

"Take a break," Shawna said, leaning over and squeezing her arm. "We'll get it." And Shawna swung round and wandered off the set.

"Shit," Anna said under her breath. The focus of the scene was almost completely on her, and they were at full crew and cast today, just so everyone could see her fuck up.

She'd known the script word perfect, then been floored by the late changes. She hadn't realised how dependent on rehearsal she'd been in the past and she wasn't as quick at picking up lines. Plus last-minute changes didn't happen too often with Shakespeare. Anna tapped her fingers agitated against her head. The original text was stubbornly embedded.

"Hey." Jess appeared by her side, holding a pile of sheets which Anna assumed was her script. "Do you want to go over it while everyone's on a break?"

Anna sighed irritably at herself. "Thank you," she said, with an apologetic look to Jess. "I would."

Jess had been word perfect every single take. Anna had appreciated first hand why Jess was so popular on set. Courteous, professional, focussed, exceptional.

"These were very late changes," Jess said, reassurance in her voice.

"But it's only me who's fucking up."

"You have the most lines."

"All the more to foul up," Anna said. "I'm sorry," she added. "I used to be quicker and we'd rehearse of course. I always picked up lines better aurally during read-throughs."

"I don't think you need to apologise." Jess shrugged. "People learn in different ways and they didn't give you time to pick them up in the way you needed."

She could have hugged Jess for her understanding, yet at the same time this was the person she didn't want to disappoint most of all. The realisation made Anna pause. The night of the preview, they'd cleared the air between them and they'd spent more time together in breaks – she and this young woman who'd charmed and coaxed her from her reclusive existence all those months ago. Anna's heart beat in her chest. Her hopes and expectations were building higher with every moment she spent with her.

Stop it, Anna told herself. Jess was a beautiful, talented, phenomenally successful young actress in demand across the world.

"Thank you," Anna said. "I would appreciate another read through."

Then after the break, another take and another mistake. This time by the extra, and the way his friends in the cast railed against him, Anna knew patience was wearing thin.

It was like the whole stage was holding its breath on the next take. Anna's shoulders knotted as she held her arms aloft. Her voice was losing its power. She wasn't breathing into her stomach with her body so tense and she was croaking by the end of her speech when the camera operator panned round to finish on Jess.

There was an audible sigh of relief when the assistant director called cut. They all turned to Shawna.

"I think that's the best we're going to get my loves," Shawna said. "We can probably dub over Anna fluffing that last bit."

And Anna's humiliation was complete.

She picked up the train of her gown, not caring if she revealed her legs. She couldn't leave the set fast enough. Anna could tell people watched as she left. She swung out of the huge sound stage, raced into the corridor and straight into a trolley of equipment.

"Sorry, love," a voice came from behind a mound of cabling.

Anna put out an arm to the wall to steady herself.

"Fine," she spat, then squeezed her way along the wall.

She wanted to be home, away from all of this. She marched along the corridor, face down to hide her humiliation, only half registering that it took longer than the route to her dressing room. She stopped and swayed, disoriented at a fork at the end, but instinctively turned left in her haste and punched at a door's metal lever to enter another corridor.

When she stepped into darkness the anomalies finally grabbed her full attention. Her momentum took her forward and she stumbled, her heels sinking into gravel and cold night air chilled on her face.

Wrong turn. She could have made several. She swung round, but not in time and the door clicked shut.

"Shit."

She staggered back to the building. It was pitch black outside. She patted around the doorway, but save for its outline it was smooth. There was no window to peek through or through which to be seen. She pawed across it. No handle. She swiped around the edges onto the corrugated surface of the huge studio building. No buzzer. No intercom. She must have stumbled outside through an emergency exit.

Her eyes were beginning to adjust but except for a strip of low-energy lights at the bottom of the building it remained dull. The orange glow of Richmond blazed in the distance, but the studio was surrounded by the woodland of a large park. Staring out, all she could detect were the large looming shapes of trees and little else.

She hammered on the door.

"Hello?"

Then waited for a response.

Nothing.

She pounded harder. "Hello! Can anyone hear me?"

She put her ear to the door, the cold metal a shock against her cheek. A door slammed muffled down a distant corridor, then nothing above the distant hum of the city.

"Shit," she said, her voice shaky.

She crossed her arms. It was cold in the April air, spring still mean with its warmth. It must have been late in the evening, her foul ups pushing the schedule out. She pounded the door again.

"Hello!" She shouted at the stop of her voice.

Oh god.

She crunched across the gravel, away from the glowing strip of lights around the exit. There must be a way around somewhere. It was disconcerting, advancing into the cool blanket of darkness. The chilly air stroked across her face, tickling her cheeks. There could have been anyone or anything in the dark and she hugged herself tighter as she stepped forward.

Nothing there it seemed. She thrust her arm into the black void and edged on, until her heel sunk into ground softer than the gravel and she stumbled onto cold and wet grass. Moisture seeped through the dress where she knelt on the ground, her hands claggy with mud where she'd broken her fall.

She was exposed, on all fours, surrounded by darkness and she shivered. She had no idea how far the studio grounds extended into the park and headed back to the building.

Hammering on the door brought no response and she felt her way around the edge of the building. The strip of lights ceased a little way off but she persisted, dabbing her way along the corrugated exterior. At least she couldn't stray too far this way.

But the building was huge. The corner she could discern in the faint glow didn't come quickly and by the time she reached the end, the light from an office blinked out.

"Please!" she shouted. "I'm stuck outside!"

The light didn't come on and her panic soared as she realised the building was shutting down for the night. She stumbled forward quicker, hoping to find a window to hammer on but ran straight into a wire fence, her finger bending at the collision.

"Oh fucking hell."

She held her finger to her mouth trying to squeeze away the pain while shaking the fence with her other.

The darkness and indistinct shapes in the park were disorienting and her head began to swim. Oh god. Would she be out here all night? She hugged herself in her thin costume wondering what state she'd be in by morning. She became aware of noises. The crack of a twig. The snuffle of breathing. Was she hearing things? Her own breathing hitched in panic.

She was by a park and it was probably deer, but her brain wouldn't listen. That fear that she'd never completely shaken descended – a sense of being watched and followed, always looking over her shoulder, never seeing but always suspecting. His presence had always been there even when he hadn't.

"Fuck," she gasped.

Her stalker had been dead years now, but still he haunted on her worst days.

This is why she'd stayed in her comfort zone for so long. This is why she hadn't stepped beyond her flat, her walks and work until a few months ago. She'd been a bloody fool coming here. She squeezed herself tighter and sank against the building until she sat on the sharp gravel, hugging her knees and shivering.

"I want to go home," she whispered into her hands, her breath moist on her fingers. "If I can just get back home."

The freezing night bit deeper and she started to quietly weep. She curled up in a ball, resigned to the imagined presence all around her, spirits sinking and waiting for whatever lurked in the darkness to take her.

"Anna?"

It was a muffled cry a distance away and Anna realised in her sluggishness that the voice had cried out before.

"Anna?" it said again, louder this time, as if someone were casting about in the darkness.

"Jess?" she croaked.

The voice came again, but fainter this time, and Anna scrabbled to her feet. "Jess!" she managed louder.

Her name was thrown back to her, clearer again, then quick steps crunched on the gravel, at the pace of someone running.

"Oh Jesus fucking Christ," Anna stuttered, wiping away at her tears and nose. She swept the hair from her face which had become plastered to her cheek.

The noise of the person approaching became louder. "Anna? Are you there?"

It was definitely Jess.

"Here!" she yelled, her distress breaking in her voice.

The footsteps slowed and the noise of a hand running across the corrugated building became louder.

"Are you there? I can't see a thing," Jess's voice came.

"Here," Anna said reaching out, and her fingers encountered Jess's warm body, her eyes at last making out Jess's shape.

Strong arms clung to Anna's waist and with intense relief she stretched up and threw her arms around Jess's shoulders.

"I was stupid. I took a wrong turn and ran outside," Anna babbled.

"You're OK," Jess murmured, her lips warm on Anna's cheek. "You're all right."

All the rising panic and fear channelled into intense relief and Anna held Jess tight. She couldn't stop pulling her as close as possible. Jess's toned shoulders were vivid beneath her arms, and breasts soft on Anna's belly. The shape of her was suddenly everything in Anna's mind and gratitude, desire, relief all melted and flowed inside her.

"I couldn't find you," Jess said. "I tried your dressing room and your driver said you hadn't gone home."

Anna clutched Jess's head. She couldn't stop chattering with relief. "I'm sorry. I panicked. I took a wrong turn. I got stuck outside. I thought someone was watching me."

She was dizzy in the darkness, shivering with cold, burning with relief and a jolt of attraction shot through her, the kind that explodes after a heightened state of fear. Her hands ran down Jess's slender but firm shoulders, squeezing them with nervous relief and powerful need. She couldn't help her admiration of the delicious curve of toned arms. The familiarity and physical intimacy of the only person she'd slept with for years was irresistibly suggestive and her fraught body responded. She longed for reassurance and erotic comfort and it was almost unbearable.

Anna had to pull back. She held Jess's shoulders at arm's length.

"Thank you," she gasped. "I'm not sure what kind of state I'd have been in by morning." Her words sounded slurred.

"You're all right now. Let's get you inside," Jess said, and she pulled Anna under her arm.

Anna almost burst into tears. Her body was confused, her mind in panic, and she let Jess take her inside.

49

Asking security to open up a star apartment and wrapping Anna up beneath a duvet had been a good idea. Jess getting in with her, not so much.

In fairness, Jess had been concerned about hypothermia given Anna's clothing, how long she'd been outside and her babbling. It was Jess or the security guard and seventy-year-old Bob Baxter, a traditionally minded old soul, suggested Jess was more appropriate.

"Don't let her fall asleep yet," he said. "Make sure she warms through and talks sensibly to someone before she's left alone. Give me a ring if you need anything." And he'd left, turning the lights down to a comfortable low, to do his rounds.

They were snuggled on the bed beneath the duvet, Jess wrapped around Anna and attempting to keep at bay thoughts and feelings which Bob would have considered anything but appropriate.

"Don't fall asleep," Jess said, squeezing Anna.

"You're a hard task mistress," Anna muttered. She gave another shiver and snuggled into Jess.

"I'm serious."

Anna felt cool against her chest, while the rest of Jess roasted under the duvet.

"Look at you," Anna said, still sounding a measure or two worse for wear. "You're even wearing your superhero costume." She stroked the thin material on Jess's chest.

"All in a day's work," Jess said.

Anna smiled, then drifted again.

"Oh no you don't."

Anna grumbled then blinked herself awake. She wriggled to get comfortable and Jess was grateful that Anna resembled a block of ice when she writhed against her legs.

"I got myself into a state," Anna said quietly. "Thank you for finding me. I couldn't think clearly."

"Why did you run from the set?"

"I feel stupid," Anna said. "I was freaked out by someone I used to work with, a guy who saw me freeze on stage and derail an entire run at the Globe. I could tell what he was thinking."

"What?" Jess gently asked.

"That I was a flake. I've had so many people say I should just get over it. It's just stage fright. Stop stressing about a man who's not even alive anymore."

"People telling you how you should think? Telling you how you should be?"

Anna nodded. "They'd say 'Get over it. What's wrong with you? Stop being so pathetic.'" She squeezed Jess, but still looked ashamed.

Jess took a moment. "I've had that my whole life too. Be louder, be quicker, do small talk, but not like that, speak up in class, only like men, look me in the eye so that I think you're listening but now you can't, say thank you to the creepy dude who complimented you, be fun even though you can't even think above the noise, why do you do that with your hair, that makeup's wrong on you, too geeky, not geeky enough, people shouldn't lie, why can't you lie." She took a breath and gazed at Anna. "For so much of my life, I've been told that I'm wrong – the way I look, the way I think, the people I love. So I hear you. I might not always know what you're thinking or understand why you're having a bad day. And sometimes, often even, I will get things wrong. But I will listen, and I will learn, because we're all different."

Anna attempted a tight smile. "I relapsed a little out there with the fear of being followed"

Jess nodded.

"It's been a while now, but it haunts me at times and then my fears escalate out of all proportion."

"I understand that," Jess said.

"The night we met," Anna started, "in the Underground, did you ever find out who was following you?"

Jess winced at the allusion to that night and her deception, but relaxed when Anna remained motionless, apparently open to whatever Jess might have to say.

"No," Jess said. "In the last year, my profile has gone sky high and I've had all kinds of people track me on social media to the point of obsession, some high-profile themselves, others ordinary people. Some want to support me, others, well, I seem to stand for everything they despise. I was terrified one had found me that night." She shivered and was grateful for the gentle hug that Anna returned. "I had to change my phone recently. The number must have got out somehow and I was getting nasty calls."

"Oh," Anna said, then she hesitated. "I tried to call you," she confessed, "at Christmas."

Jess's heart thumped in her chest.

"I wanted to apologise," Anna continued, "and say hello. Actually I'm not sure what I wanted, but your phone number was out of service."

Jess's whole body tingled at the thought that Anna had been receptive to her back then, that perhaps not all had been lost.

"I didn't know if you'd want to hear from me," Jess said. "So I didn't send you my new number."

Anna nodded, the movement caressing Jess's chest. She didn't dare move. She waited for Anna to say more, her body primed with anticipation.

"I don't blame you," Anna murmured at last, and when she stroked up Jess's arm, the thrill of it shot through her entire body. Jess cleared her throat desperate for distraction from the awakening inside.

"You're sounding more coherent," she whispered.

"I am?" Anna murmured. "Does that mean you'll let me sleep?" Jess could hear the smile in her voice.

"Yes. I'll let you," she said and they both deflated, Anna perhaps with relief that she could succumb to tiredness, Jess that she'd soon have a reprieve from this intimacy. They'd been getting on so well. She didn't want to mess this up. At the same time it was increasingly difficult to hide her desire from Anna, for her company and physically.

Jess waited, listening to Anna drift into a slumber, waiting until Anna's body was the same temperature as her own, then slipped into dreams herself.

And what dreams they were. Anna sought more warmth, stroking her soft fingers beneath the seams of Jess's suit, running her hand beneath the silky material and caressing Jess's skin with the delicate pads of her fingers. Anna's hand explored, round the shape of Jess's breast, tweaking the peak of her nipple, then drifted lower following the burning that ached between Jess's legs.

Just as Anna's fingers found the heat they desired, Jess woke with a yelp. Anna lay half on top of her, cradling her breast, her knee snug between Jess's legs. Jess's whole body thrummed with desire, an embarrassingly short way from peaking and the heat pulsed where Anna rubbed her knee.

"Oh fuck," Jess gasped and she twitched away from Anna.

Daylight blazed into the room and she squinted.

"What time is it?" she said, alarmed in every way and sliding from under Anna and out of the bed. She snatched her phone from the bedside table.

"Is it late?" Anna moaned, her eyes scrunched and her hair a gorgeous mess.

Jess gawped for a moment. She'd forgotten how heavenly it was to wake up beside Anna and she stared captivated by the woman bathed in morning sunshine.

"We need to get ready for on set," Jess smiled, unable to take her eyes from Anna.

Anna leant up on her elbows, her gown slipping open at the chest so that the curve of breast was deliciously apparent, and Jess audibly sighed.

Anna smiled, her cheeks pink. "I feel stupid about yesterday."

"Don't" she said. Did Jess's face betray total admiration and besotted longing? She was unable to do a thing about it. "You had a bad day. You've seen mine."

"I fucked up in front of the whole cast and crew, then shut myself outside and had to be rescued," Anna said quietly.

"I froze in front of several thousand people and needed the same."

They both laughed.

"What a pair we make," Anna said, then she paused, seeming to fear the implication.

Was it Jess's imagination or were they both glowing?

"I need to get ready," she said reluctantly. What she would give to stay here and watch Anna Mayhew all day, ruffled and luxurious in bed.

"Me too," Anna said, a goofy gorgeous smile on her face.

"I," this was going to sound painfully eager but Jess couldn't help herself, "I can come by your dressing room and run over the script before shooting if you like."

"Thanks," Anna said, her voice husky. "But I don't think there'll be many changes today."

"Oh?"

"It's the revival scene."

"Oh," and Jess's heart leapt into her throat.

Oh god. The revival scene. Of all the days.

—

"So?" Matt said, striding beside Jess along the corridor. "Ready for your Anna Mayhew kiss?"

"It's not a kiss," Jess grumbled. "It's a resuscitation."

"They're legendary you know," Matt said, an extra bounce to his stride.

Jess flipped up the hood on her arctic coat, hoping to hide behind the fake fur lining. "It's a revival scene. It's going to be more like a medical procedure than anything more salacious."

"See, I was definitely hoping for salacious," Matt said, growling the last word, making it sound impossibly rude.

They turned into the cavernous sound stage and approached the corner, set up with snow covered boulders.

Shawna was conferring with her assistant who was marking out the stage floor.

"Wahey," Shawna said, with a grin when she saw them approach. "Ready for your Anna Mayhew kiss?"

Oh bloody hell.

"It's not a kiss," Jess said between her teeth.

Shawna lifted an eyebrow and wiggled her hips. "Oh yeah?"

"Just fuck off the pair of you."

Shawna threw her head back and filled the entire stage with a laugh.

This was the worst day possible for this scene. Jess's body was already primed with desire for Anna. How was she meant to dispassionately lay on the floor unconscious with Anna kissing, no, reviving her? This was going to be challenging.

"Am I late?" All three of them swivelled round at the sound of Anna's honeyed voice. She glided forward, a white gown flowing at her feet and her face hidden in the same style arctic coat as Jess. How did she manage to look even more magnificent in that, the shadow and softness of the hood accentuating the size and shine of her eyes, the fullness of her lips, the glow on her cheeks.

"Not at all, bab. Hope you've both dressed light under there. Could get hot," Shawna said, her grin expanding.

Jess cleared her throat. "T-shirt and jeans."

The roll of Shawna's eyes had a gravity all of its own. "You have no sense of occasion."

Jess wasn't quite sure what she meant by that and didn't want to think about it too much.

"Should I change?" Anna said, with a slight frown, innocently seeking clarification. Jess wanted to kick Shawna.

"You're fine," the director said, squeezing her arm. "Right, let's get down and dirty then," she said with glee.

Jess shot her friend daggers then obediently lay down on her mark and waited for the crew to dust her with snow. She closed her eyes and tried to think of anything to reduce her heightened state. It was to no avail, because as soon as Anna leant over her, liquid warmth suffused Jess's entire body. The beautiful woman, on all fours, hands either side of Jess's breasts, one knee between Jess's legs the other astride her thigh, and the growing desire had Jess on the verge of groaning.

"You OK?" Anna whispered, her face a few inches away.

Jess gazed up into her eyes, melted at the sight of her smile, inwardly groaned at the flush across her cheeks, and sighed at those soft lips. "Amazing."

"Wait!" Shawna shouted.

The intimacy was broken by the appearance of Shawna's face and abundant hair between them. She tweaked a stray ribbon of hair into Anna's hood and gave Jess a grin. "Cosy?" She didn't wait for an answer and bustled away and a camera drew up to them in her place.

The assistant director started the run through. Sound. Camera. Then silence.

Jess closed her eyes and let her cheeks go slack. Her head lolled to the side as she relaxed her neck muscles and she slowed her breathing. She was a picture of oblivion and even her heart rate slowed.

But the anticipation, what a killer that was. A shadow stroked across her eyelids. The air between them became balmy and Jess sensed Anna getting closer. The temptation to meet her was colossal and even though she managed to suppress a twitch across her cheeks, her chest began to heave with expectation.

Then Anna's lips touched hers. Those succulent, most tender lips surrounded her. The contact was like gentle lightening, hot, instantaneous, burning but delightful, all at the same time. The exquisite sensation made Jess's body thrum. How Anna managed to caress with such delicacy but at the same time stunning command, Jess she had no idea. Anna's lips slipped over Jess's and as she drew slowly away, Jess's whole being was drawn after her, and she lifted her head from the floor, loath to break contact.

"Cut!"

Jess snapped her eyes open and stared right into Anna's. Were her co-star's cheeks flushed? Were those dark pupils large with the same kind of longing that made Jess's body pulse?

"Right," Shawna shouted, "that was quite a lot of movement for an unconscious body."

Jess's cheeks burned.

"Let's try again. And," Shawna shouted, "can we get some blue light on them? These two are positively glowing with good health."

And Jess's cheeks shot up another few degrees.

"OK?" The assistant director ran through to silence again.

"Stay still," Jess chanted mentally, while trying to keep her body limp. Don't react.

Again the anticipation heightened her senses, from her tingling lips, through her inflamed body, all the way to her toes. Anna lingered this time, the warmth of her face caressing Jess. Her breasts pushed down and Jess couldn't help the moan that escaped her lips.

"Keep rolling."

Drawing deep on will power, Jess suppressed her reaction, keeping her body supple and supine. Anna's breath was humid on Jess's lips, her breasts cushioned into hers, her knee brushing inside her thigh. Jess kept herself limp but the heat building inside threatened to burst.

Then came the kiss. Another divine kiss from Anna. More fluid this time. Was there more intent than just revival? Jess couldn't help herself and she moved into the kiss. She reached up to hold Anna's side, the curve of her breast discernible and teasing in her palm. Jess's body wouldn't pretend. It twisted with longing and just as embarrassment and awareness threatened to intrude, Anna slipped the tip of her tongue inside Jess's mouth and the whole of her body burst into flames.

"Cut!"

Jess blinked. She let her head fall back to the floor and she stared up at Anna whose rose cheeks were definitely as involved as Jess's burning body. She was breathing hard and Jess gazed with inflamed disbelief at Anna.

"Sorry," Jess whispered, but Anna remained silent.

"OK," Shawna shouted. "I think we need more blue light. Let's roll again."

Jess's mind raced, wishing the scene over. She cursed Shawna for shooting from several different angles then insisting on a tracking shot around them both.

Did Anna feel that? Was she as overcome as Jess or was this torture?

Her mind was in turmoil and Jess lay, take after take, wound with nerves and twitching with desire, wishing an end to it so she could talk to Anna.

"Alrighty then!" Shawna shouted. "Not what I had in mind, but I'm gonna take that and roast it."

Anna sat back, took down her hood, her cheeks blazing.

"Are we done?"

"We certainly are. Jess you're finished for the day. Anna I need you in twenty."

Jess stared, as Anna rose to her feet. Was she avoiding her gaze? She watched as Anna made her way across the sound stage, unbuttoning her coat as she went.

Shit. Had Jess thrown away all the progress she'd made with Anna? But how could she not react to that, after a night in her arms and a kiss that seduced like an instant liquid drug it was so overpowering.

She scrambled to her feet. "OK," she muttered as she passed Shawna, wilfully ignoring her friend's gleeful expression.

"Anna," Jess said, rounding the corner, but Anna was already half way along the corridor towards her dressing room.

Jess broke into a run. "Anna!" she shouted. Surely she could hear her.

Anna was stepping inside her room when Jess caught up and she put her arm out to stop Anna from closing the door. Her heart jolted with surprise as Anna reached back and pulled her inside. The door slammed, Anna pushed Jess up against it and Anna's wonderful hot lips smothered her with delicious hunger.

Jess groaned and wanted to slide down the door it was so exquisite. She held Anna's head and instantly deepened the kiss, the heat from them both driving their passion.

"God," Jess gasped, as Anna's leg pushed between hers, the warm pressure so achingly welcome.

Anna tore at her coat, pulling the buttons apart, as she writhed between Jess's legs, sending Jess higher and almost agonisingly into desire. She was soaking wet against Anna's leg.

Thrown up against the wall, by someone Jess had craved for months, it was fucking heaven.

Her hands explored Anna, desperate to find a way in. Anna was direct and adept, pushing Jess back, her hands undoing Jess's trousers, dipping her fingers inside and stroking straight over Jess's clitoris.

"Oh fuck," Jess gasped and she caved in rhythm as Anna circled her centre with a sure and hungry touch. Just as Jess became comfortable to her rhythm, Anna pushed her higher against the door and slipped her fingers inside. Jess moaned loudly as Anna filled her so that her body was consumed all the way to her chest. As Anna thrust her fingers inside, her thumb circled her clitoris so that Jess groaned with every motion. Oh christ she wouldn't last long like this.

She desperately tried to find Anna's body, stroking her hands beneath her dress, eager to touch her, and suddenly her hands encountered her naked chest. She panted in time to Anna pushing inside her and squeezed Anna's breasts with dizzy rapture. The woman felt phenomenal.

As Jess's arousal built, Anna quickened her rhythm, pushing her higher. Jess stroked her fingers down Anna's waist and slipped her fingers between her legs. She was soaking, the warm slickness making Jess's head spin, and Anna's cry as Jess circled her sent delicious shivers through Jess that heightened her arousal and her whole body prickled with expectation at the orgasm to come.

Her body tensed from her core to her fingers, ready to explode and they both cried out as they came together.

50

They stood trembling, Jess's breath humid beside Anna's ear. Her chest heaved with deep inhalations. Jess sank down the wall and Anna to her knees and she stared at Jess's beautiful face, which still reeled with the shock of orgasm.

Anna cupped Jess's soft cheek and sighed at this wonderful woman. Eyes like conkers. Jess's description always made her smile. Anna traced her fingers lightly over Jess's features. The full lips that felt delicious against her own. Her black hair, which had been straightened but now curled in the perspiration of their activity. Her toned shoulders and smooth skin. Her elegant, strong arms. Her long slender fingers that enjoyed Anna's body. The way they fit together. She adored it all.

Anna's heart sank. "I probably shouldn't have done that."

"Why?" Jess gasped.

Anna peered at her. "What are we doing?" she whispered.

"Falling for each other?"

Anna smiled sadly.

"I don't understand," Jess said. Anna could hear the hurt in her voice. "I think we make a great couple. I'm bonkers about you."

Anna had to breathe in to keep a level head and stop her emotions from rising.

"Your life," Anna said. "You. Your fans. I'm not sure if I can afford to fall for you. I'm already in deep and I'm scared."

"Of what?"

"You're young and superstar, wanted all over the globe. You're under immense scrutiny and I'm not sure I'd cope well with the increased attention. I've already trespassed beyond my comfort zone and I haven't coped well at times. I don't want to have to check over my shoulder."

"But I'd be with you."

"Would you? All the time?"

"If that's what it takes."

Anna's chest swelled with affection for this kind and genuine woman.

"Maybe now," Anna said. "But you're young. What happens when the passion wears off? What about when an opportunity comes your way and you need to travel? Because you are going to get those offers, no doubt. Then there's the fact that I'm a middle-aged woman who values her independence. I don't want for you to have to be always around."

Jess was silent.

"I'm falling for you so badly," Anna said. "You had me right from the start, but I have to be realistic."

"So....So what...." Jess was struggling.

Anna sat back and waited, realising Jess needed time to think.

"It's not just you who's scared of my life," Jess started. "I've had trouble with fans in the past. I tend to shut down any attention quickly, but I've had people who think we have a connection when there's none. They've watched me for hours on film, read every article and interview. I think they get attached to that. Maybe they forget that I don't know them and that's not me up there on the screen." She paused. "So I do understand."

Anna nodded.

"That's why," Jess continued, those beautiful eyes filling with hurt and longing, "I need a break. And I don't mean an escape for now, I need somewhere to come home to. Staying with my parents helped, but most of all I want you. I want a real life. I want pancakes in the morning. I want walks in the park and to wake up with a woman I love. I want to chill out with a book and have somewhere familiar to retreat and recharge. And I love acting, have lived for *Atlassia*, but I can't do it any more without a real life too, without my own story."

Anna listened, her forehead pounding with yearning for this to work. "Can you even have that?" she murmured. "Are you so well known that it's not possible anymore?"

"I want to try," Jess said, her tone desperate.

There was a knock at the door and they both flinched.

"A minute please," Anna called out.

"Ms Mayhew, you're needed in Stage 4," came a man's voice.

"OK. I'll be right there."

Anna waited until the footsteps receded down the corridor. She opened her mouth to speak, but Jess cut in.

"I know you have to go, but..." Jess shook her head annoyed with herself. "I don't think well on my feet. Just, don't dismiss this. Please." And big brown eyes looked at Anna and she could see they were filling with tears.

At least Anna had time to think with Jess away on location, except every time Anna did she went through missing Jess, aching for her with so much strength Anna felt she could overcome anything, then relapsing into fear about what lay ahead.

Midweek, Anna joined the crew on location in a Midlands wood for a heavy schedule before spring arrived in force and the barren chill of winter couldn't be pretended anymore.

Anna hung back from the shooting, behind the perimeter of tape, grateful for her arctic coat costume and her breath clouding in the cool air of the woods. The fallen leaves of autumn were still bronze and rustled beneath her feet, but spring was definitely threatening and she twirled a bud on a branch between her fingers, the leaf inside almost ready to unfurl.

A little way through the woods was a village and a handful of locals had turned up to watch the shoot.

"This is where it all began," a woman further along the tape said, her strong voice lending the sentence the grand promise of story. "This is where she and her friends from school shot their version of *Atlassia*. It had millions of hits and won her the role."

Anna's ears pricked up as she realised the woman was talking about Jess.

"I think it's wonderful that the producer wanted to acknowledge those beginnings by including the location in the new series and making our little village famous." The woman said the last word with a growling gusto.

Anna's interest must have been obvious because the couple next to her, a tall middle-aged white man and a black woman with a short pixie haircut of tight curls, kept peeking towards her.

"She's talking about Jess's film," the woman said, her accent local, "the one her friends put on YouTube. It got her the audition."

"Oh," Anna said, smiling. "I didn't know that."

"The kids were always acting their favourite scenes from the graphic novels in these woods." The woman wore a fond expression as she gazed around the scene and a beaming smile filled her face. "Amazing isn't it," the woman said, stepping closer to Anna. "Who'd have thought that she'd be a big movie star and be back with a proper film crew." And she shook her head.

They both glanced at the scene being prepared for Jess. There was kerfuffle about missing props delaying shooting.

"Erm," the woman from the couple, said quietly, "I hope you don't mind me asking, but–"

"Sorry?" Anna said coming to.

The woman hesitated. "Are you Anna Mayhew?"

"Yes?" Anna said surprised. There was something about the woman's approach that put Anna at ease rather than on alert, her genuine interest and politeness perhaps.

"I'm Trisha," the woman said, her face breaking into that big smile again and putting a hand out. "Trisha Lambert. Jess's mom."

"Oh," Anna said, and she was stunned into silence. It took more than a few seconds to recover. There wasn't much that made Anna speechless but this had taken her entirely by surprise. And that big shining smile looked awfully familiar now that she thought about it. And the man too, from Jess's family photograph.

"Oh my god!"

Anna didn't have time to respond to Trisha, because the enthusiastic woman with the animated voice was striding over towards them, hands stretched out. In fact, as she approached Anna noticed a certain similarity between the women, similar expressions, heights and physique.

"Anna Mayhew!" the woman shouted. "We've been dying to meet you."

"Sorry?" Anna said.

"Jess talks about you all the time," the woman drew out with satisfaction. "Anna this, Anna that, it's all we ever hear these days."

"Sorry, I–"

"Mom," the younger woman growled in warning. "I don't think Jess–"

"Rubbish! Oh my god, you are beautiful!" the woman shouted, and she clapped her hands on either side of Anna's arms. "No wonder my granddaughter is so taken with you."

"Oh," Anna said, in realisation. "You're Jess's Nan."

"That's right!" the woman said. And she gave Anna the kind of hug that thumps out breath in a way that only a grandmother could.

The woman leant away and laughed. "Oh my god. Where is that girl anyway?"

"Mom," Trish whispered again, harsh at the back of her throat.

"All we ever hear when she comes home is about this goddess Anna who's joined the cast," Jess's Nan continued. "How you floored an entire audience with your sexual power. How you had thousands of people in your grasp."

"I think Jess may have exaggerated–" Anna started.

"Had them grovelling on their knees."

"That's too kind—"

"And how you put that bitch of a journalist in her place."

"Nan!" The yelp had come from the direction of the shoot, followed by a quick rustle of footsteps through the leaves and the rapid appearance of Jess with eyes as wide as saucers.

"There she is! My lovely granddaughter. We've met the goddess Anna Mayhew."

"Nan!"

"Mom!"

The two younger women growled at the same time.

"I didn't ever call her a goddess." Jess's voice pitched high with consternation.

"You didn't need to. We knew what you meant and she's here now and I can tell with my own eyes."

Anna stood with her mouth open, entirely surrounded by Jess's family, voices coming from all directions.

"Well," Anna said, breaking into a smile, "hello," and she offered her hand to Jess's Nan.

"Pleased to meet you," she said and she gave Anna another enormous, breath-defying hug and a squelch of a kiss in return.

"Trisha," Anna nodded.

"Pleased to meet you, bab."

And she turned in the direction of the tall man who Anna assumed was Jess's father.

"Hi," Anna said.

"Bill," he said, and his amused tone said everything. "This is our son Jack," and he stepped aside to reveal a boy, almost as tall as the man, who waved and grunted a little.

"Well," Anna said, "I'm very pleased to meet you all."

"I'm really sorry you've been ambushed like this," Jess said quietly by her side.

"Nonsense!" her grandmother shouted, missing nothing. "Have you finished shooting for the day?"

"Yes. We've left the scene props at the studio and we'll have to start again in the morning."

"Excellent! Then we can all go home for tea. I have a stew in the oven."

And before Anna could think of a polite excuse, and Jess was no help at all there, Nan had offered her arm and was escorting Anna through the woods.

51

Once Anna had persuaded Nan to let her change out of costume, the whole family walked home.

"We moved here when Jess was eight."

"Seven," Jess muttered, walking beside Nan.

"Whatever, seven," Nan carried on. "Like a little stick she was back then. Can't believe she would grow into this woman here." And she patted Jess on the hip.

Anna couldn't see Jess's expression past Nan, but she imagined it wasn't best pleased.

"She was such a timid little thing. I used to braid her hair, shout a thousand times for her to get dressed in the morning and drag her to school. No matter how early I got her up we were always late. She'd be last at the school gates, a piece of toast and Nutella-"

"Marmite."

"Breakfast still in her hands, school clothes already covered in crumbs and sticky patches of Nutella on her cheeks."

"Marmite," Jess repeated.

Anna couldn't help smiling. It sounded adorable and she wished she could reach out to Jess to try to put her at ease. At this point Jess jogged around them both and appeared at Anna's side.

"Hello," Jess said quietly, which made Anna smile even more.

"I worried about her when she came out as a lesbian," Nan carried on.

"Queer," Jess said.

Nan batted away Jess's objection. "I know, but I love saying 'lesbian'," and she shouted it out into the woods. "Has a power about it, don't you think? Really gives some people the heebie jeebies. Always telling everyone that my granddaughter is a lesbian, especially those who come to the door preaching about sin. Why would God not love lesbians?" And she gave the sky a cursory wave.

Anna laughed and drew Jess closer.

The woods opened out into a churchyard, then a village with a group of trees in the centre of a green.

"This is home," Nan said grandly, and she led Anna across the green to a terrace of cottages. "Watch your head," Nan fussed.

There was a heavy clunk as the latch handle opened and the door creaked inwards as Nan pushed. Anna was met by a waft of warmth suffused with the rich aroma of spices and stew. She instinctively closed her eyes and inhaled. There was ginger, chillis, rich gravy and it made her mouth water.

"That smells delicious," Anna said.

"My favourite stew," Nan said, "with dumplings. Except I have to cook a bean version because these two," Nan flailed around towards Jess and her brother, "want to eat less meat. Then," Nan put her hands on her hips, "I can't use my usual cuts of beef, because this one," she pointed towards Bill who was dipping under the doorway, "needs to watch his cholesterol. But," Nan threw her hands in the air, "it's still delicious."

"Come on in," Trisha said, at Anna's elbow. "Dinner will be a while so make yourself comfortable."

Trisha led Anna around a large kitchen table, through to a sitting area, Anna having to duck under a low beam across the cottage, and offered her a sofa by the window, an expanse of green and a small building of some sort visible outside. The tinkle of wind chimes reached Anna and she remembered Jess's phone call and guessed that was where Nan lived. It struck her how ordinary it was, as ordinary as when she'd pictured it on the phone with Jess, before she knew she was a star, before Anna had been blinded by the deception and the fame of *Atlassia*.

"Can I get you a cup of tea?" Trisha said.

"Thank you," Anna said. "With milk please."

"Won't be a tick," Trisha replied, politely. Then, as Jess's brother slumped next to Anna on the sofa and a bright TV flashed on beside them, "Switch that thing off Jack."

There was a groan from Jess's brother which broke over several octaves.

"Help your Nan in the kitchen a minute," Trisha said.

The teen tutted next to Anna. "You wouldn't mind if I played on the console would you?"

Anna smiled. "It's not my place to say."

"Mom," he moaned. "She doesn't mind."

Anna caught Trisha desperately beckoning him away. "Give her some peace a minute would you."

"But Jess is here too," he groaned. "Can't she help with tea."

"Just get," Trisha growled.

Anna realised she and Jess were being set up.

"How about I take Anna into the garden for a bit," Jess said.

"That sounds nice," Anna replied, realising Jess's need to escape scrutiny and her brother to do XBox."

"Oh go on then," Trisha said. "That thing goes straight off at tea time though," she said, jabbing her finger towards Jack.

The boy growled a "yes!" then high-fived his sister.

—

"I'm so sorry," Jess said as they stepped out of the back door. "It's like you've been abducted."

Anna laughed. "I wanted to meet your family. You always talked so fondly about them."

"Right now I have no idea why. Bet your family's nothing like it."

"No," Anna shook her head, "unfortunately not."

Jess led her across a lawn and beneath trees Anna assumed were fruit trees of a small orchard, and onto the veranda of Nan's home. They sat on a sofa, Jess spreading a couple of blankets over them both and snuggling close, though not as close as she could. Anna guessed at her reticence with how they'd left things back at the studio.

"They're everything a family should be," Anna said.

"What? Annoying?"

"Yes," she laughed, "bickering, getting on each other's nerves, helping each other, most of all being together."

There was a beautiful warmth about Jess's family and it wasn't just the comfort of the stew cooking in the stove. Food, chatter, commotion. It was a home, a proper home. It was nothing like the stage of her mother's house, everything cool and precise and ostentatious, to be admired. This house breathed as part of a family, alive and imperfect. Anna suddenly had a greater sense of Jess after seeing this side of her.

"I can understand why you missed it so much."

"Yeah," Jess sighed, beginning to unwind from the chaos. "I have. And Jack, Jesus, he's as big as me now. I'm glad I've spent time with him again. Admittedly it's been playing computer games most of the time, but I can cope with that level of bonding," she said.

"Your Nan…" Anna started, but she couldn't help smiling.

Jess laughed. "Wish I was like her." Then she stopped, thoughtful for a moment. "She would have coped with all this."

"With what?" Anna asked gently.

"Fame, adulation, all the hate too," Jess said grimly. "She'd have handled the exposure like a boss, put any detractors in their place and bulldozed on through. She did it when I was little, settling here, and when Mom was young apparently," Jess said with a shrug. "But I'm not like that." She turned to look at Anna. "I'm quiet, more like Mom and Dad. I think Nan despairs of the lot of us. But then other times I wonder if underneath she's like the rest of the family, especially when she wants a quiet game of chess or retires early to bed with a romance novel. Her need for greenery and quiet made her move to this village after all."

As always when Jess talked of her folks, the local accent came to the fore, especially tonight in her family's presence.

"They're nice," Anna offered her genuine opinion.

"They are," Jess replied. "I envy them," she said quietly. "Never thought I'd say that but I do."

"In what way?"

"They're happy. They've got each other," Jess said, and the weight of her envy and longing hung over her and Anna couldn't miss her meaning. "That seemed so boring growing up, but it's something I want most of all now."

Anna didn't know what to say. Her heart swelled in her chest, aching for Jess and grieving that this was unlikely for them. At least hearing it and seeing Jess at home, Anna could believe it. She could imagine Jessica Lambert, the star, wanting an ordinary life.

"They got married when Mom was twenty-three and Dad was thirty."

"Wow, young," Anna said.

"Younger than me."

And Anna felt a lump in her throat and there was silence at the implications.

"I'm serious about you," Jess said quietly, staring towards the house, as if not wanting to catch Anna's reaction.

"I know," Anna whispered. And they were quiet for a while, huddled up beneath the blankets, the sky above deepening to indigo.

"I've been thinking of getting a place out here," Jess said, suddenly.

"Really?" Anna turned to look directly at her.

"A little cottage, not much different to this. Somewhere I can escape to."

"Oh," Anna said.

Jess near her family. Countryside to allow her to breath. Sounds of birds and fresh air. Anna could imagine it recharging Jess. "That sounds wonderful," she said.

"Yeah?"

Anna couldn't miss Jess's hopeful tone, but she shook her head. "Would you be safe though?"

"Perhaps," Jess said, looking at her and seeming to will Anna to try. "I don't really have a choice," she said, again waiting for Anna's decision. "I am who I am."

Anna knew she was seeking her approval, hoping for her to take a step.

Was it possible? Could Anna move out of her comfort zone again for this incredible woman? The weight of expectation and problems hung heavy in the air. She was about to tell Jess a hundred reasons why it would never work, when they were called inside for dinner.

And it was the messy chaotic dinner of an ordinary family and Anna's heart both grieved and celebrated. Jess and her brother teamed up in camaraderie against their Nan. Trish was pulled between the generations, siding with her mother one minute, berating her for her attitudes the next, Bill, the voice of calm reason, ignored one moment then exalted the next. The flow of conversation, the laughter, the food, the cat stealing the stew, the dumpling rolling under the table, the glass too many of wine, the embarrassing story of Jess's childhood, the revenge from Jack about Trish and Bill's adult hugs ban – it was like life happened in this household and Anna couldn't help but be swept up by it.

When Anna left for the studio car outside, she was showered with affection and hugged to oblivion. She rode on a wave of love and happiness and the slap of cold air when she stepped outside was a rude awakening.

Jess accompanied her up the steps and onto the pavement. Anna stood at the car door, wondering how she should say good bye. She didn't know where they stood. Anna knew what she wanted, but not whether it was possible, and the more she saw of Jess, the more she had to lose and the more it hurt.

Jess waited, beside Anna, close enough that she could feel her warmth. Anna was torn between wanting to promise Jess the world and embracing this wonderful woman, and her head that cautioned her.

She peered down at the pavement and Jess's shoes scuffing the ground. "I–"

"Do you want to go on a date?"

Anna looked up in surprise. "A date?" she said, with disbelief.

"Yeah." Jess was grinning. "An ordinary date. Meet up. Spend some time together. Me and you. I don't think we've ever been on one."

Anna mulled it over. "You know, I don't think we officially have."

"So?" Jess beamed.

Oh it was hard to resist her when she was like this. Anna had been caught up in her youthful enthusiasm before.

"So," Anna said, gathering her poise and trying hard not to smile, "we've spent several nights together, had wonderful sex." Did Jess twitch with embarrassment at that? "We've fallen out and argued, saved each other, had steaming sex, I've met your family…"

Jess shuffled.

"…and now you want to go out on a date?"

"Yeah." And there was that grin of Jess's that you could see from space.

"Well." Anna thought. It was as though she put all her worries and complex scenarios to the side for a moment. "Why not?"

52

"Meet me at the end of Warwick Lane in the City," Jess had said, and she'd messaged to say she was already there, ready and waiting for her.

Anna emerged from the London taxi at the inauspicious address into cool spring air and bright morning sunshine, a small tree at the edge of a square beginning to unfurl into fresh leaves. Anna shaded her eyes from the low sun that beamed over a silhouette of an enormous stone building, one with two pointed towers, dark shadows between columns and the suggestion of a dome further beyond the facade.

"St Paul's," Anna breathed with a laugh.

Jess had remembered – the one place in London Anna wished she'd visited most of all and had never got round to. Of course Jess had remembered. It was from their conversation on Bonfire Night when they'd walked up Primrose Hill full of excitement and returned home to make love. For the first time in a while the memory filled Anna with elation so that it brimmed in her heart and burst into a smile on her face.

At that moment she recognised a figure walking towards her across the square, tall and striking in her long winter coat, with the confident stride of a superhero, hair bouncing in curls on her head and a smile bright and wide. Anna couldn't stop grinning as Jess approached, and she felt like a shy goofy teen when Jess stopped before her. They stood close enough to lean together and kiss, but stayed a fraction apart.

"Hi," Jess said, and Anna could tell she was both as shy and eager as she was.

"You remembered," Anna said.

Jess nodded. "Do you fancy it? Today? With me?"

"Very much," Anna murmured, taking in every bit of Jess's beautiful face. She wanted to kiss every inch of it.

"Shall we?" Jess said, holding up her elbow.

Anna took Jess's arm, pulling her near and hugging it into her chest. Jess responded, gazing at her and holding her arm with a hand, the affectionate squeeze saying so much. Jess opened her mouth as if she wanted to say something and her chest heaved against Anna's hand. Jess was so large a presence to Anna, it was as if she filled her whole world with light. She wanted to know every thought in Jess's head, reach up and stroke and explore every part of her body, hold her in her arms and never let go.

The words and thoughts seemed too many to say, and they both laughed as if their hearts were too full to acknowledge.

"Let's go," Anna said at last, pulling Jess a little closer, and savouring the glow where their bodies met.

Across the bumpy stone cobbles, over smoother paving, up the wide steps that ran the length of the Cathedral front. They dipped into the shadows of the entrance and the atmosphere changed immediately, from a slight fresh breeze of the spring day to the cool still space of the colossal cathedral. The sounds of the city fell away, replaced by the sonorous echoes of the cavernous interior surrounding them, people shuffling, talking, a door closing with a crack.

"It's huge," Jess said, and the words repeated sweetly down the airy nave.

Anna smiled. "Never been?"

"Never been." Jess shook her head. "It must be over a hundred metres to the altar."

They strolled along the generous nave, shoes clicking and echoing on the marble chequerboard floor that swept the length of the cathedral.

"Doesn't this make you feel small?" Jess said, gazing up. "I mean that in a good way. Something as wondrous as this makes you appreciate how enormous and amazing the world is, and all your problems disappear for a moment."

"I know what you mean," Anna said, holding Jess close.

It was like they were walking in the park again, all those months ago, the two of them alone at last. Just Jess and Anna, removed from the complications of life, simply two people enjoying each other's company.

"It's bonkers," Jess laughed. "Think how many people it took to make this thing. How long to carve a single block of stone for that arch?" And she pointed ahead and up, then, "Oh wow."

The vast dome opened up above them as they passed beneath the high arch. Jess spun around, gazing up. A halo of light beamed high above from the windows in the dome with another glimpse of daylight further up again.

"That's where we need to go," Anna said, pointing to the ring at the base of the dome.

"Up there?" Jess squealed.

"That's where the Whispering Gallery is."

"How the heck do we get up there?"

The answer was up two-hundred and fifty-nine steps of stone spiral staircase, a fact announced by a small boy accompanying his mother in front of Jess and Anna and who was determined to verify the fact. Anna smiled as the boy counted, and they all climbed at a steady pace, Anna pulling on the cool iron rail that wound around the stone walls.

"Tired," the boy complained, and they all rested a moment. "Naawww, I've forgotten what number I was up to."

"One hundred and seventeen, mate," Jess said.

The mother swung around. "Thank you," she laughed. "Oh…"

Anna could hear the astonishment in the mother's voice and see it on her shocked face. The woman did a double take at Jess and Anna only now realised that Jess had made no effort to disguise herself – no beanie hat or fashion glasses – and she seemed most like herself today.

"Oh…you're…" the woman said. "Sorry…I'll let you get by…"

"You're OK," Jess said. "We're in no rush."

"No, you must."

She turned to Anna and her attention lingered. "Oh," she said again in surprise at Anna this time. "Well, you're…."

"Hi," Anna said.

"Hi," the woman replied, with a wave.

"Do you know them?" the boy asked.

"No, no, no," the woman said. "They're on the telly. Sorry, you really must go ahead."

The young boy gawped at them both.

"Try not to stare, sweetpea," the woman muttered, then she stared, at them both, expectantly, unremittingly.

At this point, Anna decided to take pity on the babbling parent and climbed past.

"Thank you," Anna said. "Enjoy the Whispering Gallery."

"Have a… have a day… nice," the woman said as they went by.

"You too," Anna said.

They continued on, the stairs circling endlessly round, Anna climbing in an easy rhythm with Jess by her side.

"Are you OK?" Anna ventured. "You didn't wear anything to disguise yourself."

"I didn't want to hide anything today," Jess said, squeezing Anna's arm. "Sometimes people are lovely. Other times I will need to retreat and take a break from the world. But I wanted everything to be open today."

Anna nodded. "To prove we can do it?"

"Yes," she said.

They carried on climbing, the sound of the boy's counting getting further away.

"I would give it all up you know," Jess said quietly.

Anna stopped.

"I would quit acting, modelling, everything," Jess said beside Anna, but staring ahead. "I would walk away from it all."

"I don't want you to do that," Anna stuttered, conflicting thoughts and feelings swirling inside. "I know how much I missed it and this chance to act again has been everything to me. I'm not like my old self." She had to stop and ponder. "I'm not who I used to be. I'm several years older and people change over time, but acting nourishes a part of me that I must keep alive. I don't want to take that away from you."

Jess wouldn't look at her.

"Let's at least try this," Anna said. "Don't give it all up yet."

Jess turned to her at last. "I would though, if it meant it would keep us safe and together."

The incessant counting of the small child broke through and they set off again, Anna's heart thumping with more than the exertion.

They climbed on in a silence full of things not yet said. Jess slipped her arm around Anna's waist, her company intimate and comforting, but she wouldn't look at Anna. It was as if she were bursting with thoughts that she didn't know how to articulate. Anna had to stifle her need to hear them, to give Jess time, and herself time. She didn't know what she'd say to the turmoil that preoccupied Jess.

They broke out into light again, the dome expanding around them. Anna stepped across the walkway that circled around the inside of the dome and clutched the cold metal rail that ringed the cavernous space. It was impossible not to gaze up into the painted heavens of the dome, then down over the rail to the grand sweep of the cathedral floor far below. Anna gasped as her head swirled with vertigo and she stretched back to the walls of the dome and the circular stone bench that ringed the space.

She sat down, the coolness of the stone seeping through her coat and dress to her thighs. She curled her fingers over the smooth lip of the bench. It was all so vivid. The colossal space, the light, the echoes, the sensation of the hard unyielding stone beneath her, as if she really were there. And Jess, who sat beside her, her presence large and vital, her whole being exuding warmth.

They sat in silence as the boy and his mother walked past and round the gallery and a tour group filled the space with noisy chatter. One or two of them seemed to linger, perhaps recognising Jess, but they moved on and out of the gallery to climb further up the dome.

"I nearly gave it all up you know," Jess said quietly, when they'd gone.

"When?" Anna said, turning to her surprised.

"When I arrived in London."

Jess didn't look at her. She wrapped her fingers around the edge of the bench, her hand touching Anna's. Such a small amount of contact, their little fingers side by side, but it was like Jess in her entirety, almost as if Anna could feel the living pulse of her beside her.

"I was in a bad way. I'd pushed myself too far, or let others push. I'd had too many years on the road and not enough time to recharge and be quiet and exist as just me. I think I came very close to breaking down."

She almost glimpsed at Anna.

"Then I met you." Her hand nudged ever so slightly at Anna's, as if craving contact and reassurance but afraid to take it in hers. "That weekend with you, of peace and ordinary life, in your apartment full of beautiful everyday things. That time, simply being together." Her voice wavered. "If someone had said choose then, I would have chosen a chance with you."

Anna didn't know what to say. The urge to take Jess's hand and hold it to her heart and promise her everything was overpowering.

"What if we're wrong?" Anna murmured. "What if it doesn't work out? What if you're hounded? *Atlassia* will be in the public consciousness constantly now it's airing on TV."

Jess hesitated. "I don't have all the answers. I don't think there is a right answer here. I can't tell you the future and can't guarantee happiness whether we're in the public eye or not. But I can tell you what I feel." And Anna could sense how much Jess wanted to hold her hand, her fingers edging over hers. "I don't fall in love easily. I'm even careful about the friends I make. But I adore you."

When Anna didn't say anything Jess added quietly, "Our business doesn't nurture relationships. If we don't try, things will never work."

Was it the confidence and recklessness of youth talking, that ability to dive in and risk all consequences?

Still Anna didn't say anything.

"You know how people wait for all the signs to add up?" Jess ventured. "For all the right qualities to be checked before they know someone is right for them? Maybe they realise they like the same food, or laugh at the same jokes. Maybe it's when they notice how good their partner is with kids. Sometimes that takes years, but with you it's been like dominoes falling one after another."

Jess turned to her at last. "You were kind," Jess said. "That's been so rare it blew me away. And sexy, I don't know even where to begin with that."

Anna couldn't meet her eyes but knew she was smiling.

"I love how you tease me, even more than teasing you." Jess held her hand at last. "I don't know the last time I met someone I wanted to hang out with all day, every day, doing everything and nothing. You understand so much about me already, you read me so well and you're open to learning more. And that's before considering that you appreciate our work and the pressures we're under. That counts for so much when it comes to supporting each other. I respect you as an actress. I'm in awe." She squeezed her hand tighter. "My family are besotted and I might find them annoying at times but I trust their judgement when it comes to folk."

Jess took a breath before carrying on.

"It took me a while to work out why you fit me so well, but I felt it right from the start. And when I say it out loud like this, I think, why wouldn't I want to grab and hold onto this with all my strength."

Jess squeezed her hand, then raised it to her lips, pressing a long kiss to Anna's fingers that spoke of the depth of her feeling even more than her words.

Anna didn't know if she'd been breathing and she inhaled sharply so that it juddered in her chest. She gazed at the young woman beside her, a young woman who threw her everything into her acting, who was dedicated to the creators and crew of the films, someone who stuck to her principles.

"You don't do things by half do you Jessica Lambert?" Anna had meant to say it lightly, but the tremor in her voice gave her away.

Jess laughed gently. "No, I don't."

It hit Anna hard then, just how much Jess had become invested in her.

"So," Jess said. "How about we see if this Whispering Gallery really works."

Anna gulped at her reprieve, her chest still full of everything she felt.

"I read that you can hear someone whisper from the other side of the dome," Jess said. "In fact words whispered into the curve of the wall are meant to travel better than anything louder. Want to try?"

Anna nodded, keeping everything inside that threatened to burst out.

Jess took a few steps around the circular walkway and leaned into the wall.

"Can you hear me?" she whispered.

Anna pressed her ear close to the wall. She nodded. She could see Jess from the corner of her eye only a few feet away. Jess walked a little further, curving around the dome and behind Anna's view.

"How about now?"

Anna hoped Jess was looking because she couldn't speak and she nodded again.

"I'm going to try from the other side." Even with a whisper Anna could hear the excitement in Jess's voice and Anna began to smile.

She caught herself. This is what Jess did time after time for Anna, she made existence exceptional. A kiss had Anna floating on air. A tease brought her back to earth with deft tenderness. A compliment uttered without guile resonated deeply until her heart swelled with love. Everyday became magical again in her company.

As Jess walked further away, her footsteps curving around the dome, the truth of what she'd said settled deeper. Jess had blown Anna's world open, but it scared her still. There were so many issues and traps in the road ahead. But when Anna considered turning away there were no other roads. Her conviction that this was the only road was suddenly overwhelming and Anna realised her heart had already made her choice long ago. It all came out at once.

"I love you," she whispered, before she'd realised she was speaking.

She struck out her hand to the wall to steady herself, the smooth surface cool against her hand.

"I love you, Jess," she uttered again, before she could stop herself.

Her heart cantered in her chest at what she'd done.

There was silence. Had Jess heard? Anna waited for a reply, perhaps in a whisper that slipped around the walls of the great building. But none came. She leaned towards the wall, her ear pressed to the stonework. Nothing, but the beat of her heart, the distant shuffle of tourists far below in the cathedral and fainter again traffic in the world beyond.

Then footsteps, not from below, or from the stairs. Louder they came, then quicker, into a run, and Anna turned to see Jess rushing around the walkway and sweeping down to her.

In a fluid movement Jess embraced her, drawing Anna to her feet and taking her lips into a sensuous kiss that obliterated everything else.

"Take me home," Anna gasped.

53

The temptation to indulge in stolen kisses in the back of the taxi home was torture, but pictures would appear in the media the next day.

Their embrace and kiss in the Whispering Gallery was probably already online.

Anna trembled with expectation and the words she'd said. They'd given her release and freedom but she shook at their impact. She could feel the same excitement and need through Jess's fingers as they climbed the steps to her apartment.

Anna lowered the blinds, her fingers clumsy on the controls, willing them to shut faster, and the flat was dimmed into diffuse spring sunshine. She hurried to Jess who was waiting eagerly by the bed.

"Take these off," Anna murmured, pulling at Jess's coat lapels, then hungrily slipping her fingers around Jess's belly and lifting her T-shirt, her soft skin against Anna's tantalising. Jess crossed her arms and lifted her T-shirt over her head and Anna stared at her chest, her bright white bra contrasting with her beautiful brown skin.

Jess didn't wait there though, she'd already unhooked her bra and was slipping it away and Anna blushed, staring at the shape of Jess's naked upper body. She so badly wanted to touch her, to stroke her fingers around the gorgeous shape of her breasts, to trace the definition of her nipples, but Jess was at a disadvantage.

Anna slipped off her coat, throwing it to the chair, and unzipped the side of her dress.

"Help me please," she said, tugging at the dress, for the first time not wanting to hide any of herself.

Jess hesitated, perhaps wondering if Anna was sure, then carefully pulled the garment over her head. Jess was as unsubtle as she was. Anna could feel her gaze taking in her body.

"And this," Anna said, reaching behind to unclasp her bra and Jess, trembling, lifted the straps from her shoulders and threw the underwear down. Anna could hear Jess's breathing, see her whole body lifting with excitement.

"These too," Anna said, dipping her fingers underneath the waistband of Jess's jeans, the warm sensuous flesh there so tempting she almost collapsed to her knees to kiss her. The combination of firm fit physique and that layer of softness that Jess had made Anna's head spin. She undid the button and as Jess reached for her underwear they both carefully removed each other's clothes, their breasts so very close to touching.

Then they were naked and the warmth between their bodies was dizzying. Anna reached up and slipped her arms around Jess's neck and slowly stepped in to her.

The first touch of their breasts together made her gasp. The spark electrified her whole body and she couldn't move. Jess slipped her hands around Anna's sides and gently pulled her nearer, her breath hitching with every inch of their bodies caressing together. Anna moaned at their breasts touching, at the exquisite smoothness of Jess's thighs against her own, and Anna arched her back so that her stomach sealed with her lover's and she could feel the whole length of her body.

It was beyond erotic. The sense of being as close as possible to Jess was overwhelming. She held her tight, wanting nothing more than to enjoy her lover against her body. She loved this woman and with everything stripped away she gave in completely. She closed her eyes and bathed in the glowing elation of loving someone and having them so sensually near.

"I love you," she sighed.

She couldn't stop thinking it now. Her whole body was saying it – the way she nuzzled into Jess's neck, the way her fingers curled and stroked around her head taking her in, the way she arched into her body for as intimate a touch as possible.

But when Jess started to move her hands up her back, massaging with firm fingers and definite intentions, Anna's body responded immediately and wanted more. Every touch ignited pleasure. Jess moved eagerly, working her way up so that burst after burst sent dizzying spells of arousal to every part of Anna's body. She groaned. She couldn't help it.

"Lie down," Jess whispered and Anna's senses heightened at the promise of more.

She lay between the sheet and duvet by her side. Even the smooth material seemed erotic today, stroking her back and delighting every nerve ending that was usually protected beneath clothes. But it was nothing to the feeling of Jess's soft lips at the top of her cleavage, or the warm hand that gently cupped her breast.

Anna wanted to say how good it felt, how much she desired Jess, but she couldn't speak. Jess's kisses were gentle but urgent and every contact stepped up Anna's desire so that she nearly panicked at how intense it was.

She groaned as Jess took her nipple in her mouth. The warmth of her lips, the luscious kiss, the exquisite suck on her nipple; it had her whole body pulsing with heat from her breast, through her belly, right to the swell between her legs. She moaned as Jess kissed her, every gentle nibble, every delicious squeeze, building her higher and higher.

Fingers dipped between her upper thighs and Anna breathed in sharply as if she might come. She waited, panting with anticipation for Jess's touch, and when she parted Anna's legs with a silky sweep of her hands, it was almost unbearable.

"I can't–" she groaned. I can't bear it, she wanted to say.

She didn't need to wait long. Jess hungrily trailed down her body, her lips and kisses inflaming Anna, and her movement betraying her eagerness.

"Oh god," Anna gasped. She was wound tight from her neck to her toes, her arousal climbing ever higher.

Jess's lips seduced her stomach. Her kisses explored the top of her thigh. The tip of her tongue parted Anna's lips.

"Oh fuck," Anna cried.

Then slowly, with a perfect luscious lick, Jess slipped her tongue over Anna's centre and her whole body caved. Anna shuddered with the pleasure pulsing through her, then swam in dizzying waves of ever growing arousal as Jess licked over her swollen clitoris.

She clutched the sheets in her fists, arched up to Jess's mouth, who took her with ever hungrier kisses. Anna was rigid with paralysing excitement, afraid of how tightly wound she'd become and desperate to tip over the edge. Then Jess gently sucked her into her mouth and the engulfing warmth and firm stroke of her tongue sent Anna tumbling.

Wave after wave of powerful orgasm ravaged her. Anna groaned with heavenly release. She swore like a fucking sailor and the way Jess held her to her face, murmuring appreciation, Anna could tell Jess revelled in it as much as Anna.

She lay exhausted on the bed, racked with deep breaths and blissfully obliterated by intoxicating hormones.

"Oh you are gorgeous," Jess sighed and Anna smiled, as Jess's breath tickled over her clitoris. She sounded drunk.

"Come here, please," Anna said, smiling down at her.

Jess climbed up the bed and over Anna, covering her with adoring kisses as she went. Anna pulled her in, kissing her lips, both groaning with appreciation.

"I love you on top of me," Anna whispered, and Jess's reply was incoherent.

Anna's hands explored down her lover's quivering body, admiring her firm torso, the roundness of her buttocks, then slipped around her thigh and into the slickness between her legs and over her swollen centre.

Jess almost collapsed with her whole weight on top of her. She seemed to have only enough strength to arch her hip to let Anna inside.

The sensation of Jess's clitoris, wet and firm beneath Anna's fingertip as she circled around and around the nugget of pleasure, oh it put a smile on her face. She breathed in time with Jess, almost overcome again, as Jess tensed and pulled Anna's into her arms. The cry Jess gave was of anguished ecstasy and Anna was lost mumbling incoherent delight.

—

Anna gazed at Jess, her lover's eyes closed but mouth curved up with pleasure at the attention. Anna stroked her fingers around Jess's curling hairline, then around her ears, curiously soft and firm at the same time. She kissed her cheek then above her eyes, her silky smooth eyebrow faintly salty on the tip of Anna's tongue from perspiration at their love making. It was intimate and comforting, touching from her head to toes.

"I want this every day," Anna said, her heart full. "I want all of this. Dates at St Paul's, rushing home to bed, waking up with you in my arms."

Her heart lurched at the thought of not having that. She wanted it so badly, the possibility of it ever disappearing made her world tilt, her head reel and her body cry out. The idea of being apart made her feel the chill of exposure even though their bodies still met.

She'd feared falling in love with Jess for so long. Now that she was in deep, she felt the full force of it, good and bad, that intense living and horrible possibility of loss. The fear turned to urgency to keep her lover close and they sought each other, kissed and tenderly reassured, their caresses becoming erotic once again.

"I always feel calm here," Jess said later, enclosed in each other's arms. "Ever since the first time I stayed."

"You certainly made yourself comfortable," Anna smiled, teasing Jess at falling asleep on her bed that first night.

"With your company and this safe haven, I never want to leave."

Anna hesitated. "Then don't."

Jess looked at her.

"Stay here. When you can," Anna said. "When you need to be in London."

Jess kissed her. "Are you asking me to move in, Anna Mayhew?"

How quickly the tables turned with their gentle teasing, and a thrill of excitement and tickle of amusement filled Anna's body. That's always what Jess did, made her come alive in so many ways. The world had so many dimensions when she was with Jess.

"I am. Jessica Lambert, superstar, I'm asking you to move into my tiny London flat."

It sounded ridiculous, and Anna's confidence wavered. "If you want to. If it's practical. You know you can leave overnight things. Your London pied à terre."

"I want to more than anything else in the world. I want to move in and wake up with you every day." Jess paused. "And more."

It was loaded with meaning, with promises, questions and hope about the future and Anna felt the enormity of it all. Jess didn't say any more but Anna knew she watched and waited.

"Let's see how this goes," Anna said. "A lot of things might change."

"They will," Jess said, "and how we live may need to change several times, but I want to do that together."

And Anna kissed her, reeling with the breadth and depth of her feelings at Jess's words.

54

"Is that all you're bringing?" Anna asked, after she'd frowned and puzzled over Jess's luggage.

Jess put the modest suitcase on the floor of the flat and dumped the holdall from over her shoulder. Jess had stayed every night at Anna's, moving over in dribs and drabs. Toothbrush, underwear, tablet for reading and music. But with the shooting schedule she hadn't had time to pack and check out of her room. So, today was official moving-in day.

"There's more than enough room for those," Anna said, relieved. "Is that all you need to bring?"

"That's all there is," Jess said.

"In London?"

"Anywhere. I suppose there are a few boxes at Mom and Dad's, but I never use them."

"Really?" Anna looked bewildered, the crinkle in her brow and wrinkle of her nose bewitching Jess and making her want to swoop her up already. She looked divine. The spring sunshine had brought out the dusting of freckles across her nose and a light rusty tan on her arms more obvious against the loose white linen shirt she wore over comfy faded jeans.

"This?" Anna motioned to Jess and her luggage. "This is Jessica Lambert's whole world?"

"Yeah." Jess laughed.

"Well, OK," Anna said, lifting her eyebrows. She smiled at last, then stepped forward and cupped Jess's cheeks in her hands and placed one of those delicious kisses on her lips. The one that made Jess float on air, close her eyes in submission and curl her toes in delight. The one where Anna's lips caressed over Jess, and even when she pulled away, Jess was irresistibly drawn after her.

"Hello," Anna murmured, and Jess sighed at the sound of that silky voice.

"Hi," she moaned. "I don't suppose we have time for more of those, do we?" Jess said, plaintively.

"Later," Anna purred. "You have a busy day. Let's get you unpacked."

Anna sat on the armchair next to the bed and alongside the shelves that ran the length of the room from window to eaves.

"You sacrificed CD space!" Jess said.

Drawer-boxes now sat on the shelves where Anna's CD collection had been previously.

"Well," Anna replied. "I use the digital player more often anyway."

"You moved," Jess said with great gravitas and a hand over her heart, "antiquated music formats for me?"

"I had to make room somewhere and I never–" Anna whipped her head round and scowled at Jess, all the while her cheeks twitching with amusement. "Watch it," she growled.

Jess leant down and kissed her lover who was having a hard time maintaining her chagrin. "I love you," Jess said, her cheeks tight with a grin.

"Hmm," Anna said, her mock indignation still present and Jess couldn't resist softening her further, caressing across her cheek, nibbling her earlobe then trailing butterfly kisses all the way down her neck.

Anna gulped. "Stop it, or we'll never get unpacked."

Jess drew back, her grin ever bigger. "I like this, kissing whenever we like."

Anna was unable to hold the pretence of irritation and her whole face lit up, her love and happiness shining out at Jess.

"Me too," she said, and it made Jess giddy. "But," Anna said raising her hand to indicate gravity. "I need to remind you to be tidy. Otherwise I'm going to be tripping over your shoes in this small flat and the new robo-vacuum is going to choke on your shirts."

"I can do tidy," Jess said, with a confidence that could take on the world today she was so high on Anna. She dragged over her bags and pulled out piles of folded T-shirts and jeans and placed them in drawers.

"I don't have much to be untidy with," Jess continued, "which is part of the point. When I had stuff at home I left it all over the place and forgot about it. So I gave up having any."

"Seriously," Anna said with a strict schoolmarm voice and twinkle in her eye. "Keep it tidy here."

"Oh," Jess purred. "I like strict Anna, one of my favourites," and she threw Anna her best sultry smile. Anna's eyes lingered on her lips, then she licked her own. Jess definitely caught that.

"Stop it," Anna said, smiling. "Concentrate. We have to get you unpacked, practise your interview and see Penny before you leave for the studio tonight."

Anna's pretence of command and voice of authority really did reach places in Jess.

"Correction," Jess said. "I love strict Anna." Her eyes dipped into Anna's shirt, open to the top of her cleavage and the skin pale where the sun hadn't reached yet. "Especially when she isn't wearing a bra."

Anna's face flushed and her lips twitched. "We really don't have time."

"But," Jess said. "I'm done. That's me unpacked."

"Already?"

"Yup. I've been living out of hotels for years. I have it down to a fine art. So," Jess drew it out suggestively. "Perhaps we have time…?"

"No." And before Jess could seduce her with a kiss Anna had leapt from the chair and was crossing to the kitchen corner.

"I'm going to get us a drink," Anna said over her shoulder. "Then we'll practise some likely interview questions for tonight on the show, to stop you fretting or seizing in front of the audience."

Jess grumbled a note of acquiescence.

"Tea?"

"Yes, please." Jess loved that Anna knew what she preferred to drink this time of day.

"Then get comfortable and ready for your questions."

Jess sat on the floor and crossed her legs. She watched Anna make two cups of tea and wander towards her, frowning a little in concentration, a cup in each hand. Jess tilted her head, appreciating the sway of Anna's hips as she curved past the kitchen island, around the end of the shelves demarking the sitting area and leant down to offer Jess a cup, her shirt opening as she leant and offering a peek of curving white breasts within.

"Mmm," Jess said, without even pretending she meant the tea. She put the cup down and peered some more. "Do we really have to practise?"

Anna stroked her index finger under Jess's chin and tilted her face up. Jess blinked lazily at the soft sensation of Anna's touch and her humid breath on her mouth. It was like being bathed in pheromones.

"I'm only thinking of you," Anna said, her eyes dark and her lips full.

"I'm thinking of you too," Jess moaned.

Anna arched an eyebrow. "Plenty of time for whatever consumes your thoughts, but after your interview tonight."

That was far too long to wait.

"So," Anna snapped, but with a smile. She sat back on the chair, shuffled between the cushions, crossed her legs and assumed a serious demeanour. "Jessica Lambert, star of the *Atlassia* blockbusters, Bond girl and in-demand fashion model," Anna continued, "what's been keeping you in London these past few months?"

"Seeing a wonderful woman," Jess sighed.

"Be serious." Anna threw one of the cushions.

The cushion sailed past. "Wonderful, but who's rubbish at throwing."

Anna threw the other and it made its mark, pummelling Jess in the face and wafting the curls of her fringe. "Who's actually pretty accurate."

"Be serious!" Anna said. "What's keeping you in London?"

Jess knelt forward. "Honestly, how can I concentrate?"

"What is wrong with you?"

Jess shook her head slowly and deliberately from side to side. "Well it's just this woman. I don't know what it is about her."

Anna sighed with exasperation. "So you're working with Anna Mayhew?" she said in a desperate attempt to keep the interview on track.

"That's the one," Jess said, her voice drugged with glee and desire.

"Well, what's she like?" Anna smiled with a knowing pinch in the corner of her mouth.

"Oh, well," Jess murmured, coming closer, "I can talk about her for hours."

Anna licked her lips. Jess doubted she was even aware she had.

"Go on," Anna said.

Was that a tremble of anticipation in her voice? Jess needed little more encouragement.

"She has a face like a goddess," Jess said and she reached out and touched Anna's cheek that ever so slightly flushed rose. She trailed her finger down her neck, around her collar and down to the shallow beginnings of her cleavage.

"She wears these classic-cut clothes. Very proper," Jess grinned. "So that when you peek beneath," and here she hesitated and with a barely perceptible movement slipped open the top button of Anna's shirt, "it's an insanely sexy surprise to find these bare breasts."

She slipped her hand inside, a smooth breast filling her palm. Anna gulped and began to writhe a little in her seat.

"It's so very," Jess breathed, "very, distracting."

She leant in and placed a kiss on Anna's breast, one that took a little of her inside Jess's mouth so that she could taste her skin and lick over Anna's nipple, enticing a moan from her lover.

"And what I really want to do," Jess murmured with husky nonchalance, as she kissed further down Anna's belly slipping open her shirt as she went, "is cover every inch of her skin in kisses, so that her whole body tingles."

Anna was writhing now.

"...Until she's gasping with anticipation." Jess unzipped Anna's jeans. "Almost begging."

Jess slipped down the trousers and underwear, Anna eagerly lifting her hips to rid herself of them.

"...When I ever so," Jess teased Anna's thighs apart with her fingers tips and slipped her arms beneath her buttocks, "...ever so gently..."

She breathed over where Anna trembled with desire. Jess couldn't speak any more and had to pause to stop herself succumbing to dizzy arousal. Then she tipped down her chin and, with the very tip of her tongue, lapped at her clitoris.

"Oh!" Anna's body seized.

Jess hugged Anna's naked thighs not wanting her to move away with the convulsion. She pushed her tongue inside while Anna's body moved to meet her. Jess closed her eyes and moaned, enjoying the taste of the woman she adored and the ecstasy that every stroke of her tongue elicited in her lover.

She could have stayed there all day, savouring Anna's flavour and luxuriating in the abandoned rapture of her lover. Jess groaned again, her lips against Anna's slick tenderness and feeling her building excitement pert beneath her tongue.

Jess relented a little but didn't pull far away. "Sorry." It took great effort to sound at all serious. "I got distracted. Should I get back to the interview?"

"Don't you dare," Anna moaned, gently cupping Jess's head and encouraging her to stay exactly where she was.

Jess didn't hold back and dipped her face into Anna's desire until Anna tensed into her silent thrall of oblivion and collapsed gasping into convulsions of delicious aftershocks.

Jess rolled away to sit on her feet, licking her lips and stroking gently where Anna was most sensitive. Anna looked divine, elegantly lounging on the chair, shirt undone and breasts bare, one leg hooked over the arm so that Jess's view of her glistening satiated thighs was unhindered. Jess sighed. She wished she had a painting of this view.

"So?" she grinned. "How's my interview technique?"

"I don't think Graham Norton would be impressed."

But the ravaged and blushing Anna clearly was.

—

A shower and a seduction later where Anna turned the tables spectacularly on Jess, they left the flat and walked towards the coffee shop. They didn't seem to be able to keep apart or their hands from touching for more than a second. Jess wore one of the beanie hats she'd got into the habit of wearing around town and she grinned with the sunshine on her face and Anna's hand swinging in hers at her side. She was filled with elation and high on love and happiness, so much that she decided to bring up a prospect she'd been delaying.

"It's the TV awards soon," she said.

Anna murmured a response, a satisfied beam on her face lingering from their erotic shower.

"I wondered," Jess said, "I mean, I know you're a guest already, and you're definitely going, and that you have a dress organised for you."

"Uh huh," Anna said nonchalantly.

"But. Well I hardly ever do this. And I suppose we'd look like co-stars arriving together anyway, but…" She took a deep breath. "Would you like to come with me? Like be with me? As in, each other's dates?"

There, she'd said it.

Anna slowed their pace and they came to a stop. Jess's heart pounded in her chest. She knew Anna still worried about stepping back into the limelight as an actor herself and her exposure would be tenfold at Jess's side.

Anna turned to her, gaze fondly casting around Jess's face. "Is this our coming out to the world as a couple?"

Jess stuttered and checked her shoes, "Well, people might not assume, and like I say we're co-stars anyway, and I have attended awards and premieres with other co-stars, and…" she peered up at Anna's face, her eyes sparkling, her mouth curled in amusement and what Jess recognised as adoration – something so miraculous to see on the face of the woman she was besotted by.

"I want to go with you," Jess said. "I love you and I don't want anyone to think I'm with anyone else." She looked Anna directly in the eye. "I don't want rumours to start about me and other co-stars. They always do. But most of all I want to be with you."

Anna reached up and lightly stroked her cheek.

"I'm not one to announce things like this," Jess continued. "I don't like the attention really. But I like things to be honest."

"Are you sure you want to appear with a lesser-known actor?" Anna replied. "Would Femi approve? Will it detract from your hot-young thing and available status?"

Jess could see she wasn't being serious.

"Actually, Femi approves of you no end. You keep me happy and sane."

Anna leant forward and placed a delicate kiss on her lips that conveyed a deep sense of regard.

"I would love to," Anna whispered.

Jess grinned, but was jittery with nerves. "It might mean you start to get more attention from the media."

"I know," Anna sighed.

Jess held Anna's hands and squeezed them, unable to hide her concern and empathy for Anna's anxieties.

"You might need to be more careful about how you travel," Jess said.

Anna nodded, a frown crinkling her forehead.

"We don't have to if you're not ready." Jess wondered if she was pushing too quickly, but Anna looked up with a face full of beguiled wonder again.

"I want to and especially for what it means to you. But," Anna hesitated with a frown, "I think it's time I told my mother a few things."

"Oh?" Jess tried to keep it light. She'd heard a little about Anna's family, most of it neutral and polite, and it was obvious there was discord.

"I haven't seen her for a while," Anna clarified, and she stroked Jess's cheek perhaps to reassure her. "I had to cancel the last couple of lunches because of shooting schedules." Anna pursed her lips together. "I haven't told her about putting the coaching on hold and taking this role for a start."

"Oh." Jess nodded.

"But I will," Anna said softly. She took Jess's arm and faced down the hill. "Let's get back to living," Anna said, as they walked to the café. And Jess couldn't take her eyes from her, hair flowing in the breeze, cheeks flushed from their love making and face euphoric.

They ducked into the café, blinking with the change of light. A couple of customers did a double take, but with her ordinary clothes and hat guarding against most second looks and regulars now accustomed to seeing the young star in their café, Jess's presence went unremarked.

Penny and Bibs were in their habitual booth by the window. Penny glanced up then rolled her eyes and did nothing to suppress her smirk. She scuttled out of the booth and enveloped them both with a hug, her head buried in their bosoms.

"You two," she said pulling back, "look appallingly loved up. No need to ask why you're running late."

"Actually," Jess said. She couldn't help the stutter, "It was my fault. I needed to chat, to Anna, about something."

Penny sniggered. "You're such a shit liar."

"It's true," Jess squealed.

"Whatever it was," Penny said, pointing at Anna, "it didn't put that smile on my best friend's face," and she spun on her heel and shot a grin over her shoulder.

Anna shook her head and they both slid into the booth seat.

"Jess!" Bibs exclaimed. The little toddler's arms shot in the air when she saw her. "Knee!"

Jess was something of a favourite with Bibs at the moment. After Anna and Pen had claimed she was getting too big to carry all the way from the playground in the park, Jess's young fit physique had come to the rescue, and perched upon Jess's shoulders was now Bibs's favourite mode of transport.

"Hey kiddo," Jess said. She extracted the child from the high chair and plonked her on her lap. She was rewarded with sticky hands holding her cheeks and a slobbery nuzzle that smelled of strawberries.

Anna gave her a smile and squeezed her hand and Zehra came over promptly, clucking around her favourite customers like a mother hen. And Jess sat back in the warmth of the sunshine through the window and this bubble of affection.

This was the life.

55

Anna smoothed down her dress, again, and gazed into the mirror by the flat door. Her hair was pinned high and her face had a light touch of makeup. She would glam up for the awards night later, but this was to present to her mother. It was more coverage than she'd applied in recent years and would invite comment, but Anna appreciated the armour today.

She looked down at her crease-free dress that had been stroked relentlessly by her jittery hands. It reminded her of the time she prepared to inform her parents that she would be going to drama school at eighteen. She almost wished for her young bravado, obstinate teenage belief and resilience in front of the world. Age brought competence and confidence but also nuance and doubt, and of course vulnerability from failures.

Anna was suddenly aware of the stillness of the flat. She peeked up to see Jess regarding her from the foot of the bed, her hands curled over the edge of the mattress.

"Is there anything wrong?" Anna murmured, trying not to be defensive.

Jess looked away as she so often did when she needed to think through her answer and Anna waited. When Jess caught her eye there was sadness in her beautiful face.

"I might not always be the quickest at understanding people and duplicity confuses and unnerves me, but honest feelings I empathise with more than many." She looked at Anna. "And you're wavering. I can see your confidence slipping away," Jess hesitated, "and I don't know what to do about it."

The honesty of it and its pin-point accuracy was crushing. Anna could see the mirror of her dejection in Jess.

The impending lunch had weighed on Anna for days – the prospect of telling her mother about her tentative return to acting and embarking on a new life with Jess. She was terrified of the scorn her mother could pour on it all. It wouldn't change Anna's mind, but it added to pressures that made life challenging.

"Walk you there?" Jess offered, quietly.

Anna nodded.

The late spring air and Jess's presence on her arm was invigorating and Anna was once again thankful for her company.

"I could have done it on my own," Anna said gently, as they walked together along Kensington Road.

"I know," Jess replied. "But I like hanging out with you and I'm trying to keep you relaxed."

"Thank you."

Jess shrugged. "This is how it works. You help me. I help you."

The world seemed so simple when Jess said it like that.

"Do you want me to come in and say hello?" Jess asked.

Anna didn't answer straight away.

"I'm guessing," Jess started, "by the way you're gripping my arm like a vice that you're not keen."

"Oh," Anna exclaimed. She relaxed her fingers which were indeed embedded in Jess's bicep. "Sorry." Her whole body had tensed right up to her neck. She stopped and blew out a frustrated sigh.

She sought Jess's eyes with a heavy apologetic smile. "To be blunt, she's unlikely to warm to you or any girlfriend of mine. She has enough difficulty liking her own daughter. I wouldn't wish her upon you, but perhaps you should see the person who's compulsory in my life."

Jess stepped closer. "Would you like to get this meeting over and done with?"

Anna nodded.

"Then I accept your challenge."

Anna laughed. She lifted a hand to stroke Jess's cheek. "I love you."

Jess clutched Anna's fingers to her face. "I am so in love with you."

"Come and meet my gorgon of a mother then."

Jess giggled. "Great."

They turned into a side street of well-heeled residential Knightsbridge and towards the exclusive restaurant in a four-storey town house.

"It's almost empty," Jess said as they walked past the windows. "There's a group of businessmen and a smartly dressed woman with ash-blonde hair."

"That's probably her."

"Oh, she's spotted us. Make that a smartly dressed woman, with ash-blonde hair and a pissed off look on her face."

"Definitely her."

A waitress led them through a deceptively modest room with white walls, white table cloths and darker floor.

"Morning Mother," Anna said cheerfully. She was determined to stay in charge of her temper today despite every needling insinuation and outright attack her mother might throw at her.

Her mother didn't rise to meet them. "I wasn't expecting company," she said, her voice and face tight.

"This is Jess," Anna replied. "She accompanied me here. I've mentioned her before, do you remember, and we've been seeing a lot of each other. I thought you should meet."

"Pleasure to see you, Mrs Mayhew," Jess said. She offered a hand, but Anna's mother didn't take it.

"Perhaps another time might have been better," her mother said, replying to Anna and seeming to ignore Jess. "We haven't seen each other for a while and I imagine there's lots to catch up on."

"I'm not staying," Jess said. Anna marvelled at her equanimity in the face of outright hostility. "I'll see you tonight," she murmured by Anna's ear, then her soft lips pressed a kiss onto her cheek and Anna couldn't help but close her eyes and enjoy the welcome comfort. "Have a good lunch both," Jess said more loudly.

Anna had to steel herself and resist the urge to chase after Jess and abandon her mother. She heard the front door to the restaurant close and she sighed at Jess's absence.

She slid off her coat into the hands of the waitress and took her seat opposite her mother, gently leaning her elbows on the table cloth and interlinking her fingers in a graceful pose.

"Was that really necessary?" Her mother tutted.

"Was what necessary?" Anna smiled, innocently.

"The kiss? In front of everyone?"

Anna peeked round the quiet restaurant, the businessmen in the corner engrossed in conversation, and Anna was certain that no-one would have noticed.

"It was a farewell kiss," Anna said lightly. "Hardly controversial. I'd expect Dad to do the same with you."

That silenced her at least.

"Well," her mother said, recovering. "Good to see you at last, darling. We haven't seen each other for weeks have we. What on earth have you been up to? Well anyway," she moved on quickly perhaps not wanting to hear the answer, "I've lots to tell you."

And that apparently was the last her mother wanted to hear about Jess or the rest of Anna's life.

Her mother ordered for them both, Anna accepting her suggestions without quarrel, letting the irritation wash over her today.

"Has your sister caught up with you yet?" her mother said. "Celeste's been trying to talk to you for days."

"I'm hoping to catch up with her this weekend. I said I'd ring." Guilt pinched at Anna who'd been wrapped up in work and Jess and unable to take her sister's calls.

"Well, I'll tell you her news anyway," her mother said with obvious excitement in her voice and leaning forward. "She's expecting again. Isn't that marvellous?"

"Oh," Anna said, a genuine smile lifting her mood. "Good for her."

"She's had such trouble since little Toby. I thought she'd never have another at this rate. I said," and her mother leaned in further, "she should try with help from the clinic now she's getting on."

"She's only thirty-five?" Anna said, puzzled.

"Ancient for a mother. I had you all before I turned thirty, thank god. But with these clinics and procedures you could be a new mother well into your forties."

Anna decided to be generous and assume her mother referred to the impersonal 'you' rather than being so very personal.

"Which is what I always point out when Cameron asks after you."

Anna stared. So that assumption was wrong.

"I imagine," Anna ventured, "that's of little interest to him."

"On the contrary. It'll be a consideration even if he doesn't realise it."

"Mother," Anna said sharply. "That isn't appropriate." Then she composed herself. "Mum," she said more gently. "I'm in love with Jess and we're living together." There didn't seem to be any other way to break it to her other than starkly, given her mother's lack of interest. "Please don't imply to anyone that I'm available."

Silence.

"Well," her mother muttered. "As long as you're happy." Then a second later the words "for now," crawled out.

Her mother sniffed and dabbed at her mouth with a napkin. "Anyway, Sebastian sends his love. I saw him last night…"

So another change of subject. Anna found herself trying to unpick her mother's motivations today. What did she want? What was her strategy? How exhausting it all was. And she suddenly smiled at how she didn't have to do that with Jess. She'd been clear about what she wanted from the start. Jess wasn't without fault and she certainly messed up from time to time and had her own difficulties. But Anna would take those any day of the week compared with unrelenting games.

"Don't you want to know anything about Jess?" Anna interrupted.

Her mother was unresponsive.

"Is this because Jess is a woman?"

Her mother tutted. "Good god, you're not playing the gay card again are you. Nobody cares, Anna. Your father and I aren't bothered about whether you see a man or woman. I just don't see why you have to go on about it. Your sort have got equal marriage. What else do you want?"

It was funny how, for someone who was unconcerned about gender, it was always Anna's male partners who were considered suitable and there was only ever a list of objections for anyone else. She wondered at her mother's prejudice against Jess. The depth and breadth of her mother's bigotry was plain and Anna had no compulsion to subject Jess to this woman again.

"Well go on then," her mother said, dropping her napkin and leaning back, arms crossed. "Tell me about this Jess."

"She's an actress," Anna began.

"I thought you said she worked in publicity," her mother parried.

How annoying that her mother had been paying attention and Anna winced at her spotting the incongruity.

"Promoting the *Atlassia* films is part of her job," Anna recovered. "You may have heard of them. She's the lead character? Perhaps you've caught her full name, Jessica Lambert?"

"An actress," her mother sighed. "Yes, the name's familiar, although I wouldn't have recognised her."

"We've known each other for a few months–"

"How old is she? She seems very young," her mother interrupted.

Anna had to force herself to sit straight, to counter the sense of being on the back foot. "She's in her mid-twenties and has been working for eight years–"

"You're a great deal older."

Anna paused, took a breath and rode over the attack. "She's had a busy few years, filming abroad, but she's based in London and–"

"I've seen her in a Bond film, haven't I?" her mother said, an amused sneer twisting her words. "There was an article about her in the Sunday paper, I remember now, flicking past some ludicrous shots of her half naked."

It was like wading through mud while under fire. And they hadn't even got to the part Anna dreaded most yet.

Her mother was still amused by her recollection. "So, a real-life movie star. I imagine it makes you quite jealous." And Anna regretted every bitter feeling she'd had against Jess as she saw her own envy reflected in her mother's words. "How on earth did you meet?"

It was like her mother had a sixth sense about every sore point. Anna maintained her poise. Unlike Jess, thinking on her feet and improvisation had always been her forte.

"We met by chance," she said evenly, despite frustration threatening to boil to the surface. "But we work together now."

There. She'd made it. Her confession at last.

"You work together? Are you consulting on her film? Coaching?"

"No," Anna said. "I've taken an acting role on the series they're producing for TV."

"Good god, Anna." Her mother spat out every word. "What on earth were you thinking?"

Anna closed her eyes a moment, imagining her mother's words bouncing off her skin. She opened them again, ready for more.

"I thought your name was mud as an actress these days." Her mother threw her hands in the air. "Is it this Jess? Has she been calling in favours? Did she ask them to find you something? She may be besotted with you for now, but don't expect that to last forever."

Anna opened her mouth to respond but her mother jumped in again.

"Honestly, Anna, after everything, don't you think this supremely unwise? You could have another John Boyd after you. I think this a terrible decision. Then again, perhaps you won't attract that kind of adulation now you're older." She waved her hand dismissively.

Anna wished she could capture the conversation and show Jess. If ever anything encapsulated everything that had eroded her confidence over the years this conversation was surely it.

"And alongside this…this…Jessica Lambert, you could be in more danger. I can't see the attraction quite frankly, but I know she has rabid fans. If you associate with someone like that, you will get all sorts of cranks after you."

Anna breathed out, a slow steady exhalation like she practised in yoga.

"You're right, Mother," she said, with a sad smile, trying to suppress the tremble in her arms. "I fear all of those. I've been hiding away because of everything you've mentioned."

Her mother was silent at last and Anna had time to notice how her mother's words, although painful and brutal, hadn't penetrated so deeply this time. She was filled with love from Jess, strengthened by her support and bolstered by her own growing confidence that had been building for months.

"I can't keep hiding." Anna shook her head. "I don't want to live like that anymore."

"These people may threaten your life," her mother shouted, her composure gone.

"They might," Anna said. "It's true. It's definitely a possibility. But at this point I'm not sure if they're a greater threat or you are?"

"What on earth do you mean?"

Anna tried to look at her mother, catching a glimpse of her enraged glistening eyes.

"After everything's considered," Anna said, calmly but the words beginning to stick in her throat, "I think you've had a worse effect on my happiness than my stalker ever did."

"Ridiculous," her mother breathed. "What the hell are you talking about?"

"I won't change my mind," Anna replied, her body swirling with opposing emotions of fury and distress. "I love Jess. I'm extremely lucky to have a role acting beside her. I'm luckier still to receive her love."

"You think a young starlet will remain by your side?"

"Yes, I do," Anna said, smiling genuinely this time with the reminder of Jess. "I have more faith in Jess than anyone else I've ever been involved with."

"Another actor?" Her mother tutted. "Someone else who doesn't live in the real world?"

Anna took a moment, a little like Jess did. "Funnily, for someone whose career it is to pretend to be someone else, she is more strongly herself than anyone I've ever met. I think it's down to her honesty. I never appreciated how much simpler life is when you strip it down to that. It's a revelation. It's so freeing." What a weight was lifted, not having to worry about all the machinations and motives, when Jess talked plainly to her.

"Maybe we won't stay together for ever," Anna continued, "no-one can guarantee the future, but I would be a fool to let her go. She is kind, loving and a person who it's fun to be quiet with. I feel like my soul is recharging when we hang out. And she is as sexy as hell."

Her mother was mortified. "Anna, for god's sake."

"I'm in love with her. I'm lucky to have found her." She looked unwavering at her mother. "You have never made an attempt to understand me, from who I loved to what I thought and what made my life worth living. I'm glad I didn't make that mistake with Jess and I will continue to listen to her."

Her mother was still speechless.

"Now," Anna said, dabbing her mouth with her serviette and putting it aside on the table. "If you can't even try to understand and accommodate anyone else's point of view, then I'm afraid we are done with this conversation."

"But this girl," her mother spat out the words, "she'll be gone in a matter of weeks and you'll be left looking a fool."

"I doubt it. I've rarely met anyone more loyal to friends, work, family or her lover. She is remarkable." Anna breathed in. It was time to be blunt. "If you try to undermine my relationship with her, like you have with everything else in my life, from my work to my sexuality, you will inflict more damage than anyone else." Anna hoped the trembling in her limbs didn't show. "I will not let you do that anymore. If you cannot support my decisions and cannot support me and Jess, then I will no longer see you."

She stood up. Her mother stared, her mouth gaping open in shock for a moment before a veil of fury hid it. Humility wasn't immediately forthcoming and if it happened at all it would have to be in her mother's own time, not Anna's.

"Until then," Anna said. "Goodbye Mother."

She turned and walked across the room, struggled to ask for her coat, fumbled with the door, but remained composed right until the other side and into the street.

Anna expected to choke on tears. She waited for a blow of loss to crush her. But instead, a weight lifted. Anna would no longer have to live with those thousand small acts of aggression from her mother. The exhaustion from never meeting her expectations was relieved. Life would have its challenges, but Anna didn't have to face them shackled by her disapproval.

56

Jess blinked in the onslaught of cameras flashing in the London night. She raised her arm to cover her eyes.

She wasn't comfortable with this. A red carpet. Journalists. Paparazzi. Agents. Stars. All out for the awards evening in the West End theatre. And the noise. Traffic, shouts from fans, demanding journalists, it all drilled at her head.

She fidgeted with her tuxedo jacket, pulling the lapels together protectively then forcing herself to drop her hands and square her shoulders.

Someone called out her name. She registered that it had been called several times but it had taken a while for her to focus on it. It was likely a hack in the crowd behind the barricades somewhere. She waved and cameras turned their full force of fire on her, flashing and clicking. She tried not to flinch but couldn't help it. Tomorrow's photos in the paper wouldn't be flattering. Femi would not be pleased. Gossip would start and he'd have to firefight again.

"Jessica!" the male voice called out again. "Are you expecting an award this evening?"

It took several moments to find the source of the voice, then she recognised the journalist whom Celia described as a worm. Jess didn't want to risk opening her mouth, but then silence generated its own stories and they already had their awkward picture to go with that.

"Just presenting an award tonight," she said, realising she was speaking in a monotone. She dropped her gaze and tried to move on. Several photographers were waving to her further up the line but the pressure followed her.

"You're not with Anna Mayhew tonight?" another male reporter shouted. "You two have been spotted together a lot recently. Any comment?"

"No. She's not here yet."

Where was she? Anna hadn't come home after lunch with her mother. She said she might not have time before collecting her dress. But Jess was unnerved. Anna's mother had clearly taken against her. Jess tried not to dwell on the look the woman had given her, the one that appraised up and down and said so many things. She'd seen it a thousand times when she'd been presented – so unlike people expected in so many ways. The contempt Anna's mother conveyed though was special. Jess tried to tell herself that it said more about the older woman than Jess, a mantra imbedded by her Nan.

"I hear you and Anna have been very friendly." The hack shouted out. "Why's she not here tonight?"

Why indeed. All Jess had thought about all day was Anna and how her confidence seemed to drain away when her mother was present. Jess wanted to go home, not be here in front of hundreds of people with flashes and incessant clamouring and noise. How did anyone think above this?

She wanted to go home and wait for Anna and not be distracted by anything else.

"Not been a lover's tiff has there?" the hack shouted again.

No, there hadn't. But then she had no idea what Anna was thinking right now. Jess's brain was beginning to seize. She wasn't coherent. It was like her tongue and cheeks became swollen and she couldn't articulate the words.

"Miss Lambert! Over here!" another voice shouted.

"Jessica!" yet another came.

"Anna Mayhew hasn't been seen on set for a few days," the original hack continued. "Are there professional issues too?"

What? That wasn't even true. How did things deteriorate so quickly? Jess wished for the thousandth time her brain could cope. She could feel the panic start to creep up her back. She was breathing rapidly, she twitched, her head swirled and she stumbled a little further up the red carpet towards the old theatre, camera lights flashing from all sides.

She could see the journalist moving along the crowd to keep up with her.

"Is it true," he shouted, "that you had a breakdown when you first arrived in London?"

Her head was pounding and she could hear her heart in her ears. The crowds loomed in from both sides of the red carpet as it funnelled towards the entrance and her heart rocketed as she stumbled forward. It felt like the whole world was collapsing around her.

Then as she reached the entrance, it stopped. Soft fingers slipped between hers and a melodious voice reached out.

"Hi," is all it said and it was enough for the whole world to melt away.

Jess turned, eyes heavy and drooping with the fatigue of panic to find the beatific face of Anna. Her hair was swept back and magnificent. Her eyes sparkled blue. It was like spring sunshine after winter and Jess's anxiety seemed to disappear. The crowd receded. Only Anna existed for Jess, her fingers caressing her cheek.

"You're here." Jess couldn't help the crack in her voice.

"Yes, I am," Anna smiled. "We're together now." And she slowly held Jess's cheeks in her hands, overwhelming love and fondness shining in her expression.

"How are you?" Jess gasped.

"I'm OK." Anna smiled.

"I didn't know how it went. It didn't look nice."

A shadow flitted over Anna's features. "It wasn't," she said. Then recovering some of her levity, "So, my mother and I will be taking a break from each other, until she can find a way to be constructive."

"I'm sorry if I made things more difficult."

"You didn't," Anna whispered. "You make everything so much better."

"I was worried about you," Jess breathed hard. "Just when you were happy and things were going well for you. For us…"

It all came tumbling out, everything that had gone through Jess's thoughts, round and round ceaselessly while she waited for Anna.

"Because I want to marry you. I want a little place in the country to escape to when we need it." Jess couldn't stop now. "I want us to be together. When *Atlassia* finishes I'll take a break and follow you wherever your next role takes you, then maybe we could take turns doing that. I know this is all enormous." She paused for breath but didn't want to stop. "I'm sorry I don't do things by halves and if this all comes across as naive and youthful confidence, but I want us to do everything now–"

Anna pressed her fingertips to her lips. She was smiling. "Please wait a moment," she said, "because I want to check, did you ask me to marry you?"

Jess paused a moment. She'd been thinking of it. She'd been thinking of it a lot.

"I think so," Jess said, surprised. But then she thought of things so hard sometimes that she forgot to say them. "I'm pretty sure I did. Yes. Kind of."

"That's funny," Anna said, her eyes glistening.

Jess searched Anna's expression, wondering if she could work it out and save herself from whatever was coming.

"Why?" Jess said, not knowing if she wanted to hear the answer.

"Because," Anna whispered, "I was going to ask you too."

Jess couldn't speak. Her throat was choking on a swell of emotion that she couldn't keep down. She opened her mouth but no words came out.

"I want to marry you," Anna said, beaming.

Jess still couldn't speak.

Anna stroked her face, her eyes searching around Jess. "I wish it was more romantic," she said with a smile, "but if we're talking about it?"

"I am. I do," Jess blurted out. "And I want to."

"Me too," Anna said gently.

"You do?" Jess didn't know whether to laugh or cry.

"All of it." Anna drew her shoulders back a little. "No more doing things by halves. But…"

"But what?"

"You mentioned getting a little cottage?"

"Yes?"

"That might not be so easy."

"Why?"

"I come with baggage," Anna said, with a smile pinching the side of her mouth.

"Baggage?"

"We're going to need a spare room for Bibs and Penny when they visit." Anna grinned.

"Is that all?" Jess laughed. "They've got it."

Anna drew closer and Jess couldn't help placing her hands on her hips and drawing her nearer still.

"I love you, Anna Mayhew," she said.

"And I love you, Jess Lambert."

They both lifted their lips to meet with a delicate kiss. Jess closed her eyes, indulging in the tenderness of her most loved, the anxiety of the day only making their touch sweeter.

Their kiss didn't go unnoticed. A cacophony of camera shutters rained over them and white light exploded in the theatre entrance. Jess and Anna's gentle kiss that spoke of deep love and togetherness in the face of the world was captured a hundred times over.

And that was the photo that made the papers the next day.

THE END

Acknowledgements

I've bounced ideas and versions of this book off several people and I'm hugely grateful for their feedback. However, any errors of judgement or fact in what remains in this published version are my responsibility alone.

Jess has different heritage to me and I don't have first-hand experience of her background. I'm white with a white-centric education – the latter sadly still being ubiquitous in the UK – and although my experience and reading broadens constantly I have much to learn and unlearn. I'm very grateful to a fabulous sensitivity reader for highlighting inaccuracies and tropes that I hadn't appreciated.

In the storytelling, I'm hugely grateful to three awesome authors for their feedback. G Benson for early encouragement and listening to my regular grumps about writing. Diana Simmonds always for being Diana and getting my books like no other. Cindy Rizzo for support and always finding something to make me think differently. Wonderful writers all.

Many thanks to Dor for proofreading and the super speedy turnaround!

Thank you so much to readers who keep me writing – reassuring words make all the difference. I feel like a book isn't truly finished until it finds a reader who loves it. It's the biggest high when I hear one of my books has found someone.

And thanks to my family, who make the ordinary extraordinary.

About the Author

Clare Ashton is an award-winning indie author of WLW and lesbian fiction and F/F romances, with German translations of her work published by Ylva Publishing and Verlag Krug und Schadenberg.

Her dark romance After Mrs Hamilton is a Golden Crown Literary Society (Goldie) award winner and her first foray into romantic comedy, That Certain Something, was a Goldie and Lambda Literary Award finalist. Light romance Poppy Jenkins won the Rainbow Award for Best Lesbian Contemporary & Erotic Romance.

Clare grew up in Mid-Wales and has a brain stuck somewhere not particularly useful between the arts and sciences. She has been accused of sometimes living too much inside her head, but it turns out that this is good for writing stories. She lives in the Midlands with her wife and son and daughter who are a lovely distraction from writing.

Also by Clare Ashton:
Pennance
After Mrs Hamilton
That Certain Something
Poppy Jenkins
The Goodmans

Find out more about Clare

http://rclareashton.wordpress.com
https://www.facebook.com/pages/Clare-Ashton/327713437267566
https://twitter.com/RClareAshton

The Goodmans

EVEN THE NICEST FAMILIES HAVE SECRETS

CLARE ASHTON

FROM THE BEST-SELLING AUTHOR OF 'POPPY JENKINS'

Poppy Jenkins
CLARE ASHTON
THE BEST-SELLING AUTHOR OF 'THAT CERTAIN SOMETHING'

Love or money? Follow the head or heart?

That certain something

clare ashton

The bestselling author of *Pennance* and *After Mrs Hamilton*

Secrets, obsession, betrayal

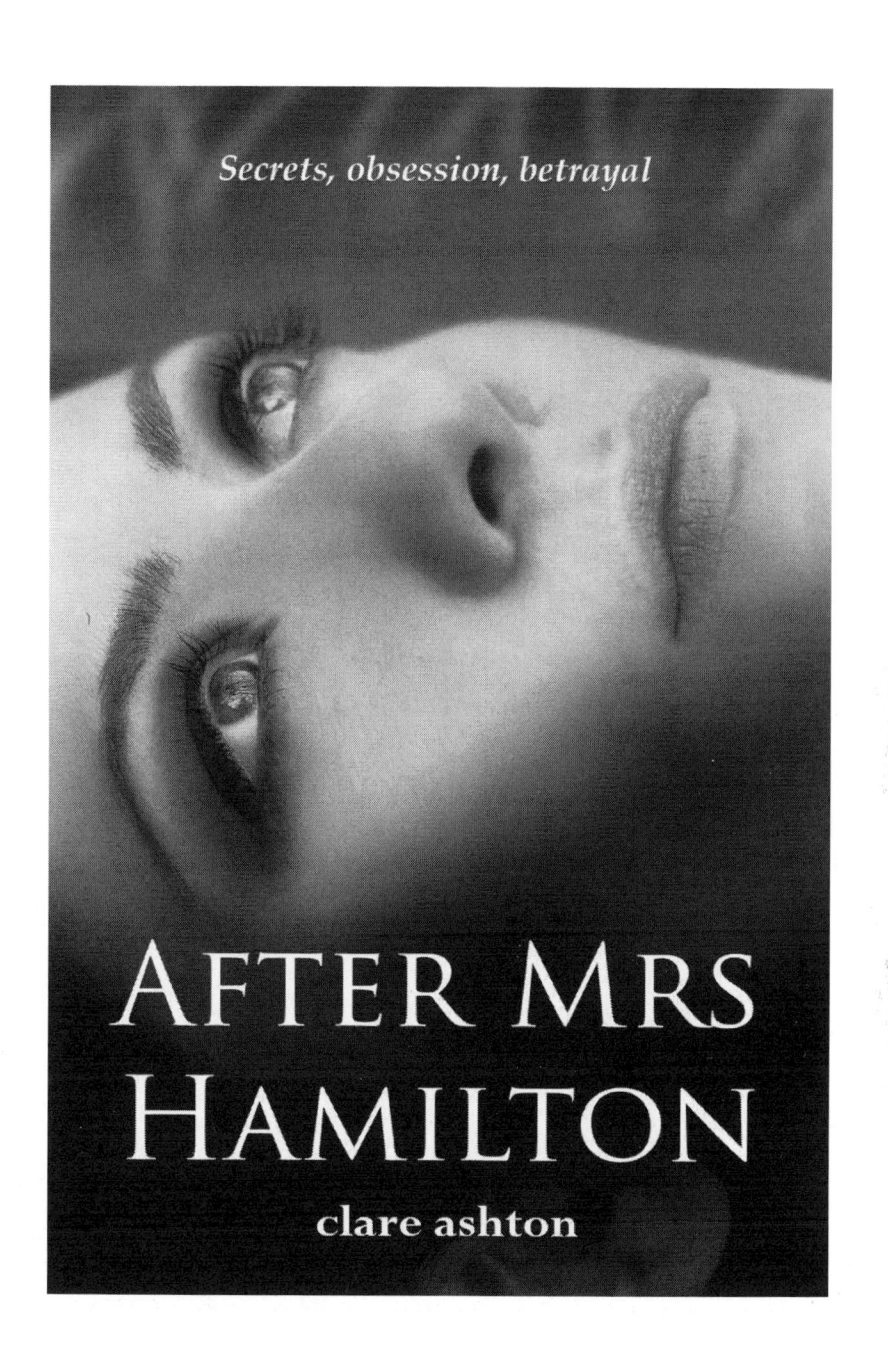

AFTER MRS HAMILTON

clare ashton

be careful who you love

PENNANCE

clare ashton

'a brilliant love story / mystery, beautifully written'
T.T. Thomas

Printed in Great Britain
by Amazon